NIKI

CHRISTOS CHOMENIDIS

Translated from the Greek by
Patricia Felisa Barbeito

OTHER PRESS
New York

Originally published in Greek as *Nikh* in 2014 by
Patakis Publishers, Athens
Copyright © S. Patakis SA (Patakis Publishers) &
Christos Chomenidis, Athens 2014

English translation copyright © Patricia Felisa Barbeito 2023

Song lyrics on page 476 from "That'll Be the Day" by
Jerry Allison, Buddy Holly, and Norman Petty, 1956.

Production editor: Yvonne E. Cárdenas
Text designer: Patrice Sheridan
This book was set in Baskerville & Alinea Sans by
Alpha Design & Composition of Pittsfield, NH

10 9 8 7 6 5 4 3 2 1

Library of Congress Cataloging-in-Publication Data
Names: Chōmenidēs, Ch. A. (Chrēstos A.), 1966- |
Barbeito, Patricia Felisa, translator.
Title: Niki : a novel / Christos Chomenidis ; translated
from the Greek by Patricia Felisa Barbeito.
Other titles: Nikē. English
Description: New York : Other Press, [2023]
Identifiers: LCCN 2022051170 (print) | LCCN 2022051171 (ebook) |
ISBN 9781635421972 (paperback) | ISBN 9781635421989 (ebook)
Subjects: LCGFT: Novels.
Classification: LCC PA5614.H62 N5513 2023 (print) |
LCC PA5614.H62 (ebook) | DDC 889.3/4—dc23/eng/20221214
LC record available at https://lccn.loc.gov/2022051170
LC ebook record available at https://lccn.loc.gov/2022051171

TO MY DAUGHTER,

AND TO ALL CHILDREN HER AGE

TO FREE YOURSELF OF THE PAST

YOU HAVE TO GET TO KNOW IT

Your likeness I hold dear, the flame I brought not near
A likeness fine and true, one daybreak I'll bring to you.

—MICHALIS KATSAROS, "YOUR LIKENESS"

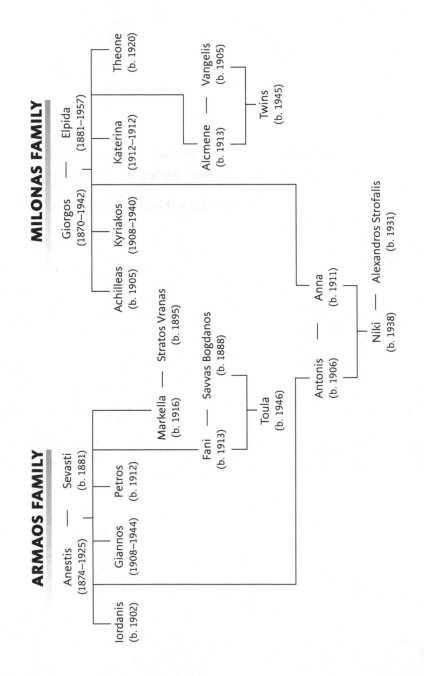

ARMAOS FAMILY

MILONAS FAMILY

AUTHOR NOTE

NIKI ARMAOS IS based on my mother, Niki Nefeloudi.

Niki Armaos, however, is a fictional character. This applies to all who appear within the pages of this novel. They are reflections of people who lived and acted in the real world as seen through the mirror of fiction. As a writer, I am faithful not to the letter but to the spirit of each person's history. And to History itself. I adapt events, at times taking creative liberties, in the hope of getting to their very core, and agonizing all the while, from beginning to end, to not diminish or wrong anyone.

NIKI

NOW THAT I am dead, laid out in my coffin, wrapped in my good white dress (the one I picked out and had dry-cleaned a week before returning to the hospital for the last time); now that I lie in the mortuary cooler waiting for sunrise on the day of my funeral; now on my way to that place where, by all accounts, there is no sorrow, heartache, or pain; now, I feel freer than ever. Free to roam the seventy years of my life; to advance, to retreat, to linger at those landmark moments—the critical decisions I took, or that others took for me—and ponder them, fully and clearly. Free to take the microscope to every tiny detail, to sift through the subtle nuances of shade that make all the difference in the end; the difference that set me apart not from other people but from the infinite palette of possibilities lying latent within me; the difference that distinguished the woman I was from all those I might have become.

When I was alive, I never indulged in reflection. Even the diaries I maintained almost without interruption since my years underground contained only facts, not their interpretation: *I went to such and such a place, and met with so-and-so, and this and that happened*...A couple of underlined words, some bracketed, even rarer exclamation marks, the only clues to my state of mind.

The day I was told I had cancer I didn't write in my diary. The next day, I listed the items I would need to pack for the hospital: a catalogue without commentary. Was I hiding from myself? Perhaps...

Or perhaps I didn't see any sense in passing judgment on a picture not yet finished. Now, that time has come.

BEFORE NIKI

I **WAS BORN** in February 1938, during a period in my parents' lives utterly inhospitable to bringing a child into the world. They had come into it in more peaceful times.

My mother was the eldest daughter of a man born to poverty who had become a wealthy landowner through marriage. I'm not implying that he married for money. On the contrary, my grandfather Giorgos Milonas had fallen madly in love with my grandmother Elpida Petmezas, all social and financial calculations be damned. They came from neighboring villages on the plains of Messenia, and I imagine they met at one of the village festivals where Giorgos played syrtos and kalamatianos on the bouzouki, and Elpida, like other young women of the time, danced demurely with close relatives. They claimed that it was love at first sight, and in terms of appearance at least, they were well matched: Elpida, a fair-skinned brunette, as pleasing to the eye as the tall, strapping, flaxen-haired Giorgos with his handlebar mustache. His was the first generation to wear European clothing; his father still favored the fustanella. Late nineteenth century in the Peloponnese...

Giorgos had no hope of winning Elpida's hand; even trying to woo her was out of the question. A gaping chasm stood between the thirty-year-old jack-of-all-trades and master of one—occasional hunter, horseman, and itinerant musician—and the Petmezases, who had forty peasants (sharecroppers, to be precise) at their beck and call. I doubt, then, that what followed gave him much pause. One day, when Elpida set off to see the dentist in Kalamata—back then, a bona fide journey from her village with two mares leading the way, another two bringing up the rear, and in the middle a donkey with the young woman perched on its saddle—Giorgos and his mates lay in wait behind a bend in the road. When the cavalcade approached, he leapt out and cut them off, rifle in hand.

"Will you give her to me for my wife?" he demanded in a thundering voice.

"You must be dreaming, man! Come to your senses!" the young woman's keepers shot back.

The gunfire that followed left one dead and three wounded, and provided Giorgos with the cover to carry the young Elpida away to a cave for the night. At dawn he surrendered to the police and was tried and sentenced—some say for five years, others seven—to hard labor at Bourtzi.[1] But it was no skin off his back: He had made her his wife and she could not be married to anyone else.

---

[1] Bourtzi Fortress in the coastal town of Nafplio was used as a prison.

Almost as soon as he was released and the marriage solemnized, the children began to arrive. First, Achilleas and Kyriakos; then Anna, my mother; followed by Katerina (who died in infancy), Alcmene (ancient Greek names were all the rage), and finally Theone, all within the fifteen-year period from 1905 to 1920.

Were the boys especially gifted students? Or was it the noble aspiration of a well-to-do landowning family to send its sons to university? In any case, as soon as both finished high school, they were dispatched to Athens: Achilleas to study theology and Kyriakos, law.

They returned to the village every summer, but instead of helping with the work on their land, they would lie in the shade of a tree, ostentatiously reading Marxist tracts. Who had introduced them to communism? It's a mystery. When Grandfather Giorgos asked them point-blank—glowering, probably, as he did so—Achilleas replied with what he believed was the perfect riposte, but to everyone else was arrogance pure and simple: "These days, if you're not a communist you're either blind or a complete idiot, like taking a position against the Revolution back in 1821." In the face of such conviction, Giorgos only shrugged.

In the evenings, Achilleas would go to the village café to propagandize, while Kyriakos oversaw his sisters' education. "Communism is Soviet power plus the electrification of the whole country," Lenin had said. Kyriakos dwelt on the second leg of the aphorism. He described the electrification of the Peloponnese, the automation of work by state-of-the-art machinery, the layers of compressed air propelling modern trains to speeds that would shrink the distance between Kalamata and Athens to next to nothing. Eyes agog, the girls consumed science fiction as political catechism.

Anna's journey to Athens via steam engine (that trusty coal-guzzler!) lasted almost a day and a half. It was preceded by three months of heated arguments with her father, or rather her father's heated arguments with himself. He could not decide between keeping his little Anna (the girl was so like him—she had such pluck!) in the village or letting her go to discover the vastness of the world. "If you are going to hold me prisoner, then marry me off immediately! The sooner I have children, the sooner I can set them free." At the end of the day, these two sentences had won the war for Anna.

She moved into her brother's student den, a room in a house in the foothills of Lycabettus, and passed the entry exams for the School of Fine Arts with the helping hand of one of the other applicants (later to become a renowned artist). Infatuated with her, he had submitted both the live-model and still-life drawings in her stead. Despite all this, she did not attend a single class. Having hastened to join the Communist Youth, she was now already working in a textile factory, charged with the mission of spreading the good word among her coworkers.

Was she a great persuader, or did her silver-spoon upbringing betray her, despite her affectations of proletarianism? I can't say. In any case, Anna was not the kind to be turned from her course once it was set. As soon as she signed on to the socialist cause, she served staunchly and steadfastly, no matter the cost.

Her brother Achilleas, on the other hand, was either less loyal or a more independent thinker, depending on your point of view. Upon his graduation, he was appointed to a theology position in a public school. His first words to the students were to admonish them to not believe in nonsense, there was no such thing as God. Needless to say, they fired him on the spot. So as not to end up in exile—where his conversion to Trotskyism was sure to put him in the crosshairs of the KKE[2]—he fled Greece. For a number of years, he drifted around Europe doing odd jobs. After the Second World War, he ended up in Israel, where he sired ten off-spring and cut a strange but well-known figure in Tel Aviv. Clad in a black suit, long hair billowing in the wind, he would stride up and down the seashore, a book conspicuously in hand, soliloquizing by himself. "I am a traveler of the mind" was how he liked to introduce himself.

In 1933, the twenty-two-year-old Anna must have been a most striking young communist: Tall, blond, and slim like her father, she possessed a rather austere demeanor that was as arousing as it was forbidding to the men around her. One day, a girlfriend told her that Comrade Armaos was eager to meet her.

"Our delegate?" Anna was impressed.

"Yes, the very same!"

---

[2] The Communist Party of Greece.

II

ANTONIS ARMAOS, MY father, was only five years older, but his life had been immeasurably more tumultuous. Born in 1906 in Mudanya, Asia Minor, he was the second son of a self-made businessman who in addition to a lucrative trade in oil also ran the town's fishing wharf. Daily, he bought the full catch and either sold it in town or cured it and sent it on to Bursa, Constantinople, and even farther afield. My grandfather Anestis traveled regularly to Varna and Odessa, smoked the hookah, and knew how to enjoy a good tsipouro.[3] He was rather short, stout, and bald, always dressed to the nines, a gold pocket watch tucked into his vest. He too had married for love, a young woman without a penny to her name, Sevasti, with whom he had six children: four sons—Iordanis, Antonis, Giannos, Petros—and two daughters, Fani and Markella.

When the Greek army landed in Asia Minor in 1919 in pursuit of the nation's lost lands, Anestis was far from pleased. Straightaway, he saw its arrival not as the vindication of "sacred national yearnings"[4] but as the prolongation

---

[3] A strong distilled spirit found throughout Greece.

[4] This is a reference to the irredentist politics of the Megali Idea (Great Idea) that aimed to establish a Greek state that would include the large Greek populations still under Ottoman rule after the end of the Greek War of Independence (1821–1830), as well as the lands that had belonged to Greece since antiquity.

of a war that boded no good. His compatriots' bombast
and bravado, their big talk of King Alexandros's corona-
tion taking place in Hagia Sophia, Empress of the Greeks,
dismaycd him.

"Where will the Turks go?" he demanded.

"To hell!" the most hotheaded spat back, scowling at his
apparent lack of patriotism.

Venizelos's[5] crushing defeat in the 1920 elections was
even more unnerving. As the Greeks marched toward the
east and the Turks rallied under Kemal's leadership, Anestis
increasingly felt like he was sitting on a powder keg. Among
his circle of friends and acquaintances, almost no one
shared his unease. He called on the cachet of his position
as a church warden and success as a merchant to convince
them, but his efforts fell on deaf ears.

In the spring of 1922, he finally resolved to liquidate his
landed property, sell his fishing wharf permit, and with his
entire family in tow relocate to the security of Constantinople, where his eldest son, Iordanis, was studying at Robert
College.

"Why are you leaving?" his friends pestered him until
the last day.

---

[5] Eleftherios Venizelos (1864–1936) was the prominent leader of the Greek
Liberal Party, and a principal promoter of the Megali Idea. In 1920 he was
defeated by the United Opposition, a pro-monarchist alliance of parties,
whose mishandling of the Greco-Turkish War is generally credited with
leading to the Asia Minor Catastrophe of 1922 and the massacre and expulsion of a million and a half Greeks from Asia Minor.

"Because the Turks are coming to massacre us!" He had grown tired of repeating this refrain. But no one believed him, and behind his back the rumor quickly spread: There was a hidden motive, a family scandal perhaps, that had precipitated this abandonment of hearth and home.

The day of departure from Mudanya was the most memorable in my father's young life. A strange, perhaps even somewhat superstitious strain in my grandfather Anestis's disposition had led him to convey wife and children to Constantinople on one ship, and all other worldly goods—carpets, jewelry, and gold tender—on another. He had assigned the responsibility of the "property" to his sixteen-year-old son. That is how Antonis, pistol in hand, ended up, from dawn to dusk, standing watch over dozens of trunks and crates stacked along the dock, waiting for the ship that was to carry them.

Pitying him as a victim of paternal eccentricity, friends and classmates kept him company under the scorching sun.

"Your father has lost his mind and you're all bearing the brunt of it," his best friend finally dared to blurt out.

Antonis glared at him, but did not reply.

"Any day now, the Greek army will take Ankara," his friend insisted. "Honestly, if I were in your position, I don't know what I would do. On the one hand, yes, 'honor thy parents' but on the other...Did you at least try to change his mind? Of course, he didn't ask you—why would he? Tell me, what would you do if you were attacked by bandits?

Would you pull the trigger? Would you risk your life for a decision that you know full well is simply idiotic?"

Without a word, Antonis aimed between the boy's legs. The bullet lodged into the wooden pier, well clear of its target, but the shot boomed throughout the harbor.

"Have you gone mad, too?" his friend shrieked. "A chip off the old block, eh?"

Antonis loaded the pistol and raised the barrel, aiming straight at the boy's head. Panic-stricken, his friend started desperately backpedaling, alternately swearing and pleading, until he tripped and fell into the water.

All the family's possessions were delivered safe and sound by the son to the father. This accomplishment had Antonis brimming with confidence: Now that he had proven himself worthy of his father's trust, he was certain he could handle anything, even the most complicated of tasks.

CONSTANTINOPLE, LATE WINTER of 1922: My grandfather Anestis (not yet a grandfather but a gentleman of leisure on the threshold of fifty) was torn between conflicting emotions. On the one hand, immense relief that thanks to his foresight he had salvaged both family and livelihood. On the other hand, terrible pangs of guilt toward his former townspeople, the ones who had remained faithful to Mudanya until the bitter end, who had survived the Turkish invasion only to end up refugees, homeless and destitute.

"I ought to have rung those alarm bells much louder," he chastised himself. "Not to mention that if you look at the situation objectively, I took them for fools. I accepted their gold in exchange for my land and my home, only for Kemal's brigands to snatch it all up a few months later."

On top of these tormenting thoughts, there was also the torture of inactivity. The business prowess cultivated in Mudanya, a town of a few thousand people, did not easily translate to a city like Constantinople. He had no connections nor did he know his way around the local block. All he had was his capital, carefully secured out of harm's way, and sufficient in his estimation for the needs of all his children, perhaps even his grandchildren. But what to do with his itchy fingers?

Some say that his fateful meeting with the deacon was accidental. Others, that it had been orchestrated by the deacon himself, who had been dogging my grandfather's footsteps for quite some time, driven by the desire for vengeance and, primarily, to line his own pockets.

"What good wind brings you to these parts, brother?" As if fallen from the sky, the deacon suddenly appeared before Anestis in an alley in the Ortaköy district. He threw his arms around my grandfather, and in keeping with his role as a man of the cloth, uttered a blessing. Anestis had difficulty recognizing him; the last time he had set eyes on him, the deacon had been a young child. The bastard son of a hapless maid—back then, no one had any compunctions about calling them "scullions"—he had aroused the pity of the parish priest, who had enlisted him as an altar boy to help carry the Epitaph[6] and shine the candelabra. At fifteen, he had left for Mount Athos and all trace of him had been lost. Now, here he was, settled in Constantinople and, as he informed Anestis, under the protection of the Patriarch himself, who—"Don't breathe a word to anyone"— had charged him with "special assignments."

"Let's go have a raki!" the deacon insisted. Anestis could not make up his mind. "I wonder if he knows he might be my son." Might he? The more he looked at the deacon, with his thick unibrow and cleft chin, the less room there was to doubt that he had been spawned on one of those summer afternoons in 1899, in the laundry room of his brother's house, where Anestis had lived before his marriage. The deacon, however, betrayed not the slightest inkling. He led him to a café with a view of the Bosporus. There, with alcohol flowing straight from glass to brain, among small plates of appetizing meze, stories of the past and laments for the Turkification of Mudanya, Anestis opened his heart wide to the deacon, confiding his innermost thoughts (silent only on the secret ties that bound them), as well as the size of his considerable nest egg.

"You have all that money just lying around?" the deacon spluttered.

---

[6] The symbolic funeral bier of Jesus Christ, the Epitaph is a canopy covered in flowers that is carried in procession through the streets on Good Friday.

"What can I do? Here, all the fishing wharves are already taken, even the stands in the fish market are reserved, and there are no oil presses in the city."

"Money, my friend, no longer reeks of fish, nor does it drip oil. In the twentieth century, money begets money!"

"I'm no moneylender!" an alarmed Anestis protested.

"God forbid." The deacon crossed himself. "You misunderstand me! I'm talking about investing. About putting your money in stocks and bonds."

I HAVE NO idea how much persuasion it took. How many visits to Pera's Bankalar Caddesi, otherwise known as "the street of banks." How many appointments with expert consultants, who bowed deeply as they welcomed Anesti Agha and made him feel like he was someone again, not an out-of-his-depth country bumpkin. I do not know, because my grandfather hid all these activities from his family. But he did repeat that aphorism of the deacon's almost fifty times a day as if it were a charm—"In the twentieth century, money begets money"—and each time seemed to find it wiser. All the more so after he had crossed the threshold to the stock market and was dazzled by the gleaming marble, the solid-gold statue of Hermes, the enormous billboard with its list of stock prices rising and falling constantly and seemingly spontaneously, although in reality it was the doing of the clerks perched on ladders behind it, as he had found out when he asked. (And no, they did not remind him of shadow puppeteers.)

In August 1923, Anestis overcame his final reservations and plunged headlong into the game. Beforehand, he had come to an arrangement with the deacon: His advisory role would be compensated with ten percent not of the winnings but of the invested sum.

"I will not be pocketing any of it. It's all going straight to the Patriarchate's benevolent works," the deacon had declared.

"Keep some for yourself," was my grandfather's response, and he vowed that, if all went well, he would put something aside for his hard-done-by son. At the very least, he would build him a church to preside over.

His story, of course, had a foregone conclusion, a well-known and tedious one to those who have spent any time in a casino or at a racetrack. At first, he won sums so spectacular that he was well and truly hooked. Then began the plunge of no return. Whenever the extent of his losses scared him to the point of contemplating withdrawal, an almost miraculous upturn would occur. Emboldened anew, he would hope against hope—"The tide has turned"—and gamble ever more rashly to recoup what he had lost. And so, he kept losing more and more. The only thing truly remarkable was the lightning speed of his fall: A respectable estate, the fruit of more than thirty years of tireless work, was all gone within a few weeks.

"What is the true meaning of wealth? He who finds contentment in having nothing,"[7] was all the deacon had

---

[7] A preaching of Cosmas of Aetolia.

to say on the day of the irredeemable catastrophe, before announcing that he was soon to return to the Iviron Monastery at Mount Athos. My grandfather almost lunged at his throat, but what good would that do? He was not by nature a vengeful man, let alone a possible child-killer. Perhaps also he believed in his heart of hearts that given his fortunate escape from the Asia Minor Catastrophe, he was owed one of a more personal nature.

"We're ruined!" he announced to my grandmother, who had the presence of mind not to press for details. They held on for another three months in Constantinople, out of inertia more than anything else. My grandmother started selling her jewelry to pay for the family's needs. Iordanis, the eldest son, withdrew from his final year at Robert College and joined his younger brother (my father, Antonis) in the daily grind. They rented a boat and rowed out into the open waters where the British warships were anchored. After a small bribe to the bosun, they would climb on deck and hawk their wares to the sailors: candy, chocolate, combs, cigarettes, and decks of nudie-girl playing cards. They must have had the gift of gab, because they sold out every day. Yet the profit from this small business barely covered their own expenses and left nothing for their parents and siblings. Finally, Iordanis despaired. He got his papers in order, pawned the violin that his father had once given him, and bought a third-class ticket to South America. "I'll wire you money!" he promised. As a minor, Antonis could not follow suit.

At first, Grandfather Anestis would not hear of their leaving for Athens as refugees to benefit from the aid offered by the Greek government to "our brethren from Asia Minor."

"Refugees? What do you mean, refugees? I wasn't sent packing by a Turk! I made my own bed!" he kept repeating, until my grandmother finally put her foot down. And so, near the beginning of 1924, the family boarded a ship headed for Piraeus.

"What did I think of the Attica peninsula when I first set eyes on it? It reminded me of a desert," Antonis would reminisce. "As for the country's so-called support of the refugees, it meant housing us in what were essentially shacks with roofs that threatened to come off any time there was some wind. Threatened? Off they blew! It's not for nothing that the residents of Peristeri are called 'wind-wrecked'!"

Despite all this, they did have some "pull." A cousin of my grandmother's was employed in the Athens municipality, in an upper-management role, with an office and an official stamp to his name. He offered to help Anestis, and indeed found him work—as a street sweeper.

Dressed in the tattered remains of his suits, freshly bathed and well-shaven, he made his way up Syngrou Avenue each morning with his cart, collecting every piece of litter he encountered, no matter how small. He poured everything into fulfilling his duties to perfection. Not because he was hoping for a promotion—what chance did a man his age have for promotion, when there were thousands of men in the prime of their working lives still unemployed?—but rather because he had hung the last shreds of dignity and self-worth onto his broom like a flag. He needed to prove, at least to himself, that he was good at something. He also needed to keep his mind occupied, even if only in the hunt of dead leaves and dog shit, so as not to keep mulling the same thing over and over again: the enumeration of his fatal mistakes.

One afternoon, kneeling and scraping at a piece of chewing gum stamped into the sidewalk, he spied Antonis approaching, hand in hand with a young woman from the neighborhood. His son, mesmerized by the young Armenian's beautiful eyes, passed by without noticing him. His father, however, was convinced that his son had avoided him on purpose.

"My own son is ashamed of me," he said. "My own son is ashamed of me," he repeated brokenheartedly to my grandmother. "And you know what, that deacon—the one who ruined me—he too was my son!" He left her dumbfounded and disappeared from the house.

He handed over the cart, broom, and dustpan to a tavern keeper in Tzitzifies in exchange for the carafe of ouzo that he drank straight, without the usual accompanying meze, after turning his chair toward the wall so as not to see or be seen by the other patrons. He staggered out and wandered the streets and fields (the thistles clinging to his trouser legs bore witness to the latter) until dawn. He smoked all his cigarettes and drunkenly singed his mustache with the lighter. On the following day, he was found cold and stiff next to a potter's yard in Marousi. At least it was a broken heart and not his own hand that killed him.

Antonis never learned of his inadvertent role in his father's death. Grandmother told me on her deathbed, after swearing me to secrecy. He was buried in a plot donated by the Athens municipality, a tribute to their exemplary employee. Three years later, his bones were exhumed and thrown in the ossuary to empty the grave for someone else. His gold teeth, removed earlier and given to his family, were the only patrimony he left behind.

IN 1970, WHILE rummaging through a drawer, I pulled out a yellowed photograph. It was taken on the day of the funeral, in the yard of the house. Anestis presided over the center of the frame in a tilted plank coffin, the top resting against a table, the bottom on the ground. The dead man's head was flanked on the one side by my grandmother, dressed in black, a kerchief covering half her face, on the other by my father, wearing a tie and cap, both of them perched on stools. At the dead man's feet, the remaining children were sitting cross-legged: Giannos, a precocious and boisterous adolescent, hair gleaming with brilliantine and thumbs rakishly hooked behind his suspenders; Petros, four years younger, the faint shadow of a mustache tracing his upper lip; Fani, shrinking from the camera with virginal modesty rather than grief; and at the very edge of the frame,

Markella, in her third year of elementary school, all roguish airs and clutching a cat that her mother clearly had been unable to persuade her to put down.

I was taken aback, almost shocked, by this macabre scene, until a little later I learned that it was common practice at the time for photographers to immortalize mortality.

III

WHEN ANTONIS, AS the eldest remaining son, stepped into the role of head of the family at the age of nineteen, he was a tall, personable young man, whose wide, full-lipped mouth gave him a certain likeness to a dolphin. He was almost always smiling; the social disgrace, the dashing of his personal dreams did not dishearten him except very fleetingly.

"I was planning to enroll in the Hellenic Naval Academy. Or the Polytechnic," he was saying one day to Anaïs.

"Don't let it get you down," she replied, stroking his head.

"Get me down? Of course not. We're the ones with our hands on the wheel!" he reassured her.

Who was he referring to with this "we're the ones"? To the two of them? The lovebirds who trysted in the most unlikely of places—including a secret recess in the church forecourt accessed by a trapdoor—and who exchanged many more kisses and caresses than words? To his mother and siblings, who looked on him like a god after his father's death? (An exceptionally awkward situation given that he did not particularly care for either Markella bringing him his slippers or Petros plying him with questions about math problems.) To his compatriots from Asia Minor, most of whom insisted on deluding themselves with dreams of a return to the homeland? Antonis had no sense of himself as a refugee; he was well aware of the whys and the hows of his family's downfall. So, no. This "we" had an entirely different meaning, one which escaped him for the time being.

For the time being, he slaved away copying sheet music. He had come about this work completely by chance. He was strolling on Stadiou Street one day when he spied a want ad in a shopwindow: *Calligraphist needed.* He recalled his early years of elementary school and how his teacher had praised his remarkable performance in Turkish, taught to them as a native language and rendered at the time in the Arabic alphabet. He was the only child whose board— those small, individual blackboards that each student used to carry and write on with slate pencils—was not covered in chicken scratch but might well be mistaken for a page from the Quran. Confident as usual, he strode into the shop. The owner put him to the test then and there and had him copy the introduction to the operetta *Miss Sorolop* by Theophrastos Sakellaridis, who at the time had taken Athens by storm. Impressed, the man offered half a drachma per page, much less than the fee for having the pages printed or importing sheet music from abroad. Antonis accepted without bargaining, the work had seemed exceptionally easy.

"You know how to read music, don't you?" his new boss asked, and Antonis immediately responded in the affirmative because he wanted the job. After agreeing to transcribe them seven times over within three days, he left carrying two oratorios by Verdi. But his lie caught up with him immediately. Without any knowledge of music, the notes made no rhyme or reason; they were nothing but tiny marks scattered randomly on the staves. Not to mention that the special, indelible ink he was using meant that the smallest of slipups obliged him to scrap the page and start again. Accordingly, he had to glance up and down constantly from the original to his copy. Progressing at a snail's pace, sweating with the effort of it all, he refused to succumb to his frustration. Only when his hand started to tremble did he go out to the garden for a smoke. Working night and day, he completed the order with only minutes to spare. His boss received the scores and paid him, adding a small tip.

"Beethoven is up next. A beauty, even though a little challenging," he explained. Antonis glanced at the callus on his finger, but dared not refuse. He needed the money.

YET THE FAMILY'S fortunes were taking a turn for the better, and they were, in fact, much more comfortable than most of their Asia Minor compatriots.

After a brief sojourn in Argentina, Iordanis had finally settled in Santiago, Chile, from where he mailed them a respectable sum every two months.

Esteemed mother, beloved siblings, began the almost identical postcards accompanying each remittance. *I am in good health and I hope the same is true of you. I send you this photograph so that you may admire the magnificent valleys of Casablanca* or *the Santiago Cathedral* or *the Presidential Palace. In this country, the weather is mild and the people, openhearted. I look forward to a speedy reunion.* He would conclude this brief note by signing his name all over the bottom. But he never said a word about what he was doing.

Giannos, too, was invariably silent about his "affairs." On the sly, he began slipping generous amounts of pocket money to his younger siblings. After my grandmother caught Markella with fifty drachmas tucked into her garter and forced her to confess that it was a gift from Giannos, she cornered him and grabbed him by the hair.

"Hey, you! A petty thief, is that what you've become?"

"No, Mother, I swear!" he whined.

"Where did you find all that money?"

She would not relent, threatening to spill the beans to Antonis until Giannos pulled a deck of cards from his pocket and demonstrated his prowess.

"Oh, so you're a cardsharp?"

"I play clean, I swear on all that is holy!"

"Cut it out!" my grandmother snapped. But she did not betray him. Deep in her heart, she believed that he too would find his way, and that like all her children, he had his own personal guardian angel watching over him.

THE YEAR 1926 was one of upheaval. In February, the family moved from the refugee shacks in the Brahami district to a little house in Kallithea. It had only one floor with barely three rooms to it, but it was newly built and well-situated in a quiet oasis in the city center.

In April, Anaïs made Antonis an unexpected pro-posal: One of her late father's aunts, a childless and wealthy widow, had invited her to Marseilles.

"Let's go together!" she suggested excitedly. "The Armenian community there is big and powerful. They can find us good jobs, perhaps even help us study!"

"And what will I do with my mother and siblings?"

"You'll send them money, like Iordanis."

"They need a man in the house—"

"There's Giannos."

"I wouldn't trust Giannos even with our chickens!"

"What are you going to do? Rot here in Athens, going blind copying out that sheet music? I, for one, am not staying here any longer. I've had it up to here with being called 'slut'[8] at every turn and helping my mother with the sewing!"

"Don't you love me?"

"It's because I love you that I want to take you with me. I'm not even asking you to marry me. Let's go to France and see what happens."

Antonis sat up on the mattress—taking advantage of the fact that her mother was out, she had smuggled him into her room—and stared at her, more intently than ten-derly. She was short and swarthy, with curly hair and perky

---

[8] Indigenous Greeks denigrated ethnic Greek women from Asia Minor.

little breasts. More than anything she enjoyed a good roll in the hay, and was always hot to trot when there was a man around. She was only fifteen and had already lost her virginity when he first met her. But as soon as she fell in love, she was faithful and relinquished her games and her wanton ways. "My family is just an excuse," he admitted to himself. "The real issue is whether I could live my life with Anaïs." He lit a cigarette and inhaled in silence. Something did not sit right with him, arguably something really inconsequential: the scent of her skin, or the way she rolled her *r*'s, a little like *l*'s, and which strangely enough I "inherited," the daughter he had with another woman. Something held him back from tying his lot irrevocably to Anaïs's. He got up, dressed, and walked out the door.

Two weeks later, Anaïs left Greece for good. Remarkably, they maintained a secret correspondence until their late old age. She called him "my pasha" and he called her "my little filly." He stored her letters in a suitcase with a combination lock, and after his death, I had to cut through the leather with a knife to open it.

In July 1926, Antonis resigned from his position as sheet-music copyist. He had found less-grueling and better-paid work at a carpet merchant's behind the Church of Panagia Kapnikarea in the city center. He had first entered the shop on an entirely different errand. His mother had given him a small, extremely beautiful bouchara carpet that she loved dearly but had heavyheartedly decided to let go because she believed it to bring bad luck.

"Sell it, but for the love of God don't give it away for a pittance!" she had pleaded. And so as not to disappoint her, at the age of twenty he had discovered the dormant Anatolian within: He drove a hard bargain for about an hour, at times pretending outrage; at others, feigning capitulation; at yet others, appealing to the merchant's sense of honor; a couple of times, he even turned on his heel as if heading toward the door. He managed to raise the price from the one hundred and fifty drachmas the shopkeeper had originally offered to eight hundred.

"Will you take a coffee?" the latter had asked, after counting the money. He was a lanky, cross-eyed man of around sixty, with long monkey hands that he kept regularly disinfecting with cologne. "You've got talent for driving a bargain, my young friend. Do you have any experience as a salesman?"

"My father was a merchant."

"Where are you from?"

Antonis provided a synopsis of their story with some strategic embellishments: He claimed that his father had been butchered by the Turks and that all traces of his brother had been lost.

"In other words, you alone are supporting your mother and siblings," the merchant remarked, visibly moved.

"All refugees are in the same boat, more or less," Antonis said, and shrugged.

He did not like pulling on the man's heartstrings in this way, yet it was necessary, he knew, in what he sensed were ongoing negotiations.

"And how do you put food on the table?"

"Odd jobs here and there," Antonis started to say, but bit his tongue. He did not want to weaken his position by appearing desperate. "I translate from French and also Turkish."

"You speak French?"

"My parents made sure I got an education. They had big dreams for me."

"How much do you make from these translations?"

Antonis realized that his future was hanging in the balance—his immediate future at least. He decided to toss the dice: "Between a thousand two hundred and a thousand five hundred drachmas on average." He doubled the amount he made as a copyist.

"Per month?"

"Yes."

The merchant scratched his bald dome and peered at him.

"I'll give you nine hundred," he said finally. "And three percent on each sale. Your shift is from eight in the morning to eight at night. You can take a nap in the attic after lunch and use it to stay overnight whenever you need. Coffee, small bites, and an afternoon ouzo with meze are on me. You'll learn the ropes and they will open doors for you. Your father, watching us from above, will be bursting with pride to see you follow in his footsteps."

Antonis counted until one hundred under his breath, pretending to think it over. "Eight hundred drachmas in salary, but six percent on each sale," he countered.

"I like it when young people believe in themselves!" The merchant beamed, and finally introduced himself. "Emilios Lichnarakis. Don't be misled by the 'akis.'[9] I am not from Crete. I'm a true Athenian born and bred!" he added proudly.

Uncle Milios's business depended on a two-way exchange: He bought carpets, mainly from refugees, at the lowest possible prices, which he then sold to the local residents at the highest possible prices.

"Under no circumstances must the two cross paths! As soon as you see a buyer on the threshold, any Turk-spawn[10] go straight up to the attic—"

"For the moment at least, I can't do any of the buying," Antonis interrupted before he could continue. "I too am Turk-spawn. I just can't be that cold."

Despite his initial disappointment, Uncle Milios soon accepted their division of labor. In any case, the young man's record was impressive. Within five months, the business had almost doubled its profits.

How did he sweet-talk them into it? How did he manage to convince their customers that the success of the inauguration of a doctor's office, or even the anticipated prosperity of an impending marriage, depended on the purchase of a carpet? His courtesy and eloquence certainly contributed,

---

[9] The suffix "akis" is a very common ending for Cretan surnames.

[10] A derogatory term used by indigenous Greeks to designate ethnic Greeks born in Asia Minor.

but more than anything, it was the brightness of his face and the sense of largesse he emanated—one could easily take him for the son of a good family, if not of noble stock. It never even occurred to the men that the young gentleman might be leading them up the garden path, while the women just did not have it in their hearts to disappoint him.

"The lad certainly appeals to the finer sex," Lichnarakis mused to himself, his left eye wandering to his daughter, who was sitting at the register batting her eyelashes at Antonio.

IV

THE NIGHT BEFORE Christmas Eve 1926. Dusk. A man of around thirty years of age, wearing a fedora, monocle, and trench coat, stands before the shopwindow, eyes darting from the carpets on display to the interior. Eventually, Antonis gets up and opens the door. The man hesitates.

"I don't—you know—I don't intend to buy anything…I'm just killing some time until dinner…"

"That's all right. The demonstration is free, and I guarantee you'll be impressed!" Antonis says, smiling broadly. "Come in, you'll catch your death in that cold."

The man finally enters and Antonis helps him off with his hat and coat.

"I didn't expect such cold in Greece."

"Where are you visiting from?"

"Alexandria in Egypt. Adam Kremos."

After shaking his hand, Antonis immediately begins to roll out rugs, extolling their "excellent quality" and "unparalleled designs" as if he had handwoven them himself. Kremos nods along to all the praise, but it is clear that he is only playing a part. He is much more interested in the salesman than his wares.

"So young and yet so accomplished!" is his clumsy compliment.

"Oh, I'm just a humble clerk," Antonis replies.

"My wife and I are in Athens for our honeymoon and we need a guide. Someone with your esprit, your joie de vivre."[11]

"You flatter me, but I too am a foreigner. I came to Athens as a refugee."

"But this is where you live, and I bet you know the place inside out, all the fine places."

It occurs to Antonis that he knows not a single "fine place." Two and a half years in Athens and he has not even set foot in a tavern. The only entertainment in which he indulges is going to the cinema. Twice a month he enjoys a comedy or a melodrama, American or French preferably, at the Attikon Cinema. In the past, he used to go with Anaïs; now he takes his little sister Markella, who dreams of becoming an actress and is always agog at the sight of a movie star.

---

[11] A language favored by intellectual elites throughout the Greek diaspora in the early twentieth-century, French words and terms are peppered throughout the Greek text.

"It goes without saying, of course, that you'll be compensated for your services," Adam Kremos presses his suit.

There is no longer any doubt in Antonis's mind: He smells a rat. But his curiosity is well and truly piqued.

"But I can't just leave my boss hanging, can I?" he asks, speaking mainly to himself.

"Not to worry about that," Kremos reassures him. "I will take care of getting you time off work. By the way, are you married? Engaged?"

"Single."

"Excellent. Will you do us the honor of dining with us this evening?"

THIS IS HOW Antonis wound up crossing the threshold of the Hotel Grande Bretagne into an imposing hall with chandeliers, a grand piano, and liveried waiters.

Kremos rescued him from the dilemma of having to choose from a menu of dishes that he not only had never tasted but had never even heard of: entrecôte bordelaise, two-salmon tartare with asparagus and truffles, filet tartare. The maître d' stopped at their table to recommend a sparkling Russian wine—"better than the best French champagnes"—from the 1906 vintage.

"It was an excellent year for the Odessa vineyards," he sniffed nostalgically.

"I was born in 1906," Antonis blurted in order to say something but immediately regretted what struck him as a rather gratuitous, if not completely daft remark.

Nevertheless, it brought Mrs. Kremos out of her reverie of indifference. Her listless eyes finally lit up. "Really? You look so young! I'm only three years older. Would you like a cigarette while we wait for the hors d'oeuvres?" she extended her gold cigarette case.

Antonis had difficulty believing that this vamp with the crimson lips, perfect curls, and fur stole thrown somewhat carelessly over her shoulders was not yet twenty-five years old. "All that lipstick and powder age her," he thought to himself. "Even the mole on her cheek is probably painted on."

Time slipped away, smoothly, easily, until midnight. Antonis kept peppering the newlyweds with questions, betraying such an interest in life in Egypt that it was as if he were preparing for an imminent emigration. When it was their turn to ask, however, he avoided answering with any specificity. But this did not seem to concern them, as if the mere act of observing him sufficed to quell their curiosity.

"So will you tour us through Athens?" Adam Kremos repeated his offer at the end of the evening.

"With pleasure. But as I explained, I don't have the time."

"I'll have everything arranged by the day after next," Kremos pledged rather patronizingly. "Tomorrow night we'll have seafood at Aktaion."

THEY MET THERE, at the pride of the Faliron Delta, in the restaurant of the magnificent hotel, which was partitioned into private rooms called *separées* with doors that the waiters, summoned by the press of a button, could shut for the diners' discretion. And it was there, over the empty shell of an enormous lobster, that the reason for the Alexandrians' extravagant interest in the young refugee finally came to light.

"Our situation is rather unusual," Adam began hesitantly, while Clary urged him on with her eyes. "We are, as you know, married, newlyweds, but we do not have relations. Carnal relations, that is."

"Why?" Antonis asked, like a wide-eyed innocent.

"Let's say we have different tastes."

"Let's say that Adam is not partial to women," Clary further specified, but without a trace of bitterness in her expression.

"In any case, that's our way of life and we have a terrific, absolutely idyllic time of it, as you can see."

Antonis smiled awkwardly.

"There's only one problem: Marriage creates certain expectations, and especially when you are the only son of a wealthy family, these expectations become demands. You must... no, in fact you are duty-bound to bring an heir into the world, someone to continue the family name and inherit the paternal estate. Do you understand what I am getting at?"

"Yes," Antonis replied.

"This is where you come into the picture," Kremos added, getting down to brass tacks. "On our return from our honeymoon, it would be a true blessing if Clary were pregnant. You cannot imagine the joy it would bring to our families as well as the entire Greek community, not to mention the Patriarch of Alexandria. Since I am not that kind of man, we kindly ask you to take on the duties of insemination. For a price, of course!"

"What do you mean?" Antonis asked stupidly.

"Duties, my foot!" Clary feigned offense. "Adam, my dear, you may have other interests, but this young man won't be having a bad time with me!"

"I don't understand what exactly you're asking of me..."

Kremos turned to Antonis, his tone businesslike, almost stern: "We're staying in Athens for another three months. Our proposal is that you spend that time sleeping with Clary. Should she fall pregnant, we will compensate you with a sum of five thousand gold English sovereigns. Needless to say, after our departure, we will cut off all contact. Agreed?"

"Why did you pick me?"

"Isn't it obvious? Don't you see?" Kremos smiled. "Because we look alike, my friend. We look so much alike that no one will doubt that your child is mine!"

For the first time, Antonis looked Adam Kremos up and down and admitted that despite the latter's dandified airs, their features were indeed very similar.

Had he known of the blood ties that bound his father to the despoiling deacon, Antonis might have reacted differently. Perhaps the Kremos proposal would have terrified him; perhaps he would have turned tail and run. Now it only dumbfounded him. Smoking an aromatic Egyptian cigarette, he managed to steady himself and consider the situation clearheadedly. In essence, what were they asking of him? To sell his sperm, and at an astronomical price! Five thousand sovereigns would forever change his and his family's fate. It would free them once and for all from poverty and an uncertain tomorrow. And what would he have to do? To get the lady pregnant and then forget the whole thing. Come to think of it, that Clary was not without her attractions. There was a certain hardness to her face and bearing, but many men would pay a good price to have her in their beds. Their proposal had initially seemed bizarre, immoral. Immoral? According to which moral code? After all, he would be bringing happiness to two human beings, their families, and the Alexandrian Patriarchate into the bargain, he smirked to himself. As for the child that he would never meet, it would be born with a silver spoon in its mouth and a gilded future lying in wait.

The couple did not wait for Antonis to say "I do"; his faint smile sufficed. The agreement was sealed with an improvised ceremony: The three of them drank out of the same glass, which later Kremos, now drunk, hurled "for luck," smashing it to smithereens on the oak door of the *separée*.

"Shall I return to work tomorrow?" Antonis asked.

"No, of course not! I'll come and pick you up at your house."

"Better avoid the neighborhood gossips. I'll wait for you nearby, in the forecourt of the Church of Saint Eleousa."

With the exception of a humiliating examination at the Hospital of Venereal Diseases—"Forgive me, but we don't buy a pig in a poke," Adam said by way of apology—the couple all but laid out the red carpet for Antonis.

V

MR. AND MRS. Kremos had settled into a two-floor villa in Ampelokipoi, back then almost a country suburb. They had shipped all their household goods from Egypt—from dishes to curtains—as well as two dark-skinned, tight-lipped servants, the giant Mehmet and "Auntie" Leila. A taxi lay in wait outside the house all day and all night. As soon as Mr. Kremos got into it, another taxi arrived to take its place in the event that Mrs. Kremos wished to take a jaunt.

The couple's bedroom was on the second floor. Adam handed Antonis over to Clary and hastened to get ready for a night out on the town.

"I will be very discreet," he said to set their minds at ease. "Whenever I stay over, I will sleep in the room downstairs, even though I have also rented a room at the Hotel Excelsior."

Clary stretched out on the sofa. She was wearing a very short silk Chinese robe and nothing underneath.

"It is customary for us women of the Orient to wax off all our body hair," she explained to Antonis. "Besides the hair on our heads and our eyebrows, of course. I hope that doesn't bother you."

"Not at all," he assured her.

"Would you like a pastis?"

"Isn't it too early for alcohol?"

"Probably," Clary conceded, glancing at the little gold watch hanging between her breasts.

The huge canopied bed lay in readiness, strewn with half a dozen velvet pillows that might shortly prove to be useful. But the two of them hung back awkwardly. The familiarity that had begun to grow between them over the previous days seemed to have taken wing.

SUDDENLY, ANTONIS REMEMBERED an image from his very early childhood. It was insemination season and Mudanya's stockmen had pooled their resources to pay the steep leasing fee for the most fertile stud bull in Bursa. The animal was so prized and pampered that its owner had insisted on sparing it the rigors of the dirt road. Traveling the distance in a cart drawn by two oxen (two eunuchs of its kind, in other words), the beast had been dismounted in the square so that the entire village could pay tribute before it was led to its brides.

"Let's go see the beast!" his father had said, taking Antonis by the hand. Beast, indeed: back rising to a grown man's height, black coat glistening in the sun, head like a giant anvil capable of bending the hardest metal, nostrils spurting plumes of steam as if from an inner heat. A thick chain around its neck and another one around its middle held it in place. The surrounding crowds had initially kept a safe distance but inched closer and closer as they gradually grew bolder. Superstition had it that touching the beast would grant the men strength and the women fertility.

"You, too. Grab its horns!" his father had commanded, and without asking, lifted him high in the air. Practically trembling with fear, the five-year-old child came face-to-face with the beast. And that's when he had what was perhaps the first great surprise of his life: As close as they were, the bull's eyes had nothing threatening or even fearsome in them. They emanated a deep melancholy, absolute resignation. Antonis burst into tears, not of fear but of pity.

"Now is not the time for such thoughts!" he admonished himself as he dismissed the memory with an uneasy brush of his hand. In the meantime, Clary was winding up the gramophone. On a shelf next to the window there were stacks of two dozen or so discs—heavy and fragile 78 rpm records, which cost more than the entire budget for the average Greek household.

"Do you like 'La Violetera'?" she asked as she plucked it out. Antonis nodded in affirmation, even though he had no idea what she was talking about.

"Let's dance to it then!" Clary exclaimed, placing the needle in the groove.

As soon as the first notes wafted out of the horn, she spun around twice and came to a stop in front of him, holding the tango's opening pose. Antonis did not know the first thing about Argentinean dance, so he got up and instead of swinging her around, he grasped her waist and threw her on the bed.

"Better a stud than a sissy!" he thought as he entered her.

DESPITE THEIR DEDICATION to their charge, despite the aphrodisiacal tidbits that Kremos fed them—royal jelly, oysters, sea urchin salads—the first month remained fallow.

"It's here," Clary announced to Antonis with a defeated look, while "Auntie" Leila delivered discreetly wrapped sanitary napkins.

Kremos made no comment on this failure, but Antonis thought he discerned a hint of reproach in his eyes. "Could I be infertile? A eunuch?" Anxious, he started to count the days to the end of Clary's flow so that he might throw himself with renewed vigor into this bedroom campaign.

A few days later, as they were lying in bed in the afternoon, exhausted after sex, Antonis leapt to his feet.

"Let's get out of here! Everything is as sterile as a hospital. We will never conceive a child surrounded by all these French perfumes, silks, and porcelains! And you know what? If you continue to think of me as a chore, just lying there waiting for me to finish while I pant and sweat over you, then it's truly hopeless."

"I have to want you on top of everything?" Clary asked sourly.

"In that moment, at least. Pretend that I'm making love to you and not simply siphoning sperm into you!"

They told Kremos that they were taking a trip to Delphi, where the poet Sikelianos[12] was organizing some festivals. Instead, almost dragging her by the hair, Antonis took her to a hotel on Peraiki Avenue, a place of ill-repute frequented by sailors and prostitutes. The room reeked of sweat and hashish. The bed shuddered and groaned. In place of a toilet, there was a chamber pot that the bellhop emptied each morning and evening.

Either because the place frightened her, or because she had been freed from her habitual environment, or simply because of the cold piercing through the unplastered walls, for the first time Clary curled up into Antonis's arms. For the first time, she told him about herself, about all the hopes and dreams she had for her marriage to Kremos.

"Make sure you get me pregnant before I fall in love with you," she said finally, avoiding his eyes. "Otherwise, it'll be the end of us both."

"And what if I get you pregnant and then don't let you leave?"

"You would be condemning our child to squalor and poverty. I did not think you were so selfish."

---

[12] During the 1920s, Angelos Sikelianos (1884–1951), a lyric poet and playwright, along with his wife, Eva Palmer Sikelianos, organized a series of festivals in Delphi—musical and dramatic performances, athletic games, and art exhibitions—aimed at reviving the Delphic idea.

FOR SOME REASON, Clary reminded Antonis of an olive, the fleshy green kind that dribble oil when you take them out of the barrel. He felt that she was always slipping out of his grasp, that he could not hold her still long enough to get to the pit within. But he had to. He was gripped by such stubbornness that nothing would have turned him from his course, not even if he were told that Clary, like a praying mantis, would bite his head off as soon as he got her with child.

During their third night in Piraeus, he got up to take a piss. Afterward, he stood naked in front of the window, smoking a cigarette and staring at the full moon flittering over the sea. The dark mass of a ship was slowly entering the harbor. Its first blare echoed in the squawks of hundreds of seagulls. The second was drowned by a factory siren summoning workers in the wee hours before dawn. The third sounded a battle cry to Antonis, a sign that the moment had come. He turned Clary on her back and thrust himself between her legs. Without opening her eyes, she pulled him into herself.

Adam Kremos waited until Clary's period was four weeks late before making an appointment with the chair of the Obstetrics Department, who diagnosed his wife's pregnancy amid hearty congratulations. That very same day, Kremos handed Antonis a leather bag—so heavy it could barely be lifted—laden with a hundred bundles wrapped in paper bearing the stamp of an Egyptian bank.

"Count it. Tear the seals and count the gold coins!" he exhorted.

"No need, I believe you," Antonis replied.

"It was a pleasure to have met you." Kremos dismissed him with a shake of the hand.

"May I say goodbye to Clary?"

"The lady has gone to lie down." Kremos's tone was suddenly chilly. "The doctor advises that she remain resting in a supine position and avoid visits during this first period of the pregnancy. She asked me to convey her warmest wishes."

He walked Antonis to the door and directed the taxi driver to take him to Kallithea.

"DON'T ASK ME where it came from and, above all, don't tell me where you are going to put it," Antonis begged his mother as he put the bag down on the kitchen table. "It's for you to spend on your children as you see fit."

My grandmother pulled the wrapper off one of the bundles and a golden cascade poured out.

"Are these stolen?" she asked, her eyes wide with alarm.

"I earned it all with the sweat of my brow, on my word of honor. Let's say that I reclaimed the fortune poor father lost in Constantinople. Finally, we are our own masters again, and we can use it to realize our dreams," he said, with a big smile.

For the next two and a half days, Antonis basked in the triumph of a victor laden with trophies. He whistled as he walked, daydreaming as he faced the future. In no hurry to give shape to his plans, he indulged in some unprecedented luxuries: a gramophone for the house, along with its inevitable companion, the record of *La Violetera*, as well as two made-to-order suits from the most expensive tailor in Kallithea. On the third day, he went to see Emilio Lichnarakis and tendered his resignation. The latter did everything in his power to keep him there, offering to make him a partner in the business and even proffering his daughter's hand in marriage. Antonis, however, politely turned him down. He bowed and left, leaving the other man staring after him openmouthed.

Antonis decided to go have a coffee at Aigli in Zappeio, the favored haunt of the golden youth of Athens. He now felt equal to them, part of the in crowd, not because the five thousand sovereigns were such a fabulous sum but because he had come about it so easily, due entirely to his charisma. There are people who, if manna were to descend on them from the heavens, shudder and quake in anticipation of the blow of fate that will balance the scales. My father's temperament tended to the opposite extreme: He wholeheartedly believed that life belonged to him, and now he had incontrovertible proof.

As he was crossing the Royal Garden, he heard a crack followed by a burning sensation in his left ear. The second report dispelled all doubt: Someone was shooting at him. Instead of taking to his heels, he turned to look for his would-be killer. Behind him, on the pathway through the woods, a couple of nursery maids were pushing prams.

"Where are you, you bastard?" he cried, and then the snap of twigs spun him toward a thick cluster of trees. He lunged through lacerating thorns and managed to clinch the culprit by the neck. Astonished, he dragged him to the ground and stripped him of the ivory-handled Smith and Wesson 45.

"What are you doing? What have you done?" he yelled, yanking on the man's necktie as if to strangle him.

"Don't you see?" spluttered Adam Kremos. "You know my biggest secret! You are my biggest secret! How can I let you live?"

"Why didn't you kill me at your house in Ampelokipoi?"

"At the time, I did not realize how dangerous you might become. Clary brought me to my senses. She said that you would hold it over us all our lives."

"Don't drag Clary into this mess." Antonis slapped him hard across the face. Yet he sensed that, despite his madness, Kremos was telling the truth.

"Even if Clary did send you, it's not because she fears that I will extort you!" he added, kicking Kremos in the groin. "It is because she has fallen in love with me!"

A BRAWL OF that magnitude in such a well-frequented location could not fail but draw police attention. Two baton-wielding officers pulled them apart and hauled them to Syntagma Station. During the initial interrogation conducted by the officer in charge, Antonis described the attempted murder, while Adam brashly stated that Antonis, "a youth unknown to him," had tried to rob him.

"Very well, when the commander returns tomorrow from Farsala, you can explain everything to him," said the rotund young man sweating through his assistant patrol leader's uniform as he washed his hands of the situation.

"At what time do you expect us here tomorrow?" Kremos asked, simpering obsequiously.

"What makes you think you're going home tonight, my friend?" the young man chuckled, before instructing his officers to lock one of them in the roof cells and the other in the basement. As he tumbled down the stairs, Antonis heard Adam screaming bloody murder and threatening the guards with a world of trouble: they had no idea with whom they were dealing. As soon as the door to his filthy cell, with its earthen or possibly manure floor, closed behind him, he heard a gruff voice: "Welcome, young man!"

It turned out that Adam Kremos did indeed have some strings to pull with the local police (or at least had obtained them with some generous palm greasing). The following morning, they were let go.

"We'll consider this matter closed," the commander said to Antonis. "And don't let me see you occupying the authorities' time again," he added sternly.

If wishes were horses, then beggars would ride. By the time dawn broke over the prison, Antonis Armaos had become a communist.

VI

WHO WAS IT that succeeded in converting my father within a few hours? A former priest of a church in Chania who, despite casting aside his robes in protest at the use of religion as the opiate of the masses, had not discarded his preacherly talents. After hearing out his young fellow inmate's story—Antonis only omitted mentioning the gold sovereigns and portrayed himself as a victim of the Kremoses' evil machinations—he heaved a deep sigh. "Is it not enough for them to suck the blood of the working man, now they must also steal his sperm?"

"Who?" Antonis wondered.

"The bourgeoisie, my boy. Capitalism."

In a handful of simple sentences free of all theoretical obfuscation, the defrocked priest described the world from the beginning. All that Antonis learned later in his study of Marxist-Leninist texts was but a complement or embellishment to that first lesson.

What was it that had captivated him, that led Antonis, on his release from the police station, to already view himself as a soldier of the revolution? The battle between good and evil, which was necessarily and deterministically destined to lead to the triumph of the former. Deterministically not because the outcome was ordained by the arc of Justice, or the will of God, but rather because it was the intrinsic law of all-powerful History.

"To put things a little abstractly, when there are changes in the means of production, the relationships underlying production change, too. Initially, the feudal lords were in charge, then the bourgeoisie, but the twentieth century belongs to the working classes!"

"Who are the working classes?"

"We, who enrich the fat-cat industrialists with the exploited fruit of our labor. But their thrones are unstable and on the verge of toppling! In the Soviet Union, in Lenin's Russia, a new world is being built, free of poverty, squalor, and the oppression of human beings by other human beings. The Soviet Union is a torch bringing light to the globe!"

"Have you been there?" Antonis asked, impressed.

"Me? I'm a tubercular old man. You, the youth, will go and learn. Do you know what communism means?"

"No…"

"From each according to his ability, to each according to his needs."

"And how do I get to Russia?"

"Join the Party and you will find the way," the defrocked priest promised.

Until that night, Antonis had never thought about politics. In the darkness of that stinking cell, the words of the defrocked priest began to give new meaning and direction to his past and future, to the entire course of his life. What was the Greco-Turkish War? An imperialist battle waged for control of the Straits and Middle Eastern oil reserves.

Why did Kemal win? Because he mobilized the Turkish people and allied himself with Lenin. Who destroyed his father? Constantinople's stock market. Who almost killed him in the Royal Gardens? A sponger who lived high on the hog by exploiting the Nile's dark-skinned laborers. What lay behind the Kremoses' apparent liberal-mindedness? Corruption, decay, and bourgeois decadence. Clary? A woman so alienated that she rented out her womb in service to her fake marriage and acquiesced to the murder of her child's biological father.

"How do I join the Party?"

"Go to Ideal, the restaurant on Panepistimiou Street, and ask for a waiter called Vrassidas, better known by his nickname, Carob. Tell him that ExComm sent you to connect with the Athens branch. He'll take care of everything else."

IN 1927, THE KKE's ambitions were wholly disproportionate to its actual powers. The ten parliamentary delegates granted by the four and a half percent of the vote the Party had won in the previous year's elections in no way justified its declared, immediate objectives: the calling of a general workers and farmers strike, the seizure of power, and the establishment of a Soviet Greece. The only trouble was that the type of Marxist-Leninist analysis practiced by the heads of the Party seemed to mathematically lead to the conclusion that capitalism was in its death throes worldwide and that countries like Greece—semi-agricultural and underdeveloped—were its soft underbelly. Circumstances therefore demanded that local communists rise to the call of History and take the lead among the workers and peasants as they collectively prepared to "storm the heavens."[13]

"Does this mean that the revolution is near?" Antonis asked Carob, with the exhilaration of a man who has contrived to jump on the ship a split second before it weighs anchor.

"If we rise to the occasion, it is well within the bounds of possibility that in six months you'll see the red flag flying over the Acropolis."

"What can I do exactly?"

Carob did not hasten to respond. It was past midnight. They were sitting at the café in the Museum Gardens, at the most secluded table. At long last, he loosened his waiter's bow tie, rolled up the sleeves on his white shirt, and scrutinized the neophyte that ExComm had sent him.

Antonis struck him as exceptionally bright, yet at the same time so ignorant, so ideologically unschooled that he was like a babe in the woods. This, however, was an asset. How much longer could the Party remain in the hands of the old-guard highbrow cobblers and Salonika Jews? They were unparalleled in their grasp of theory, but with all their cud-chewing and hairsplitting day in, day out over

---

[13] Karl Marx's phrase used to describe the actions of the Paris Commune, the revolutionary government that seized power in Paris from March 18 to May 28, 1871.

revolutionary tracts, they were steadily losing the hearts and minds of their audience as well as their own anchor in reality. There was an urgent need for new blood, for people of action, who would bloom not in frowsty hiding places[14] but out on the streets and in the factories. This refugee lad with the charming face was a new type of communist. Provided that his enthusiasm came with an ironclad backbone.

"Do you fully understand, lad, what you're getting yourself into?" Carob asked in a tone calculated to be daunting. "Joining the cause of Marxism-Leninism is not fun and games. It means that you must forget all the dreams that to this day sustained you and all the joys that brought you comfort. Communists know nothing of holidays or leisure. They don't sit at the table to eat hot meals served by their wives; they don't play with their children, and even if they do, they know that at any moment the police might burst in and drag them back to the labor camp or exile. On top of it all, they must serve as role models, as a constant source of light and inspiration to their community. Gambling, womanizing, drunkenness are all strictly off-limits. Even idling around at the café—the men's talk that happens over a game of backgammon, for example—is not in keeping with the expectations of a warrior in the vanguard. If you resolve to move forward, study, study, and struggle, these are the things that will become the chorus of your life. How

---

[14] Persecuted and outlawed throughout its history, the KKE members often had to meet in secret.

did Lenin put it? 'Study, learn more, learn forever: learn, learn, learn!'"

"Communists don't get involved with women?" Antonis asked.

"Of course they do. They're not monks! But what unites a couple most of all is the shared, coordinated struggle toward a common good. It's neither dowry nor the bedroom that binds them but rather the rocky road they choose to walk together. That's why I warn you: Steer clear of all this. Find yourself a nice young woman and a good, stable job, set up house…"

Like any young man with red blood instead of water running through his veins, Antonis took offense. "Who does that nitwit take me for? A milksop?" he asked himself.

"How would you like me to prove that I'm worthy of being a communist?" he asked, throwing down the gauntlet.

"Tell me, lad, are you ready to die for your beliefs?"

"Absolutely!"

"Don't expect a reward in heaven. There is no heaven."

"You think this is news to me?"

Carob got up and approached Antonis. He leaned toward him, as if to whisper something in his ear, and without warning struck him a powerful blow to the chin. The room spun around Antonis. It took all his strength not to fall out of his chair, but he didn't waver for an instant as to how he ought to respond. He swept his hand over his burning face and with lightning speed balled it into the fist he rammed smack in the middle of Carob's brow. For three minutes or thereabouts the waiter was counting stars. As soon as he came to a little—and while Antonis steeled himself for the next blow—he rewarded Antonis with a big smile and lifted his arms high in a sign of surrender.

"Welcome to the Party, comrade!" he said, and kissed him on both cheeks.

VII

BY JOINING THE KKE on an impulse, my father obtained in under two weeks something that would have been almost impossible had he opportunistically joined Eleftherios Venizelos's Liberal Party or the promonarchic People's Party: He was hired to a post on the Athens–Piraeus Electric Railways. Initially as a ticket collector, but the contract he had signed stipulated that after the successful completion of six months in service he was to be trained as a train driver. Only after the scheduled promotion and attendant tenure would he openly declare his ideological convictions and begin his true work.

As soon as she heard the news, my grandmother was floating on air. The sovereigns he had entrusted to her safekeeping were a great boon to her children's future security (she had them hidden out of harm's way and spent them only sparingly, at times of urgent need), but Antonis had to have gainful employment. *He who does not work, neither shall he eat*, Saint Paul had said. Far better to be an employee—and at a large company for good measure—than getting embroiled in business ventures and losing everything, like her husband had done. The only thing she had difficulty believing was that he had been hired, as he himself had explained, by the Bolsheviks.

"Do the Bolsheviks truly run the Athens railway?" she asked him.

"Under cover, so as not to come to the attention of the big bosses. Our hiring manager is a Bolshevik," he explained, laughing.

"He must be a good person to recognize the value of your moral strength and work ethic!" my grandmother retorted.

"He is a good person, but he didn't hire me out of the goodness of his heart." Antonis revealed the whole truth. "To be of any use the Party, I must be part of a booming workplace where I can meaningfully coordinate the class struggle."

"I don't understand what you are saying."

"I'm saying that if what you envision for me is the quiet and settled life of a complacent citizen, think again. Persecution, imprisonment, perhaps even the firing squad or noose lie in wait for me. Take care of my brothers and sisters and be ready for anything."

"You'll come to your senses as you grow older," my grandmother insisted.

My grandmother clung to this idea so doggedly that the photograph of Antonis she had hanging over her bed next to the icons until her death was not the one of him speaking to the May 1st assembly, red flags waving in the background; nor was it the one of him proudly holding a copy of *Rizospastis*.[15] Her pride and joy was the picture of him in his train driver's uniform: felt jacket and cap with the gold-plated Electric Railways braid. When I was in kindergarten and asked her for the first time what my father did, she answered proudly, "He drives the train!"

The truth is that my father genuinely enjoyed his years at the railway. While he was still a ticket collector, he probably felt some misgivings—especially when he caught fare-dodgers and had to hand them over to the authorities—but as soon as he was promoted and installed in the pompously dubbed "navigator's booth," he was buoyed by the exhilaration of someone who holds both untold horsepower and the lives of hundreds of people in his hands. Later in his life, while studying Russian, he wrote down and underlined the following words in his notebook: *voditel* = driver, *rukovoditel* = leader.

DID ANTONIS ARMAOS always have leadership ambitions? Even if he had, he would have found it near impossible to act on them. On the threshold of the 1930s, the KKE was more akin to a cult dedicated to self-destruction than to a

---

[15] The official newspaper of the Communist Party of Greece, published since 1916.

political party. With barely a thousand members scattered throughout Greece and constant internal strife among the "liquidarians" and the "anti-fractionalists," the "crypto-Trostkyites" and the "true Third Internationalists," it floundered in a quicksand of its own making.

Each congress concluded in the departure and occasional expulsion of half its members. Each leadership gathering turned into a free-for-all with inflamed ideologues bickering through the night in the stumbling dialect of "pure" demotic[16] sprinkled with Marxist jargon. All things considered, the KKE's electoral results were almost miraculous. Largely due, no doubt, to the Party's persecution by the successive governments that believed they were acting preventatively by outlawing it, by throwing its leaders in dungeons or banishing them to exile on arid islands—in essence, by turning them into heroes. "The Bolsheviks, too, were the underdogs shortly before the October Revolution" must have been the thought in every communist's mind at the time.

Whether by intelligence or by instinct, Antonis avoided entanglement in these intraparty scraps. He followed their conflicts in silence, and whenever it was his turn to speak, he steered the conversation to practical issues.

"Are you aware that certain reformist elements are attempting to infiltrate the Party? What is your opinion on

---

[16] Vernacular Greek, spoken by working people, as opposed to the "pure," Katharevousa Greek that was modeled on ancient Greek and used in politically conservative circles.

the matter?" the secretary of the Athens chapter said one day as he tried to bait Antonis.

"I'm not equipped to say one way or another," Antonis replied with a humility that left his interlocutor speechless. "My contributions to the struggle are through my cadre at work. When the left takes the lead on the rights of the working man, it gradually wins over the people. No?"

There was no arguing against that point. The two strikes that he had almost single-handedly organized within a three-month period had rallied an unprecedented number of participants (before his arrival, the Electric Railways communist cadre was a small, somewhat somnolent minority). His bravura on these occasions had been the talk of the town. When scabs attempted to start the trains, he had lain on the tracks and refused to move, even when the bumper of an advancing locomotive grazed him. A photograph taken while he lay on his back, fist raised high, had made the front page of all the newspapers over the caption "Worker-Warrior."

"Meeting striker demands is not always a good thing," the secretary of the Athens chapter plowed on. "Minor and meaningless improvements in a working man's daily life can dampen his revolutionary impulse. In one sense, the worse things are for him, the better!"

"What's the point of unions then? Why fight for a more humane workplace?" Antonis asked, appalled.

"To a communist, a union is nothing more than a gateway to the Red Army!" the secretary pontificated. "As for our syndicalists, they ought to always and absolutely adopt the Party line, avoiding all improvisation and false heroics," he added with a look heavy with innuendo.

Antonis swallowed the insult, but not without difficulty. During his almost two years with the KKE, he'd had more than enough time to realize that open conflicts, especially with one's superiors, were never worthwhile.

WHAT WAS IT that drew Antonis to the revolutionary life? What was it that had him making a beeline to the printer after a hard day's work to pick up the proclamations and brochures he would then deliver door-to-door, sowing them throughout Athens until midnight? What kept him plumbing his reserves of eloquence in the hope of winning over to the communist cause someone, anyone, stranger or acquaintance, who betrayed the least inclination to listen to him? What helped him endure the leadership's baiting and bullying, the routine police beatings during demonstrations, their trespasses into his home? (Almost once a month, under the pretext of a search, they would break in and wreak havoc, tearing pillowcases and even rifling through Markella's underwear.)

It must have been his faith in the triumph of communism. Even if, whenever he was being truly honest with himself, it seemed increasingly out of reach.

It was also the feeling of belonging to a select, if not actually anointed few, who operated in a realm above that of mere mortals, beyond their tired platitudes and practicalities. Observing passersby on the street, he found them terribly insipid, sadly floundering in their own tiny worlds. "I could never tolerate the hand-to-mouth life of the work mule," he would think to himself. "To have no other ambition than to get through the day. To not raise one's head for fear that it may get cut off. As for the bosses, their greed disgusts me. Their bottomless thirst for food, for fun, for fucking. If they're fit to burst and fully sated, why are their souls always so empty?"

In other words, while a part of Antonis teemed with an absolute, almost Christian love for his neighbor, another part of him felt only deep disdain.

This internal contradiction tormented him for some time, until he came across an essay taking stock of ten years of Soviet rule. In it he found the key to his dilemma: *Our goal, is not the establishment of a just socio-economic system,* the author argued. *Our goal is the creation of a new man. Freed of the bonds of necessity, socialism's New Man will acquire a depth of conscience, a strength of will, and reserves of energy inconceivable to us today. Indeed, in studying the past, socialism's New Man will be astonished by the servility and primitivism of our times. His will be a superior form of life. Let's not mince our words: His will be the life of a Superman!*

Antonis learned this passage by heart. While he never uttered it out loud for fear of being taken for a dreamer, every time he exhorted his comrades to switch off their engines and gather in front of parliament to trumpet their demands, he became increasingly convinced that each mobilization, each confrontation with authority, each sacrifice, no matter how large or small, transformed their lead actors, creating minuscule cracks in the shell of routine and alienation, in the shell that one day would be fully shattered by the emergence of the New Man awaiting within.

The ability to see those around him not as they really were but, in his estimation, as they might come to be, became one of my father's fundamental attributes.

VIII

AFTER THE PASSAGE in 1929 of the law of special illegal acts,[17] which in addition to subversive actions also penalized subversive ideas, Antonis was taken into custody, and when he refused to renounce communism, he was sentenced to three years in prison. Almost at the same time, he was informed of his summary dismissal from the Electric Railways. He viewed this sentence as a badge of honor: He was so feared by the regime that his freedom of movement could no longer be tolerated.

For communists, prison served as a sabbatical of sorts, an opportunity to focus on self-improvement. Older inmates

---

[17] The Idionymon, a 1929 law passed by the government of Venizelos, was the first in a series of legal actions targeting the Communist Party of Greece, in particular its calls to revolution. The law continued to be used to repress communists, trade unionists, and anarchists until the fall of the Regime of the Colonels in 1974.

prompted first-timers with the following message: "Cherish your cell; eat your chow; and read, read, read." Those with higher levels of education offered lessons not only in Marxism but also in subjects ranging from literature to biology. Attendance was mandatory. The more athletic encouraged physical exercise, even organizing volleyball championships in the recreation yard. The conditions of enclosure and sexual deprivation demanded physical release of some kind. These odd-duck communists greatly amused the criminal offenders. Instead of smuggling in tsipouro, drugs, or the occasional bouzouki to help pass the time more easily, they had turned their cells into study halls and borrowing libraries.

"A labor camp within a labor camp is what you've got here!" a notorious burglar taunted them one day. "Aren't the warden's rules and regulations enough for you? You need to add some of your own? Are you at least allowed to jack off under your blankets, or has Stalin done away with that, too?"

Noticing that a longshoreman was about to lunge at him, Armaos intervened. "We don't react to the provocations of the lumpen elements," he admonished. "Just ignore it."

The following week, however, he had to swallow his pride and approach this very same lumpen element, who often boasted of having eviscerated every safe and strongbox in Athens and its broader regions during the span of a thirty-year career.

"We're planning an escape." Antonis got down to business right away. "Can you help?"

"Ha! Already getting bored in here, my friend?"

"This isn't for me."

"Who, then?"

Antonis bent down (the burglar's size, barely five feet, was clearly an asset in his line of work) and whispered a name.

"But he's one of ours!"

"He's a member of the Party."

"Isn't he in here for murder?"

"The murder of a policeman, but in self-defense. He'll be sentenced to death."

The burglar didn't give a damn, and my father had to surrender ten of his gold sovereigns to win him over. The operation was planned and executed with surgical precision.

"You're absolutely sure you don't want me to get you out, too?" the burglar kept asking until the final moment.

"My place is here inside for the time being," Antonis replied.

THE "RED SLASHER'S" prison break made the headlines. The entire police force, both regular and military, along with handpicked military units, a total of twenty-three thousand men in uniform, were charged with hunting him down. Opposition parties denounced the government for unacceptable, if not downright suspicious negligence. *Rizospastis* announced the event in the most pithy and provocative way possible: *Following a resolution by the KKE's Political Bureau, Comrade Alexandratos broke out of the Averoff Prison.* In other words, the Party was more powerful than the state: When it put its mind to it, neither prisons nor legal systems could stand in its way. The investigation dragged on for a number of months to no avail. In the meantime, every neighborhood rung with the mocking lyrics and brisk tempo of the song hurriedly composed in commemoration: *Oh, the bourgeoisie, they tremble in fear / Building dungeons far and near / Locking up the children of the poor / With one strong fist, we knock down the door / Smashing their dungeons forevermore!*

Alexandratos had disappeared into thin air somewhere in the depths of Siberia. Yet he had fully risen to the call of History by providing the KKE with its first hero.

The success of this coup was in large part credited to Antonis Armaos. So much so that a year later, when the Communist International, with which the KKE was affiliated, decided to intervene, ousting the existing leadership for weakness and indecision and replacing it with new blood, Antonis shot to the top of the hierarchy. In one night, he found himself a member not only of the Central Committee but also of the Political Bureau. He was now one of five Party strongmen.

"How can I fulfill my responsibilities from prison?" he asked the intermediary who had brought him the glad tidings.

"Don't worry, soon enough you'll be passing through not one but two big doors!" was his reply.

Taking advantage of a temporary lull in government persecutions, the KKE took part in the 1932 elections. Without asking him, they registered Antonis to run for the Athens candidature. He had assumed that they simply needed names to fill the ballots. Having no sense of his reach and popularity, he believed he was known only among his Electric Railways colleagues and Party comrades.

So when, on a Monday morning, he was summoned to a meeting by the warden, who treated him to a coffee before announcing, with great formality and respect, his release to facilitate "participation in parliamentary proceedings," Antonis imagined he was the butt of a ridiculous prank. It was only when he saw his face on the front page of *Eleftheron Vima*[18] (with his name printed in huge letters across the top) that the truth sank in.

"What is 'Attica's new strongman' referring to?" he asked.

"To the fact that you received more votes than all your opponents!"

"Me?"

"You. Not your party."

"How is that possible?"

"Electoral law allows voters to black out names on their party ballot and write in the name of a candidate from a

---

[18] Now known as *To Vima*, *Eleftheron Vima* was a prominent daily newspaper known for its coverage of political issues.

different party. Even though many voted for the Liberals or the People's Party, they chose you as their delegate."

"What a law! To enter the ballot box arm in arm with the Crown."

"Well, that's democracy for you," the warden replied in a conciliatory tone.

AS SOON AS Antonis hopped off the tram at the Kallithea stop, he was recognized by local youths, who began cheering. They wanted to lift him up on their shoulders—like they did with sports stars—and when Antonis protested, they grabbed his battered prison suitcase and carried it to his doorstep like a trophy. His brothers and sisters were waiting for him dressed in their Sunday best; his mother had roasted lamb and potatoes; and there was even a bottle of wine on the table, a gift from the tavern keeper. Three of their neighbors had sent trays of desserts drenched in syrup. The house was abuzz with people coming and going to congratulate him.

Antonis's initial alarm gave way to anger. "What has come over you to open our door and let everyone in?" he railed when he collared his mother in the kitchen. "What do they imagine? That I'm going to run around putting in a good word whenever they want? A communist delegate is worlds away from a bourgeois party leader!"

"Understand them, son," she replied, in a tone more stern than contrite. "They were kicked out of Asia Minor and arrived here in rags. Ever since they've been treated like animals, called every name under the sun: 'Turk-spawn,' 'dirty slut.' Now, ten years later, one of their own enters parliament. It makes no difference to them whether you're with the king or with Lenin. Now, please go out there and celebrate with them!"

Until midnight, Antonis shook hands and raised his glass.

IX

MY MOTHER AND father's union would have delighted Charles Darwin, substantiating as it did his theory that the male selects the most attractive female, and the female succumbs to the male powerful enough to provide safety and healthy offspring. Even the revolutionary, or at least rebellious, communist milieu was not immune to love's biological imperatives.

One autumn afternoon, my mother's friend from the Communist Youth, whom my father had asked to intervene, went to my mother's house to pick her up and accompany her to the Panathenaic Stadium. The entire way there, Anna was silent, almost grim.

"He's waiting across the street. There he is, smoking under the tree! Go on, hurry up!" the friend prompted.

"Will he recognize me?"

"He knows who you are. He's seen you many times, and he fancies you."

"But he hasn't seen me up close, and we haven't talked—"

"Well, you'll talk now."

"What if he's disappointed?"

"What if you're disappointed?"

Neither one was disappointed. They walked to and fro the length of Alexandras Avenue several times, talking about their lives (Antonis skipping a number of scandalous episodes; Anna slightly exaggerating her contributions to the Party), and when they sat down to drink an orange soda, Antonis asked whether, moving forward, she was ready to walk beside him on a shared path.

"What do you mean?"

"It's what a bourgeois might call a marriage proposal," he said and smiled.

"But you've known me for less than two hours!"

"If she wanted nothing to do with me, she would have said, 'But *I've* known *you* for less than two hours,'" Antonis thought to himself and his smile widened.

"Two hours are enough for me, but if you need more time, I'll wait for you," he responded, as if doing her a favor.

"But we haven't even kissed," Anna stammered and immediately bit her lip.

"No sooner said than done!" Antonis said and pulled her into his arms. Anna gave him her lips without opening them, like a five-year-old girl. This pleased him; he would have found a more brazen response alarming, especially on their first meeting.

"Whom do I ask for permission to marry you? I've been told that your parents live in the village, and that your brother Kyriakos is doing his military service. Your brother Achilleas is a Trotskyist. You must understand, I cannot ask anything of a Trotskyist."

"I understand. So how about you just ask me."

And so, on an autumn afternoon in 1933, my father asked my mother for her hand in marriage. She held it out to him, pale and cool, and he clasped it in his.

HAD HE FALLEN madly in love with her? She was certainly, in the words of the song, a catch fresh and fluttering,[19] so beautiful to his eyes that not even movie stars could hold a candle to her. The cloud of gold curls crowning her head, her at times blue, at times gray eyes, lent a certain wildness to her beauty. She was also as tall and lean as a candle, with long, tapered legs, narrow hips, adolescent breasts. She didn't look very Greek. Or rather she looked like the kind of Greek dreamt up by a philhellene.

Had he fallen madly in love with her? Burned from the bitterness of the Clary Kremos episode, Antonis had ruled out all prospects of romance. During his early years in the Party, he had confined himself to the occasional fling: one of the salesgirls at the farmers market, a rather masculine woman in her forties, who had made sweet eyes at him and

---

[19] From "The Fisherman," a song by Giorgos Bilis: *A fisherman at dawn, makes the rounds of the neighborhood streets, crying out as he goes: "A catch so fresh and fluttering. No one who buys ever regrets the treat."*

lured him into a warehouse, where he laid her on a mound of dry onions; a young wife from Charokopou, with whom he would tryst on Sunday mornings while her husband, who was a cantor, was in church. He lied about his name and identity, not so much because he feared possible complications but rather because he wanted to remain a nameless shadow, a complete and utter stranger to them.

But after he was locked up, the more time passed, the more it gnawed at him that he didn't have anyone out there, a girl to wait for him and send him letters. After his triumphant release, he also realized that his position and the conditions of his daily life had changed for good: As long as the Party was officially recognized, he and his Political Bureau and parliamentary comrades functioned as its public face. They could not afford to expose themselves and the Party to scandal of any kind. And if the KKE were to be outlawed once again, trawling the neighborhoods for a bit on the side was completely out of the question. He therefore needed a committed partner, someone who would be willing to stand by him through any and all adversity.

So had he fallen in love with her? Even though I am their daughter, the fact that I am dead allows me to see with absolute clarity. I would say that he found in her exactly what he needed. And there was another reason: Anna's character was much simpler, or perhaps more intransigent, than his. It never occurred to her to reconsider a decision, not even to equivocate before taking it. Like a wild goat, she kept going, one foot in front of the other, never dreaming of turning back or looking down.

AT THE TIME, marriage for communists involved no ceremony, either religious or secular. The beginning of their life together as a couple required nothing more than cohabitation. When they lay down together on a shared bed, that's when their marriage was truly consecrated, both in fact and in feeling.

My parents' engagement could not have lasted more than a week, the time it took for Antonis to find a ground-floor apartment in Petralona. Even though Anna offered to help prepare their new abode, her betrothed turned her down: The apartment, in any case, was rented fully furnished and was even equipped with an icebox, he told her to set her mind at ease. On the morning of their wedding, they met on Filopappou Hill. When they turned the key to open their front door for the first time, Antonis wanted them to be holding it together.

"I have a comrade who is a taxi driver," he said to Anna. "I'll ask him to move your things."

Anna showed up with an enormous box in her arms. "This is my dowry," she explained timidly. "I've been working on it since I was six."

Once in the house, doing her best to conceal her agitation and hoping to delay, if only slightly, the moment when she would give herself to him, she took the lid off the box. A traditional wedding dress spilled out, with elaborate hand-embroidered designs on the bodice and a silk scarf for a veil.

"See these buttonholes? My father promised to hang gold coins through them," Anna said, pointing to the scarf's border, without a trace of regret in her voice. Instead, she

seemed proud of the fact that her father would not be handing her off to her groom decked out like a festooned barrel
organ.[20] In any case, her parents' marriage in a cave years
before they appeared in front of an altar had not been very
different.

No matter the depth of one's revolutionary conviction,
the need remains to mark the most important moments of
one's life, to invent personally meaningful rituals. At seven
the following morning, after a long night of conjugal bliss,
Antonis tiptoed out of the house and returned with a bouquet of chrysanthemums and a bag of steaming fritters. For
each wedding anniversary that they shared, he gave Anna
these same gifts.

X

THE SUNDAY AFTER their wedding, Antonis took Anna to
Kallithea to meet his family. My grandmother, who was
lurking out on the street to catch them before they got to the
house, hastened to slip the wedding bands she had ordered
at the local jeweler onto their fingers without asking for permission. Originally, she had wanted to ambush them with
a priest and give them no choice in the matter but, fortunately, had reconsidered for fear of her son's reaction.

---

[20] Akin to saying that one is decorated like a Christmas tree, as barrel organs
were covered in a profusion of baubles and trinkets.

They gathered around the table. Dazzled, Antonis's brothers and sisters stared at Anna, her beauty almost exotic to their eyes. She, in turn, was trying to get a sense of who they were without betraying her curiosity with too many nosy questions.

It was difficult not to notice Giannos—he made an immediate impression. A real man about town, he was clearly itching for the end of the meal to rejoin his merry band of miscreants. He was twenty-four years old but looked eighteen, even in a starched shirt, tie, and the beloved suspenders that he kept nervously snapping like rubber bands. He was an itinerant gramophone operator. In other words, he had commandeered the gramophone purchased by Antonis with the Kremos gold and installed it in a cart that he used to make the rounds of all the neighborhood festivals, wandering up and down, here and there, playing songs on demand.

"I have more than fifty records!" he boasted to Anna. "Something for every taste, from waltzes to Anatolian laments!"

"Do you make money out of it?"

"You bet! People love to have a good time! So much so, that in a couple of months I will be buying a delivery tricycle! Then, I'll be able to get to Kifissia, even out to Loutraki!"

There was no doubt in Anna's mind that in addition to his official employment, Giannos was also dabbling in all manner of petty swindles and scams. It was clearly distressing for Antonis, who was of the same mind, to see his brother puffing and preening like that. But he didn't say a word: Giannos was under his mother's protection.

At twenty-one years old, Petros was in business school, finishing a degree in accounting. Gaunt, prematurely balding, and wearing round glasses, he looked like a bookworm, in other words, a complete apple-polisher. He didn't say a word during the entire meal. But afterward, when the boys went out to the yard for coffee and cigarettes, leaving the women to "their chitchat," he pulled Antonis aside and asked whether he would help him join the Party.

"What do you know of the Party?" asked my father, surprised.

"I already have a very developed class consciousness," Petros responded, with the sentence he had prepared.

Antonis looked him up and down. "A slap or two from the police, and they'll wipe the floors with him," he mused. But he could not simply say no.

"Join the Communist Youth," he suggested. "Anna can make some introductions."

"Why won't you do it?" Petros protested.

"I'll be gone in a few days...What's the matter? Don't tell me you're embarrassed by Anna? She's your sister now!"

At first glance, Fani looked like the female version of Petros. With her modestly downcast eyes, bun, and unflattering pair of glasses (always slowly and painfully sliding down her nose) swallowing almost half her face, she could have been a catechism teacher. In actuality, she had recently been hired at one of the central banks as a secretary typist.

"I'm an excellent touch typist and stenographer!" she declared, vainly hoping that her sister-in-law would go on to describe her own talents. She liked to think of herself as the household's guardian angel: her mother's constant helper with the housework, her younger sister's mentor and protector, her brothers' tender confidante. To her great disappointment, none of them took her seriously.

Least of all Markella. That Markella! Had my mother watched any movies at all, her younger sister-in-law would surely have reminded her of those child wonders tap-dancing their way through American musicals. Short, sassy, sporting bright rouge and girlish pigtails, Markella bounced and bopped and chirped incessantly.

"Our little Markella is studying classical voice at the Conservatoire."

"I can do lighter, contemporary songs, too, Mother!" Markella chided. And without any prompting whatsoever, she ran off to fetch a small accordion and began singing—right there and then, in the middle of the meal!—anything and everything that popped into her head. Antonis tapped his fingers to the rhythm, following her every move with eyes full of tenderness.

"This one is either going to end up a prostitute or marry above every possible expectation," Anna thought to herself.

"Do you, my dear, have any brothers or sisters?" her mother-in-law asked.

"Achilleas, the eldest, is a theologian," Anna replied, without further elaboration. "Kyriakos just finished law school and is doing his military service at Kalpaki in

Epirus." She did not mention that he was in a penal bat-
talion, sensing that my grandmother would not be pleased
to learn that there was another communist in the family.
"My sister Alcmene lives in Kalamata and is married to
a lawyer. The youngest, Theone, is still in school at the
village."

"May the good Lord bring us all together one day," said
my grandmother as she poured homemade liqueur into tiny
glasses.

"WE'LL BE KEEPING the apartment, of course, but Anna will
always be welcome here, too, won't she, Mother?" Antonis
broke the big news as they were leaving.

"Why, where will you be?"

"In Moscow, for a few months. The Party elected me as
their representative to the International."

"And what about parliament?"

"I'll resign, of course."

"So you're leaving us for good?"

"Don't be silly, Mother! By summer, I'll be back."

It was October. Together, my mother and my grandmother began silently counting the months.

"You could have told me earlier about the trip," Anna
complained as soon as they were alone.

"It wouldn't have changed anything. We're talking
about one winter when we have our entire lives in front of
us," Antonis replied, wrapping his arms around her waist.

"Couldn't he take me with him?" Anna wondered. He certainly could have: Official representatives to the Communist Party had the right to be accompanied by their wives. But Antonis had not considered it for a second. Partly due to excessive rectitude ("The proletariat should not be bearing the cost of hosting my wife"); partly, to calculation ("The distance will show whether our relationship is built to last").

This is how, because of my father's male stratagems, my mother was denied the opportunity to meet Stalin.

REVENGE CHILD

I GREW UP believing that my conception was an accident, a mistake. How could two people living amid such uncertainty, with no regular (and at times no) income, without a home, facing relentless persecution by the authorities, even dream of having a child? I was certain that I owed my arrival into the world to an erroneous calculation on my mother's part, or a defective condom.

I was mistaken. There was indeed an accident involved, but it had nothing to do with me.

Shortly after my father's departure to Moscow, my mother discovered she was pregnant. At the time, however, they could not communicate. To be precise, my father was able to send her brief messages once a month via comrades, but she had no way of responding. On her own, then, she decided to keep the baby. Three months later, she was arrested at a rally. Once at the station, she did not disclose her pregnancy. The police had done their due diligence; they knew that she was the companion of one of the KKE's top dogs, and they treated her accordingly. Two kicks to the stomach prompted the miscarriage.

When Antonis returned to Greece, Anna brokenheart-edly recounted what had happened. His fury was terrible to behold—it was the first time Anna had seen the veins in his temples bulge and throb like that. He asked her for the name of the officer leading the interrogation. "One day, he will get his just deserts," he vowed between gritted teeth. (Under the Occupation, the officer in question transferred to the Security Battalions,[21] and during the Dekemvriana[22] was found with his throat slit in a vacant lot in Peristeri. To the day of his death, my father denied any involvement in the incident.)

"The best way to get revenge will be to have another child," he added. "In any case, who says that communists shouldn't have children? We believe in a new world, and we

---

[21] Greek collaborationist military group formed under the Occupation by the government of Ioannis Rallis in 1943. The Security Battalions supported the Nazis and the collaborationists in the battle against communism and were later deployed by the British against the EAM-ELAS.

[22] "The December events," a series of clashes during World War II that occurred in Athens during a monthlong period in December 1944 through early January 1945 between communist partisans and the Greek government army in collaboration with far-right militias. While the British supported and armed far-right militias like X, on December 1, the British commander Ronald Scobie ordered the unilateral disarmament of the EAM-ELAS thus reneging on previous agreements established during the Lebanon Confer-ence. A rally was called by the EAM on December 3 to urge for the immedi-ate punishment of collaborationists, the withdrawal of the "Scobie order," and an end to British intervention in Greece's internal affairs. The British opened fire on the peaceful rally, which was attended by 200,000 to 500,000 Greeks. This led to a full-blown confrontation, initially between the EAM and government forces, and then the EAM and the British.

pursue it by any means necessary and under any circumstances whatsoever!"

It took four years and those circumstances to hit rock bottom for vengeance to assume flesh and bone. My flesh and my bone.

WHEN I WAS born, in February 1938, the KKE was at the lowest point since its founding. The Metaxas dictatorship had not only arrested most of its cadres but also succeeded in sowing confusion among those who remained at large. It had created dummy cells (veritable nests of snitches) run by flunkies of the Special Security Directorate. They published a second, dummy *Rizospastis* that spread a fake political line to its readers. In a nutshell, the Party was trapped in a labyrinth of distorting mirrors, where everyone was groping around in the dark because no one could trust anyone else. A truly unthinkable situation, given that only two years earlier, in the 1935 elections, the Party had taken ten percent of the vote, was holding the reins to dozens of unions, and had the mayors of a considerable number of towns on its side.

After August 1936, my father was a wanted man. He had to circulate in disguise, and spent his nights in the unlikeliest shelters, from the trailer-trucks he crawled into to lie down to sleep, to caves or fox lairs in the foothills of Hymettus. One evening, as he was walking on Acharnon Street, believing himself protected by the cowl and robe of a Capuchin monk, two hulks approached him quickly from behind and wedged him between them. Before he knew what was happening, they had put him in handcuffs and tossed him into a black limousine.

"You're toast, Mr. Delegate!" the one on the left announced as the one on the right threw the first punch.

"You've got the wrong man!" my father protested.

"You're not Antonis Armaos?"

"No!"

"Who are you?"

"Who are *you*?"

"We're the ones asking the questions!" said the one on the left, landing the second punch. Antonis's nose started gushing blood, soaking the front of his robe.

The limousine careened into Omonia Square, but instead of turning toward the General Security building, it veered onto Stadiou Street. "Where are they taking me?" Antonis wondered. They cut across Syntagma Square, then flew past Evangelismos Hospital and the refugee shacks at the end of Alexandras Avenue. The farther they left the city center behind, the more my father was sweating bullets. When he saw Marousi's marble works in the rearview mirror, he no longer had any doubts: "They're going to kill me. Out here, where no one will see or know, and then they'll bury my body out in the sticks." He immediately thought of Anna, his Anna, so young and beautiful. He ought to have made her promise that if some evil befell him, she would not grieve for long but would get on with her life.

Upon arriving at Kifissia Square, the limousine took a left turn onto a dirt road. His kidnappers, who had been staring at the road for some time, resumed their interrogation, their ferocity redoubled.

"Are you going to tell us where your boss is hiding, you piece of shit?" Both of them were raining blows this time.

"You won't get a word out of me!" Antonis replied, struggling to defend himself even though his hands were tied behind his back and his feet were pinned under their hobnailed boots.

"Talk or you're mincemeat, asshole!"

The car turned into a driveway and stopped in front of a formidable iron gate. The driver jumped out and pulled it open.

"Last chance!" the two hulks howled. A three-story mansion loomed at the end of a large garden. "Where is Nikos? Tell us if you don't want to lose your head!"

"I don't know!" my father cried, before they shoved the barrel of a gun into his mouth. The driver then honked the horn in what was clearly a prearranged signal, and the two kidnappers burst into laughter, saying, "There he is! There's Nikos!" Antonis watched him dash toward them from the bottom of the garden, cool and cocky in a fresh white shirt, his hair slicked back with brilliantine.

"Congratulations, comrade! Again, you prove yourself hard as nails!" Nikos said, throwing his arms around him.

"This was all a test?" Furious, Antonis pulled away.

"I prefer to call it revolutionary gymnastics," Nikos replied, holding out a cigarette. "As well as an invaluable lesson for our younger recruits," he added, pointing to the two hulks and the driver. "They need to understand what it takes to be a communist leader."

"Where did they bring me? Where are we?" Antonis glanced around suspiciously.

"The perfect hideout. A lady of the aristocracy has given us the use of her gardener's house. She's the widow of a count from Corfu, a traitor to her class. The police will never think to look for us here!"

"And that's her car?"

"Yes. She is in Switzerland with her tubercular daughter. After the defeat of the Venizelist movement in '35,[23] the entire family bolted out of there. The count died soon afterward. The son is here with us."

"How can I let my wife know?"

"Just give her a shout. She's in the kitchen with my wife, cooking fish."

As Nikos stood there savoring the end of his little performance, Antonis was thinking that if any other member of the Party had dared to act with even a fraction of his audacity and recklessness, a definitive expulsion would be the lightest punishment he would have to worry about. But Nikos was not just anyone...[24]

---

[23] Pro-Venizelist factions in the armed forces attempted a coup d'état against the People's Party because of concerns about the future of democracy in the country. The failed attempt led to the violent persecution of Venizelist leaders and Venizelos's exile in Paris. The monarchy was reinstated and Ioannis Metaxas was installed as dictator in 1936.

[24] The character of Nikos is based on Nikos Zachariadis (1903–1973), the general secretary of the KKE from 1931 to 1956.

SO, WHO WAS Nikos?

Antonis had first met him four years earlier, when Nikos was working as an interpreter at the headquarters of the Communist International in Moscow. He spoke Russian, Turkish, and Greek fluently, and could get by in Polish and Czech. He was a swarthy young man, whose pronounced cheekbones and sloe eyes gave him a some-what exotic air. Without a doubt, the blood of many nations coursed through his veins. He, however, was proud to call himself Pontian, born in Trapezounta of a Greek father and an Armenian mother. After the Armenian and Pontic genocides, the entire family had sought refuge in the city of Gori in Georgia. From there, he had gone to study in Moscow.

They had met for lunch at an outdoor restaurant in Gorky Park. Nikos was wearing an army jacket without stripes and was devouring piroshkis and downing vodka like there was no tomorrow. He had a quantity of ques-tions about Greece, which Antonis readily answered. Like many diaspora Greeks, he was ambivalent about the "mother country": On the one hand, it beckoned as both a distant point of origin and a final port of call; on the other, it was fundamentally foreign to him. They arranged to get together again soon, but Nikos was transferred to Kyiv and they lost track of each other.

The next time they met was at the official Labor Day celebration in Red Square. At the end of the procession, Antonis, along with two hundred or so Party representatives and foreign delegates, was led to a huge reception room in the Kremlin to greet Stalin. As he waited in line, Antonis felt a tap on his shoulder. He turned and was astonished to see Nikos standing behind him: What was a humble interpreter doing among the frontline cadres? The mystery only deepened from there. Enthroned in a velvet armchair and indolently sucking on a pipe, the leader of the world's proletariat barely deigned to shake Antonis's hand—he, the chosen delegate to the Greek Communist Party!—yet he beckoned Nikos nearer, and with the latter stooping toward him, chitchatted for some three (perhaps as many as five!) minutes before dismissing him with a playful pat to the cheek. As they headed toward the exit, Antonis could not resist asking about this surprising familiarity.

"My folks live in Gori, two doors down from Keke," Nikos replied without missing a beat.

"Who is Keke?"

"His mother!"

THREE WEEKS LATER, during a white night in June that was pouring buckets of tepid rain, Antonis boarded a train for his return to Athens, taking the same route he had traveled to Moscow: via Constantinople, armed with fake papers that had him masquerading as a captain of the merchant marine. When he entered his train car, he saw Nikos lounging comfortably on the top berth.

"I arranged to have you upgraded to first class so that we might travel together!" Nikos announced, his tone all earnest generosity.

"Are you telling me that Stalin's mother is paying for my ticket?" Antonis retorted, trying to make light of his irritation.

For the entire trip, Nikos did everything in his power to win over his travel companion. He had a certain disarming boyishness that soon overcame Antonis's reservations. Whenever he spotted a blast furnace or tractors plowing the endless plains, he would cheer: "Look, Look! That's socialism in the making!" As soon as they crossed the border into Turkey, however, he became a changed man, instantly shedding his schoolboy earnestness and assuming the role declared on his passport: an Anatolian tobacco trader, traveling on business.

In the dining car, Nikos met some Belarusian émigrés, whom he quickly proceeded to fleece at poker. A couple of hours later, he buttonholed a young Circassian widow traveling to Constantinople for an arranged marriage. In no time at all, he had his hands all over her and was also trying to pass her sister off to Antonis, even though the latter had no desire to cheat on Anna mere days before their reunion.

"Where are you going, my friend? Stay and sleep on the bottom berth, or watch if you're so inclined!" Nikos suggested, but Antonis preferred to spend the night smoking in the corridor.

About half a mile before arriving at the Thessaloniki station, Nikos hoisted his seabag over his shoulder and opened the window wide.

"Will you finally tell me who sent you to Greece and why?" Antonis asked him for the umpteenth time.

"You'll find out soon enough!" Nikos promised, and jumped out of the speeding train.

IT WAS EIGHT months before Antonis received an answer, and in the most unexpected and staggering way. One morning, he opened *Rizospastis* (as a member of the KKE leadership, he was ostensibly responsible for its content) and came face-to-face with a picture of his traveling companion under the headline "Our new leader!"

Our Party Congress has confirmed the election of Comrade Nikos as general secretary, the article read. *The appointment of a leader is an act of major political significance, bearing witness to the Party's rapid expansion and the emergence of warriors entirely committed to the cause, of whom Comrade Nikos is the most shining example. Leaders of bourgeois parties and fascist groups are now up against Comrade Nikos, a fast friend of the people at the vanguard of the fight for their rights…A new wind invigorates the Party's sails, and all now know that there's a strong, firm hand at its wheel.* This was followed by a cryptic biography that alluded to great feats of organizational prowess, heroic clashes with the enemies of the working man, and epic escapes, even implying at one point that the fugitive Alexandratos and Comrade Nikos might well be one and the same man. *Nikos's editorials and speeches are like a torrent of molten lead*, continued the article. (Editorials? Speeches? Really?) *Now, here he is, general secretary of the Party, leader of the Greek people. It is to the honor and glory of the KKE that someone like Comrade Nikos was nurtured at its breast.*

My father could not believe his eyes. He made a beeline to the *Rizospastis* press offices to confront the editor in chief, restraining himself from seizing the man by the lapels.

"Who wrote that article, and who approved its publication?"

"The Soviet embassy sent it to us at midnight, fully translated and with explicit orders that it appear in today's issue. I had to change the layout of the entire paper to fit it in," the man protested, almost apologetically.

"No matter where he says he comes from, here in Greece no one knows of Nikos. At least, almost no one," said Antonis more to himself than to the editor, who, it was clear, had had nothing to do with the piece. "In any case, shouldn't they at least have given us a heads-up so that we could have laid the groundwork for the Party?" he added in a gentler tone.

Nikos, and especially whoever was responsible for appointing and foisting him on the KKE, had no intention of providing explanations to anyone, either in advance or as an afterthought. This became clear during the following session of the KKE's Political Bureau. Nikos, who was the last to arrive, strode in and sat down at the head of the table as if it were the most natural thing in the world. He then announced the agenda and proceeded to lead the discussion. Bureau members, most of whom were setting eyes on him for the first time, were staring at him as if he were the messiah come unto them. Nikos, for his part, treated them with fraternal familiarity, as if they were old friends. From the details he shared about Party matters, it was clear to Antonis that since the day they had parted in Thessaloniki, Nikos had received intensive training. Even his Greek had improved—he had shed the heavy Pontic accent.

My father struggled to make his peace with this new state of affairs, as well as to digest the fact that everyone called Nikos "Chief" and not "Comrade Secretary" as they had his predecessors. "The Party must need a strong, uncompromising leader to bring a definitive end to our complete disarray," he thought to himself. "It makes sense to bring in new leadership from outside, bearing Moscow's incorruptible stamp of approval. After all, our Party is a branch of the Communist International, which advocates for and defends the interests of the working classes the world over. On the other hand, when all is said and done, what exactly are we looking at here? Stalin handpicked and then sent us his mother's young neighbor. Why? Here we have cadres aplenty who are no strangers to revolutionary struggle." Whenever he felt his indignation rise to the boiling point, he would admonish himself: "Antonis, my friend, local syndicalist leaders are one thing, and revolutionary leaders another thing entirely. And let's be honest, didn't the International also catapult you to your Political Bureau and parliamentary positions?"

Truth be told, after Nikos's arrival, a fair wind filled the Party's sails. Communist organizations and voters were burgeoning, and the Party's pursuit of concrete, realistic demands—like a decrease in the price of bread—rallied growing numbers of people. Communism was also gradually catching fire among intellectuals, who were being invited to the Soviet Union on a regular basis. After touring all the sights, factories, and kolkhozy, and staying at magnificent dachas, they would send enthusiastic dispatches to Greece. After reading their impressions in respectable newspapers, even the most conservative citizens gradually stopped thinking of Lenin and Stalin as Satan's minions. While many were held back by their social standing from openly joining the KKE, they supported it behind the scenes, offering assistance and protection whenever it was needed.

It would be difficult to concretely quantify what Nikos contributed to these successes, to credit him with a truly dazzling idea or initiative. Yet it was also impossible not to acknowledge that he led the Party with an iron fist. He condemned every deviation, muzzled even the most minor disagreement, and he did so masterfully, avoiding the personal conflicts unworthy of a leader. All who met him sang his praises, raving about his warmth, about the sincerity of his feeling not only for the class struggle but also for each and every one of their own family trials. Indeed, one day, he might be shedding tears with a comrade over a sick child and drawing money from the Party coffers to help him buy medicine, and on the very next day ordering that comrade's expulsion for bourgeois tendencies or lingering religious beliefs. He often expelled people for trivial reasons, sometimes for no apparent reason at all.

"The Party grows stronger when it purifies its ranks," he would repeat with the expression of those doctors of yore who specialized in bloodletting. Yet he avoided the sight of blood. Distasteful decisions never bore his signature. And all those who paid the price of his censure believed, deep down, that if only they might speak directly to Nikos and explain themselves, they would be exonerated.

The only time that Antonis saw him lose his composure was after the 1936 elections. Even though *Rizospastis* and communist organizations had mounted a furious propaganda campaign to support his candidacy in Thessaloniki, Nikos had not succeeded in his bid. He had come in a distant second, lagging far behind Euripides Lachanas, a fisherman from Karabournaki, who had become a hero after almost dying on a hunger strike during his time as a political prisoner.

"Who is this Lachanas?" Nikos had asked, as if he had no idea. "The whole story stinks. The results must have been doctored at the election centers," he asserted, completely out of left field.

"Lachanas is planning to step down in your favor," my father informed him.

"I don't give a damn about a seat in parliament!" Nikos replied, aggrieved. "I don't want anything to do with a bourgeois, corrupt, rotten-to-the-core legislature. It's a waste of time for a Party leader to be locking horns with Venizelist and monarcho-fascist bigwigs! To effectively direct the proletarian movement, he must remain in the shadows!"

In any case, the government of 1936 was not destined for longevity. A few months later, Metaxas had installed his dictatorship, and before year's end, my parents found themselves, along with Nikos and his Hungarian wife, confined to their gilded cage in Kifissia.

"WHEN DID HE marry that Magyar? When did he bring her to Greece?" my mother wouldn't stop asking, as if personally offended by the presence of that great mare of a woman, with her rosy cheeks, braided hair, and wooden clogs, who insisted on communicating by gesture and pantomime, instead of learning a few words of Greek.

"I have no idea," my father replied.

"The other day, Antonis, she undressed in front of me and asked me to get into the tub with her so that we might soap each other up! Not even my sister has asked me to do something like that!"

"Different countries have different customs, Anna. I am sure she doesn't mean anything by it."

"When will we finally be able to leave this place? We're neither free nor imprisoned! It's just a waste of time!" exclaimed my mother, railing against her lot.

Truth be told, from time to time the inactivity also tried Antonis's patience, but Nikos was adamant about not deviating from their plan: "If we are arrested, the Party will be rudderless. It would be foolhardy to risk it."

"How long will we stay holed up like this in Kifissia?"

"Patience, comrade. Don't forget that Lenin stayed in Zurich for three years. In 1916, would you have advised him to return to Russia and fall into the hands of the Okhrana?[25] Don't worry, Antonis, History has its ebbs and flows, and soon we will find ourselves riding its crests!"

It was impossible to know from where he drew such optimism. He meant it, however; he fully believed it. Every evening for two months, he locked himself in his room to write feverishly. He had asked the young men in the black limousine, who kept them supplied with food and cigarettes, to bring him stacks of books, political and economic tracts, mostly in foreign languages. One day, when he ran out of ink, he became so agitated that, unable to wait until the following day, he claimed his wife's one and only lipstick.

Finally, one spring evening, he called Antonis, Anna, and Irmoushka into the garden, and in a deep voice quivering with emotion began to read out loud the work he had just finished, titled *The KKE's Governance Plan, or, On the Construction of a New Soviet Greece*. Over more than three hundred pages, Nikos described in exhaustive detail what the Party would do as soon as it rose to power. It addressed almost everything one could imagine, even the professional reorientation of the priesthood. When he finished, it was almost midnight. His expression left his audience of three with no choice but to stand and deliver a lengthy

---

[25] The secret police in imperial Russia.

ovation. The rooster in the neighbor's coop woke up and began crowing.

"So? Questions? Comments?"

"Where are you publishing it?" Antonis asked.

"I'm not publishing it. I'm going to actually do it," Nikos replied in the tone of a prime minister waiting in the wings.

"Do you know something we don't? Is the Red Army getting ready to invade Greece?" my father finally baited him openly.

"If speech is silver, then silence is gold, comrade!" Nikos said enigmatically and immediately changed the subject by announcing Irmoushka's pregnancy.

I WANT TO linger a little longer on that night in 1937. Four very young people (Irmoushka was not even twenty years old) in an almost Edenic environment beyond space and time, all passionately devoted to the same cause, all inflamed by the conviction that historical destiny lay in their hands, that they could feel the grain of every one of its twists and turns on their fingertips. A romantic image, isn't it? The daily struggle and anguish of the last few years—above all, the constant worry about the Party, how to get it to stand on its own two feet, how to grow its influence, vote by vote—had begun to fade from their memories amid their living conditions of forced leisure. Even my father, the one whose feet were planted most firmly on the ground, had to keep reminding himself that big revolutionary movements were always founded on the backs of a handful of dreamers.

IN HIS EXCITEMENT, Nikos convinced my father to break into the empty villa—thus trespassing into the only place declared strictly off-limits by the still-absent mistress of the manor—to filch a bottle of wine from the cellar with which to drink to the health of the new child on its way and the new world about to be born. This romantic image also includes me. Because Anna, too, was pregnant. I would like to believe that the second bottle of wine for which they returned to the cellar an hour later was opened for me. Even if none of them knew it.

Nikos and Irmoushka's baby was born on the day before Christmas at the poshest maternity clinic in Athens, owned by a secret supporter of the Party. As soon as the Magyar's water broke, the famous lurking limousine whisked her off to Kolonaki. She registered under a false name, posing as the wife of a Soviet diplomat. A week later, she returned to Kifissia with a chubby infant boy in her arms.

My mother was nowhere near as lucky. On January 5, Nikos was arrested. He had ventured out the previous afternoon for what he had described as a critical meeting, the details of which he had not disclosed even to Antonis. Night fell, and then dawn broke on the day of Epiphany, and there was neither hide nor hair of Nikos. The remaining occupants at Kifissia were like cats on a hot tin roof. Until nearly noon on the feast day of Saint John the Baptist, when the limousine sped by the grounds and, without braking, the driver tossed a freshly printed issue of *Kathimerini*[26] through the iron gate. "Leader of KKE Arrested. KKE Breathes Its Last" the headline declared triumphantly over a picture of Nikos in custody. He was sporting a wide, clearly forced smile, which was probably meant to cheer his still-at-large comrades.

"At least he looks well," Antonis said, trying to console Irmoushka.

"What am I supposed to do now? What will become of him?" she wailed, pointing to the newborn at her breast.

"Ah! So, you do speak Greek, Irmoushka?" Anna glowered, completely out of left field.

"I'm ashamed to speak with you. The words just trip off your tongue, and I'm ashamed," Irmoushka exclaimed, racked by hysterical sobs.

With one young mother with a baby at her breast, his wife about to give birth, and the limousine no longer delivering supplies, my father was on the brink of tears himself. Burdened by these responsibilities, he broke into the villa and resolved that if he didn't find anything to eat, they would turn themselves in that very same day.

But he did find food. The pantry behind the kitchen was packed with sacks of flour, sugar, and rice. There were

---

[26] Founded in 1919 by a prominent anti-Venizelist, *Kathimerini* remains one of Greece's leading conservative daily morning newspapers.

also two amphorae of olive oil, and another enormous one containing an entire salted pig suspended in its own fat.

"We'll make it through the winter!" he rejoiced. "But we're worse off than castaways." Almost immediately afterward the thought occurred to him and his mood darkened again. "At least castaways are buoyed by the hope that a ship may appear, whereas for us, almost all ships are those of the enemy."

What distressed him most was that everyone on the outside seemed to have completely forgotten about them. No one denounced them, but then again, no one extended a helping hand. As if both friend and foe had struck them off the annals of the living. The indifference, the silence were a torture. One day, it occurred to him that the police might already have them surrounded, that they were simply waiting to take them in at the most advantageous moment for the regime. "In any case, how does that change anything for us?" He shrugged.

He saw no reason to make plans for the future. The anticipation of my birth was both his greatest joy and his worst nightmare. At first, he had decided take Anna to the maternity clinic in Kolonaki by taxi and risk be damned. But what if things did not go as planned, and both mother and newborn fell into the hands of the pigs? The thought of losing a second child, and in such a similar manner, was unbearable! But was there an alternative?

An alternative did present itself entirely out of the blue.

"You and I will attend to your wife when she gives birth!" Irmoushka declared one fine morning without batting an eye, revealing, in her broken but newly confident Greek, that she was a trained midwife, licensed by an institute in Budapest.

"Do you trust her?" Antonis asked Anna.

"Yes. God help me." It was the first time he heard her utter the word "God."

In the middle of January, with freezing temperatures transforming Kifissia into an Arctic landscape in a matter of hours, my father overcame his remaining scruples. Taking the women and newborn under his wing, they moved from the gardener's cottage to the villa. They lit a fire in every room, threw open every wardrobe, slipped into furs and silk pajamas, and nestled under plush quilts and thick blankets. In that haunted mansion, empty and abandoned by its fleeing owners, Antonis once again lived the life of a bourgeois, more luxurious even than what he had experienced with the Kremoses in Ampelokipoi. Once again, it was for the sake of a child—or rather two, this time around.

THEY SAY THAT at the moment of death, your life flashes before your eyes. In my case, however, the moment of my birth contained the seeds of my life to come.

Even though I was born into an aristocratic environment, it was completely foreign to me—I neither aspired to nor was I entitled to it. I was pulled out of my mother's belly by a man who had passionately longed for me years before my arrival (I was, after all, his revenge), and who fell in love with me instantly, as soon as he laid a finger on me, before even seeing my face or my sex. A young woman from foreign parts, a good fairy from another world, stood by his side, guiding him along, but with one eye wandering constantly to her baby, wailing nearby in its improvised cot. That, in effect, was my destiny: cross-eyed and star-crossed, with forces external to me always conspiring to trip me up.

In the meantime, my mother had spiked a high fever. She ranted and raved, quivered and shook. When the shivering turned into full-blown convulsions, her teeth chattering and eyes bulging, the question spontaneously popped into Antonis's head: Who would he rather lose? His wife or his child? "Neither one!" he vowed to himself furiously. "I'm not losing either one!"

I believe that this determination of his, his refusal to bargain with the lives of his loved ones, kept us both alive.

II

I WAS BARELY seventy days old when a squad of police armed to the teeth raided the Kifissia property and arrested us all. The operation had been organized as if they were expecting resistance from the fugitives. They handcuffed my father and the two new mothers, left the babies bawling in their cots, and began an exhaustive search of the gardener's cottage, the mansion, and the grounds. Their only find worthy of note was Nikos's magnum opus: *The KKE's Governance Plan, or, On the Construction of a New Soviet Greece.*

Soon afterward, they published a bastardized version, "so that the public might hear, right from the horse's mouth, about the kind of hell that the communists are planning."

After fingerprinting them all, the squad commander did them the great kindness of divulging their fates.

He started with Irmoushka: "The foreigner and her little bastard will be deported back to where she came from. As for you," he turned to Antonis, "there's a first-class cell at the Corfu Prison in your near future. You'll be sharing a wall with your boss. And your wife over there, we've found a lovely little island where she'll be spending some quality recreational time. Your daughter will be brought up as a true Greek Orthodox in the municipal orphanage."

"Out of the question!" my mother screamed, beside herself. "I'm not going anywhere without my child!" and she clasped me to her chest.

The officer sneered like a fairy-tale villain, but when my father took him aside and bribed him with five gold sovereigns—"Go to Kallithea, 6 Vrisiidos Street, and ask for Mrs. Sevasti"—he immediately changed his tune, extolling the "natural laws that bind the lactating mother to her child," and even ordering that the exiled woman and her baby be handled with kid gloves.

IN 1938, THE Cyclades, with the exception of some shipping villages and the relatively industrialized island of Syros, were the picture of abject poverty. Most of the men went to

sea and, once onboard, traveled constantly with almost no
shore leave. Whenever they happened to be sailing through
the open waters near one of their islands on their way to or
from the Black Sea, they tossed packages of letters and gifts
overboard for their families, to be fished out later by local
boats. The women spent their lives bowed over tiny strips of
arable land. A recent law of the Metaxas regime mandated
the regular whitewashing of Cycladic homes in "the interests of public health."[27] To the people of the islands, there
was nothing either poetic or picturesque about this obligatory whitewashing.

My mother's sentence of exile was based on the theory
that by separating delinquent elements from their social
and geographic contexts, they would be either chastened
or safely neutralized. In the Greece of the interwar period
there were three kinds of exiles: livestock rustlers, mainly
from Crete; drug addicts in need of detoxification; and the
regime's political opponents.

Under Metaxas's ruthless dictatorship even centrist officials and notable members of the haute bourgeoisie were
summarily dispatched to the Aegean, where they rented
picturesque island villas and dreamt of the restoration of
democracy while listening to the waves breaking on the
shore. The communists who comprised the large majority

---

[27] An outbreak of cholera prompted this law because the limestone in the
whitewash used at the time was considered a powerful disinfectant. Unifor-
mity and the "purity" of the white color were also symbolically important
to the dictatorship, an idea that was reprised by the Regime of the Colonels
(1967–1974).

of exiles, however, had little opportunity to enjoy the natural beauty of their surroundings. They lived in small cottages, usually on the outskirts of the village, that they rented collectively in groups of five or ten, scraping together the rent from the meager savings sent to them by their families after untold privations. If there were any men among their number, they were housed separately so as to avoid potential romantic entanglements.

Their daily regimen was demanding, almost as demanding as that of prison: housework and cleaning, reading, exercise, and the ideological instruction of those lower in rank by their superiors. Every morning, the exiles had to put in an appearance at the police station. When necessary, and only insofar as the island folk trusted them, they joined in the farmwork and were paid in kind: eggs, olive oil, the occasional chicken or rabbit.

The local community's ingrained biases—taught, as they had been, that communists were predatory atheists—gradually diminished when faced with their irreproachable behavior. If they happened to have in their midst a doctor or agronomist who offered their services for free, their prestige shot through the roof. So much so that some of the locals—taking, naturally, all necessary precautions—began to lend an indulgent ear to communist propaganda. Aware of the risk of ideological contamination presented by the exiles, the authorities made a practice of relocating them to a different island at six-month intervals.

Sifnos, Kimolos, Serifos, Sifnos again, and then, out of the blue, Gavdos, south of Crete, and a long and perilous journey by boat from the Cyclades to the Libyan Sea in the middle of winter. Before spring had fully arrived, we were back on Sifnos for a third and final time.

THOSE EARLY IMAGES of my life have not lost any of their sharpness, not even after my death. The only difference is that now it's as if I am looking at the past through two distinct points of view, two separate focal points. Anything that I experienced myself, I see again through the eyes of a child. Everything else—by dint of the immateriality that allows me to move freely through space and time—I behold from above, as if in flight. Fortunately, I can descend and even burrow deep into the human heart. But I don't always do so. Occasionally, a girlish delicacy holds me back.

IN THE SPRING of 1939, I took my first steps. I was living with my mother and another handful of women exiles on a farm in Kimolos. They treated me like a living doll, squabbling over who would get to change me, who would get to bounce me on their knee. Despite all this attention, I managed to escape the house unnoticed one afternoon and, half crawling, half walking, made my way out into the surrounding fields. Suddenly, I felt something clinch the back of my neck and lift me up into the air. A donkey, the possessor of what was clearly a strong maternal instinct, had taken me for a defenseless orphan, seized me between her teeth—very carefully, so as not to hurt me—and was carrying me to her manger. Catching sight of me through the kitchen window dangling from the beast's muzzle, my mother panicked. Fortunately, she pulled herself together and realized that if the donkey startled, the consequences might be fatal for me. She got up and followed us silently, on tiptoe, waiting until the beast laid me gently on some hay before picking me up and making off with me in her arms.

MY SECOND MEMORY takes place a year or more later. We are on Sifnos again, for the second time. Three doors down from our house, living in a ruin under thoroughly wretched conditions, is an exile whom both locals and communists contemptuously call "the junkie." He is, in fact, the most talented folk musician of his time. His songs, which will be recorded after his death, are considered small masterpieces to this day. The people on the island at the time have no sense of his genius. The baglamas, which they sometimes see him playing while seated in his doorway, only makes matters worse.[28] In any case, he does not show his face often. As a substitute for heroin, he knocks back tsipouro straight from the bottle all day long and is in a perpetual state of semi-drunkenness. Yet he keeps a hold on himself,

---

[28] A smaller, higher-pitched bouzouki, the baglamas is one of the main instruments used to play rembetiko, a style of music that was prohibited for being linked to marginalized Anatolian communities and the urban poor.

neither provoking nor disturbing anyone. He is also hand-some, extremely handsome, of an ethereal, almost angelic beauty.

Taking pity on him, the communist exiles send him something to eat every day at noon.

"See this plate? Take it to him," the woman doing the cooking that day says. "Mind you don't let it fall and break, you hear me? Put it outside his door, knock, and then run back. Whatever you do, poor dear, don't step into that filthy hovel!"

I do exactly as she instructed, except that when I put the plate down on the ledge, I hear something like moan-ing coming from inside, interrupted every now and then by a rippling laugh. I'm thoroughly confused. If it's some-one in pain and needing my help (mother has taught me to help all who are in need, starting with kittens and puppies), then why are they also laughing? If something is causing the laughter, then why the moans? After a momentary hesita-tion, I give the unlocked door a little push. And I see them: The junkie is lying flat on his back, and there's a woman on top of him, rocking back and forth. From my vantage point, all I can see is a back and a disheveled cloud of blond hair. Suddenly terrified, I turn tail and run, bursting into tears along the way. To avoid the exiles' questions, I crawl into someone's yard and stay there until I calm down.

The reason for my distress is as clear as it is unmen-tionable: Either by instinct or genetic memory, I know what those two were doing on the bed. I can also guess to whom that back belongs, even though my mother has never given me reason to suspect, in the many years that followed, that she ever acted on or even harbored desire for another man besides my father. And yet even now, when I can fly unperceived and find myself face-to-face with the woman making love to the junkie, even now I don't dare. The truth that might appease me might also, at the same time, disappoint me.

BESIDES ALL THIS, I was a tall and lanky child, with braided ash-blond hair covered in a straw sunhat that my grand-mother had sent from Athens. My mother wouldn't let me associate with the local youngsters, so I spent my time almost exclusively surrounded by adults, by "aunts" and "uncles," who called each other "comrade." As I have already mentioned, I was cherished and pampered by all. On the islands we were sent to, there were almost never other children among the exiles. The women knit me clothes, while the men whittled wooden toys for me—wood carving and chess were favorite pastimes among communist men. They also taught me revolutionary songs; I was two and half years old when I first faltered through "The Internationale."

Sometime later, in September 1940, I contracted dys-entery. My rapidly deteriorating condition, and the fact that there were no medicines to be had on the island, led almost everyone to give me up for dead. This became the cause of an open and unprecedented conflict between the locals and the exiles. The villagers firmly and unshakably believed that infants and young children who died without having been anointed in the baptismal rite turned into *kallikantzaroi*,[29] condemned to haunt the place of their death. The communists, on the other hand, were just as firmly and unshakably opposed to having one of their own be subjected to the obsolete, not to mention degrading, procedure of a Christian baptism. Besides, all that splashing in the baptismal font might well finish me off. The entire island of Sifnos sent an ultimatum to the exiles: "Either you let us baptize her, or pack your things and leave today." The comrades decided to ignore it. Before two hours had elapsed, some hundred locals led by a priest had surrounded the house where we lived.

In defiance of her more hardline companions, who were ready to go to battle rather than have me fall into the hands of the local yokels, my mother finally relented. She wrapped me in a blanket and took me to the church, surrounded by a hostile procession.

"What's her name?" the priest asked.

"Niki!"[30] my mother replied. Was she invoking the victory of socialism or my victory over the disease? I doubt that even she knew. But the following day, I passed the crisis and began to recover.

---

[29] Malevolent goblin-like creatures rife in Greek folklore. They are associated with the underworld and are said to haunt or attack humans who are in vulnerable or liminal states (unbaptized infants, for example).

[30] The name Niki means victory in Greek, derived from the ancient Greek Nike, the goddess who personifies victory.

III

UPON THE DECLARATION of the Greco-Italian War,[31] the KKE rallied behind the embattled state, even accepting the direction of the Metaxas regime. This position had beneficial repercussions on the daily life of the exiles. For one, the police acknowledged their patriotism and stopped treating them as if they were vermin. While communist applications to enlist were generally rejected, the doors to people's homes were finally thrown wide open.

At the café in Artemonas,[32] high festivities were underway—I remember the smell of lamb on the spit tickling my nostrils and my mother stuffing a piece of crispy crackling into my mouth. Were we celebrating the Greek victories at Saranda or Korytsa?

JANUARY 1ST AT the Apollonia school playground, two large packages of letters from the front are being distributed after arriving on the island with more than a month's delay. Most Sifniote men not at sea on October 28th had been sent to

---

[31] Launching the Balkans campaign of World War II, the war was declared on October 28, 1940, after Metaxas rejected Mussolini's ultimatum that the government cede Greek territory. When the Italians tried to invade the country through Albania in the north, they suffered an unprecedented defeat at the hands of the Greek forces.

[32] Artemonas is one of a collection of villages that make up the capital on the island of Sifnos.

the front lines. Flanked by the teacher and the priest, the postman is standing at the head of the stairs and calling out the recipients' names. Alerted by the envelope, he is the first to know the nature of the news awaiting the soldier's loved ones. If the address is written by hand, then the lad is alive, even if possibly wounded, and writing from one of those shacks acting as hospital wards in the mountains of Epirus. If the address has been typewritten, then the family will be preparing the memorial kolyva.[33]

Perched on the school fence, smothered in the make-shift coat that my mother has fashioned out of a flokati rug (which, now that I think of it, looks more like a Mexican poncho than a coat), I soak in every detail of that awfully dissonant and poignant spectacle. As the letters are opened, one after the other, mournful laments intermingle with cheers of joy, thankful blessings to the Virgin with maledictions hurled at the heavens.

Within a period of ten minutes, an elderly couple receives a summons from both heaven and hell. In the first letter, their eldest son notifies them that his bravery has earned him a promotion and a transfer to the rear guard, because *the army does not want to risk losing such a crack wireless operator.* The second letter, sent through official channels, announces that their younger son has *fallen in the line of duty.* Weeping, wailing, beating their breasts, the elderly couple

---

[33] A dish based on wheat berry, nuts, raisins, and pomegranate that is an integral part of the Greek funeral and memorial liturgy.

instantly forget their eldest son's joyful news. My current, incorporeal self stoops to whisper in the ear of the little girl of yesteryear: "Sorrow always steals the show. Perhaps because we believe, mistakenly it turns out, that happiness is our due."

A MONTH AND a half later, a letter bearing similar tidings arrived for my mother, sent from Kalamata by her sister Alcmene, who was married to a lawyer. In a formal tone that she seemed to borrow directly from her husband's documents, Alcmene, instead of beginning by saying "We've lost our Kyriakos!" thought it proper to copy word for word the army's official death notification: *Admitted to the 3rd field hospital, Ward 5, on 12/20/1940. Wounded in Përmet on 12/12/1940 by shrapnel during an air raid in the left shoulder and left shin. Admitted in great distress: temperature high, pulse weak and thready. Purulent exudate from abscess at site of wound necessitated surgical intervention. No shell fragments found or retrieved. Wounds packed, dressed, ice packs applied. After symptoms of advanced progressive heart failure, the patient succumbed to his injuries on this day at noon.*

On the second page, Alcmene finally changed her tone to a more intimate one: *My dearest Anna, this great misfortune will live forever in our heads and our hearts. But what can we do besides be strong? You see, we are the first to make the ultimate sacrifice for our beloved country. Mother and Father are inconsolable and spend all day weeping. I fear that the weight of their sorrow will send them to an early grave. As soon as I heard the sad news, I hastened to the village to provide them and our younger sister with some assistance. I have been here for two weeks now and have been trying the entire time to convince them to come live with me in Kalamata, but in vain. Please write to them and tell them, too, Anna, because if mother stays here, she will surely die. She spends all day weeping and singing funerary laments. Please write to me too, I beg you.*

Write to them? Was that all? Anna was suddenly racked with remorse. Since she had taken that train to Athens twelve years ago, she had returned to the village only three times, and never for more than a week. With Kyriakos and her sisters, she corresponded rarely. As for Achilleas, she had disowned him after he had become a Trotskyist. It had never occurred to her to take Antonis to her place of birth to pay his respects and kiss her father's hand. And when I was born, she had not even attempted to find a way around our confinement to announce the joyful news to her family.

"Why did I turn my back on them? Do I hate them deep down?" she asked herself. Yet they were more deserving of her love than her hate. Owing to them, she had only the sweetest memories of childhood. Every time she thought about how she would never again see her dear Kyriakos—that gentle giant with his huge hands and the bright eyes of a faithful dog—she felt a stabbing pain in the heart. "How can I dedicate my life to the common man, and then disregard my own blood like that?" she rebuked herself. "If my parents die without my seeing them, I will never forgive myself. Never!"

Such was her determination that she would have found a way to escape even if we were under lock and key in a labor camp. Since the surveillance of the exiles had become almost nonexistent, it didn't take much: She confided her plans to her comrades who, sympathetic to her situation, gave her their blessing and pitched in to pay for our travel. In mid-February 1941—I was turning three at the time—we boarded a fishing boat in the middle of the night and left Sifnos once and for all.

The captain had agreed to let us off at the Port of Kalamata, but once out at sea, he changed his tune, citing inclement weather. "I won't be responsible for the child!" he said, pointing to me, and finally set us down, twenty hours later, at Faliro. Anna still intended to take me with her to Messenia, but her mother-in-law, my father's mother, Grandmother Sevasti, wouldn't hear of it. She invoked the cold, the halt to public transportation due to the war, the aerial bombardments, until Anna relented. "In any case, I'll be back in a few weeks," she thought. Little did she know that it would be another three and a half years before she saw me again.

"HAIR DOWN DOWN down to your butt, girl up up up to the sky!" Grandmother Sevasti sings to me as she untangles my braids with a mother-of-pearl comb, which, she says, she inherited from her grandmother, who had it from her grandmother, who had it from hers, and "so on and on and on through time immemorial." It is evening in the kitchen of the house in Kallithea. Sevasti, short, stout, and sixty years old, sits on a stool in front of the woodstove and holds me in her arms. A few feet away, red mullet are frying on the stove. Suddenly, Mister, her one-eyed black-and-white tomcat leaps on the chair, snatches a fish from the pan in one impressively agile swoop, and jumps into the yard through the half-open window. "You hooligan! May your whiskers fall off!" my grandmother curses him. Two hours later, Mister returns and, still as cool as a cucumber, climbs onto her bed, curls up on her enormous breasts, and joins his percussive purring to the crescendo of her snuffles and snores.

IV

IN THE WINTER of 1941–1942, thousands of people died from hunger in Athens. Many crippled on the Albanian front had been unable to return to their villages and were trapped in the capital, begging and sleeping on the sidewalks. Children with bellies swollen from starvation huddled together for some warmth over subway grates in Omonia Square. Every morning, municipal carts gathered the corpses and tossed them into mass graves. The most central burial ground occupied a vast vacant lot in Kanningos Square. After the war, there was no retrieval of bones or even prayers for the dead. They simply drowned the whole area in cement and erected the Ministry of Commerce.

Yet I, the daughter of a communist delegate languishing in a Corfu dungeon, experienced nothing of this. Or almost nothing. Occasionally, faint cries of "I'm hungry" reached our ears from the road, and immediately Fani would turn up the volume on the radio to hear Markella giving one of her Italian canzonet recitals at the Zappeion studio. My grandmother would make a big tray of halvah, with real sugar and real semolina, to share among the neighborhood.

"On whose side are you, anyway, Mrs. Sevasti? On your sons' or on your daughters'?"

"I'm with all my children and all the world's children."

FANI AND MARKELLA: my aunts. It was not planned, I'm sure of that. The fact that they found themselves in the opposite camp to that of their brothers was not the result of premeditation but rather the hidden workings of circumstance.

By 1938, Fani, a typist-secretary at the bank, had become the governor's trusted assistant. Initially, he had been impressed by her dedication and her aptitude with the typewriter, which she used with both admirable speed and precision and remarkable noiselessness. He began taking her with him on trips—the first time, he had even tactfully asked for her mother's permission in writing, even though Fani had long come of age.

One morning, as he was sipping his coffee—sweet and dense, the way he liked it—over breakfast at a hotel in Thessaloniki, he looked up and saw her, for the first time, as a woman. "Well, well! She's really quite a fine specimen! It's just that she hides her charms out of an excess of timidity!" The governor believed that a man of true taste should always be able to pick a diamond out of the mire.

"Fani, dear, do me a favor and take off those glasses, will you?" he said lighting a cigarette. "Pull your hair back, too. I want to see your sweet little face."

Surprised, my aunt obeyed.

"Like this. See..."

He got up, leaned over (enveloping her in a cloud of the French lotion that he always applied too liberally after shaving) and undid the top two buttons on her blouse. Fani almost fainted from embarrassment. But the governor did not so much as graze her pearly skin. Instead, he returned immediately to his seat to appraise from a distance the effect of his interventions.

"Magnificent!" he said and gasped.

Two hours later, Fani, who until that day had always dressed her hair herself with tongs heated over the wood-stove, was marching into the most expensive hair salon in Thessaloniki. On the return train, the porter had the Herculean task of trying to wedge into their compartment five cases of freshly purchased dresses and three hatboxes. As they neared Athens, the governor pulled Fani into his arms and without preamble slipped a diamond the size of a chickpea on her finger.

"My fiancée," is how he introduced her to Metaxas three months later at a reception. "Foteini Armaos. She goes by Fani."

"Armaos?" the dictator exclaimed. "Don't tell me she's related to that communist delegate!"

"Ah, she is, Ioannis!" said the governor, with a playful twinkle in his eye. "She is his little sister!"

Metaxas opened his mouth, but then thought better of it. What could he possibly say to the man lauded as a hero of the Asia Minor campaign, who had orchestrated the monumental task of resettling almost half a million refugees in the villages of Macedonia and been decorated by the United Nations, the American vice president, and the heir to the British throne? At fifty years old, Savvas Bogdanos had nothing left to prove and no one to fear. Except perhaps for the shadow of his first wife, taken by cancer in the flower of her youth, whose portrait—at the hand of none other than Parthenis[34] himself—presided, and would continue to preside, over his dining room.

"Foteini—what a fitting name for such a radiant young lady!" Metaxas quickly regained his composure, drawing himself up as my aunt curtsied down to his height.

"My very best wishes for a joyful life together, Savvas!"

THE WEDDING WAS officiated by the archbishop at the Metropolitan Cathedral of the Annunciation. There were two notable absences: my father, who was behind bars, and therefore kept away by circumstances beyond his control, and Uncle Petros, who had chosen to go into hiding like the

---

[34] Konstantinos Parthenis (1878–1967) was a distinguished Greek artist born in Alexandria, who broke with the Greek academic tradition and introduced modern elements combined with traditional themes in his painting.

most militant members of the Communist Youth. Swaggering in the tuxedo his sister had bought him, Uncle Giannos walked the bride down the aisle before handing her off to Savvas Bogdanos. He had every intention of stealing some hearts at the party that was to follow at the famous Attik's Barn, and so emulate his sister's good fortune by ensnaring a "young lady of the aristocracy." Unfortunately for him, fate smiled on Markella instead.

Markella, a graduate of the National Conservatoire, and now in her second year at Drama School, made sure to shout from the rooftops that her life was consecrated to her art. That short of treading the boards of the theater or lyric stage, nothing, absolutely nothing, interested her. It was what she told her mother. It was how she turned down presumptive suitors: young working men but also neighborhood merchants who whistled at her as she walked down the street and even, on occasion, slipped love notes into the letter box. It was also the argument she used to silence Petros when he tried to win her over to the revolutionary cause. "My passion lies elsewhere!" she had said, turning on her heel.

Deep down, however, Markella had no illusions. She knew full well that she belonged to that most numerous and hapless category of artist: those talented enough to have a career, perhaps to even make a decent living off it, but who will never shine; those born to the second tier, condemned to lurk in the shadows cast by the stars, to perform during intermissions and keep the audience warmed up for the true holy monsters on either side—monsters of the stage, the pen, and the full palette of color.

Mediocrity: That was the word. No matter how much Markella spurned it, she felt it constantly, an indelible badge of infamy tattooed on her skin. It had first tripped off her tongue on the day she listened to her Greek-American classmate sing "La Habanera."

"Spare me! That's no Carmen, with her double chin and custard arms!" whispered, all venom, another classmate, who believed she had inherited some talent from her great-grandfather, the composer Nikolaos Mantzaros.[35]

"Except that she truly is Carmen! While we simply pretend to be," Markella had replied bitterly. "Kalogeropoulos soars on gossamer wings; we stumble around in leaden shoes."

Since she was fully aware of her limitations, since she had mustered the courage to compare herself to Kalogeropoulos—later to become "la Callas"—and to admit that there was no comparison, why did she not give up? "And do what instead?" she would have replied. "Live the life of a proper little housewife in Kallithea? Sit around moldering for a few more years with my mother, before moldering for good in my husband's house?" Besides, one of her Drama School professors had given her and her classmates a wise piece of advice: "Those among you with a true gift will go far, as long as

---

[35] Nikolaos Mantzaros (1795–1872) is known for composing the music to the Greek national anthem.

you never leave your art behind. Those without a gift will go even farther. As long as you leave at the right moment."

Markella had pinned all her hopes on that "right moment": on that opportunity that she firmly believed would one day be given her to leap off the thin nutshell of her talent onto a big ship sailing smoothly into open seas.

THAT SUMMER NIGHT, Attik's Barn was packed to the rafters. It was swarming with tailcoats, official uniforms covered in medals, evening gowns imported from Paris, and rifle barrels, meant to protect the nation's elite, radiating from the shrubbery. An enormous bouquet of flowers sent by the heir to the throne, Pavlos, and his wife, Frederica, almost fully covered the central table. For an entire hour, Attik himself feted the newlyweds by playing all of his most beautiful songs on the piano and adapting their lyrics, whenever possible, to reflect Savvas and Fani's romance.

He did so with a willing heart. From his vantage point onstage, this man of great sensibility could see that he was not dealing with a marriage of convenience between a gold-digging, penniless typist and a besotted old fogy. It was clear that they were bound by reciprocal and authentic feeling; as clear as day, in fact, that they were right for each other. Fani nestled like a cat in Savvas's sturdy arms, while he seemed rejuvenated by her youthful touch. The two deep wrinkles that had creased his cheeks after the death of his first wife appeared to have softened. Every so often, he would lean protectively in the direction of his new relatives, filling Markella's and Giannos's glasses, saying a tender word to Sevasti, whom he was already calling "Mother." The mood threatened to turn when Konstantinos Maniadakis, the infamous Minister of Public Order and a pitiless persecutor of communists, approached to wish them well.

"Ah, my dear Mrs. Armaos!" he had the effrontery to say to my grandmother. "If only we could knock some sense into your son Antonis's head, he'd be living like a king!"

"Don't mention it, son," she replied with a serene smile. "To each his own."

Next in the line of guests waiting to congratulate the newlyweds was a blond man of some forty-five years of age, whose twinkling eyes and sunburned face betrayed a life of ease. He hugged Bogdanos with the warmth of a close friend, kissed Fani's hand, and without beating about the bush brazenly pointed at Markella and asked, "Who is this enchanting creature? Don't tell me she's your little sister! What a pleasure, my beauty! Allow me to introduce myself: Lieutenant Commander Stratos Vranas, of the navy, discharged." From the manner in which he squeezed her hand, Markella understood that she had finally found the big, safe ship that she had been waiting for.

OH, THE DINNERS, the excursions, the nights spent dancing at exclusive clubs! From the day that Markella and Stratos became a couple, the Armaos sisters and the two brothers from different mothers became inseparable. Savvas rejoiced to see his philandering friend finally settling down, and Fani was infinitely relieved that her "little one," as she called Markella, had become enamored not of a disreputable artist but of a serious businessman.

Stratos Vranas, a serious businessman? One had to not know him very well and be ignorant of his past to use these words. In fact, after he'd quit the navy (the scandal of his escapades with the admiral's wife had been quickly quashed and the dishonorable discharge transmuted to an honorable discharge by virtue of the royal favor enjoyed by the Vranas family) and turned his hand to business, he had almost lost everything multiple times and brought ruin on anyone who had trusted him. No, he was not a crook, nor was he a swindler who tried to pass off pigs' ears for silk purses. It was just that his eyes were bigger than his stomach, and he had an inordinate amount of confidence in himself. Not only did he pour money down the drain but, to cap it all off, he found regular work unbearably tedious. There were only two things he was truly passionate about: women and cars. He was one of the first Greeks to participate in a rally race, as well as the first to choose a woman co-driver. Despite his strong ties to the Athenian upper crust, no one thought particularly highly of him, and no one would have bet a cent on his future as a businessman. This all changed one day in 1938, when he proudly returned from a trip to Berlin with a contract in hand: He was now Volkswagen's exclusive authorized distributor in Greece.

The contract was not just a piece of paper, it was a key to every door. Governor Bogdanos received him immediately and awarded him almost the full amount of credit he had requested to open offices, garages, and showrooms in Athens and Thessaloniki. As a token of his gratitude, Stratos Vranas offered him a Beetle, "the people's car," and the brainchild, according to legend, of Hitler himself.

"I don't accept gifts," Savvas objected.

"But it's barely worth a thousand marks!" Vranas exclaimed in surprise.

"Another reason not to, then!" the governor retorted, laughing.

For some reason, Stratos inspired both the governor's liking and his trust. In his opinion, a business venture that grew out of such deeply rooted passions could not but flourish. Both confirmed bachelors and past their marrying prime by the standards of the day, they began spending time together. Bogdanos quickly assumed a paternal role toward Vranas, and when Fani came into his life, he could not have wished for anything more than to see Stratos marry Markella and so become his brother-in-law.

At the time when my mother left me at my grandmother's on her way to the Peloponnese—February 1941, that is—it had become the rule for the two couples to dine together every Sunday at the house in Kallithea. The men brought the food and the wine, the women cooked, and Sevasti savored the pleasures of family. That is to say, she did as much savoring as a woman can do when she has one son in prison, another in hiding, and a third, Giannos, wandering around all day doing God knows what.

My arrival created a tidal wave of excitement. A child, albeit the child of a brother or brother-in-law, was the ideal cherry on top of the cake, the crown to their shared good fortune. My aunts were fairly jumping for joy when they first set eyes on me, declaring me adorable, exquisite, but also neglected and scrawny because of the trials I had endured *through no fault of my own*—the emphasis they placed on these words was the only barb against my mother. Hand in hand, we made the rounds of the shops to buy me clothes and toys (the war was raging in Epirus and Macedonia, but the Athens shopping district was doing business as usual, or almost). They were refugees, girls who had experienced great privations in the tenderness of their youth. By dressing and primping me, they were soothing old wounds.

And what about me? How did I feel about the sudden upheaval in my life? Island vistas, windmills, and the bleating of sheep had been supplanted by the teeming streets of Athens and the screeching of braking trams. My mother's comrades in exile, gruff and rough around the edges even when at their most affable, had been replaced by my aunts' elegant friends.

Even though three-year-olds often do not have the words to articulate what they are feeling, this does not mean that they do not notice and judge everything. Their capacity to adapt is in inverse proportion to their age. In a few weeks, my memories of exile were already fading. My grandmother's

unwavering presence consoled me almost completely for my
mother's absence. I was not a neglected child. On the contrary, I felt secure, loved, and pampered beyond measure,
and this reconciled me to the fact that my parents were
detained somewhere far away because, as my grandmother
explained, they were fighting for the common good.

V

ON APRIL 6, 1941, the Germans invaded Greece. On April
19, they occupied Larissa. On the following day, the first
protocols of surrender were signed by General Tsolakoglou.[36] On April 23, King George and Prime Minister
Tsouderos evacuated to Chania as the Greek fleet made
its way to Alexandria, Egypt. On April 27, the Germans
entered Athens. By the beginning of June, Crete had fallen
and all of Greece was under Occupation.

During this entire time, Savvas Bogdanos was on ten-
terhooks. As governor of the second-largest bank in the
country, he ought to have played an active role in the
unfolding events. Strangely, however, no one had asked
him to. The bank, of course, contributed to the national
effort, especially during the early months of the war when
the enemy was forced to retreat to the Albanian mountains. But after the upheaval following Metaxas's death,

---

[36] Giorgos Tsolakoglou (1886–1948) was installed as prime minister by the
Germans to lead the collaborationist government.

and above all after the German invasion, the bank was essentially paralyzed.

When the government decided to go into exile and continue the struggle under the aegis of the Allies, Savvas had no doubt that a place had been reserved for him on one of the departing warships. He even hastened to inform Fani of their impending departure. My aunt asked if the rest of the family would be joining them. Savvas shook his head. Fani raised her voice: "Don't you understand that I cannot leave my mother behind?"

The quarrel that followed was for naught. From the beginning of April, hundreds of prominent Athenians had received a discreet summonses to prepare themselves. Bogdanos waited in vain for his turn. On the day the front fell, he put his pride to one side and visited Prime Minister Koryzis.[37] Without beating about the bush, he asked how he might be of use to the homeland.

"The country has a variety of needs, as much on the front line as behind it," Koryzis prevaricated as he gently walked him to the door. On the following day, Koryzis killed himself, and Bogdanos was left spinning his wheels and waving his handkerchief at the ships weighing anchor.

"WHAT DID YOU expect, Savvas? You never took part in their cliques and byzantine intrigues. It's only natural that they

---

[37] Alexandros Koryzis (1885–1941) was appointed prime minister after Metaxas's death.

would now give you the cold shoulder," Vranas observed, trying to sugarcoat the pill.

Summer was approaching and the paths through the Field of Ares Park, sublimely indifferent to war and foreign occupation, were in full bloom.

"I did not ask you here to console me, Stratos. I need your advice. I received a strictly confidential communication from General Tsolakoglou. He's offering me a cabinet position."

"Which one?" Vranas exclaimed excitedly.

"To oversee food supply."

"And you're dragging your feet?"

"The last thing I want is to go down in history as a traitor."

"Why a traitor, Savvas? Because you haven't tied yourself to the British apron strings? Have you forgotten the contemptible role they and the French played in the Asia Minor Catastrophe? Have your forgotten about their warships, anchored in Smyrna harbor while the city burned, and they just sat there and watched as the Greeks fell into Kemal's clutches?"

"That's no reason to cast my lot with the Germans."

"Who's talking about the Germans? You will be serving your country, like you've always done. You will be protecting the little people from starvation. If upstanding characters like you don't forge a solid front and act as a buffer, the Reich's generals will install their strawmen at the helm and run all over us."

"But you are with the Axis, so you would say that—"

"You're wrong! I am with anyone who gives me work. I leave religion and ideology to more romantic souls. You, however, are of a different caliber, a public persona, an *homme d'état*," he said, all praise and adulation. "Which is why I swear to you on everything you hold most dear, Savvas—indeed, I would bet my head or anything else on it—the Axis will win. We need to keep this in mind as we look ahead."

I don't know how much Savvas was influenced by Stratos. The very next day, however, he was sworn in as minister. To the end of his long life, he insisted that while this decision proved fatal to his reputation, it saved the lives of many people.

VI

AS SOON AS he assumed his duties, Uncle Savvas was assigned bodyguards who were always by his side. Whenever he visited us in Kallithea, the house would be surrounded by plainclothes security units, and a German sidecar motorcycle, engine still running, remained parked by the front door.

It was not insurgents they feared, at least at first. It was the gangsters, the black marketeers, against whom he had declared full-blown war, turning a blind eye to the fact that the fish rots from the head down and that all the bullies busily fleecing the little people maintained secret relations with both the deep state and the occupying forces. When the occupiers claimed that they wanted to see the Greeks happy and well-fed, Bogdanos took them at their word, believing that it only made sense. He was, after all, a bit of a Don Quixote.

IT MUST HAVE been the spring of 1942. My grandmother and I were returning from the baths (that is to say, the hammam), which we visited every Saturday as was the custom in Asia Minor, when we noticed a crowd gathered in the square. My grandmother wanted to keep going but finally let me drag her by the hand—me and my child's curiosity!—ignorant of the spectacle that awaited us. Two men were strung up in trees, one on each side of the fountain. The sight will remain forever burned into my memory: the ghastly grayness of their skin; the bulging glassy eyes, like those of fish past their prime; the purple tongues protruding from their gaping mouths. Cardboard signs were pinned on their chests.

"What does that say, Grandma?" It was as if she had turned into a pillar of salt. "What does it say? What does it say? Tell me!" I demanded, tense and impatient. I knew one of the men, he owned the neighborhood café and was the father of my friend Lilika.

"They were black marketeers," my grandmother stammered. "In exchange for a dry crust of bread, they take all your belongings. They got caught and they were punished."

At that moment, a large, heavy woman, Lilika's mother, seized my grandmother by the collar. "Your son-in-law killed my husband!" she shrieked, right in her face.

"Bogdanos has orphaned my children! Justice? You call this justice, eh?" Her entire body was shaking. "But you, your bellies are full, aren't they? And the Germans, they shower your granddaughter with chocolate. Shame on you, you Turk-spawn!" she cried and spat in her face.

A couple of men grabbed her and pulled her away. My grandmother wiped the spit off her face, and we walked home in silence.

What the evil tongues in the neighborhood whispered among themselves was slander pure and simple. Mrs. Sevasti was not profiting from her sons-in-law; she had not strategically pushed her daughters into their arms. Because of the carefully hidden cache of Kremos gold, entrusted to her fifteen years earlier by Antonis and still almost intact, my grandmother had no need of either Bogdanos's or Vranas's largesse.

IN THE SUMMER of 1942, Stratos finally decided to marry Markella. The wedding was going to take place in Corfu. Partly because it was his mother's birthplace and she still lived there, partly because he wanted to cultivate the Italian Occupation authorities with the aim of building business relations with the "Republic of the Ionian Islands,"[38] as the Heptanese were called.

---

[38] In 1941, when the Axis occupied Greece, the Ionian Islands, which had long been the target of Italian expansionism, were handed over to the Italians. When the Italians left in 1943, the Germans took over.

One sweltering afternoon in early August, a limousine drew up to the house in Kallithea to take us to Palaio Faliro, along with bags and bags of luggage containing everything from my aunt's wedding dress to my beloved dolls. A hydroplane that Vranas had hired especially for the occasion was waiting for us there. It was the first time flying for both me and my grandmother. For Markella, too, I believe. After personally buckling our safety belts, Stratos donned a helmet and took the copilot's seat. My grandmother was a bundle of nerves. Until we splashed down and moored at one of the piers under the shadow of Corfu's old fortress—in other words, for the entire span of five hours—Sevasti did not stop reading out loud from the prayer book she had propped open on her knees.

I was a bridesmaid, or, as my grandmother explained to me, a "little bride." The ceremony took place on August 12th, on the day following Saint Spyridon's big festival.

I remember that the previous evening, as a token of honor, the bishop had taken us into the crypt to watch the preparation of the saint's relics for the holy tabernacle. After fitting him with new slippers (they changed them once a year, because the story was that he wore them out on long walks along the shore that left seaweed and small pebbles embedded in the soles), they lifted and placed him in a stand that looked like a telephone booth. In the gloom and doom of the Occupation, the litany provided an occasion of unbridled festivity. Three brass bands led the way, and the rest of the population, dressed in their Sunday best, followed in their wake.

The wedding, as well as the reception that followed in a manor house outside the main town, were equally festive. Once there, Markella, dressed in the traditional Corfiot costume, used a golden spoon to feed a kumquat to each guest in turn while I giddily clung to her skirts. Then she proceeded to sing her entire repertoire.

The Italian commissioner was giving out golden pins in the shape of the fascist double-headed battle ax. Sevasti wavered momentarily, but in the end she refused to wear it and slipped it into her pocket. Her age and position protected her from the malevolent looks.

ON THE FOLLOWING day, I was woken at the crack of dawn.

"We're going to see your father!" my grandmother announced, without further explanation. What I knew was that my father was fighting for the common good, but I had not been told, or else I just hadn't understood, that he was actually in prison, and in Corfu at that. The best that Bogdanos as a government minister had been able to do for us was an hour-long visit. The prison was a ten-minute walk from our hotel. On the way there, my grandmother brought me up-to-date—no doubt so that I would not have the opportunity to ask questions—as quickly and as simply as possible, about the fault line that separated our family.

"But we all love each other! We all love each other very much!" she added. Then she asked me not to mention

Markella's wedding to my father, "because he will be sad that he was unable to attend."

I remember the bolting and unbolting of numerous doors. I remember a dim and twisting corridor that led to a damp room illuminated by a bare ceiling bulb surrounded by flittering gnats, a wooden table, and one sole dilapidated chair. My father was sitting on it. When I set eyes on him, I burst into tears. He was swimming in his striped prison uniform. On purpose, they had forced him to go unwashed and unshaven for a week so that he would look frightening to me.

"Shush, little one, it's your father," Sevasti said, while on the sly, she slipped him a toy car so that he could pretend he had bought me a present. But it failed to calm me. I refused to accept this big bad wolf as my father. When he pulled me into his arms, I tried to throw them off and slip away. But when he looked into my eyes and smiled that kindly dolphin smile that lit up his face and everything around him, the evil charm was dispelled in the blink of an eye.

"Yes, this is my father!" I declared, and stroked his hair and pressed my cheek against his even though his beard tickled.

A ludicrous performance ensued: Sevasti, Fani, and Markella didn't say a word about the wedding. They pretended that this visit was the only reason for their voyage to Corfu. Antonis, in turn, pretended to believe them, and in general, asked nothing about their lives. As if he already knew everything.

Most of the time, he focused on me. He whistled two songs—he whistled incredibly well—and then, interlacing his fingers, made shadow puppets on the wall: a rabbit, a cat, a rooster. I watched him, mesmerized.

When a guard entered the room, we knew the visit was over. Now, I did not want to leave my father for the world—arms wrapped around his neck, I begged him to take me with him wherever he went. My grandmother moved heaven and earth to get me to let go, but I wouldn't budge. Then, he had an idea: He took an olive pit out of his pocket and gave it to me.

"When you get back to Athens, plant it in the yard," he told me. "It'll grow, you'll see—first there will be a little sprout, and then there will be leaves and branches. When it blooms its first flower and grows its first fruit, that's when I will return. And I will stay with you forever...Don't ever forget it, eh, my little Niki?"

"I won't forget!" I promised.

"Hurry then! Hurry!" He pointed to the door.

On the way back to the hotel, I was lost in thought. I wasn't sad—that's not really the right word. I had fallen prey to a new and complicated feeling for my four and a half years. I felt, I knew, that I belonged to two contradictory worlds, which despite their apparent coexistence were, on a deeper level, waging a battle to the death. I sensed—as the Virgin is my witness—that one of these worlds was feeding on the blood of the other. No one had asked me yet to choose one over the other, but I was absolutely certain that sooner or later that moment would come.

VII

IN THE AUTUMN of 1943, my grandmother put me in the nursery school run by Mrs. Styliani at her house only five doors down from ours. The idea was to cut the apron strings, but without having me run completely loose. I suspect that she was also motivated by the desire to help Mrs. Styliani, a widow with an only son who had been blinded in Albania. We were a handful of children all in all, no doubt the most well-off in the neighborhood. Mrs. Styliani did not have the faintest clue about pedagogy, but she did have the right balance of discipline and affection for her role. We drew and played with Plasticene, and she taught us songs, primarily religious in nature. To this day, what I remember most clearly is her son, Dionysis. A tall, strapping young man who had been a talented carpenter in his past life, he was withering away in the house with never a word of complaint. Mrs. Styliani encouraged us children to lend him a hand with all the day's little tasks, and so we helped him on with his shoes and vest, and two of us would walk him to and from the café. To thank us, Sakis, as we called him, gave us candy. A fallen eagle at the mercy of little sparrows.

IN FEBRUARY 1944, a tragedy occurred. One afternoon, Bogdanos traveled to Loutraki for an appointment with the owner of the local casino. He had made it his mission to convince the man, by hook or by crook, to shoulder the cost of financing at least one of the large soup kitchens in Athens. It had been his idea, and the Occupation authorities had not raised any objections. Since it was impossible to fully extirpate the black market given the considerable number of Greeks who were getting rich on the backs of the needy and celebrating their new wealth in the flashiest and most sordid ways possible (cabarets and clubs were making money hand over fist, and the stock market, too, was thriving), the only realistic option was to go to where the gold was plentiful and confiscate it. Bogdanos was not a moralist, nor did he have anything against gambling and prostitution. It was just that he had resolved to help the poor and thereby protect them, among other things, from the "virus of communism."

The casino manager received him with the honors worthy of a maharaja. Initially, he tried to induct him into the pleasures of life in Loutraki, then to bribe him, and finally to threaten him: The tide would not be long in turning and those who had openly collaborated with the Germans would be in need of special protection. Bogdanos, however, stood his ground. "If you refuse to finance the soup kitchen," he said narrowing his eyes threateningly, "I'm going to lock up this shithole. Or perhaps I'll just burn it down."

The casino manager folded but returned to the bargaining table with a new hand. They both proved to be hard nuts to crack. Instead of sedating them, the alcohol and smoke acted as stimulants, keeping their negotiations at such a steady boil that the sun was rising by the time they shook hands. The casino finally committed to "contribute to the national struggle" in the sum of two thousand gold sovereigns each week.

"I want the first installment now, in cash!" Bogdanos demanded.

The state car and escorting motorcycle were barely a thousand yards outside Loutraki, when they saw a small German patrol blocking the road and signaling them to stop. The chauffeur stepped on the brake, but in the nick of time Bogdanos noticed that the squad's weapons were a strange, motley assortment: He spied a sawed-off shotgun and an antiquated Gras rifle.

"Step on it!" he growled. "Open fire! They're not Germans, they're crooks!"[39] He fell from the seat onto the floorboard, rolled the car window all the way down, and started firing his revolver. It was a bloodbath. The motorcycle driver took a bullet to the neck, and the chauffeur was wounded in the left shoulder but continued firing. Finally, Bogdanos opened the door and lobbed the grenade he always kept in his coat pocket. The explosion was deafening. The ELAS[40] combatants in their borrowed uniforms (looted during a recent raid of the Lanara textile factory, which was running production for the Occupation forces) scattered, leaving behind one dead body. An ambush like

---

[39] A term used by the right to denigrate the partisans.

[40] The Greek Liberation Army, the armed branch of the EAM (National Liberation Front), was founded by the Greek Communist Party but included membership from a range of political parties on the left.

that had not come about by chance, and Bogdanos's suspicions about who had leaked the information were confirmed when he came face-to-face with the corpse: Giannos Armaos, his wife's brother.

MY UNCLE GIANNOS. A born hustler, a "hellion" as my grandmother called him. He had never had it in him to do an honest day's work. A cardsharp until he was banned from every gambling den in Athens and its broader regions, he then turned his attention to "the arts" as an itinerant gramophone operator. But among the crowds congregating around him in the squares to request Anatolian laments and "European" songs, there was always an accomplice charged with filching their wallets.

The Occupation fucked him over well and good, as he used to say. All his little schemes had been figuratively dealt a swift kick to the nuts. Even dealing drugs was pointless because hashish was selling for next to nothing. Worn out and backed into a corner, he began stealing cargo, tires, and sometimes even gasoline from German vehicles: a difficult and dangerous pastime. At first, he worked alone, or at most with someone else serving as a lookout. But he was affable and persuasive (something he had in common with my father), and he soon had an entire gang at his beck and call. A gang of underaged boys, youngsters whom he conscripted from the poorer quarters—Dourgouti, Brahami, Petralona—based mainly on their physical attributes. The smaller and nimbler the boy, the more successful the prospective "jumper."[41] Needless to say, no one knew Gian-nos by his real name. He had them call him "Panagis" and passed himself off as a native of Thessaloniki.

Month by month, the gang grew, and at their zenith numbered between two to three dozen "little Panagises." The eldest was seventeen, the youngest, only ten. Naturally, Giannos never deployed them all at once. After each heist, he would gather the participants to allot them their share of the spoils. In the autumn of 1943, he successfully orches-trated one of the most intrepid plots yet. One moonlit night, they broke into the vehicle depot at the German headquar-ters, emptied the gasoline tank, and drove off with three army trucks and two motorcycles. Enraged, the Germans resorted to something extremely rare because it amounted to an admission of their inability to maintain order: They put a bounty on the burglars' heads, wanted dead or alive. Soon thereafter, Giannos and his staunchest disciples joined the ELAS.

Had playing cat and mouse with the Germans aroused his political consciousness? Or was he simply seeking refuge in the bosom of a large armed organization with whom he shared a common foe? At any rate, had Giannos been solely concerned with saving his own skin, he could have joined the Security Battalions, which in addition to offering amnesty also came with a host of legal advantages.

---

[41] A term used because these boys or young men would jump on the German trucks to rob them.

In his role as both jumper and combatant of the Resistance, Uncle Giannos always went incognito. Not even his brother Petros, who was the liaison between the EPON[42] and the ELAS in Peristeri, had a clue about his machinations. As for his mother and the rest of us, we all believed him to be working as a warehouse clerk at the Lanara textile factory. We also were aware—at least, the adults among us were—that he was living in Kokkinia with a divorcée. He would visit Kallithea once in a blue moon, always dressed to the nines, his famous suspenders on display, and always with a wisecrack on his lips, at times amusing, at others disconcerting to his sisters and their husbands. Only one thing was certain: No one took him seriously. Which is why Bogdanos, in his presence and without thinking twice about it, revealed his intention to go to the Loutraki casino and personally "levy the taxes they owe."

SAVVAS WAS BESIDE himself. "What truly terrifies me is that your brother and his cronies did not want to assassinate me for political reasons!" he exclaimed to Fani. "What they were after is the money!"

"What terrifies me is that I've lost my brother! How can we break the news to Mother?" she replied, pulling at her hair in despair.

---

[42] The United Panhellenic Organization of Youth was the youth wing of the National Liberation Front that was active during the Axis occupation.

"There's no need to go into the details," Bogdanos decided. "We'll say that we were notified by the morgue."

And that's what they did. But my grandmother knew. She knew straightaway. No charitable soul had to go whisper it in her ear. Her heart had told her by suddenly shattering in the middle of the night. And the fact that she didn't completely fall apart, I'd like to think, is due in some measure to me.

They brought Giannos to us in a closed plank coffin. It was a radiant, cloudless morning. The entire neighborhood had rallied around Sevasti. They put him down in the middle of the living room. After lifting the lid, she took him in her arms and clung to him for several minutes, as if hoping that the heat of her body would breathe life into his, but she let go before anyone had to intervene and pull her away. She arranged his tie, placed the icon of Saint Barbara that she had brought from Mudanya over his crossed hands, and slipped a copper coin into his jacket pocket "to pay the ferryman." Then she took a large basket filled with the flowers she had cut the night before in nearby gardens and began covering him with them. "Oh, Sleep, come and take him to the gardens; cover his bosom with roses and sweet violets."[43]

The house smelled of frankincense and fish soup. Feverishly, my aunts dashed to and fro like headless chickens, buzzing around their mother, running into the kitchen to stir pots, accepting condolences. Stratos Vranas was in

---

[43] A traditional lullaby from Asia Minor.

charge of arrangements. He had talked to the priest, the gravediggers, and the café owner, who was now carrying dozens of cups of coffee on a tray for the visitors.

The only words that brought true comfort to Sevasti came from Stratos. She had collapsed into an armchair and was wailing: "Where are my sons? Iordanis lost at the end of the world, Petros in hiding, Antonis in prison—"

"Antonis is no longer in Corfu," Vranas interjected.

"Where is he then?" my grandmother asked, alarmed.

"He escaped to the Middle East," he told her. "Probably planning his return as we speak, and thinking about how best to take our heads." By the look on his face, it was clear that he knew exactly what he was saying.

"Word of honor, Stratos?" she asked. Her face looked about to light up, but then her eyes fell on the coffin.

In the meantime, I was paralyzed by shyness. An irrational shyness. I just wanted to close my eyes and disappear. In the little black dress sewn by Aunt Fani after they had not been able to find any mourning clothes for children in the shops, I kept myself to myself as much as possible. The entire time, I wanted to pee and I kept biting my nails. At some point, I escaped into the yard. That's where Bogdanos found me and took me under his wing. He was clearly even more ill at ease than I was, even though he had made sure to spread the rumor that Giannos had been killed in Piraeus in a confrontation with persons unknown. He was smoking one cigarette after the other and glancing repeatedly at his watch and winding it as he exchanged hurried half sentences with his bodyguard under his breath. Seeing him like that, with the implacable sun of Attica right in his face, I became conscious for the first time of his age. "Uncle Savvas is an old man," I thought.

Then Markella came and took me indoors to kiss the dead man before the procession began. I had never touched a corpse, and I confess that my curiosity was as strong as my apprehension. Stretching up to my tiptoes, I saw, smack in the middle of his eyebrows, a third eye: the hole left by the bullet that killed him.

"Is that where his soul came out of?" I asked Markella, but she looked down at me sternly and told me to cross myself and pull up my socks.

The burial took place at the Third Cemetery. Giannos's lover from Kokkinia appeared and went to stand by my grandmother's side. An extremely tall and imposing figure of a woman, a "stone-cold fox" to echo the popular phrase I learned years later. When the casket was lowered into the earth, a salvo sounded at a dozen or so headstones' distance. It was my uncles' comrades, all come to pay their respects. "EAM, ELAS, power to the people!" they cried as they ran off and disappeared behind the cypress trees.

VIII

WHEN DID THE possibility of an Axis defeat first become felt? Was it after the attack on Pearl Harbor and the United

States' entry into the war? After Stalingrad? In any case, by the spring of 1944, it was common knowledge throughout Greece that the Occupation had one foot out the door. That Easter Sunday, people kept wishing each other a "Happy Resurrection!"

"But didn't Jesus rise yesterday?" I asked my grandmother.

"They're talking about a different kind of resurrection," she replied.

During that time, the Resistance intensified day by day, barely outstripping its bloody repression. Every evening, as soon as it got dark, the "funnel" resounded throughout Kallithea, a bullhorn through which a woman's voice generally emanated. "EPON here!" she would begin, vibrant and clear, and then proceed to inform her listeners of the latest developments in the struggle for liberation. Each new day saw more walls covered in slogans. Each new week, we heard of another blockade[44] that had led more people to either their deaths or to the camps' barbed wire. My grandmother, especially after losing Giannos, made no bones about both her desire and her impatience to see "the Krauts finally clear out."

To the poisonous tongues in the neighborhood that asked, "Good for your sons, Mrs. Sevasti, but what will happen to

---

[44] The Germans and Security Battalionists would encircle a particular neighborhood, assemble all the men, and use hooded informants to identify communists and Resistance fighters.

your sons-in-law?" she replied with a line from the Gospel:
"Those who have done good to the resurrection of life; and
those who have done evil to the resurrection of judgment."

For the first time, her sons-in-law had parted ways.

Bogdanos, on the one hand, at peace with his conscience and convinced of having acted in the line of patri-
otic duty, had decided to stay in the ministry until the final
day to personally hand over his files to the government-
in-exile that was returning from the Middle East. He had
also compiled a full report of his accomplishments, which
he believed was sure to mollify the most uncompromising
skeptic. One could not read it without exonerating him or
singing his praises.

Vranas, on the other hand, was under no illusions. After
making money hand over fist in his multiple dealings with
the Germans, he knew that his fate was sealed as soon as
they left Greece. He could, of course, attempt a softer landing by wrapping himself in "the cloak of anti-communism,"
or, more to the point, by liberally greasing the palms of
Greece's new strongmen. But he told himself that if he did
so, he would always be beholden, always at their beck and
call. In his view, there was only one option: to follow on the
departing heels of the occupying forces and tie his lot to
theirs, once and for all.

He started to lay the groundwork at the beginning of
the summer. By the middle of August, he finally had something concrete in hand. He had been informed by a trusted
source that a train was scheduled to leave Athens at night,

carrying on board a handpicked group of the most prominent and irredeemably compromised collaborators. After a
brief stop in Thessaloniki to allow the "fighters" of northern
Greece to embark, it was destined for Vienna.

"Save me a window seat!" Stratos said and hastened to
pay a king's ransom for two tickets, one for himself and the
other for Markella.

"When should we be at Larissa Station?" he asked.

"We're not meeting there," they replied. "We want to
keep the lid on this as long as possible, so we will gather
earlier at the Black Cat. You know, at the corner of Agiou
Meletiou and Acharnon. When the time is right, a truck
will arrive to take us. Only one bag per passenger, mind
you." Stratos was not happy, but he agreed—in any case,
he had no other choice.

IN ORDER TO take me with her to the Black Cat, my aunt
Markella had to kidnap me—literally. What business did
a six-year-old child have in a dive like that? She told my
grandmother that she was taking me to a children's variety
show at Zappeion, and promised that she'd have me home
in Kallithea by nine that evening at the latest. On the way,
she revealed the truth to me: "I'm going to show you how
grown-ups have fun!"

As soon as Stratos set eyes on us, walking in hand in
hand, his face fell. (Stratos and Markella had parted ways
early that morning. She had stayed at their house to pack all
the essentials; he had wandered around town, taking care of

final loose ends—for only God knew when they'd be back. Perhaps never.)

"Have you gone mad?" he exploded. "Why did you bring that one here?"

"I wanted to spend my final night in Greece with her!" my aunt replied without an ounce of apology in her voice.

"Don't even think of secretly carting her along with us on the train!" Stratos groaned. All the tenderness and affection he had lavished on me during the last three years had abruptly vanished.

"Is that who you take me for?" Markella threw him a poisonous look.

"Here, sit, my dear!" She patted the seat next to hers at the table. "And you, why don't you order us something to eat. The child is hungry."

Since my birth, I had seen a thing or two compared to the overwhelming majority of my peers. I was used to things new and strange. Yet everything I witnessed and heard at the Black Cat that night remained indelibly etched in my memory.

It was a basement room with a sawdust-strewn mosaic tiled floor, containing approximately twenty wooden tables covered in wax paper. At the center of each table was a big oil lamp whose intensity could be turned up or down to the patron's taste. As a result, a penumbra prevailed throughout the room. Despite the darkness, waiters dashed back and forth, carrying trays overflowing with sheep heads and roast chicken, grilled steaks and seafood, and as side dishes, entire hills of spaghetti and mountains of potatoes.

That night, the Black Cat was filled with passengers for the train to Vienna, all intent on as much revelry as possible before their departure. Corks shot out of champagne bottles, cigars flared, hookahs gurgled. I looked around more in amazement than shyness. Women kept arriving—in the middle of August, mind you—wrapped in furs and with fingers, arms, and necks laden with jewelry, their work-around for the baggage restrictions. Men, among them Stratos himself, had no qualms about planting a revolver next to their plates.

"Put that away immediately!" Markella hissed. He bridled for a second, but then tossed a napkin over it.

When everyone had feasted to their heart's content, a band of musicians filed into the room—two bouzouki players, a guitarist, an accordionist, and a red-haired young woman holding a tambourine—and pulled five chairs into an impromptu stage. Besides the junkie on Sifnos, I had never heard anyone play rembetiko before, and the entire scene was completely new to me. At first, it sounded monotonous and somewhat weepy, but the more time passed, the more it grew on me, aided and abetted no doubt by the vapors of "incense"—hashish, in other words—smoldering in the hookahs. Fledgling babe, chick barely hatched that I was, I soon found myself in a strange, dreamlike state. Heavy-limbed, I curled up in my aunt's arms, but every time I opened my eyes, a new psychedelic image flitted before me: five men, arms around each other's shoulders, in a frenzied hasaposerviko, feet stomping the mosaic floor (they must have been wearing iron-studded soles judging by the thundering noise they made, as if an entire herd were on stampede); a man dancing zeibekiko, a knife between his teeth, while his friend poured alcohol on the floor and set it on fire; the singer shaking her tambourine in a Dionysian frenzy as two customers lifted her up in a chair and paraded her around the room (because of their difference in height—one was big and tall, the other Lilliputian—this improvised and listing throne had her intermittently shrieking in fear and screaming with laughter).

Tipsy now, Stratos's high spirits revived along with his affection for me.

"I can't bear the thought of leaving the little one here!" he proclaimed to Markella. "Ah, what the hell, in for a penny, in for a pound, let's take her with us!"

A cold sweat came over me. Of course, they had not told me where they were going, but I feared the worst.

"Niki has parents!" my aunt interrupted, no doubt the only one in the entire place still completely sober.

"Bah! It's been years, and neither hide nor hair..." Stratos sneered and filled her glass to overflowing with champagne. Markella saw red, a fearful scene would surely have erupted had not the Germans barged into the Black Cat at that very moment.

As soon as their uniforms appeared on the threshold, the music stopped, and the customers began to gather their belongings.

"Ladies and gentlemen, the train is ready for boarding," the platoon leader, sporting a white trench coat, announced in a metallic voice. "Please get into the two vehicles waiting outside. They'll take you to Larissa Station. Before that though, as a formality, we are going to conduct physical searches. The bearing of arms is forbidden during the journey. We will hold on to them and return them to you on our arrival in Vienna."

Even though the high-ranking collaborators had good reason for outrage, they had no choice but to comply. After settling their bills with the Black Cat's maître d', they lined up to put their guns down on a bench and succumb, arms high and legs spread, to the soldiers' rough handling. The women were no exception.

Long before our turn arrived, Markella rose from the table.

"Where are you going," Stratos asked.

"To put Niki in a taxi and send her back to her grandmother. I won't be a minute!" she replied, tugging at my arm. Eyes to the ground, we passed in front of the Germans, and as soon as we were outside, we started running. At the corner of Agiou Meletiou and Patision we hailed a taxi.

"Hotel Cecil in Kifissia!" my aunt cried.

It didn't take Stratos long for the penny to drop. Did he waver so much as one second, I wonder? Did it occur to him to stay behind for Markella? Even if it did, he strangled his qualms like a newborn kitten. "Every man for himself," he thought and shrugged it off.

"Didn't you pay for two tickets, Mr. Vranas?" the platoon leader asked snidely. "If you are, in fact, traveling alone, I'm afraid a second bag is out of the question."

Stratos glanced resentfully at Markella's suitcase. He had bought it for her: It was of the finest leather and was now almost bursting at the seams with silks and jewelry. Then, noticing the musicians still sitting around one of the club's tables, he promptly grabbed the suitcase and deposited it at the singer's feet.

"All I ask is that you occasionally light the lantern on my father's grave at the First Cemetery," he told her.

At exactly the same time, twenty minutes to three in the wee hours of the morning, Stratos Vranas, on board the train, and Markella Armaos, in the Hotel Cecil, were removing their wedding rings, thereby dissolving their marriage by mutual accord.

THE FOLLOWING MORNING, when we returned to Kallithea, Grandmother Sevasti was waiting for us at the front door. I had never seen her in such a state before. She was beside herself, on the verge of a paroxysm. Markella stammered vague excuses—"I couldn't find a way to alert you"; "Are you saying you don't trust me, Mother?"—but Grandmother was not having it. She grabbed us both by the hair and dragged us into the house.

"You go and wash." She pointed to me. "Lord only knows what that good-for-nothing daughter of mine roped you into! And you, shameless hussy, sit there and spill the beans, and don't dare leave anything out!"

Even had she wanted to, Markella could not have hidden from her mother's relentless scrutiny. Every word out of her mouth only increased Sevasti's fury.

"Why did you have to take Niki with you?"

"I needed a reason to leave."

"A reason or a pretext? A grown woman and you hid behind the child? And all this to ditch your husband when he's already taken hard knocks aplenty? Is that how I brought you up? To be a fair-weather wife? All this time, when everyone else was going hungry and putting their lives on the line, and you were preening in your well-feathered nest, it was all fine by you, wasn't it?"

Under this merciless barrage, Markella burst into tears.

"Don't cry. You won't soften my heart. Instead, do yourself a favor and find a way to get to your husband! Take an airplane to Thessaloniki, meet him at the train station and fall at his feet!"

"But I don't love him anymore." Markella sniffled.

"You don't love him anymore?" My grandmother's tone changed instantly. "You really don't love him?" My aunt nodded. "In other words, you'd have left him even if things had turned out differently?"

"Yes... We haven't shared a bed for months."

"You swear?"

"On the holy cross, Mother."

Sevasti then threw an inquisitive look at Fani, who was silently following the conversation. She confirmed her sister's story.

"If you are in earnest, then I forgive you. You should have left him earlier. What about you, Foteini, do you love your Savvas?"

"I'd climb to the gallows with him if necessary!" Fani replied.

"May you be blessed," my grandmother said.

This is how I learned that the measure of all things is devotion. And when devotion catches fire, as Markella explained, it turns into love.

IX

THE GERMANS WITHDREW from Athens on Thursday, October 12, 1944. It was done with such coordination and control it was as if their retreat had been planned since the day of their arrival, three and a half years earlier. At eight in the morning, a detachment placed a garland on the Tomb of the Unknown Soldier, and at a quarter past nine a corporal took down the Nazi flag from the Acropolis. In the surviving images (someone filmed him as he folded the flag, tucked it under his arm, and descended the marble stairs, head held high), it looks like he is deftly rushing through a simple formality, without sparing a thought for the villages razed to the ground, for those who died of starvation and in the battles of resistance.

A long convoy of German vehicles was leaving the city, coursing through all the central thoroughfares, while church bells rang as if raising the dead. In record time, the roads filled with jubilant crowds. In our house in Kallithea, my grandmother was in a quandary: She longed to take me and join the people out there, but she feared a physical or verbal attack. And what could she say in reply? That three of her four sons had fought in the Resistance? When people are liberated, it's resentment rather than respect that first rears its head.

IT WAS ALMOST noon when the bell rang. I liked to welcome visitors, so I dashed to the door, opened it, and found myself in front of two lacerated legs in a pair of battered work boots. I looked up: a mop of hair as tangled and unruly as a briar patch, a face ravaged by the sun, a mouth grimacing in an attempt at a smile. When the scarecrow's arms reached toward me, I panicked and slammed the door shut.

"Who is it?" asked my grandmother.

"A Gypsy woman...a beggar."

She opened the door and the scarecrow fell into her arms.

I started shrieking.

"It's your mother, my child! Your mama!"

That was my mama? Impossible. I no longer remembered her, of course; I hadn't even set eyes on a photograph, but everyone described her to me as a very beautiful woman, like a fairy. Well, fairies don't broil in the sun; their skin is translucent, like silk, not at all like this leather mask.

"The Gypsy has cast a spell on my grandmother," I thought and took to my heels. I hid behind the urn of olive oil and held my breath, but to no avail. The Gypsy flushed me out in two shakes of a lamb's tail, and she lifted me in the air and pinned me to her chest. Crushing me in her arms, choking sobs racked her body. I was suffocating. Besides everything else, she also stank like a billy goat. I tried to extricate myself but she wouldn't let me. We were both now bawling our eyes out, but for very different reasons.

While Sevasti heated the water for her bath, Anna, without stopping for breath, recounted her adventures: how she had stayed in the village for months because of her father's stroke and had taken to the mountains only after his death; how she had tried to get to Athens three times, but had been prevented by her superiors; how she had learned how to use weapons, but had also been trained as a nurse.

"Big things are brewing up there!" she announced excitedly. "A new Greece is being born!"[45] From behind her glasses, my grandmother peered at her skeptically.

"Didn't you get any of the messages I sent you?" my mother asked.

"No, nothing."

"About a month ago, I decided I would come find you, even if it meant the end of the world, even if it meant being accused of desertion! As a matter of fact, that's what I did:

---

[45] In the spring of 1944, the EAM had organized elections throughout Greece and created the Political Committee of National Liberation (PEEA), also known as the "government of the mountains." This government existed in tandem with the collaborationist government and the official government exiled in Cairo. At the end of the war, many of its members joined the government of national unity.

I deserted. I left in the middle of the night and walked all the way here."

"On foot?"

"I crossed half of the Peloponnese on foot. Of course, I did not have a travel warrant, nor could I rely on anyone's help, not even that of the Resistance. A woman alone—you can imagine the dangers. That's why I avoided the main roads and took only footpaths and trails. I thought to myself: Better to be devoured by jackals than fall prey to humans."

"What about water? Bread?"

"Blessed be the shepherds and monks. I would tell them that I had taken a vow to walk all the way to the Holy Monastery of Daphni and kneel before the altar. I carried a small image of the Virgin Mary in my bodice. All I had to do was show it to them and they believed me."

My grandmother, on the contrary, remained skeptical.

"And how did you manage, my child, to arrive right on the day of liberation?"

"I arrived the day before yesterday, but stayed in hiding. It would have been dangerous to come here earlier. Dangerous for you…"

My grandmother was suddenly overcome with shame for grilling Anna with questions like an interrogator. It was her wretchedness talking, all those pesky worries constantly picking and poking at her.

"Welcome, my dear Anna!" she said, flinging her arms wide again.

"I am so happy to see you, Mother!"

It took two sponges and an entire cake of green soap to scrub off all the grime. When she had dried herself, combed her hair, and slipped on one of Fani's dresses, she finally just about approximated the image of the mother in my mind's eye. Her hair, now blond again, was a halo of curls around her face. Her gray-blue eyes had a somewhat remote expression, due—as we found out much later—to the beginnings of early-onset cataracts. My aunt's dress, which was really more of a tunic, was short on her, and her legs were long, slender, and shapely. She could have been taken for Artemis, the goddess of the hunt, whose image I had seen and admired in a mythology book. In this sense, her looks perfectly complemented the story of her peregrinations through the mountains of Arcadia and Corinth. I stared at her in wonderment, but it was not enough to vanquish my distrust.

"Are you in school? Which grade? Are you a good student?"

Grandmother replied for me.

I stood at a safe distance, my arms crossed over my chest, on the defensive.

"Do you know any songs?"

"Go on, child, why don't you sing 'Up on the Mountain, Ever So High'?"

Even if I had wanted to, my agitation had driven it clean out of my head.

"Why don't you show your mother your dolls! Show her your father's olive tree!"

In our courtyard, I had planted the pit that Antonis had given me in Corfu. It was already a sapling but had not yet borne fruit. I checked on it religiously every morning and evening, and even mentioned it in my prayers, sure that my father would return on the very same day the first olive appeared.

"Your father is here," Anna announced. "We can go to him now!"

"How do you know?" Grandmother asked her.

"At dawn this morning, two military ships docked in Piraeus full of Greeks from the Middle East. I'm sure Antonis is among them!"

"How will you find him?"

"Before our arrests in '38, we agreed on a place to meet when we were freed. Come on, Niki, let's go!"

Grandmother's eyes urged me on. Finally, I deigned to slip my hand into my mother's.

X

IT WAS PANDEMONIUM in the streets. Flocks of people hung from balconies and passing trams. Others were waving flags—Greek, British, Soviet, where had they been hiding them all this time?—singing, cracking red Easter eggs.[46] We had no hope of finding a ride. My mother removed the

---

[46] A Greek custom to mark the resurrection of Christ.

clogs my grandmother had given her and stuffed them in
her canvas bag: the soles of her feet were as hard as hooves
and she was more comfortable without shoes. We climbed
Filopappou Hill, and gazed down at the celebrating city,
before descending on the Acropolis side. My mother was
aware that Thisseio and Petralona were Chite[47] lairs.

"If we're stopped and questioned, no matter what it's
about, don't open your mouth!" she said, squeezing my
hand. I had begun to warm to her. I liked her bouncing
step —my aunts carried themselves like staid little ladies
compared to her. I also liked the confidence in her voice,
which made me feel that at her side I had nothing to fear.

We roamed around for a while before reaching our destination. I don't know if she had forgotten the way or she
was trying to cover our tracks in case someone was following us. Finally, we found ourselves in front of a small cottage
on a narrow dirt lane.

"This is where your father and I lived during the early
days of our marriage. This is where we arranged to meet,"
she said.

She planted herself on the doorstep, and I took a seat
on the stairs to rest. The longer we waited, the more pronounced her apprehension. Clearly on pins and needles,
she kept dashing out to the middle of the road and looking around to see if anyone was approaching. The sun was

---

[47] Members of the monarchist and anti-communist militia called X (*chi* in
Greek) founded in 1941 and armed by the Germans.

harsh and burning; the summer heat, stifling. I demanded water, but of course, she didn't have any. "How long are we going to wait?" I asked myself, and imagined with horror having to spend the night there, bedding down on that dirt road, parched with thirst, our stomachs empty.

Suddenly, I heard a shutter open behind my back. A very old woman, with an incredibly wrinkled face and a goatee on her chin, loomed against the window frame.

"You're Armaos's, aren't you?" she asked in a cavernous voice. "Your husband is waiting for you at the Kommandantur."

"Where's that?"

"Kommandantur, my girl, the Krauts! Hurry! Go find your man!"

"The Germans have him?" my mother cried, without thinking.

"No, he's the one that's got them!" The old woman cackled and closed her shutters.

The Kommandantur, the German garrison headquarters in Athens, was on Korai Street. The closer we got to it, the thicker the crowds. From Klafthmonos Square onward, we were cheek by jowl and could barely move. My mother was not discouraged: Pushing, prodding with her elbows, she managed to clear a path for us.

We arrived in front of the building just in time to witness history in the making: Three young men, straddling the balustrade of the main balcony, were sawing through the chains holding the sign with the swastika and its Gothic inscriptions. Clapping together in rhythm, the gathered crowds were spurring them on.

"Move back! It's coming down!" the ringleader warned. People quickly stepped aside leaving an open semicircle.

"Heeeyyy, ooooop!" I remember the metal sign coming loose, taking a half turn in midair, and exploding with a deafening clap on the sidewalk. Immediately, people began jumping on it. One man drenched it in red paint. Another brazenly pissed all over it. It was the first time in my life I saw a pecker.

Two men, armed from head to toe, were standing guard at the entrance to the building.

"Anna Milonas," said my mother, but her patronymic left them completely unmoved.

"ELAS Ninth Regiment."

"What do you want?" they asked, grudgingly.

"I'm Antonis Armaos's wife."

Straightaway, they stepped aside and let us through.

A terrible racket reigned throughout the building. Its new occupants were ransacking every drawer, every cabinet for information the Germans might have left behind. But they had, of course, burned everything. We went from room to room looking for my father and finally found him on the top floor, in the only office with a locked door, in the middle of convening an important committee.

He too no longer corresponded to the image I had of him. Instead of prison stripes, he was now wearing a starched white shirt, a double-breasted suit, and a silk tie.

His face was closely shaven and tanned by the Egyptian sun. He took me in his arms.

"Did you plant the pit I gave you?" he asked me conspiratorially.

Even though duty called, before returning to the table for the planning of the *Rizospastis* relaunch, he pinned onto my chest a brooch that he told me had been sent by "someone very close." I dared not ask who. It was a hammer and a sickle in pure gold.

We remained in that building for many hours. The earlier feverishness was now turning festive. Demijohns of wine and spit-roasted pork wrapped in wax paper appeared out of nowhere. A rough-and-ready orchestra was formed—an accordion, guitars, and trumpets—and the musicians congregated on the side balconies to play folk music, but also tangos and, needless to say, revolutionary songs. And there I was, their little mascot, giddily waving a red kerchief at the crowds. When I'd had enough of that, I ended up with a brush in hand that I was dipping into a can of gold paint to help color in a huge wooden *E*. Three letters were going to be placed on the building's facade: *E, A, M*.

When we walked out onto Korai Street, night was falling. I was over the moon: Finally, I was walking hand in hand with my parents, returned to me victorious. We climbed into a military vehicle that took us to Kallithea and my father's mother. When my parents asked me if I preferred to sleep there, or go with them to "their own house" in Patissia, I had no qualms at all, even though I had no idea what they meant by "their own house." Grandmother packed me a little bundle with my nightgown and my favorite doll, Dadouna.

XI

IT WAS NOT a house but an old hotel, or perhaps a sanatorium that had been requisitioned by the EAM. Resistance fighters were billeted throughout the enormous courtyard. They had lit fires in metal barrels and were sitting around them, drinking and smoking.

We entered a room on the first floor containing three metal beds. My parents pulled two of them together, side by side, and pushed the third one, destined for me, as far away as possible. I began to feel ill at ease. My mother undressed me, rather clumsily it must be said, and then told me to get up on my tippy-toes and wash in the sink that was next to the door.

"It's cracked!" I cried, almost with disgust.

She did not reply—what could she say?

"Do you need to go wee-wee?" she asked.

"Pee-pee not wee-wee!" I corrected her, annoyed. Pee-pee is what my grandmother called it. We walked to the end of a dim corridor, locating the public toilets by smell.

When we returned to the room, my father was already in his undershirt, smoking and lying under a sheet of dubious cleanliness.

"Come here and let me give you a kiss, my little one!"

I bent over him.

"It's so good to have you near!" His lips barely grazed my forehead.

My mother tucked me in. Accustomed to sleeping with my favorite doll in my arms every night, I asked her to give her to me. My mother looked surprised but did as I asked. Five minutes after she had switched off the light, I cried that I needed to pee-pee again. She heaved a deep sigh but got up and took me back to the toilets.

"Now, go to sleep!" she ordered.

I closed my eyes but could not calm down enough to fall asleep. Shouts and laughter echoed from the courtyard; a tidal flow of whispers came from my parents' conjoined beds. Even though I tried to listen in, I couldn't make out any words. Suddenly, I really missed my grandmother. At Kallithea, when I couldn't sleep, I'd jump out of bed and without saying a word, I'd slip into hers. She would sing me a lullaby and stroke my hair. Deciding to put myself to sleep all on my own, I began quietly humming a tune.

"Shhhhh!" It was my father's voice.

Throwing a furtive look in their direction, I saw through the darkness a mountain rising under the sheets. "Have they climbed up on top of each other?" I wondered. I buried my head in the pillow, which gave off a strange, sweetish smell, and squeezed the doll between my legs.

I don't know how much time had passed—I must have dozed off—when I was startled by a deafening clap, an explosion or shot. I leapt to my feet, crying: "Mama! Papa!" No response. I ran to their bed. It was empty. They weren't there. They were gone. They had abandoned me. Distraught, I rushed into the corridor, careened down the stairs, dashed across the yard—my nightgown flapping behind me in the breeze—and found myself out on the street. I had no idea where I was going. All I wanted was to get to my grandmother as quickly as possible.

Unfamiliar with the neighborhood, I drifted around in the moonlight, turning innumerable times to the left, to the right, around and around myself, not knowing which direction to go. The silence and solitude were misleading. Homes and shops were tightly shuttered, but even I, a mere child, could tell that inside there were guns, cocked and loaded.

At one point I came to an avenue, but I didn't dare cross it, as if it were a river infested with moray eels, so I ducked back into the side streets. The moon, in the meantime, had hidden behind red-tinted clouds. I suddenly felt something warm and slimy under my feet—horse dung probably—and slipped, falling flat on my back on the pavement.

Complete despair came over me then. Bawling my eyes out, not daring to touch my dirty feet, I crawled to a lamp-post and collapsed at its foot. Burying my face in my hands, I prayed with all my heart for a genie to come and either take me and deliver me into my grandmother's arms or to kill me then and there. Utterly exhausted by that interminable day, without really knowing what I was doing, I curled up around the post and fell into a deep sleep.

A grim-looking man with a handlebar mustache and a bandolier across his chest shook me awake.

"Whose are you?" he asked in a heavy accent.

"A-A-A-Armaos is my father's name," I stammered.

"Ah, thank God, child! Where have you been? Your parents are losing their minds!" He grabbed me by the back of the neck and tossed me on the seat of his motorcycle's sidecar.

My mother threw me a look like a slap in the face. My father came between us and took me in his arms. The episode was closed, over and done with. We returned to our beds fully reconciled. Yet there had been no explanations. Do I truly think it was necessary, you might ask, for them to explain that after six years of forced separation they needed to be in a room by themselves, just the two of them? I would say, yes, I do. And too bad if it shocked or even angered me. It would certainly have been preferable to erecting a wall of silence between us from that very first night.

XII

"I AM ANTONIS Armaos's daughter!" Pleased as punch, I would take every opportunity to declare it or actually show it. My father took me with him wherever he could, and I would swell with pride at his side when I watched people on the street shake and kiss his hand. "When will we have the opportunity to vote for you again, Antonis?" they'd ask him.

"If all these people had voted for me back then, we'd have been running the country before the war," he whispered in my ear one day, laughing.

We had all moved to Kallithea as a family. I remember that autumn of 1944 as an endless party. Streets festooned with flags and people out all day, never leaving the squares. Front doors always open, or at least that was the impression I had, since our living room was never empty. My grandmother was still in mourning for Giannos, of course, but every now and then a smile crept to her lips, especially when she had us all around her at the table.

All of us? Uncle Petros would visit almost every day, swaggering in his ELAS uniform. He was a political instructor in the western suburbs: Aigaleo, Dafni, Chaidari. He drove around in a jeep, accompanied by a bodyguard, and now instead of a teacher's pet, he looked like a tigerish revolutionary. Markella's separation from Stratos Vranas, even though largely forced by circumstance, had led to her forgiveness for consorting with collaborators during the Occupation. She had returned to the stage, replaced lyrical song with light music, and was taking part in the first variety show to be performed after liberation.

"When are you going to come see me, Antonis? I am even singing 'Kalinka' in Greek!" she said to my father in a coquettish tone.

But Fani, faithful Fani who steadfastly stood by her husband, the ex-minister of the collaborationist government, what had happened to her?

At first, she avoided coming to the house. Grandmother made no mention of her name. Everyone was waiting for Antonis to broach the subject.

"Where's Fani?" he finally asked one afternoon.

"She doesn't know if you want to see her. That's why she hasn't come," his mother explained.

"What on earth are you talking about? Tell her that I am inviting her to lunch tomorrow!"

I remember her entrance: eyes cast down, face bare of makeup, sheathed in a black dress. Antonis and Anna hugged her; Petros settled for an offhand "Hello." She turned toward the kitchen to help my grandmother, who was preparing a moussaka.

"Come sit here, Fani!" Antonis called to her and poured her an ouzo. They began to break the ice by talking about the good old times, their childhood, their father. Antonis offered her a cigarette, and despite the fact that she never smoked in front of her mother, Fani took it.

"How is Savvas?" he asked, lighting it for her.

"How can he be? He's sequestered in the house, waiting to be arrested."

"He could give himself up. That would surely count in his favor."

"Give himself up to whom? And why? Savvas does not consider himself either a criminal or a traitor. He believes that he helped lessen the suffering of the Greek people. That his presence hindered, even if only slightly, the occupiers' cruelty. He bore his cross, knowing full well that sooner or later he would be stoned for it."

"And you, what do you believe, little sister?"

"I stand by him. Not because he is my husband but because he is right!"

Antonis was wise enough not to get embroiled in a discussion about what Bogdanos had or hadn't done.

"Listen, little sister: Savvas will probably go to trial, and he will be given the opportunity to defend his rights. If he proves that he acted in the interests of the country, even if somewhat unorthodox in his methods, then the verdict will be a favorable one for him. No matter what happens, though, you are our blood. Don't you ever forget that!" he said and kissed her on both cheeks.

That's when Fani cracked: "I'm scared, Antonis! I'm scared to death! The fear is with me when I wake and when I sleep! Savvas is so pigheaded. He's refusing to go live at his brother's, on Stisichorou Street, behind the Old Royal Palace, even temporarily. He insists on staying in our house on Kypselis Street! So what is to prevent the OPLA[48] from knocking on our door? Or someone from shooting him down on the street? Besides, he saunters around as if he doesn't have a care in the world!"

"Why doesn't he ask the fine lads at X for protection?" Petros taunted her, but Fani ignored him.

"It's not a trial that I fear, Antonis, but a knife in the back. Can you guarantee that nothing will happen to my Savvas?"

---

[48] The organization for the protection of the People's Army, an armed group created in 1943 by the KKE and the EAM to ensure the security of its leadership and defend their demonstrators in Athens against the authorities.

"I can't guarantee anything. I don't have any jurisdiction in that area." He cast a quick glance at Petros, who was seated behind Fani, and quickly averted his gaze.

"You must relocate to Stisichorou," he advised her, his tone stern. "You're his wife. It would really take the cake if you, of all people, can't convince him!"

ANTONIS WAS NOT indifferent to Bogdanos's fate. When he professed a lack of jurisdiction, it was not due to reluctance but rather powerlessness. Though many people, and most of all his kith and kin, still considered him the KKE's powerful second-in-command, it was becoming increasingly apparent, on a daily basis in fact, that circumstances had worked against him, had left him unmistakably on the sidelines. While he was in prison in Corfu, and then in the Middle East, a new crop of cadres had taken the Party's helm. They had done the work of rebuilding the Party and taking the lead in the Resistance. Having not participated by force of circumstance in the establishment of the EAM and the blooming of the insurgency, Antonis had returned to Greece at the precise moment that the partisans in the mountains and the cities, still stinking of gunpowder, were champing at the bit to reap the fruit of three years of bloody struggle. They were interested neither in ceding the helm nor in getting up to give him a seat. And there was no chance in hell that they would be interested in protecting a collaborator who happened to be his brother-in-law.

Prewar hierarchies had been definitively and irrevocably overturned. At the dawn of a new era, new strongmen were leading the people's movement.

He had been appointed the director of the EAM offices. From the balcony overlooking Korai Street, he kept his eye on Kolonaki, the home of the enemy, and Kaisariani, the bastion of insurgency. His duties, however, were limited to the oversight of the buildings' cleaning and employee salaries. He was not invited to any meetings of importance. Even though every day brought its share of complicated problems, his opinion seemed to be of interest to no one. Antonis would not have been surprised to see his name left off of the ballots at the next elections, even if, at thirty-eight, he was not at all ready to be relegated to purely honorific functions—and that was the best-case scenario.

He wondered if his marginalization was due solely to time and circumstance or if he was being held accountable—without anyone actually telling him to his face—for missteps and omissions that had damaged the Party.

Did they hold him responsible for the Middle East uprising that had erupted among the Greek army and navy and been extinguished only after hundreds of leftist foot soldiers and officers were safely behind the camps' barbed wire? Did they believe that he had the power to contain the righteous rage of those foot soldiers and sailors? No longer willing to serve under rightist generals or monarchist admirals, horrified at the prospect of seeing Metaxas's zealots and the parasites of the House of Glücksburg[49] return to govern in Greece after the war as if nothing had happened, they had stormed the naval base at Port Said without warning in April 1944, raised the red flag over the prow of the legendary battle cruiser *Averoff*, and taken the upper hand almost without any bloodshed before the British cannon annihilated them.

Rather than hasten to condemn the Middle East uprising as "a risky operation instigated by provocateurs," the KKE ought to have learned something from its fate and realized that one does not mess around with the British. When their interests were at stake, they did not hesitate to mobilize all their military firepower. If the EAM had hopes of manipulating them to their own ends or of presenting them with a fait accompli, then they were sorely mistaken—that was Antonis's opinion. But no one was interested in his opinion, even if only as an eyewitness to what had transpired in the Middle East.

The thought that his disgrace might be due to his disputes with Nikos in the Corfu Prison also often preyed on his mind. Yet Nikos had been captured by the Germans and his fate was unknown. He could just as well be languishing in a camp as be buried at the bottom of a mass grave. It was highly improbable that the new leadership had gotten wind of something that was now five years in the past.

---

[49] At the time of the uprising, the king of Greece was Georges II, Prince of Denmark, of the House of Glücksburg. He ceded the country to the Metaxas dictatorship in 1936.

In any case, there was only one thing of which Antonis was certain: He was suffocating. In leaving Egypt and setting sail for Greece, he'd had only one burning desire: to throw himself, heart and soul, into the struggle; to be, as was his wont, on the front line of events. Instead, he was in charge of the soap for the Korai building's bathrooms.

Increasingly often, he kept thinking back to that unexpected and oh-so-tempting encounter he'd had a few months earlier, on an evening in February at Alexandria's Délices.

XIII

IT WAS ONE of those rare occasions when he went for a coffee by himself. He had just left an interminable, hourslong meeting of the Greek community's Antifascist Youth, and realized that he needed to clear his head of his comrades, of their feverish conversation, of their ideological and organizational fervor. He needed to unwind, to finally find himself in a setting where no one knew him, where no one had any plans to run by him or, most important, advice to ask of him.

A towering doorman the size of a harem eunuch bowed respectfully at the entrance to the chic patisserie. The window displays were practically bursting with syrupy cakes, and the ceiling looked about to come down under the weight of chubby Cupids entwined with voluptuous Aphrodites carved in stucco. He walked through the dining room and out into the courtyard in the back, and chose a table at a distance from the water-lily fountain, whose perpetually gurgling waters always made him want to piss. Happily, he ensconced himself in an armchair and asked the waiter—a young Arab barely fifteen years of age in a white tuxedo—for a cardamom coffee with plenty of sugar and a hookah with apple essence. He closed his lips around the ivory mouthpiece, took a deep draw, and shut his eyes.

He had been in Egypt for ten months. Memories of his previous life had begun to fade: his five years in prison under conditions that would have broken—mentally at least—anyone who was not committed, heart and soul, to a greater plan; his fantastical escape after the Italian retreat from Corfu and shortly before the German arrival; his earliest adventures, from the time he had joined the Party, but also before that, when he was still seeking that elusive "we" to give his life breath and meaning. In short, all his years in Greece and all those near and dear to him were dimming slowly but surely.

He took another, longer draw, sucking the aromatic smoke down deep into his entrails, and his head whirled with it. When the cloud cleared, it was as if he had been magically transported to Mudanya. Strictly speaking, the town was faintly discernible in the distance. He, on the other hand, was paddling a boat on the Sea of Marmara. It was September and the sea was like an enormous pond, magnetizing in its sheen. He let go of the oars, took off his shirt, and noticed with surprise that his chest was still

hairless, young. He leapt to the prow and prepared for a
nosedive, the famous tumbling dive of his invention that
always had Mudanya's youngsters applauding like mad
and all the girls ready to give him their hearts. But suddenly he lost his nerve. "What if a huge wave steals the boat
away and scatters the oars like matches over the sea?" he
thought. There was no logic to his fear, but it was paralyz-
ing. He sat on the gunwale and gazed at the water as if it
were a prohibited paradise. "Too bad," he said. "Let me
get a little wet at least." He lay belly-down on the deck and
plunged his arms up to the elbow in the water. And then—
miracle of miracles!—schools of fish and sea creatures of
every kind, garfish tapered like swords, silvery bream, wily
squid squirting ink, lobsters armored like knights, appeared
out of nowhere and started dancing around him. So many
of them that he could catch them in his bare hands, pluck
them out, throw them in the boat, and return to the harbor
triumphant. He would be the talk of Mudanya for months,
and the story of his great exploit repeated over and over
again: how Antonis Armaos had carried the catch of five
caïques in his one little walnut shell and so fed a dozen families in need! But he couldn't do it, because he no longer
belonged to that world there but to this world here. He too
had turned into a sea creature: a young dolphin basking in
the sun before plunging into the crystalline depths.

Lost in his daydreams, Antonis did not notice the
young woman sitting at a nearby table, who, after staring
at him for quite some time, asked the waiter in English if

the patisserie had a telephone at the clients' disposal. She disappeared into the interior of Délices and on her return had a glass of champagne sent to Antonis.

"From the madam!" said the boy in the tuxedo, as he poured the bubbly into a crystal glass.

"To your health!" the woman cried, raising her glass—she would have been beautiful were she not as gaunt as a scarecrow.

"Yours, too!" replied a smiling but puzzled Antonis. "Have we met?"

"Aren't you delegate Armaos?"

"Ex-delegate," he corrected her. "Who are you?"

"Elizabeth Charalambis, or Sissi. You have no reason to know me. I'm only a mere mortal."

Was she flirting or mocking him? Or was she one of those well-heeled Greeks who were financing the antifascist struggle sub rosa? Out of courtesy more than anything, Antonis invited her to his table. Half an hour of small talk followed; in other words, their talk of cabbages and kings did nothing to enlighten Antonis about the lady's intentions. She was, as she herself bragged, an honors graduate of the famous Averoff Girls' School in Alexandria, and the heir to a textile business in Tahrir Square, right in the middle of the city.

"Do you make a habit of offering champagne to strangers?" Antonis could not resist asking. "I want to know if I should be flattered," he added to soften the irony.

"We're not the strangers you believe us to be," Elizabeth-Sissi retorted with a sly smile. "We have friends in common. Very soon, you'll have the key to the mystery."

As he watched her flounce smugly into the Délices courtyard and then park herself in the armchair across from his, he didn't recognize her. When he did, his mouth dropped open.

It was Clary Kremos, seventeen years on and some fifty pounds fleshier: a buxom forty-year-old who had not lost any of the sparkle in her eyes. As if they had parted only days earlier, she began recounting the city's latest news, chattering about everything, from the winter weather— "Unusually damp this year!"—to the literary evening in commemoration of "our great Cavafy" scheduled for the following Sunday.

"I must leave you," Elizabeth-Sissi said, offering her tiny gloved hand to Antonis. Clary Kremos beckoned the waiter to refill their glasses: "A bottle of champagne, please!"

"I moved heaven and earth to find you, and now here you are! I knew you were in Egypt, but I thought you were based in Cairo."

"Cairo is indeed my base. Why were you looking for me? To kill me?"

"Kill you? Why would you say that?" Clary exclaimed, feigning astonishment remarkably well.

"You're right! Ladies of your station never do their own dirty work. But you might foist the chore on your dear husband again, or on one of your henchmen."

"What on earth are you talking about, Antonis? Don't you know that poor Adam is dead? No, of course, how would you know? A terribly aggressive cancer…poor thing just withered away. Three months and it was over. Five years ago now. Just stopped wearing my widow's weeds. But I go to the cemetery every Sunday without fail. And then once the war broke out, we couldn't travel anyway."

"My condolences," Antonis said, rather coldly.

"Where do things stand, tell me? With that dreadful Hitler? Is he finally going to leave us in peace? Is there light at the end of the tunnel? A leader, a commander like you, with a finger in every pie, you must have reliable information! I was right when I told Adam: That young man has rare gifts! He will go far... Why are you looking at me with that mournful expression? Are you homesick?"

Antonis could not stomach her for another second. He stood up and pulled out his wallet to pay.

"Where are you going?"

"Lovely to see you, Clary."

"You have no interest in meeting your son?"

"My son?"

"You'll see! It will be like looking at yourself in the mirror! Only back when you were a teenager. You're two peas in a pod. Imagine, one day Chrysanthos happened upon a picture of you in our community paper and he couldn't put it down. 'Mama, that man looks awfully like me,' he said. I did not have it in me to tell him the truth. Perhaps you should be the one to do it."

"His name is Chrysanthos?"

"Yes. We gave him my father-in-law's name. But he goes by Chrys. Come on, let's go! I already told him that we have a special guest joining us for dinner tonight. No need

to wait, they'll send the bill to my home!" she said, taking
his arm.

IN NO TIME at all, they were in Clary's Rolls-Royce convertible (with her at the wheel, honking madly and narrowly
skirting bicycles and horse-drawn carriages), had gone the
length of the Corniche (the avenue running along Alexandria's waterfront), and gained the city suburbs, Aboukir first
and then Montazah.

"This is where my dear Adam was laid to rest," she said,
as they passed the walls of a cemetery. "I have twelve people
taking care of him, night and day."

"What do you mean?"

"Our mausoleum is so large it holds an entire family of
Arabs."

"You buried them in there with him?" Antonis asked,
horrified.

"No, of course not, silly! What do you take Adam for?
A pharaoh? They just live there, in the mausoleum, and
tend to it, polishing the marble. I send them rice, dates, old
clothes. Every three months or so, one of their women gets
pregnant!" It was clear that she was not telling him this
story to play the philanthropist but rather because she found
it amusing.

After ten minutes or so, the Rolls came to a halt at the
entrance to a building. Strangely, the Kremoses did not live
in a mansion but in an *okela*, a four-story structure rising

in the middle of an oasis of palm and olive trees. Two servants hastened to open the car doors, while a third who was manning the elevator bowed deeply before pressing the button for the fourth floor. Even though he thought it highly unlikely that Clary had laid a trap for him, Antonis clutched the grip of the pistol he carried in his trousers.

"For the past five years, Chrys and I have lived all alone in this mausoleum! My in-laws built it, idiotically assuming that Alexandria would extend rapidly toward the east. They died, as did Adam. Many of our friends emigrated because of the war, either to London or to South Africa. At times, I get so blue! You cannot image... Of course, we also keep an apartment downtown, but our son's health is quite fragile, and the doctors advise that he stay out in the country."

"Our son!" Before introducing him to their son, Clary gave Antonis the tour of the house. Had he ever traveled to England, he would have noticed that everything was distinctly British in style: the furniture, the wallpaper, even the melba toast and chutney accompanying the gin. By the time they settled into two plush armchairs, they did not know what to say to each other. Clary kept trying to lighten the mood, but Antonis remained taciturn. He smoked and glanced constantly at his watch. His train to Cairo was leaving at six thirty in the morning. It was imperative that he get four to five hours of sleep at his hotel room across from the train station if he wanted to be bright-eyed and bushy-tailed for the following day's journey, which he planned to spend writing a detailed report, destined for the

EAM-ELAS headquarters in the mountains of Greece, on political developments in the Middle East. Then, in the evening he had to meet with the director of TASS, the unofficial but legitimate representative of the Soviet state.

"Why are you staring at me without saying a word? What are you thinking about?" Clary asked.

"Will Chrys be long?"

"Goodness! Are you that hungry?"

Suddenly, Antonis began to doubt the child's existence. "Where is he?"

"He's working in his studio, on the second floor. These last couple of days, he's been finishing his grandfather's portrait."

"He's an artist?"

"I didn't tell you? He's considered a prodigy in Egyptian art circles. The sperm you gave me was of exceptional quality!"

"He's not going to school?"

"He gets his lessons at home. Don't worry, our Chrys will be here at any moment. In the meantime, may I ask you something?" she said with all the subtlety of a cat in heat, as she leaned toward him, revealing her opulent décolleté. "Don't you like me anymore?"

"What makes you think I ever liked you?"

"Oh, come on! You did it only for the money?"

"That was ages ago."

"People don't change just like that. I know what you are going to say: that you've become a communist, that you've been to Calvary and back. I have done my research, and I know everything. But, Antonis, I fell in love with you back then!"

"Is that why you wanted to have me killed?"

"Perhaps that was part of it. I swear to you, a day hasn't gone by that I haven't thought of you!"

Antonis lit a cigarette with the smoldering butt of the one he had just finished.

"Stop smoking so much!" Clary admonished with pretend peeve. "Take me in your arms, give me a kiss—"

"What would be the point of that?"

"You have every reason to believe that I lured you here on a whim. But to me, you are an Odysseus, finally returned to hearth and home!"

Realizing that her amorous advances were falling on deaf ears, Clary changed tack. She turned serious, her tone more confiding: "I used to think that if I became a widow before I was too old and doddering, I'd throw myself into burning the candle at both ends, free of the social constraints imposed on me by marriage. That wasn't the case at all! When Adam died, I mourned him fully and truly, and realized that, even though I am a hot-blooded woman, I am no libertine, no bed-hopping man-eater. I need the firm and stable presence of a man by my side. Naturally, I received loads of propositions. From within our Greek community, but also some French and British gentlemen, and even an Indian prince—they all asked for my hand in marriage. As you can see, I rejected them all. I kept saying to myself: 'The first time I got married it was out of friendship. Adam and I were kindred spirits since childhood. When I get married again it must be for love.' Listen, Antonis, my personal fortune is in the ballpark of one million gold sovereigns, and that's not counting two big textile factories, one in Alexandria and the other in Aswan that I myself manage most capably, although at the expense of my peace of mind. You don't have to worry about Chrys, a substantial bequest, and of course his even more substantial talent, mean that he is shielded from all want. So, I therefore propose" ("Why don't I stop her?" Antonis was wondering. "Why don't I tell her I am married?") "that we sign a premarital agreement granting you fifty percent of my entire estate, as well as its stewardship. I have complete confidence in you; I know that you will neither defraud nor bankrupt me. You will surely say that you are a communist, that you renounce personal property. Well then, if you can make a believer of me—why not? Anything is possible! We'll turn the factories over to their workers! Or to the Soviet Union!"

At that moment, the living-room door swung open and a tall, thin, painfully pale boy appeared on the threshold. He was wearing black trousers and a white silk shirt with gold cuff links. His shoulder-length blond hair was combed back, draping his nape. With mincing steps, he approached his mother.

"Ah, here he is, my Chrys! Let me introduce you to Mr. Antonis Armaos, an old friend from Greece!" Antonis rose to his feet.

"It's a pleasure to meet you, sir. I think I've read some articles about you in *Tachydromos*."

"It's time for dinner!" Clary announced, linking her arms through theirs and leading them to the table.

She sat them across from each other, face-to-face, and truly it seemed to Antonis that he had traveled back in time. It was less of a challenge to identify their rare differences than to fully catalogue all of their likenesses. Chrys was more delicate of build. His skin was paler, almost translucent, his eyes and hair lighter, and he had the air of a dreamer. "At his age, I had my feet firmly planted on the ground, and the grit to squeeze blood out of a stone!" Antonis thought to himself.

"Why are you so pale, Chrys? Are you eating enough? Do you ever go out and take some sun?" he asked, his tone suddenly paternal.

"You tell him!" a delighted Clary exclaimed. "He spends all day and all night in his studio. It's been months since he has stepped outside."

"Mother, I only have until April to finish all the new work!"

"Oh, I forgot to tell you that this spring Chrys is having his first solo show at the most renowned gallery in Alexandria!" Clary boasted. "I truly hope you'll be there?"

This was his son. How could he not go?

As he deboned a delicious skate cooked with nuts in a coconut-milk sauce, Antonis attempted to sound out the boy. His responses were terse, delivered in a somewhat weary, jaded tone, yet his gaze did not waver from their guest for a moment. "Has he guessed?" Antonis wondered. He was astonished at the dawning realization that Chrys was utterly indifferent to everything he, and everyone he associated with, cared about: the struggle against fascism, young people's dreams of social justice, even the Second Battle of El Alamein,[50] whose echoes were still reverberating throughout Egypt, all were like news from another planet to him.

"What *are* you interested in?" Antonis finally exploded in frustration.

"Art, of course! My art!" Chrys replied, piqued.

"Why don't you show Mr. Armaos your studio?" Clary intervened to defuse the mounting tension.

"Only if you really want me to, Mother," the boy replied in a scathing tone.

"WHAT DID YOU think of your son's art?"

"I know nothing about painting. If the experts agree, then he must have talent."

"What about your son? What did you think of him?"

"He's just like me, but also completely different."

"Well, aren't you different from your father?"

They were driving back to Alexandria. Clary had closed the roof on the convertible, and the wheezing windshield

---

[50] Battle waged in the autumn of 1942 that resulted in the British expelling the Italians and Germans from Egypt.

wipers were struggling to slough off the muddy rain heavy with the red sand of the desert.

"Tonight, let's stay at our apartment *au centre-ville*, and tomorrow we can take our *petit déjeuner* on the balcony of the Windsor Palace Hotel. It's the favorite haunt of all the better Greeks. They'll take one look at us and wonder, 'Who is the handsome man that has stolen Clary's heart?'"

"Why don't I tell her to go to hell?" Antonis wondered. Instead, he settled for a simple: "I'm sleeping at my hotel by the station. I have to leave for Cairo at dawn."

"Of course, you have your business to attend to. Have you given any thought to my proposal?"

"Why don't I tell her about Anna? About Niki? Niki, naturally, would have a gilded childhood in Alexandria. As for Anna, only God knows where she is . . . if she is anywhere at all, that is. No, I wouldn't be staying in Egypt for the sake of my wife and my daughter; even less so for the sake of my artist son."

For a moment, he imagined himself in the role of industrialist, managing two textile factories, speculating on the international stock market and, all the while, putting theory into practice: His workers would have undreamt-of rights and benefits and would be granted shares in the business. "There are, after all, examples of enlightened capitalists," he reminded himself. He envisioned building a social experiment right there, on the banks of the Nile, akin to that of the kibbutzes in Palestine: communal property, innovative schools open to everyone, mores and a lifestyle equal to socialism's New Man. In a society of a caliber so enlightened, even Anna and Clary might coexist.

"You've had too much to drink and you're rambling, Antonis! Wake up!" he pulled himself up short. "The only battle to be waged is in Greece! Do you want to be daydreaming in Alexandria's literary salons, while the EAM-ELAS fight to give the people back their power? If the class struggle has brought you to your knees and you're now clutching at straws and thinking of sponging off a wealthy widow in the guise of being progressive, then at least come clean, if only to yourself. Forget everything that you've worked so hard to sow all these years, and go bury yourself in Mrs. Kremos's skirts!"

"Drop me off here!" he said, his voice peremptory.

"But we're not at the station—"

"I want to walk."

"In the rain?"

"For the entire five years I was in prison in Corfu, rain leaked into my cell."

"May I come visit you in Cairo next week?"

"No. I will send you word."

"As you wish."

He never got back in touch, of course. Months later, when he was getting ready for his return to Athens, he received a parcel. Inside, there was a sickle and hammer in pure gold, and a letter. He tore the letter into pieces and wiped it from his memory. As for the sickle and hammer, he pinned them to my chest.

XIV

MY FATHER SEETHED as he watched his comrades squander their energies on revolutionary exercises, while the prime minister, Georgios Papandreou, under British directives, methodically began digging their graves. My mother, on the other hand, wholeheartedly shared in the euphoria of that autumn of 1944.

She was, without a doubt, the most active member of the Kallithea Chapter of National Solidarity. Every morning, she would take me to school (I was in first grade at the time) in my blue uniform and matching hair ribbon, as well as the sickle and hammer to remind everyone whose daughter I was. After that, she would attend to her many commitments: soup kitchens, housing initiatives for the homeless (notably the victims of the Piraeus bombing[51]), and other visionary, future-facing projects. A professor at the Polytechnic, a pioneering urban planner, had suggested the expropriation of a large expanse of land in Chasani—an area that later became known by the name Elliniko—for the building of a children's city, containing orphanages and nursery schools for all the youngsters orphaned during the war. He had even built a maquette; when my mother and her comrades went to his office to see it, they were transfixed.

---

[51] Conducted by the British and Americans in January 1944 to raze German military bases, the bombing destroyed entire neighborhoods.

"My work from now on is at the children's city! It's where the new generation will be forged!" Anna declared to Antonis.

"Well, don't put the cart before the horse," he warned, bringing her back to reality. "The game hasn't been called yet."

While Anna's passions may well have centered on the revolutionary struggle, she was not indifferent to her daughter's upbringing. Indeed, she was racked with guilt for having involuntarily abandoned me for so long. And even though she felt deeply indebted to Grandmother Sevasti and my aunts, all of whom had taken good care of me, it was nonetheless also true that under their watch I had acquired certain damaging habits, which ought to be shed as soon as possible. First, of course, there was my mania for crossing myself whenever we passed outside a church, and for dashing to kiss a priest's hand whenever one appeared in my crosshairs. "God only knows where that hand has been!" she would say, invoking reasons of hygiene in the realization that I would only dig my heels in if she tried to abruptly and brutally disabuse me of my religious fervor. My reeducation had to be handled with kid gloves, in the gentlest possible manner.

At night, instead of reading "Little Red Riding Hood" or "Puss in Boots," she would recount stories from the Soviet front, the great deeds of young heroes who, under Stalin's directives, had blown up German tanks and brought down airplanes, at times armed only with a slingshot. To my eyes, Stalin was gaining the status of a god. I envisioned him perched in the Kremlin's highest tower (to me, obviously, the grandest building in the world) in the process of orchestrating the worldwide resistance to fascism. "Your father has met Stalin," my mother announced one day, and this information shook me to the core. All the more so when my father added to my new iconostasis images of other saints, like those of Georgi Dimitrov[52]—"A giant among giants that Dimitrov!"—and la Pasionaria,[53] with whom he had danced a waltz at a party in Moscow.

My grandmother had discreetly withdrawn to her kitchen, ceding the reins of my instruction to my parents.

UNTIL, ONE AFTERNOON, I flew into her arms, weeping and wailing.

"What's wrong, sweetie?"

"She wants me to give my dolls away!"

"Who? Your mother?"

"Tell her to give her own dolls away!" My mother was standing a few feet away, smiling awkwardly, not at all pleased that I had sought my grandmother's mediation but unsure about what to do to avoid a definitive rupture.

"Mother, Niki owns nine dolls!" she declared solemnly.

---

[52] The first communist leader of Bulgaria from 1946 to 1949, Dimitrov led the Communist International from 1935 to 1943.

[53] Dolores Ibárruri was a Spanish Republican politician of the Spanish Civil War, who became the secretary-general of the Communist Party of Spain and spent many years of exile in Moscow as a leading figure in communist politics.

"But they were given to me by Aunt Fani, Aunt Markella, Uncle Savvas, and Uncle Stratos!" I cried.

"Most children don't have any. Many don't even have a second change of clothes."

"What's that got to do with me?"

"So, I proposed that she invite eight classmates of her choice to the house, and give each one a doll. That way, everyone will be happy—"

"Not me! I won't be happy!"

"You will learn to appreciate the joy of sharing, what is means to be part of the brotherhood of man. If you had brothers and sisters, wouldn't you let them play with your toys?"

"I don't have brothers and sisters because you didn't make me any!" I retorted.

"Your mother is right, Niki," Sevasti stepped into the fray. "Saint Luke said it, too: 'He that hath two coats, let him impart to him that hath none.' We heard this during the liturgy, remember?"

"He was talking about coats, not dolls!"

"It doesn't make a difference."

MY DOLLS KEPT me company and were the objects of my care and concern. I combed their hair and washed them (at least the five wooden ones, and the one made out of porcelain, not the three cloth ones), and I had my grandmother sew them dresses. Most were blond and blue-eyed, of German fabrication. But I also had a little Japanese girl in a kimono.

While I was still at Mrs. Styliani's nursery school, I sometimes took them with me. But it had never even occurred to
any of my friends to ask me to give them one. Only things
can be given away or exchanged. My dolls weren't things,
they were my daughters and I was their mother!

I knew that I didn't have a prayer of finding a sympathetic
ear at home. Not only would my father take my mother's side
but he would also throw a lecture into the bargain in that
silver-tongued way of his that always had the effect of making me see red. While my mother was satisfied with simply
dictating how things were going to be, my father wanted to
bring you around to his point of view. Those who were sure
to have rallied around me were absent: Stratos in Vienna;
Fani and Savvas in Kypseli; and Markella at the theater.

I resolved to hide my dolls, to bury them somewhere
temporarily, and then tell my parents that they had disappeared under mysterious circumstances, hinting that they
had made a break for it, that they had preferred to fly out
the window rather than fall into strangers' hands. I stayed
awake until I heard everyone snoring. Then, well past midnight, I crept into the courtyard and began digging. A fruit-
less endeavor. Two hours later, the spoon I was using as a
spade was completely crooked and the big hole I had imagined was barely half a finger deep. Sweaty and exhausted, I
returned to bed, took all my dolls in my arms, and soaked
them in farewell tears.

Anna was not one to drag her heels. The awful affair was
set for the following afternoon. Eight of my classmates—using

Mother's criteria, I had selected the ones who looked the most destitute—eight ragged little girls followed me home. My mother welcomed them with extraordinary warmth. She plied them with tea and cookies, and asked about their families. To her great satisfaction, all their parents with only one exception were both wage slaves and confirmed leftists.

The dolls were lined up like toy soldiers on the living-room table, and I, like a hooded informant at an Occupation blockade, had to point them out and name them one by one. I started bawling again.

"In the socialist Greece that is coming into existence as we speak, every little girl will have dolls to her heart's content!" My mother tried to console me.

I blew my nose and began: "Helga, Marlene, Chin-Chon…"

My mother scribbled their names of scraps of paper, which she folded and tossed into a cookie tin. She shook it, mixing them all up, and then my classmates drew their lots.

"Can I leave now?" I asked, my arms tight around my beloved Dadouna, with the huge eyes that opened and shut—the only one I had been able to save from catastrophe.

"Absolutely not, Niki. You can't run off from your own party," my mother protested.

After having been paired with their dolls, my classmates lined up before me. "Thank you for this gift, Niki!" they said, one after the other, and kissed me on the cheeks. As for me, there I was, expected to be as happy as a clam, expected to be running over with emotion. Like the frissons of religious awe I was meant to experience during the Holy Communion back when my grandmother was still taking me to church. If not, it meant that I was completely insensible, incapable of true feeling. Or that there was something awfully wrong with me.

XV

THE FIRST TWO weeks of the Dekemvriana—later also known as Red December or the Battle of Athens—I spent with my grandmother holed up inside the house. My parents had vanished into thin air. One morning at dawn, Uncle Petros appeared, armed to the teeth, and attempted to put our minds at ease (so to speak) by informing us that "fired by revolutionary fervor, they had thrown themselves into battle."

The ELAS controlled Kallithea and almost the entire city. Yet it was not safe to be out on the streets. From Syngrou Avenue and the Acropolis, the British and the monarcho-fascists were shooting anything that moved. Every day between noon and four o'clock in the afternoon, there was a cease-fire to allow people to stock up on food and water. I, of course, was not allowed to set foot outside even then. Lurking behind shuttered windows, I would wait with bated breath for my grandmother's return.

This is how I chanced to see one of our neighbors, a barber by trade, who was walking on the sidewalk holding his young son by the hand, get hit by a stray bullet, stagger for a few seconds, and then fall to the ground like a sack of potatoes. The little boy crouched over him and began howling like a wild animal. Then, beside himself, he began banging his head on the ground. I don't know how I plucked up the courage to dash outside and pull him, almost forcibly, into our house. Later, my grandmother had the Herculean task of hauling the barber's corpse into our yard, where she covered it with a sheet. She didn't bring him inside to spare the child from the sight, I suppose. Until his mother arrived to pick him up at dusk—accompanied by a cousin of hers who loaded the body onto a cart—the poor little boy didn't say a word. Not one word.

After the middle of December, the situation took a bad turn. Gunfire echoed ever closer, and the ELAS partisans dashing past our door looked ever younger, mere adolescents with pimples on their cheeks. One day, a hand grenade landed in our yard. It spun around for some time, like a top, but miraculously it didn't explode. After staring at it terror-stricken for hours, my grandmother finally decided to get rid of it. First, she bowed in front of the icon of Saint Barbara, then she hung her baptismal cross around her neck and proceeded, with the precision of a surgeon—or rather of a monk carrying a holy relic—to carry it and deposit it in a vacant lot half a mile from our house.

On the morning of December 26, my parents finally appeared, both of them in a pitiful state. To cap it all off, my mother also had an enormous sty almost fully covering her left eye. They were accompanied by a handful of partisans. They appeared enormous to me and truly fearsome to behold—no relation whatsoever to the neighborhood youth who had taken up arms. They hailed from afar, from the mountains. To my surprise, the last person to leap from the truck that had brought them was Aunt Markella! She too was unrecognizable in a khaki coat down to her ankles, hair gathered in a bun, and hands and arms bare of rings and bracelets for the very first time!

"Set the table for our comrades! Bring everything you have! They haven't eaten in two days!" Antonis implored his mother. "Afterward, I need to talk to you."

"Are we going to win?" an anxious Sevasti asked Antonis.

"No, Mother. We're going to lose. Churchill himself has come to Athens to make sure of it. But don't worry about that for the moment. Tell me, the sovereigns I gave you back in 1927, do you still have them?"

"Of course. Obviously, I have spent some over the years for household needs, for your brother's and sisters' education—"

"And you did well—that's what they were there for!"

"I've still got four thousand five hundred and sixty-two sovereigns left."

"Are they close at hand?"

"I can get them to you in ten minutes."

"Don't tell me where you put them. My second question is: How much is our house worth? In other words, if we were to sell it, how much do you think we'd get?"

"How would I know, son?"

"That's right. How would you know? Let's say, then, that today or in a few years' time it will be worth four and a half thousand sovereigns."

"That's too much!"

"You know me, always throwing money around. Let's see, how many of us does it belong to—you, Iordanis, me, Petros, Fani, Markella—that's six. So, we each get seven hundred and sixty sovereigns."

"I give my part to Niki!"

"No, Mother, that's not fair. You may have other grandchildren someday. If you want, share your part among your children."

"All right."

My father put pen to paper and redid the math.

"It's nine hundred sovereigns each. I will hold on to Iordanis's share to give to him if he ever returns from America, and you get two thousand seven hundred sovereigns to distribute to the others. Now, the house is mine."

"In the midst of all this chaos, why are you meddling with questions of property and inheritance?"

"I must hold the rights to the house, Mother. If not, I can't authorize its demolition."

I DON'T KNOW, and probably my father didn't either, if our house was truly obstructing the line of fire of the ELAS mortars and if another one in the neighborhood could not just as easily have sacrificed its walls to the building of barricades. It's also entirely possible that its demolition was a way of punishing Antonis: He had dared oppose the Battle of Athens (at least as it had been executed), and had barged, uninvited, into a meeting of the ELAS leadership, where he had proclaimed in these words exactly: "You don't conquer capitals with muskets." After such open disagreement with the party line, he was no doubt expected to prove concretely, with a tangible sacrifice, his dedication to the Party. At any rate, as soon as the captain of Kallithea and Harokopio demanded it of him, he could not conceive of saying no.

He took me aside to announce his decision.

"Some people sacrifice their lives and the lives of their children to the cause. We must sacrifice our house." I was beside myself. A month ago, they had taken my dolls; now, they were going to destroy my nest! And what was I being offered as consolation? A load of hot air about the imminent advent of socialism, about global human harmony— worthless poppycock that I neither understood nor had any interest in.

"And where will we go?" I asked apprehensively.

"The three of us—Papa, Mama, and Niki—will stay some time with your uncle Petros, at a very nice place in Peristeri. Grandmother will live with Aunt Markella at her new apartment in Pangrati. Very soon, we'll all be back together again. Come on, Niki, why are you crying! For these old walls? As long as we have strong arms and strong minds, there's nothing to cry about. Builders made these walls, builders will demolish them, and builders will build them back up again!" Believing that with this final tirade he had fulfilled his paternal responsibilities by teaching me a life lesson, he turned on his heel and went to oversee the preparations.

It was the day after Christmas, but there was nothing festive in the air, except perhaps for my grandmother's kourabiedes,[54] of which the partisans made short shrift. After licking off the sugar still clinging to their mustaches, they got down to work. They were not amateurs; they had all been selected because they were munitions specialists. Their leader boasted of having participated in the team that had blown up the Gorgopotamos bridge.[55]

They began by emptying the house of its furniture. Beds, mirrors, tubs, and sinks were carefully loaded onto the back of a truck. When they hoisted the tricycle and gramophone—a memento of Giannos if ever there was one—my grandmother wiped the tears from her eyes. Afterward, we, the women, were charged with packing the clothes and pots and pans. Being treated almost like an adult—I had even been entrusted with wrapping the porcelain cups in newspaper—filled me with a pride that

---

[54] Shortbread-like cookies made with almonds and rolled in icing sugar that are popular during the Christmas season.

[55] In one of World War II's major acts of sabotage, the heavily guarded bridge over the Gorgopotamos viaduct in central Greece was blown up in 1942 by the Greek Resistance. The aim was to interrupt the flow of supplies to the German forces in northern Africa, conveyed on the railway line connecting Athens to Thessaloniki.

slightly softened my sorrow. All the while, the partisans were removing doors and windows and lining them up on the street. They were going to be used as firewood, they told us, "to warm the bones of little children." I glimpsed on the kitchen door the lines my grandmother had drawn in pencil when she measured my height at each birthday. Soon they would be lapped at and devoured by flames, and nothing would remain to attest to the fact that once I had been knee-high to a grasshopper and fit almost entirely in Aunt Fani's hatbox.

In less than three hours, the house was reduced to a shell. The explosives team then buried a stick of dynamite in every corner and tied them together with a thirty-six-foot fuse. In a heavy Roumeliote accent, their leader explained everything with great professionalism. He reassured us that the walls would fall inward and that no one was at risk. Then he handed my father the end of the fuse.

"You're the man of the house, comrade. You light it," he said.

LINED UP ON the opposite sidewalk, we look like we are posing for a photograph. It's raining melting snow. Bursts of machine-gun fire and the thunder of cannon reverberate in the distance, as they do throughout the day.

"We moved in on the seventh of February," says my grandmother. "February 7, 1926."

Markella looks at her askance; she detests nostalgia.

"Come on, Antonis, are you going to light it or aren't you? Stop acting as if we're at a funeral all of you! It's the dawn of a new day! Let's sing—come on!"

She stubs out her cigarette and strikes up the EPON anthem: "*Here comes the new guard / Spreading wings wide / Building with strong arms / A world beautiful, a world revived!*"

My mother takes over and bellows the second stanza, her voice completely off-key: "*Here comes our proud youth / Full of ardor and joy / Chains they break with their might / In their path only light…*"

My father lights the fuse. The explosion is like an earthquake; it convulses the entire neighborhood, raising a huge cloud of smoke and dust. When the cloud dissipates, our house is no more.

XVI

Whirlwinds of danger are raging around us,
O'erwhelming forces of darkness assail,
Still in the fight see advancing before us,
Red flag of liberty that yet shall prevail.[56]

February 1945, in the yard of the 2nd Middle School of Trikala, some fifty children ranging from seven to fifteen

---

[56] From the Polish socialist revolutionary song "Warszawianka" (trans. Douglas Robson).

years of age are applying themselves to so-called military exercises. In reality, we are doing Swedish light gymnastics, and then, armed with wooden rods in place of rifles, we are taught how to "port arms" and "shoulder arms." Finally, we get in line and march up and down the yard, bellowing revolutionary songs. Snow covers the city streets and the mountains across the way. But we are now accustomed to the cold. Our teeth no longer chatter. And the children in Trikala no longer ridicule us as the "Athenian crybabies." In any case, in class we put them to shame in every subject. Even in recitation. A few days ago, I learned all of "The Destruction of Psara"[57] by heart (repeating it line by line after my father because I don't yet know how to read very well). In class, I recited it with such passion that no one laughed at the fact that I can't roll my *r*'s, which I pronounce a little like *l*'s.

We've been in Trikala for about a month. As soon as Athens fell to the British and their local lackeys—"They took Athens, but only for a month" was the refrain ringing throughout Peristeri—an endless stream of every vehicle under the sun began its panting ascent toward Roumeli and Thessalia. Anyone who had championed the left, either in deed or in word, was in danger of being massacred by the Chites and the militias who were now cracking down with the arrogance of the victor.

---

[57] A poem by Dionysios Solomos (1798–1857).

My parents and I left in an ambulance, along with Uncle Petros, who had been grievously wounded by an anti-tank shell and was in a pitiful state, burning with fever. Now that I think back on it, that ambulance must indeed have been uncommonly large; it didn't just appear that way to my childish eyes. It easily accommodated not only my parents but also my uncle on his stretcher, me dozing on another one parallel to it, the driver, and two comrade nurses. They and my mother tended to the wounded man, taking turns at his bedside

"He's going to lose the leg," I heard my father whispering to my mother one night.

"I don't know about that, but at this rate, he's definitely going to get a leg *over* both our good sisters of mercy. Despite the delirium and constant pain, he doesn't pass up a chance to cop a good feel," she replied, alternating between irony and indignation.

"Do you remember how shy our Petros used to be? The war has changed him."

"Exactly! The battlefield has finally made a man of him, and in more ways than one."

A SECOND, PARALLEL procession followed us on foot by the side of the road all the way to Thebes. These were the hostages taken by the ELAS and intended to function as a human shield in case of British air strikes. Most were ordinary people who had been snatched from their doorsteps on the pretext of class enmity.

It was a heartbreaking spectacle. Grandfathers and grandmothers, women clutching young children, all wading through icy mud and trembling in fear lest they be executed on the spot by the accompanying partisan guard if by misfortune they tripped and fell or simply fell behind. After Thebes, this same procession turned around and returned to Athens. The Party had recognized its mistake, but the damage had been done. In a matter of a few days, thousands of peaceable citizens, Venizelists as well as monarchists, had turned fiercely anti-communist.

On entering Lamia, our ambulance turned off from the convoy and headed toward a huge tent lit with lanterns in the central square: a field hospital, not a circus. Escaping my parents' attention while they were helping move Uncle Petros, I managed to sneak inside.

The air was thick with medication and fumes from oil-burning heaters. Dozens of wounded men lay groaning on cots or on blankets on the ground. Brisk nurses, nerves frayed from lack of sleep, were both tending to and upbraiding them. "Why are you carrying on like that? A fully grown man like you? You only lost three fingers!" they said to a big blond bull of a man who was howling as he stared at his bandaged hand. There were also the rattles of the dying, chests painfully rising and falling with increasing difficulty until they gave up the ghost, mouths open wide. The nearest doctor or nurse then rushed over to close their eyes and pull the sheet over their heads, and the stretcher-bearers took them out the back door and lined them up, one beside the other, surrendering them to the snow's white, protective shroud.

AND WHAT ABOUT me? It bears asking how I not only tolerated the spectacle but also drank it all in, my curiosity insatiable. At seven years of age, I had witnessed two of my neighbors hanged from trees, another felled by a stray bullet, Uncle Giannos in a coffin, and Uncle Petros on a stretcher. I remembered, even if only faintly, the islands of our exile and the parties under the Occupation, when Fani and Markella danced in Savvas's and Stratos's arms, and the house bloomed with the smells of expensive tobacco and fine perfumes. After that, I had watched our house explode, then found myself in a school in Peristeri under attack by Chites, while our men clambered up onto the roof and tried to defend it. When we ran out of ammunition, we fled in an ambulance in the middle of the night.

"Where are we going?" I had asked my father.

"Where the wind takes us. Perhaps Moscow, who knows..." he replied, and even he didn't know if it was a joke or not.

At seven years old, I was sure about one thing only: that from one moment to the next, everything can turn and face the strange, that nothing lasts forever. I certainly had every reason to be terrified, apathetic, closed off within myself, blinkered to everything occurring around me. Fortunately, for me it all had the opposite effect. I regarded life as a thrilling adventure, whose every crumb ought to be savored without fear or reservation, harboring as it did a surprise at every turn, something incredibly awful, or awfully incredible.

A SUDDEN DIN announced his arrival: "The Professor is here!" A tall man, around fifty years of age, wearing a long medical tunic and the thick lenses of myopia, appeared at the entrance to the tent, flanked by a handful of assistants, all gazing at him reverentially. He hastened toward Petros's stretcher. My father shook his hand with a respect I had never seen him accord to anyone.

"Our comrade, Professor Petros Kokkalis," he introduced the man to my mother. The Professor kissed her hand and then knelt, putting himself at my height to ask me my name and which grade I was in.

"And what are you doing here, Niki?" he said, with a feigned tone of reprimand. "Would you like a nurse to take you to the church, where all the other children are?"

"No, I want to see!" I replied. My parents threw him an apologetic look, abashed by my impudence.

"Well, then, let her stay," he declared. "At any rate, in these times we're living, it's difficult to know what one ought to hide from children. Just make sure she doesn't sneak into the operating room!"

He then turned to Uncle Petros. Pulling aside the blanket, he grasped the wounded leg in his hands and deftly unwound the gauze dressing. He bore down on the wound and pus spurted out.

"Holy mother of God!" my uncle howled.

"Where were you injured, namesake?" Kokkalis asked him.

"In Peristeri. We had built a barricade to stop the British tanks. It was January second, toward the end of the day. The ELAS was fighting house to house." Despite the pain, Uncle Petros did not flag in the telling of the saga, which he knew by heart, having repeated it dozens of times in exactly the same words.

The Professor was barely listening.

"You don't have gangrene," he cut in. "I won't amputate. The bone has been pulverized, so most likely you won't be able to walk without limping, but you will keep your leg. Get him prepped for surgery," he said, turning to his assistants.

The so-called operating room was an open space in the center of the tent, rudely separated by screens arranged in a circle. Almost as soon as Uncle Petros was rolled in and for the following two hours, the entire hospital shook with his screams. The Professor emerged with a wide smile.

"We saved the arteries as well as most of the muscle!" he announced to my father. "One less invalid pension to worry about for the new socialist state!" he joked.

THREE DAYS LATER, we climbed back into the ambulance with Uncle Petros and resumed the drive to Trikala. After the Dekemvriana, that is where almost all of the EAM and KKE leadership had sought refuge. That we too had been evacuated to Trikala was perhaps a sign that they acknowledged and appreciated the sacrifice of our house in Kallithea.

We were stationed in a manor house near the river. The owner, a bachelor lawyer who lived with his elderly mother, opened his door wide for us.

"The old Armaos, what is he to you?" he asked Antonis.

"Which old Armaos?"

"The delegate."

"I am delegate Armaos."

"You are too young. I am talking about fifteen years ago."

"It was twelve years ago. I was twenty-six when I was first elected."

The lawyer's eyes filled with awe. Once again, I beamed with pride for my papa.

THE TOWN WAS nominally under ELAS control, but in fact the situation was quite unstable. The enemy, as we called them, were simply lying low and saving their strength for the next strike. We were escorted to school every morning by a partisan. A handful of little Athenians, all the children of cadres, leading the way, and he behind, finger on the trigger. Every so often, like a shepherd herding sheep, he would call us to heel in his heavy Thessalian accent: "Prrrr! Git here! Prrr! Git there!"

I was exceedingly fond of the partisans of Trikala, especially the ones who came from the mountains, the shepherds

who had taken arms. Aside from the fact that they were disposed to lay their lives on the line for us come what may, as
my mother never failed to remind me—"Mitros would be
skinned alive rather than let anyone touch a hair on your
head!"—they brought to mind big children despite their
beards and bandoliers, which I quickly got used to. In addition to watching over us, they seemed to take pleasure in
showing us how they lived.

With our parents' permission, Mitros took us one Sunday to where his family spent the winter. It was a large
wooden cabin on the far outskirts of town, locatable with
one's eyes closed from the bleating of the livestock. We
were welcomed by Mitros's "old man" and "old woman."
The former, easily mistakable for Barba Giorgos[58] from
the Karagiozi puppet theater; the latter, a tiny elfin creature in woolen slippers. They both had a spry bounce to
their step and spoke a musical mix of Greek and Vlach
that swallowed most of their words' final syllables. They
offered us milk fresh from the cow and eggs still warm
"from the chick's butt." Fotos, a ten-year-old boy whose
father led an ELAS unit, kissed me on the cheek under
cover of the cabin's dim light. As he did so, his lips brushed
mine. Horrified, I recoiled. The entire time we stayed in
Trikala, I kept wondering if he would pluck up the courage to try again.

---

[58] A character in the extremely popular shadow-puppet theater, Barba Giorgos is a mountaineer and shepherd from Roumeli.

FROM OUR VERY first days there, it became clear that nothing had changed in the KKE leadership's stance toward Antonis. While not quite relegated to the role of window dressing or set out to pasture by honorary discharge, he was nonetheless assigned only unimportant tasks. He was not invited to meetings, nor was his advice solicited on any matter. The only thing he was charged with was to deliver a series of lectures to the ELAS membership. "They must be educated and encouraged to mature ideologically," was his mandate. My father took this assignment very seriously. Ensconced for two days and nights in our landlord's study, consulting its library rich in Marxist-Leninist texts, he labored over the teachings meant to transform naïve and primitive combatants into conscious elements of a people's freedom army. Needless to say, he was aware that his prospective audience comprised men a large number of whom had not finished even elementary school. He had to start with the ABC's.

The first lecture, scheduled for an afternoon in mid-January, was to be delivered at the premises of the local merchants' association. An hour before it was due to start, the hall was already packed to the rafters. Per instructions, the partisans left their weapons at the entrance, brushed the snow off their greatcoats, and found a seat either on the ground or on one of the chairs arranged in rows. The front row remained empty, reserved for the cadres and the Party officers who would be attending not to learn from Armaos but to evaluate him.

The title of the lecture was "Which World Are We Fighting For?" It began smoothly. Antonis introduced himself not as a delegate but as an employee of the Electric Railways and described, with some embellishments admittedly, his own initiation into communism.

While he talked about strikes, prison sentences, escapes, and the other acts of bravery of his youth, the audience listened in rapt attention, interrupting with regular applause. But as soon as he got to the bottom line of the lecture—the class struggle, the alliance between factory worker and farmer against the bourgeoisie necessary to the establishment of a dictatorship of the proletariat and the abolishment of individual ownership—the men were at sixes and sevens.

"What do you mean 'we want to establish a dictatorship'?" asked one of the partisans, a schoolteacher in civilian life.

"The dictatorship of the proletariat is democratic! Lenin himself has said so!" Antonis replied.

"Are you going to take my pharmacy from me?" the man who provisioned regional ELAS units with medical supplies cried in alarm.

"Nationalization begins with the means of production and will expand gradually and progressively, without prejudicing the position of scholars or small businesses," Antonis replied, avoiding mention of the fact that in the Soviet Union he had not seen a single privately owned pharmacy.

"What about my flock? Will you take that?" a shepherd called out.

As Antonis went out of his way to reassure them, explaining that in the new Greece their labor would be better rewarded, the director of propaganda for the EPON, a short and stout thirty-year-old who had not stopped scribbling in his notebook from the beginning of the talk, suddenly rose from his seat in the first row.

"Let's be clear, comrades!" he said, his tone almost menacing. "Socialism does not mean milk and honey, it means war. When our great Stalin ordered the compulsory collectivization of all agriculture, he did so without hesitation, without hemming and hawing. And so will we! We will purge the country of the big landowners and stockbreeders, but also the petite bourgeoisie who serve at the altar of reactionism. We will smash both palaces and churches! We will eviscerate both the decadent intellectual and the depraved female who whored herself first to the Italians and the Germans and later to the British and the monarchofascists! Let's not mince our words: Those not with us are against us!"

For a moment, the audience seemed as if turned to stone, then a terrible din arose. Antonis tried desperately to pour oil on the troubled waters and continue his speech, but in vain. All he could hear were voices raised in anger; all he could see were men lost in thought or glancing around in confusion. Some were making a beeline for the exit, probably a number of the ELAS faithful among them.

"Congratulations! You really know how to foster a spirit of solidarity!" Antonis turned to the director of propaganda.

"You object to calling a spade a spade, comrade? Half-truths never won a revolution! Don't worry, our superiors will know how to set things to rights."

"Oh, you're denouncing me to the Political Bureau, are you?"

"The Party grows stronger by purging its ranks," the director replied with a direct threat and turned on his heel. Antonis was not summoned to account for himself, but at the same time he was also not invited to deliver another lecture ever again.

ON FEBRUARY 12, 1945, the Varkiza Agreement was signed. After its December defeat, the EAM had come to a provisional agreement with the conservatives and the British, accepting the dissolution of the ELAS, its military wing, as an inevitable step in the constitution of a national army and a democratic state.

The Varkiza Agreement was presented not as a compromise but as a victory.[59] In Trikala, dancing and celebration filled the streets. We were then told to pack our bags:

---

[59] Signed by the minister of foreign affairs and the secretary of the Communist Party of Greece, the agreement called for the disarmament of the EAM-ELAS and a plebiscite within the year to establish elections and the creation of a constituent assembly. Despite the disarmament of the EAM-ELAS, the provisions of the treaty were not upheld, and it was followed by mass persecution of leftists and a period known as the White Terror that led to the Greek Civil War, when, in 1946, after the restoration of the monarchy, the KKE founded the Democratic Army of Greece and took up arms.

Finally, we could return to Athens. Our new friends, the natives of Trikala, bid us farewell with tears in their eyes.

"It's all good for you, you can leave," they kept saying. "But for us here, what are we going to do?"

With the naïveté of a child, I thought they meant that they did not know what they would do without us, that they would miss us. But they were referring to how they would cope without their weapons. They were painfully aware of the fact that as soon as they surrendered them—as mandated by the conditions of the peace agreement—they would be at the mercy of rogue paramilitary bands hell-bent on one thing only: revenge.

XVII

ON OUR RETURN to Athens, we spent two days in Markella's apartment, where Grandmother Sevasti also lived. Then we moved into a bright, well-ventilated four-room unit on the top floor of the same building.

It was a stately building, boasting an elevator and even a doorman, situated a couple of hundred yards from the Pana-thenaic Stadium and the Ilisos River, which was still flowing uncovered at the time.[60] Most of the neighborhood's buildings

---

[60] The Ilisos, one of three rivers that flow through Athens, passes through the heart of the city and was paved over as part of the postwar development efforts.

bore scars from the bullets of the past December, but peace
finally seemed to prevail. The United Nations relief agency,
UNRRA, distributed powdered milk and canned ham to
young children. Tiny bars and large taverns were cropping
up one after the other throughout Pangrati. Movie theaters
screened current events and Mickey Mouse cartoons. And
Aunt Markella, her popularity rising meteorically in the
world of variety shows, her name splashed in ever-larger letters all over theater marquees, had a seamstress come to the
house to sew her stage costumes.

I, in the meantime, had changed schools for the third
time in one year and due to a decree by the Ministry of
Education for all first-year elementary students, was taking
an accelerated path through the second-grade curriculum
so as to be ready to step into third grade by September
1945. I was a good student, with a particularly strong sense
of confidence. In comparison to my schoolmates in Trikala,
those in Pangrati reminded me of little lapdogs. I had a
knack for making friends easily and, by aping Markella's
kittenish airs, had learned how to turn boys' heads. This
was a very happy period indeed for me.

My only cause of consternation was that my parents had
forbidden me from wearing the gold sickle and hammer. At
first, they had tried taking the diplomatic approach (warning me that a Chite might attack me), then they resorted to
scolding and railing. Finally, they confiscated it and put it
under lock and key. I cried for a week, not for the loss of the
symbol but for the loss of my golden brooch.

At the end of February, the collaborators' trials began. Savvas Bogdanos was among the first to sit in the dock. The judges showed him extraordinary leniency. They counted as mitigating factors both the rectitude of his former life and the distinguished role he played before the war. He was sentenced to an eight-year term ("You'll be out the year after next," they had informed him in private) to be served in the Zeliotis Prison. Located in Omonia Square, it was not so much a prison as a palace, with hotel rooms in lieu of cells, where daily visits were allowed, and guards' eyes were discreetly shut when they turned into overnight stays, especially if they involved a spouse or an underaged child. For all that, Uncle Savvas could not contain himself when his verdict was announced.

"I acted out of patriotism pure and simple!" he roared. "I demand that my name be cleared in the eyes of my compatriots! If, contrary to all logic, you judge me guilty in good conscience, then I do not accept any extenuating circumstances. Lock me in a dungeon and throw away the key!"

The judges smiled benignly at this rather quaint outburst and declared the session closed.

TWO DAYS LATER, the senior editor of *Rizospastis* came to see my father to ask that he write an article denouncing Bogdanos's parody of a verdict.

"Why Bogdanos in particular?" Antonis inquired.

"Because the scoundrel actually had the gall to try to come out on top!"

"And why must I be the one to write it?"

"What's the problem, comrade?"

"Are you joking? Savvas Bogdanos is married to my sister!"

"So what? You think he'd be galloping to the rescue if you were in his shoes?"

"All I know is that under the Occupation, Bogdanos behaved in an exemplary fashion to my mother, and, most important, to my little daughter!"

"I see! You mean, you are grateful to this traitor? Would you go so far as to testify in his defense?" the editor in chief sneered.

Antonis saw red. "Listen, Themis, can you talk plainly, without innuendo, and tell me what you all have against me? If I'm being accused of something in particular, act like grown men and stop playing dirty tricks on me! Go ahead and charge me, summon me for a hearing, so that I may explain myself!"

"All in good time, comrade," Themis quipped, and shut the door softly behind him.

It was now abundantly clear to Antonis that the die of his fate had been cast. Not only was a Party candidacy out of the question but it was unlikely that he would continue to be tolerated for much longer as member of the Party, even if only as a lowly one. That he hadn't already been ousted as the director of the EAM offices was no doubt a sign that they had not yet identified a successor. Poppycock! Any day now, he would be asked to pack his stuff and clear out of the office.

What to do? How could he defend himself in an undeclared war? He ran through every possible course of action: Draft a detailed report of everything he had done since his 1938 incarceration in Corfu (indeed even earlier if necessary), and if *Rizospastis* wouldn't publish it, then he would do it himself, in pamphlet form? Try to contact the Soviet envoy to Greece and beg him to intercede in the hope that he might better judge the true value of his contributions and dedication to the Party? Resign in protest from his position in the EAM and thereby force them to react?

No! No matter what he did, the only thing that would come out of it is that he would be found in the wrong. The Party was neither departure lounge nor debate club open to anything the wind brought in. It was run like a military unit, where iron discipline and faith in the flag were rightly revered as supreme values. To effectively voice one's opinions, to conduct a meaningful critique, one ought to remain within the Party's bosom and abide by its statutory procedures. The public airing of personal grievances—whether by a high-ranking cadre or the most recent of recruits to the Communist Youth—the crying of complaints from the rooftops, the serving of them on a platter to the enemy, even if only out of an excess of naïveté, was simply not to be contemplated! No, Antonis Armaos had not spent five years of his prime buried alive in a dungeon in Corfu only to play into the hands of the plutocracy by giving them anti-communist fodder! He had not gone without his wife and child, had not blown up his own home, to become the object of the bourgeoisie's hypocritical compassion and be canonized as the faithful revolutionary wronged by his own. It was quite likely that the Party, in this moment of confusion, would go so far as to banish him. He, however, would never betray it, would never expose it to defamation.

Perhaps, in the end, the true issue was that he could not rise to the demands of circumstances, he sometimes thought to himself. He probably had what was necessary to be a top-ranking cadre during the 1930s, when the KKE was on a tightrope waging battle between decadence and renewal, but not in 1945, now that it was at the head of a great popular movement aiming at the conquest of power. Perhaps he had overestimated his capacities and felt rejected because, his pride wounded, he was blinkered to reality. Had he joined the Party in 1927 on the condition of becoming the secretary to the Central Committee and Party delegate? No! He had joined out of genuine, disinterested excitement and the profound conviction that Marxism-Leninism was the voice of the future. And in the new socialist world in the making, everyone would find exactly the position they deserved.

"When I'm no longer a professional Party member, what will I do with my life?" Antonis then asked himself. He realized, not without some anxiety, that his objective credentials fell far short of the responsibilities he had assumed in the political arena. He had not even finished high school: The Asia Minor Catastrophe and his family's economic ruin had taken care of that. Nor had he learned the tricks of a particular trade, besides driving the engine for the Electric Railways. He had of course read many books, spoke excellent Turkish, could easily converse in French and Russian. He might find work as an assistant in charge of correspondence for a company with international business concerns; as a clerk, hotel receptionist, or in the worst-case scenario, waiter or fishmonger—there was no shame in any work.

There were also the one thousand eight hundred gold sovereigns, hidden away somewhere safe. Someone else might have invested, or started a business, any kind of business, at least until socialism abolished private enterprise once and for all. But not Antonis. By rights, he ought to have sent it all back to Clary Kremos as retroactive child support for Chrysanthos, or donated it to the Party, a concrete contribution to the building of a new Greece. Yet he could not bring himself to deprive Niki and Anna of it. What were they to count on in a future that was looking ever more uncertain? No matter how adamantly he refused to admit it, no matter how much he endeavored to be a communist liberated from retrogressive, petit bourgeois values, in his heart of hearts Antonis was a paterfamilias with an acute sense of responsibility toward his wife and child.

April 15, 1945: Antonis Armaos walked into the Athens–Piraeus Electric Railways administration offices and submitted a written application for his reinstatement.

"But aren't you the Party delegate and director of the EAM headquarters?" the personnel manager exclaimed in astonishment.

"I'm an engine driver. In the country we are building, my friend, there will be no such thing as a professional politician!" Antonis replied, suddenly feeling unexpectedly relieved.

XVIII

MAY 1, 1945: *Rizospastis* issues a special edition dedicated entirely to the breaking news: *Comrade Nikos, Heroic KKE Leader, Is Alive!*

With the collapse of Germany and the liberation of the concentration camps, Nikos, held captive in Dachau since 1941, was found among the survivors. After receiving medical care and recovering from the torments of hell, he was to be repatriated without delay.

Nikos's return from the dead, so to speak, was like manna from heaven for the left after all that had transpired. There had been the catastrophe of the Dekemvriana and the fiasco of the Varkiza Agreement (while security militia were running amok all over the country, the right accused the ELAS of surrendering only a negligible portion of their weapons and having hidden the rest to plan revenge). There had been all manner of prevarication and puerile mistakes, and it was a relief for the KKE leadership to cede the reins to their historic leader. After all, Nikos had been chosen by Stalin (and by Stalin's mother, even though this was known only to a few). Not only had his legend lost none of its sheen but it had intensified during his four-year absence. The *Rizospastis* special edition was sold out in the blink of an eye and had to be reprinted in hundreds of thousands of copies. Nikos's photograph, printed on a full page of the newspaper, hung on the walls of most left-leaning homes. At our house, it was Markella, not my father, who put it up in the dining room.

On May 30, a British airplane landed at the military airport of Elefsina. No one in Athens had been informed. Nikos took a taxi and headed straight to the *Rizospastis* offices. He took the stairs two by two and appeared, like the messiah himself, before the stunned journalists.

Two days later in the afternoon, he rang our bell just as unexpectedly. He was wearing a sky blue shirt with rolled-up sleeves, blue cargo pants, and canvas shoes. A paper bag filled with apricots was in his hand. "I saw them on my way here and my mouth started watering," he said. "Quick, put them on ice!" Our building was, without question, surrounded by dozens of the OPLA's armed men, the leader's personal retinue. Yet Nikos succeeded in conveying the desired impression: that he traveled the streets by himself, like any other working man.

He and my father retreated to the bedroom and shut the door. Their interview lasted less than half an hour.

Now that I am dead and can travel back to that exact time and place and spy on their conversation, I can confirm that my father, while still alive, described it to us almost word for word. The only thing he always omitted from his many repetitions was that Nikos had settled himself, as comfortable as a pasha, on the armchair, while my father remained standing in front of him, smoking nervously.

At first, Nikos launched a regular offensive of warmth and camaraderie.

"You cannot imagine how much I've missed our conversations all these years, partner." (This is what he had called my father ever since they first met.) "Every time things got really difficult, I'd ask myself: 'What would Antonis say? What would he advise?' But you too didn't have it easy... Tell me about it!"

My father quickly recounted his escape from the Corfu Prison and the details of the Middle East uprising. Nikos listened with great attentiveness, often nodding his head in approval.

"Then you returned to Greece and had to contend with one cretin after the other! It's truly mind-boggling! First that good-for-nothing EPON stooge not letting you get a word in! Then, they're trying to get you to denounce Bogdanos and break with your sister. To prove what, exactly? Your dedication to the Party? Aren't your struggles and sacrifices enough for them? Or all the responsibilities with which the workers and the Third International entrusted you? By rights, as soon as you set foot in Piraeus this past October, they ought to have handed over the keys to the Party. You are the first in line after the absent chief! They are all just usurpers!"

It was abundantly clear that Nikos had been briefed on Antonis Armaos's every move and every breath. Yet even if he truly intended to fully exculpate him, he would never have taken flattery to such heights without an ulterior goal in mind. Antonis knew this—knew him—and bided his time.

"Come on, let's take back our Party! Let's get rid of the Old Man and the Toad," Nikos said, referring to two members of the leadership by their aliases. "Not to mention Misery Guts, who has gotten too big for his boots and thinks he is Ares, the god of war. Hogwash, all of it! Make no mistake, partner: They're all sellouts, agents!"

Antonis stood there, openmouthed. "What do you mean 'agents'?"

"Agents of the Intelligence Services, pawns in the pocket of the British!"

"Where is this coming from?"

"The facts speak for themselves. No matter how stupid they are, they would not have made such a disaster of the people's movement had Churchill not been greasing their palms with sovereigns."

"You have definitive proof of this?"

"Don't overthink things, partner. It's as clear as day!"

"Well, then, convene a full assembly, or better yet a congress, Nikos! Publicly prove the incompetence of that entire cast of characters and demand their dismissal."

"Wasted effort. The very next day, they'd form an internal opposition faction dedicated to throwing spokes in our wheels!"

"Whose wheels? Yours? The people worship you!"

"Don't forget that the wheel of fortune turns around and around! We ought to lance the abscess while we still have the power to do so. From the moment they decided to go into the Battle of Athens bearing muskets—that's your description, partner—and allowed the monarcho-fascists to wipe the floor with them, not only in Varkiza but also in Lebanon and Caserta,[61] for me there is absolutely no question: They are informants and traitors! Can I count on your support?"

Antonis's smile was bitter. "Do you remember why we fell out in the Corfu Prison, Nikos?" he asked.

"That's long in the past—"

"Because you asked—or, more accurately, ordered—me to sign a declaration of repentance."[62]

"To get you out of there! To allow you to return and rebuild the Party!"

"You did exactly the same thing with Vozikis and Lahanas a little earlier. Then, you accused them of being snitches!"

"That's exactly what they became: stooges of the Security Battalions!"

"But you denounced them first, Nikos. You're the one who said, 'Wherever you find them, shoot them!' Of course they ran to the Security Battalions."

---

[61] The Lebanon, Caserta, and Varkiza Agreements (signed between 1944 and 1945) aimed to neutralize the dominance of the left in Greek politics after the war by annexing it under the leadership of the Greek government of national unity, which was itself under the control of the British.

[62] A declaration that Greeks suspected of communism were required to sign in denunciation. Those who signed were expelled by the Party.

"What are you trying to say, partner?" Nikos's expression hardened for a moment.

"That you play with people. That you lead them right up to the edge of the cliff, pit them against each other, and then act the innocent. And who benefits from all this? Don't even dream of arguing that this is Stalinism-Leninism in action. It's too hot to get into theoretical discussions right now." Antonis opened the door to the bedroom.

"Think it over, partner! Those not with me are against me…"

When he returned to the dining room, Nikos did not seem even slightly hot under the collar. My mother had put the apricots in a crystal bowl. He snatched two in passing, biting into one and tossing the other at me. It slipped through my fingers in midair.

"What's your name, young lady?" he asked with a big smile. Despite the hardships he had endured, his teeth were a brilliant white.

"Niki," I stammered.

"Niki? How so? Do you happen to have an uncle called Nikos?" He was insinuating that I had been named after him. I kept glancing back and forth from him to the picture on the wall. The printed page did not do justice to his charisma. I found him dazzling. He sparkled and shone. I had never met a man like him before.

"Will you stay for dinner, Nikos?"

"I'd love to, dear Anna, but I can't. The Party has me running around all day and all night!… Think it over, partner!" he turned to Antonis quickly before leaving.

THAT NIGHT, I dreamt of him. He was naked and lying face-down on my parents' bed, arms stretched wide.

"I'm taking wing!" he told me. "Pull the curtains aside, will you? I don't want to tear them when I fly out the window."

I obeyed.

"Now, climb on top of me!"

I scrambled onto his back and took hold of his muscular shoulders. When I squeezed my legs around his waist, a voluptuous warmth and wetness bloomed between them. This was my first erotic dream.

NIKOS GAVE ANTONIS less than twelve hours to think things over. The very next morning, the new director of the EAM headquarters was announced. It was the EPON's portly director of propaganda who had scuttled my father's lecture in Trikala.

XIX

IN JULY 1945, Antonis started working again at the Electric Railways. In October, at the Seventh KKE Congress, he was expelled from the Communist Party on Nikos's personal recommendation. The indictment was rather vague: He was charged with "colluding with the Corfu Prison administration, and betraying signs of adventurism and cosmopolitanism in the Middle East." Antonis attended the congress and claimed the right to defend himself, but he was not permitted on the stand. He submitted a written memorandum, which was not read publicly.

The news of his expulsion barely filled three lines in *Rizospastis*, while making the headlines of all the bourgeois papers. Journalists besieged not only our house but also the Electric Railways' train depot. At least half of them also worked for the police. Armaos didn't say a word to any of them.

Two days later, Uncle Petros stopped by to see us. "They're asking me to repudiate you," he explained to his brother, in such distress that he was shaking.

"Do what you believe is best for you," my father advised him. "Whether you repudiate me or not, my position will not change. As for you, if you disagree with my choices, don't hesitate to keep your distance," he added, turning abruptly toward Anna.

My mother burst out laughing. They always discussed all political action in depth, and since their reunion, Antonis had not moved a finger without consulting her first.

"That's right! I'm going to publicly denounce you as an enemy of the people!" she exclaimed derisively.

Petros had broken out in a cold sweat. He left, dragging his wounded leg behind him. His new Party moniker was "the Cripple."

"THOSE NOT WITH me are against me." This sentence proved to be a guiding principle not only for Nikos but also for those in the opposing camp. Because Antonis had neither renounced his ideology nor pledged allegiance to his one-time foes after his expulsion by the Party, the "nationalists"[63] continued to consider him an unrepentant communist like any other.

In early 1946, after alleged passenger complaints claiming that his driving was erratic and dangerous, Antonis was demoted from the position of engine driver to ticket collector. That summer he was fired from the Electric Railways, as was everyone who had followed the KKE's instructions to abstain from the elections of March 31.[64] Those who had shown up to vote had had a hole punched in their identity cards. "No hole" voters were ergo leftists and would suffer the consequences.

My father's unemployment did not mean hunger for the family because we still had the gold sovereigns—thank God! All the same, Antonis could not sit around with idle hands waiting for better days. Not only would he have found it tiresome but it was sure to raise suspicion and set tongues wagging. He therefore found work at a shoe shop on Stadiou Street, where he manned the register and assisted the customers.

---

[63] In other words, those on the right side of the political spectrum, who considered themselves true patriots as opposed to the communist "traitors."

[64] Because the KKE deemed the political environment inimical to the free declaration of political affiliation, and denounced the elections as a farce, they encouraged abstention by Party members. Later, this stance was considered a mistake because it ended up excluding many progressive voters from the political process for decades.

I remember passing by one afternoon with my mother. I was overcome first with shame, then rage rising to a veritable fury when I caught sight of him on his knees before a corpulent woman in the act of slipping her feet into high-heeled shoes.

"They're too narrow for me, dear boy, can't you see?" she squealed. "Bring me another pair!"

Who did she think she was talking to? How dared she refer to Antonis Armaos, the former delegate to Athens, Antonis Armaos, my father, as "dear boy"? It was the first time I knew the meaning of class hatred.

IN THE SUMMER of 1947, he was suddenly arrested, along with five thousand other leftists who the government alleged were planning to instigate civil unrest, and dispatched to the island of Psyttaleia, right outside Piraeus. For three full days they broiled beneath the molten sun, without a tent, without shelter, without drinking water. Morning and evening, they were drenched with fire hoses, and the prisoners would stick their tongues out to get a drop or two of water. The first cases of madness were recorded in Psyttaleia. The men who refused to sign declarations of repentance were sent to more permanent island destinations. The most unfortunate to Makronissos, and the rest to Agios Efstratios and then Ikaria.

In Ikaria, where he was held for six months, Antonis was considered a foreign element by his fellow deportees.

Having been expelled by the Party, he was an outcast among outcasts. To fraternize with him meant risking the Party's displeasure. They barely said "good morning" to him, and grudgingly at that. But it didn't really make a difference to him. He had become friendly with the local fishermen and spent his time reading maniacally. In his letters to my mother, he explained that he aimed to fill the holes in his education and requested that she send books of every kind, from the ancient classics to nuclear physics tomes for the layperson.

His conviction that he was in the right despite what the rest of the world might think, his inflexible spirit, if not outright intransigence, inspired both respect and, at times, acute dislike.

"History will vindicate us!" He closed almost every letter with these words.

"History will vindicate us!" my mother, his echo, would repeat to me.

And I would imagine History as the twin sister to Glory—she who walked on the *blackened ridge of Psara*[65]— arriving at our house and awarding us a medal. I could hear the rustle of her tunic on our parquet floors.

FOR MY AGE, my woes were equal to my father's. At school, I found myself between a rock and a hard place. Classmates,

---

[65] A line from "The Destruction of Psara" by Dionysius Solomos.

both on the right and the left, would point me out as "the traitor's daughter." This was their only common ground. God only knows what else I would have had to endure had not Memas taken me under his wing.

A year my senior, Memas was in sixth grade, and even though small in stature, he already looked like a little man, with his too-cool-for-school airs and a budding mustache gathering sweat above his upper lip. Memas Gasparinatos had a grandfather from Cephalonia, a priest for a father, and three older brothers at the forefront of X. The Gasparinatos clan sowed terror throughout democratic Pangrati. True gangsters, with long trench coats under which they hid their rifles, they had run amok during the Dekemvriana and had continued in the period since to persecute and menace anyone they had stamped as an "EAM Bulgarian."[66] They didn't even spare the grocer on Arrianou Street who had been crippled on the Albanian front. They demolished his shop with crowbars and would have been quite capable of burning it to the ground with the poor man inside, had they not been afraid of setting fire to the entire neighborhood.

As the Benjamin of the family, Memas worshipped the ground his brothers walked on. While he could not come

---

[66] A term used by those on the right to disparage the EAM partisans because the KKE had close ties with the Bulgarian Communist Party and because in the north of the country many members of the Slavo-Macedonian minority fought with the EAM. Equally important was the fact that Bulgarians had a reputation as uncivilized barbarians. The use of this term once again casts doubt on the "Greekness" of communists and posits them as savage traitors to their country.

to school carrying a gun, he always had a switchblade in his pocket, which he never missed an opportunity to pull out with a menacing grimace. He had been unceremoniously kicked out of the Varnava Square Elementary School (now that I think of it, I am amazed that his brothers didn't beat the living daylights out of the teachers there) and ended up in ours in March 1947. As soon as he set eyes on me, he fell madly in love. Despite the fact that I was Antonis Armaos's daughter, or perhaps because of it. Immediately, he issued a decree: "If you so much as look at Niki sideways, I'll gut you!" No one dared call me "the traitor's daughter" again.

Do not imagine that the reason I didn't rebuff Memas's love was because I wished to take advantage of the protection he offered me. He was, no question about it, a far cry from the Prince Charming of fairy tales, both in terms of appearance and smell (he always reeked of garlic), yet there was something exceptionally gallant about his behavior toward me. Every time he spoke to me, he'd go bright red. The first time he begged me to let him walk me home—"'cause there's thugs out there that might bother you"—he kept swaying back and forth, hands stuffed in his pockets, jittery with nerves. He was wearing checkered short pants, a thick jacket over his bare torso, and a leather cap—"British-made," as he later boasted. Numb with cold, his thighs were bristling with gooseflesh.

During the entire walk, he kept looking around, trying to sniff out and forestall any imminent threat.

"I'll walk with you every afternoon," he declared as soon as we arrived at my front door. "And I'll make sure to tell everyone in Pangrati that if they lay a hand on Niki Armaos, ssssnickk, they're dead!" he added, as he drew his hand across his throat.

Memas's flirting was so shy it risked going unnoticed. Every now and then he would offer me a bar of chocolate and promise that when he grew up, he would have a limousine to take me on drives to Faliro. He was satisfied with the fleeting smiles I bestowed on him. One day, he mustered the courage to ask me if at home we really threw the saints' icons to the ground and wiped our feet on them. Not only did I refute this but I told him that my grandmother took me to church very often (an exaggeration) and that his father, the priest, had once given me Holy Communion (a lie). He was over the moon. With nothing now standing between us, he closed his trembling hand around mine. Even though it was awash in sweat, I did not pull away. Far from a sense of danger, all I felt was that he had truly won over my goodwill with the force if not of his sword, at least of his switchblade. Was he to blame for the fact that his brothers were crooks? After all, my uncle Stratos Vranas had been hand in glove with the Germans! We crossed Proskopon Square hand in hand, like a couple. We must have made a hilarious sight: I, with my braids, socks pulled up to my knees, and my little coat, and Memas, a little runt of a wannabe tough guy walking on tippy-toe, straining to reach my height.

I had, of course, not said a word to my parents about my association with Memas. Grown-ups—I had realized very early on—tended to arrive at the wrong conclusions. More-over, in my childish naïveté, I believed that the neighbors would not go telling tales.

So much so that it came as a complete bolt from the blue when my mother pulled me aside one afternoon and entrusted me—those are the words she used—with a very important mission: "Tell your friend Gasparinatos that your parents are fleeing Greece next Tuesday. That they're boarding an airplane to Paris with fake passports."

I was stunned. "You're going to leave me behind again?" I asked, ready to burst into tears.

"No, Niki, of course not!" she reassured me, squeezing me hard against her chest. "Never ever! It's just that this fake story must get to the police by way of the Chites, so that they lie in wait at the airport and, when they don't find us, believe that we fled abroad using some other means."

"I don't understand—"

"You'll understand soon enough. What's important right now is that you repeat exactly what I say to the young Gasparinatos."

"What makes you think that Memas would tell on me to his family?"

"Let's hope he does. If necessary, tell him that since you will be left with almost no one, the priest and his wife will have to take care of you."

I obeyed her instructions. As soon as he realized that in the very near future I would have even greater need of his protection, Memas was so ecstatic that I doubt he succeeded in going for more than fifteen minutes before spilling it all to his mother. Boys at that age, in any case, are complete simpletons.

"I'm here for anything you need!" he said, almost standing to attention as he left me at my doorstep. Little did he know that he would never see me again.

Shortly before midnight, a van came to a stop outside our building. Hurry-scurry, we loaded everything we had managed to pack and left Pangrati: Papa, Mama, and I. It was February 10, 1948.

XX

A WEEK EARLIER, Aunt Markella had returned home in a frantic state. "You're on their blacklist!" she had exclaimed, grasping my father by the collar. "Any day now, they'll arrest, try, and execute you!"

"What's got into you?" Antonis smiled incredulously.

"Lyssandros Mavrides told me in complete confidence!"

"The delegate?"

"Yes!"

"That palace brownnoser who plays at being a liberal?"

"He's also one of my greatest admirers!"

"Just an admirer?" Antonis frowned—he had never seen anything good come out of his sisters' affairs of the heart.

IN THE COUNTRYSIDE, civil war battles were raging; in the cities, emergency court-martials were convened throughout the day and night, sending scores of communists to the executioner's block. Yet my father still felt relatively safe. Despite his dismissal from the Electric Railways and his exile in Ikaria, he naïvely believed himself sheltered from danger. After all, he would say to himself, he hadn't engaged in any direct political action since 1945. The past two and a half years he'd spent living the peaceful life of a petit bourgeois, and his former comrades had definitively turned their backs on him.

Lyssandros Mavrides must truly have been head over heels in love with Markella to show up at our house in the middle of the night.

"I'm counting on you to keep this interview strictly between us," he said to Antonis, addressing him as if they were still parliamentary peers. "You are in an exceedingly difficult position, dear colleague. As far as I can tell, you are to be the target of the next offensive in the war against communism."

"I was expelled from the Party a long time ago, Mr. Mavrides. I am condemned to complete inaction. Even before that, after liberation, I unfortunately played no part in any decision-making. What will I be put on trial for? For my prewar activity? Or for the Middle East uprising?"

"Does the name Ilias Balassis mean anything to you?"

"Absolutely nothing," Antonis replied, after thinking it over for a few seconds.

"I believe you," Mavrides shook his head. "Listen, dear colleague: As early as the end of 1941, a certain Ilias Balassis—also known as Captain Pegasus—was operating in Aetolia-Acarnania, at the head of a paramilitary group. I can't say if the EAM-ELAS central administration was aware of his goings-on. The fact remains, however, that the man in question committed a series of heinous crimes that under no circumstances can be considered political in nature. He's responsible, beyond the shadow of a doubt, for the massacre of civilians, rape, and the razing of farmhouses and even churches."

"There are harmful elements of the lumpen proletariat that infiltrate every armed struggle. Are you aware, Mr. Mavrides, of the ravages committed during the Asia Minor campaign by overzealous Greek officers who burned Turkish villages as they advanced?" Antonis retorted, as if they were engaged in an academic debate.

"All traces of Ilias Balassis were lost near the beginning of 1944," Mavrides pressed on. "His men continued to terrorize the region, but he had disappeared."

"He may have been killed, unless he defected to the enemy."

"According to the indictment they're preparing, Mr. Armaos, you are Ilias Balassis!"

"That's absurd! I was in prison in Corfu until midyear in 1943! It wasn't until the Italian armistice that I managed to escape and make my way to Egypt."

"Can you prove all that?"

"Of course!"

"No, you can't, Mr. Armaos. The court-martial will rely on the word of witnesses of their choosing and will ignore the ones who come to your defense—if, that is, there are any, which I highly doubt. Do you have any idea what has already been slipped into your security file? Antonis Armaos aka Ilias Balassis! Do you see now, dear colleague? You are not going to be tried for crimes against the nation, spying, or even high treason. You'll be sent to the block as a common-law murderer."[67]

My father was stunned.

"*Former KKE second-in-command; butcher of priests and the elderly, rapist of young girls!* That's what you will read in the newspapers. So allow me to wager that even your Party will keep its distance. As for your wife, if she does not immediately declare herself devastated by the revelations, if she does not bow and kiss the hand of the prosecutor who supposedly opened her eyes to the truth, she will grow old in jail. I guarantee it."

"Why haven't they arrested me yet?"

"You want to know that, too? Any day now, we anticipate a new counteroffensive by the insurgents in Macedonia. Your arrest will serve as a distraction, part of our propaganda."

Antonis did not know what to think or what to say. To be held responsible for the crimes of a complete stranger smacked of a nightmare, but given the realities of their

---

[67] Indeed, this is how the Greek government bypassed the stipulations of the Varkiza Agreement in its persecution of communists. While the treaty gave amnesty for political reasons, actions viewed as nonpolitical were prosecuted under the law.

present moment, it was not at all beyond the realm of possibility. Mavrides seemed sincere, and even if he wasn't, what
kind of a trap might he be laying by warning him?

"What made you disclose all this to me, Mr. Mavrides?"
he decided to ask without beating about the bush.

"You owe your life to your sister, not me," he replied
with the air of a lovestruck adolescent. "Besides, I don't
believe you to be guilty, but rather a sacrificial lamb."

"What would you suggest I do?"

"Disappear as quickly as possible! The authorities, of
course, know where you live, but they believe you to be
completely unsuspecting, as you were only thirty minutes
ago. Leave! Get yourself out of the country by any means
necessary! I wish I could help you with that, too, but alas, it
exceeds my grasp. Good night, dear colleague, and I hope
with all my heart that one day we will meet again under
different circumstances."

THE QUESTION FOR Antonis, then, was how to leave the
country. He pondered it from every possible angle, until
finally rejecting it as impossible.

Even if we managed to obtain fake passports and slip
through the police's fingers at the airport or the harbor, we
would be unable to take the Kremos sovereigns with us.
Smuggling currency out of the country was severely punished, all the more so if the currency in question was gold.
This, however, had not kept many black marketeers from

finding safe harbor for their fortunes in Switzerland. There was always the option, of course, of traveling with empty pockets, but what were we to do once at our destination? We would have to start from nothing.

The mere thought of it sent shivers down Antonis's spine. It took him back to his father, stooping over his cart, picking up condoms and cigarette butts on Syngrou Avenue. It reopened an adolescent wound much deeper than he had thought possible. Antonis could endure anything—prison, exile, torture—except for the feeling of being trapped at the bottom of the pile, a nobody among nobodies, a stranger in a strange language, banished from his Party and his homeland, only to end up the most wretched of wage slaves. What's more, he was no longer nineteen but forty-two, a man past his prime with early stages of farsightedness. His prospects included coal mining (although he'd be pushing it, at his age), street sweeping, or in the best-case scenario, dishwashing in some seedy dive. No, no matter how much he might protest to the contrary, he just did not have it in him to begin all over again, neither to recalibrate plans for an entirely new future nor to draw strength from the past. He would wither and die, and wouldn't even leave us a few gold teeth as inheritance. Unlike my grandfather Anestis, his teeth were in excellent condition.

HIS THOUGHTS THEN turned to Clary Kremos and even Anaïs, his first love, who was now established in Marseilles.

"Bah! I'm truly grasping at straws!" he rebuked himself. "Anna would never accept the help, no matter how small, of one of her rivals! Unless, of course, I introduced them as mere friends... As if she would swallow a tall tale like that! Not to mention that the woman has yet to be born who would help a married ex-lover without a second thought!"

He even contemplated the possibility of traveling under cover to Corfu or Rhodes, and from there crossing to Italy or Turkey by sea. "With thirty-six rolls of sovereigns in our suitcases? It's not a captain we'll need but a saint if we want to make the crossing safe and sound and not find ourselves at the bottom of the sea with a bullet in the head! No, there's only one real option here," he decided.

And this option is what he described to me when—a week after I had turned ten years old—he asked me to make the biggest decision of my life.

XXI

"THAT'S THE LONG and the short of the situation, Niki," he said, as he concluded. "We cannot seek refuge in the mountains—the Party has expelled your father. Nor can we leave for abroad. If they catch us, we'll be executed. No, actually, only I will be executed. Your mother will be locked up, perhaps for life, and you will be raised in an orphanage. Our only other option, then, is to go underground. To hide in a house somewhere in Athens, until all this blows over."

"For how long?"

"For a year, a year and a half... I just don't know what lies in store. You are, of course, not obliged to come with us. You can stay with your grandmother and Aunt Markella."

"You don't want me with you?"

"Who, us? You think we don't want our little girl? That's impossible! But you must be the one to decide. Know that if you come with us, you'll have to withdraw from school temporarily. That we will live our lives under lock and key; that we'll have to avoid all contact with our neighbors; that we'll never see our family. We'll have fake names, and we'll speak our closest truths only in a whisper, with doors and windows tightly shut. It will not be easy, especially for you. I want you to think it over really well."

"Why can't Grandmother hide with us, too?"

"Your grandmother has other children besides me and is now expecting a new grandchild. Aunt Fani, as you know, is pregnant." (The sixty-year-old Bogdanos had knocked her up during one of her overnight visits at the Zeliotis Prison.) "Uncle Petros is on Makronissos. The prisoners there are either tortured or tied in a sack with a cat and thrown into the sea. First, they must strangle the cat with their bare hands, then hold their breath, if they want to have a hope of getting out alive. If I'm telling you this, it's so you understand that things could be a lot worse."

The two of us were sitting in Savvas Bogdanos's brother's parlor. After fleeing Pangrati, we had sought refuge there for one night, on Stisichorou Street, a mere fifty yards from the Royal Palace. My father was drinking coffee and I, hot chocolate in a porcelain cup. Our surroundings were so idyllic—plush carpets, classical paintings by celebrated artists, pine cones flaring in the fireplace—that my father's words had the effect of horror stories told to pass the time and throw into relief one's own good fortune.

"What are you thinking about, Niki?" I wasn't thinking about anything in particular. I was simply staring at the grand piano, wondering if I might be allowed to open the lid and try to play it. I had never touched piano keys before; I knew only that they were made out of ivory. How many elephants, I asked myself, to one piano; or, conversely, how many pianos to one elephant?

"You must decide very soon, Niki. In two hours, the van will be here to take us."

"Take us where?"

"I can't tell you. If you decide not to come, you can't know where we'll be. It's extremely dangerous information, both to you and to us."

"In other words, we won't see each other again?"

"No, we will...at some point...I'm sure..."

The message was loud and clear: If I stayed behind, snug in my grandmother and Aunt Markella's good care, our lives would part once and for all. For as long as they remained in hiding, all contact was off-limits. And unlike during the Occupation, when it was circumstances that had forced us apart, this time it would be me who had made the choice. I imagined hearing one morning—from the newspapers hanging outside the corner kiosk? from my classmates at school? from Grandmother Sevasti, who would at least try to shield me from onlookers' wickedness and crocodile tears?—I imagined hearing that they had been apprehended and were being led to their execution. It would not be the loss of my parents that would destroy me but the guilt.

"What are you crying about? You turned your back on them when the going got tough." This is what I would read in the eyes of both strangers and loved ones, despite their words of consolation. Even with the passage of time— "time, the great healer," as my grandmother always said— and my parents' names slowly going silent on others' lips, guilt would hound me night and day without reprieve. For me, there would be no means of atonement, no way to expiate my sin, except perhaps by suicide.

At ten years old I could see it all very clearly. So I decided—of my own free will, as it were—to follow them underground.

My father did not react with the enthusiasm I expected. His emotion, his pride in me no doubt tempered his joy. "History will vindicate us!" was all he said as he kissed me on the forehead. Then, he turned on his heel and hurried to the bathroom to hide the tears that had welled up in his eyes.

When he emerged, all his hair had been shaved off, and he was sporting a thick, fake mustache—"Only until mine grows in," he explained. In the meantime, in the neighboring room, a trusted hairdresser brought in by Markella was finishing my mother's transformation. The cloud of blond curls had been straightened and dyed black. Her eyebrows had been completely plucked and replaced by two penciled-in arrows, as was customary among elegant society ladies at the time. Finally, it was my turn: The hairdresser chopped off my braids with two big snips of the scissors. "A short crop will really suit you, sweetheart," she reassured me. "You have such a beautiful face."

Bogdanos's brother's building must have been among the first in Athens with a basement garage, which is where the same van that had brought us the previous evening was waiting. Once again, we loaded our suitcases—"Why did we bother taking them out yesterday?" I thought to myself—bid goodbye to our family without any great display of emotion, and off we went toward a destination that to me was completely unknown.

During the journey, my father explained our new circumstances and the roles we were to play from that day on. Face against the glass, I stared outside at the passing shopwindows, restaurant signs, and movie posters. *Gone with the Wind* was playing at the Attikon. Markella had promised to take me. "By next year, it will no longer be on the bill, even if it is the biggest success of all time," I thought with sadness.

I had convinced myself, completely arbitrarily, that we would remain underground for one year exactly. It would be yet another adventure, a short-lived parenthesis that I would later narrate to my close friends at school, adding all manner of spicy embellishments.

If an invisible hand had traced the number seven on the glass, would I have kept my resolve, or would I have opened the door of the moving vehicle, crossed Stadiou Street at a run, and disappeared into the backstreets?

Now that I am dead and therefore in a position to know everything, I still don't know the answer to that question.

THE WHITE TOWER

1

IT WAS DELEGATE Lyssandros Mavrides who had found the Maestro. All for the favor of the beautiful Markella, of course. The Maestro had been a client before the war, at Mavrides's legal offices in Thessaloniki. Mavrides had repeatedly saved the man from prison and knew exactly who he was dealing with; indeed, he had him very firmly in hand.

"Don't believe for a second that because you're now down in Athens, the atrocities you committed before and during the Occupation have been erased from the record." Mavrides cut right to the chase. "Anytime it tickles my fancy, I can turn you in and send you, special delivery, straight to trial, not by the Greeks but by the Jews in Israel." (When he had to address these underworld types, Lyssandros dropped his refined register.)

"What have I done to deserve this?" The Maestro blanched.

"Nothing at all . . . as long as you cooperate. I'm sending a couple with a young daughter your way—today, in fact.

You will give them one of those damn shacks of yours and put them up for as long as necessary. Don't worry, they'll pay you rent, and a generous one at that. However, you will not ask for their papers, and what they choose to tell you is all you need to know. If the neighbors begin with questions and gossip, you will take the wind out of that sail, understand? In a word, I am making you responsible for these people's safety. Got it?"

"But what if the police come sniffing around?"

"If they come, it means someone from the neighborhood started squealing. In which case, you'll be the one to pay the price. Understood?"

"Sure thing, chief!" the Maestro replied and plucked a cigarette from the gold case extended by Mavrides.

EVEN THOUGH NEA Smyrni bordered Kallithea, I doubt that I had stepped foot there more than three times until that day. In fact, when the van stopped at the corner of Imvrou and Tenedou, I had no idea in which part of the city we were.

The truth is that the neighborhoods that had sprung up around Athens after 1922 all looked alike: the same refugee buildings surrounded by miserable shacks transformed gradually, over time, by the sweat on the brows of their inhabitants into small but respectable homes. Street names evoked lost homelands; and athletic club emblems, the glories of Byzantium. Two-headed eagles fluttered in parched stadiums, while Anatolian aromas issued from the kitchens:

eggs scrambled with pastourma, imam baïldi, spoon sweets, and syrup cake.

For almost two decades, society had remained sundered between the pureblood Greeks and the Turk-spawn. At first, the former scorned the latter, their racism bald-faced and often violent. It did not take long, however, for the refugees to level the playing field with their work ethic and business acumen. Discrimination and rivalry dissipated once and for all, and October 28, 1940, found the Greeks united as if by a miracle. A few months later, a new schism began to foment, this time between the right and the left; between "nationalists" and "EAM-Bulgarians"; between monarcho-fascists and the people's army.

A FEW DAYS before Thessaloniki was liberated by the ELAS, the Maestro had hightailed it out of there to escape lynching by his victims. He had succeeded in liquidating and carrying off only a small portion of the considerable fortune he had amassed under the Occupation. With this sum, he had bought a well-kept two-story building on Imvrou Street, in the middle of a large lot of land of more than two acres. The elderly doctor who had sold it to him and was returning to Mytilini, the island of his birth, had a passion for growing things.

The Maestro had come by a veritable paradise. A paradise on the outskirts of the city, an Eden replete with citrus and fruit-bearing trees, grapes and tomatoes on the vine, and vegetable gardens of every kind. "The fruit of this earth will fill your plate, your glass, even your cigarettes!" the doctor had proudly declared. Indeed, tobacco leaves rustled in one of the corners of the lot.

It was like throwing pearls to a pig. Within three days of assuming ownership, the Maestro had the entire grounds dug up. Then, masons arrived and began building behind the main house, half a dozen mean mud-brick hovels destined for the working poor. As well as two communal latrines, of the Turkish variety, of course. In other words, two holes in the dirt joined to a cesspool that had to accommodate two dozen tenants. As well as one communal shower. Each and every time we wanted to wash, we had to heat water in a pot to fill the rusty tank, and then keep our eyes firmly on the ground in order not to trip over the rampant rats.

The glorious orchards and gardens had been converted into a yard, one of the thousands of yards that housed the Athenian poor. As if proud of this abomination, the Maestro had ordered a large metal sign to hang at the entrance: "White Tower" it read in Byzantine characters, along with a picture of Thessaloniki's famous landmark, the Greek flag billowing at its summit.

"WELCOME!" HE GREETED us, as the driver unloaded our bags from the van. "Charilaos Ligouras, landlord! But everyone calls me Maestro."

"Pandelis—Telis—Dimitriades," my father replied, shaking his hand. "My family and I have recently arrived from New Orleans, United States of America! This is my wife, Meropi, and my daughter, Koula."

"Delighted! Come in, come in," the Maestro said, staring at us with a probing eye. The fact that Mavrides had prohibited him from asking questions did not prevent him from drawing his own conclusions.

The story my father had invented was designed for exceedingly credulous, not to say unimaginably naïve ears. He claimed he was a Constantinopolitan born and bred who, after emigrating to America in 1925, had succeeded in business and acquired a restaurant and a tobacco shop; ten years later, he had married my mother, who also happened to be the daughter of immigrants. After my birth, they were both seized with nostalgia for the homeland, but war had broken out so they had to be patient and wait. As soon as sea lines of communication across the Atlantic were reestablished, we loaded all our possessions on an ocean liner and returned to the mother country.

Why New Orleans? Because it was a francophone city (as my father had read somewhere) and he himself spoke the language quite well. My mother and I, however, had no clue about foreign languages: "If someone tries to catch us out, let's say that we associated only with the Greek community." Why had supposedly affluent folk like us arrived with only five miserable little suitcases? "We lost most of our luggage during the journey. We have already filed a complaint with the company and are asking for damages." Why did both my parents wear dark glasses and never set foot outside the house before nightfall? "We suffer from an eye ailment that takes a long time to cure. It's also, by the way, why I'm not working right now. When I'm better, I'll get back to running my businesses." And, most important, why had we decided to move into that grotesque joke of a living situation? "We are simple and sober people—in other words, we like to keep an eye on our money. We are not fans of luxury or ostentation, nor are we very sociable."

The Maestro clearly did not believe a word of what my father was saying as he proudly toured us through our new lodgings: a living room that also functioned as a kitchen, a bedroom for my parents, and a second one for me that lacked a window and was as suffocating as a closet.

Had he recognized us? "Impossible!" my father declared categorically. "I've only been to Thessaloniki once, in 1929. After Nikos expelled me from the Party, in the autumn of 1945, my photograph has not appeared in any papers. And those published earlier dated back to my time as a delegate."

"What about the neighbors?" my mother asked. "Before the war, you were constantly up and down Nea Smyrni on Party business."

"They remember a young man with chestnut hair and a big smile, not a bald and mustachioed curmudgeon. What's more, I'm going to start eating to gain weight and make myself completely unrecognizable! I'll devour an entire platter of spaghetti at each meal!" he exclaimed, suddenly doubling over with laughter, more out of the need to let off some steam, no doubt, than because he found his quip all that amusing.

I remember that first afternoon at the White Tower as one of the most dismal of my life. After unpacking our things, we sat in the living room, on three rickety café chairs around a plank table. (The Maestro—bless him!—claimed to rent out the premises "fully furnished" and "equipped" with dubious tin-plated kitchenware.) Mother had taken care to pack some provisions. She boiled rice over a portable gas stove and offered sliced bread and hunks of cheese as meze. We were looking at one another, struggling to conceal the despair in our eyes. The cold oozed through the unplastered walls. The bare bulb hanging from the ceiling leaked a wan light.

"It's not all that bad, the house," my father said to break the silence. "It just needs a little money thrown at it. Some sweat, some heart, and we'll spruce it right up! We'll paint, we'll decorate, we'll buy a radio! And a gramophone!" It was primarily for me that he was saying all this, my spirits that he was trying to buoy. "We'll also buy a couple of hens to lay us some fresh eggs. And a parrot, too, why not? A parrot that talks like a person!"

The more he talked, the more I succumbed to despair. Abruptly, my father turned serious. "If it's too hard for you, Niki, if it's truly too much, I will tell Markella to come take you," he said, looking deep into my eyes, but without a trace of anger. "As soon as tomorrow if you'd like."

Bull's-eye! He'd hit me right where it hurt: my pride. How could I ever contemplate leaving them?

"Yes, let's buy a parrot!" I replied. And with a great deal of effort, I managed a trace of a smile.

II

THE FOLLOWING MORNING, I became aware that at the White Tower we did not have neighbors so much as housemates.

At the break of dawn and the rooster's first crow, an incredible cacophony assailed my ears: Babies bawled; women exchanged "good days" and expounded on what would soon be simmering on their stoves and with exactly how many cloves of garlic; men racked by wheezing coughs hawked up their entrails and then spit, swearing loudly. Water burbled and splashed, farts tooted and popped, doors burst open and closed. After half an hour of this explosion of sound, the men began to leave for work, one by one. Only then did we dare stick our noses out the door.

In early 1948, the White Tower's mud-brick hovels housed two families of four, one of two, and another of six, plus five bachelors, all sharing the same roof. Everyone hastened to welcome us and introduce themselves. And to all, we were forced to serve the same cock-and-bull about

New Orleans and my parents' eye condition, and to endure their questions, both naïve and suspicious. From our very first day, the Maestro had made it known, loud and clear, that Mr. Telis and his women were under his protection. "We fought side by side in Asia Minor," he declared, voice quivering with emotion even though the difference in their age clearly called the statement into question. My father, of course, kept his mouth shut.

Behind their dark glasses, my parents thoroughly scrutinized their new neighbors to identify who might potentially recognize and denounce them. I, on the other hand, was contented to indulge my child's curiosity and simply stare. Since I was obliged to coexist with them, I tried to come to terms with what that meant. Most critical of all, as my father had warned me, was to learn how to maintain the correct amount of distance, to learn how much to hold back—because if not one ran the danger of letting the cat out of the bag—without being too cold and haughty.

To borrow sociological terminology, I would say that the White Tower harbored a representative cross section of the working poor and the lower echelons of the petite bourgeoisie of the period. The houses were organized in two rows of three facing each other, with the two toilets and the shower in the middle. They had no view of the street, which was blocked by the Maestro's big house, but rather of a vacant lot in the back, where all the neighborhood's youngsters congregated to play soccer. That's also where we disposed of our refuse, in three large barrels.

In the house to our left lived the Chaïtides family. Both parents worked in a tavern, he as a waiter and she as a dishwasher; their eldest son was an errand boy; their youngest, still an infant in swaddling clothes.

To our right, lived the honorable Mr. Psaltis, an itinerant fishmonger and also, curiously, a lover of opera. He hawked his red mullet and horse mackerel with the coloratura of a tenor and every Sunday afternoon would take his wife and two daughters to the National Opera.

The house directly across from ours was burgeoning with the Attonis family. In all my life, I had never seen such beautiful people, like statues in a museum. Theodoros Attonis, a six-and-a-half-foot titan with the proportions and profile of an Apollo, worked as a stonemason. His wife, Sitsa, who made even Sophia Loren pale in comparison, earned a living as a shoe-leather stitcher. They had married young and were procreating as if against the clock. The entire time we lived in the White Tower, I remember Sitsa being either pregnant or with at least one infant suckling at her breast. As one would expect, their children were truly magnificent-looking creatures.

Beauty dazzles; it disarms all judgment. It therefore took me some time to realize that the Attonises, without exception, were dull and slow in almost every way, as if they had been born in a state of semi-torpor. It wasn't that they had particular trouble functioning; they fulfilled their marital, parental, and other such duties well enough. Beyond this, however, they had no interest whatsoever in anything at all. They spoke very little—never engaging in idle talk, not even in the ubiquitous soccer discussions—and always had a vague, serene smile on their lips. Had the world come tumbling down around them, they still would not have emerged from their nirvana for a second.

Next to the Attonises lived the Karassoulases. Aristomenis and his sister, Maria, who also went by Mary. Aristomenis Karassoulas was a tsarouchi-maker[68]—to be precise, he was the tsarouchi-maker to the Royal Guard. His workshop was located in the Royal Gardens, in the Evzone barracks, and he enjoyed great attendant prestige. Framed and autographed pictures of all the kings dating back to Constantine I decorated his parlor. Each Christmas, he was invited to the reception held for the palace staff. As a taxi idled in wait at the entrance to the White Tower, he would appear dressed in a tuxedo, bald pate gleaming as if it had been varnished. His sister accompanied him to the gate, making large signs of the cross all over him.

By rights, Mr. Karassoulas, with his more than decent salary, ought to have been residing somewhere better. If not near the palace, at least in the affluent neighborhood of Kypseli. Why had he chosen the White Tower? He was more at ease there. He preferred to be first in a village than second in Rome. He had surrounded himself with poor devils who might well think or say whatever they wanted behind his back, but to his face they kept their traps shut and bowed and scraped. Besides, they had no connection

---

[68] A traditional hand-sewn shoe of stiff leather, with an upturned toe and a large woolen pompom, tsarouchia are part of the costume for the Evzones, a special ceremonial military unit.

to his workplace, and his terrible secret was in no danger of becoming known and causing his ruin.

As I already mentioned, the last of the six hovels housed the bachelors. Transient in the city, they made do for a few months with sharing both bed and toilet. Hired hands working on the extension of a neighboring cemetery, musicians and folk singers, and every once in a blue moon, a student from the provinces. Men exclusively, of course. At only a few blocks' distance from a bus stop serving the city center, the White Tower made for a convenient pied-à-terre.

The Maestro's residence and the front yard were strictly off-limits to the tenants. An invisible line separated us, breached only when we entered or exited the White Tower. Not to mention that while trespassing in the Maestro's private space not so much as a hint of gawking or dawdling were tolerated, especially when he had visitors. In that case, one had to ford the distance hunched over and at a sprint. As to actually visiting the big house itself, that was, of course, out of the question. On the first of every month, the Maestro personally made the rounds of our mud-brick shacks, knocking on each door to collect the rent. The general impression was that the responsibility for these haughty and contemptuous airs lay less with him than with Argyroula.

OFFICIALLY HIS WARD, Argyroula was, in fact, the Maestro's lover, despite an almost forty-year age difference. The brightest of stars, the most fragrant of flowers in the eyes of the master of the house, to everyone else she was the worst of whores.

"Not yet seventeen and already so rotten!" Mrs. Chaïtides whispered one day to Mrs. Psaltis in a voice dripping with venom.

"She's only seventeen?" exclaimed the fisherman's wife in astonishment.

"If not sixteen!"

"Are you saying that he corrupted her at the age of twelve?"

"They say that she's the daughter of Jews," continued the other one, even more under her breath. "Rich ones to boot. When the Germans rounded them up to send them you-know-where, she renounced her parents, converted, and latched on to the Maestro for dear life. At the time, he . . . you know . . ."

From the first time I heard them maligning her, I got the feeling that it was actually envy they felt. Even though past fifty, the Maestro had not lost any of his vigor and vim. And there was nothing about Argyroula to suggest a lost soul suffering through a relationship of convenience. Whenever I caught sight of her on the balcony of the big house, daydreaming in a kimono or gossamer negligee, all platinum curls, scarlet nails, and rosy cheeks, she brought to mind a folk painting of Genevieve of Brabant. I really liked her. She had won me over from our first exchange.

"WHAT'S YOUR NAME, little girl?" she had asked me with a big smile, when we crossed paths at the entrance to the White Tower.

"Koula," I said, introducing myself with the fake name I detested.

"Ah, so you are Koula! Welcome, welcome! Would you like a noi-sssetttte," she said with a faux-French accent, and snapping open a little clutch bag embroidered in gold, she offered me a chocolate in a gilded wrapper. (The fox fur wrapped around her neck suggested that she was headed at least to the opera and not to the neighborhood chophouse.) "This one would kill to be my aunt Markella," I thought with sympathy.

I, on the contrary, had absolutely no desire to be Koula Dimitriades, even though I had caused a sensation among the youngsters at the White Tower with my trove of fantastical stories about New Orleans, describing the Mississippi, its riverboats and plantations full of Negroes, embellishing on all that my father had told me. I felt trapped. Held hostage to a life that was not mine.

The fact that it took me ten days to poop after our arrival at the White Tower (and I almost suffered an intestinal obstruction), speaks more to my inability to accept our new life, than to the horror I felt for the WC.

III

OUR LIFE UNDERGROUND conferred me with new responsibilities. My parents very rarely left the White Tower, and never before nightfall: This was their one, fundamental security measure. I was therefore the one to do all the shopping.

Every morning, I set off with a big canvas tote bag in my right hand and my mother's grocery list in my left. I'd dart in and out of the bakery and the butcher, stop by the kiosk for my father's cigarettes, and end up, twice a week, at the farmers market housed on the street in front of the cemetery, which stayed open until late afternoon, when the funerals began. In those early days, I must have presented a particularly adorable picture: Like a well-brought-up young lady, I spoke to everyone with great politeness; I inspected peaches and apricots with the air of an experienced house-wife; and in lieu of earrings, I'd hang a couple of the cherries that the grocer gifted me from my ears. In short, I'd pretend to be all grown up.

Until one day, in the spring of 1948, I did something foolish. An admiral's funeral was taking place in the cemetery. The coffin had arrived on a hearse drawn by horses sporting black-feather plumes on their heads. His hat and sword lay on the coffin, and an undertaker at the head of the procession carried a velvet pillow with medals pinned all over it. I was mesmerized. Even though I ought to have been rushing home with all the shopping, I stayed there, rooted to the spot, in front of the brass band that was playing the funeral march. On impulse, I crept into the church, listened to the chants and the speeches, and then followed the crowd to the grave, where, as the body was being laid to rest, the commander of the detachment ordered "A three-gun salute to honor the dead!" and thirty sailors raised their rifles and shot deafening rounds into the sky. I thought of Uncle Giannos's funeral, four years earlier. I almost slipped among the grieving relatives and would have gone for coffee with them, but sudden pangs of hunger brought me to my senses.

Panic-stricken, my parents were waiting at our front door. I was an entire two hours late.

"Where the hell were you?" shrieked my mother, and before I could reply, she grabbed me by the hair and slapped me hard.

"Where were you?" my father repeated with the asperity of an inquisitor.

Bawling, I began describing the admiral's funeral.

"What is this nonsense? Tell the truth! Right now!" my mother snapped, raising her hand to me again.

"She is telling the truth!" my father said as he stopped her. "But it's clear that our daughter has unfortunately not fully understood our position. Wipe your eyes, Niki. There are serious things we need to discuss."

They sat me down on a chair and, fingers wagging, lectured me for an hour. In great detail, they enumerated all the dangers that awaited in the shadows, the disaster lurking behind every step. We had to make sure to never let our guard down. The smallest blunder, the least bit of carelessness, could turn out to be fatal. They succeeded in truly and utterly terrorizing me. From that day on, I trembled with fear at almost everything: that I wouldn't be given the correct amount of change; that I'd unwittingly be drawn into giving away information by a cunning inquisitor; that, unknown to me, I'd betray my parents; that I'd be corrupted—this fear surpassed all the others combined.

Once my father's sermon was over, it was my mother's turn.

"There are monsters out there on the streets, Niki. Dreadful men who prey on and corrupt young girls!"

"What do you mean?"

"They entice them with all kinds of bait, hypnotizing them like a snake does a chicken. Then they undress the girls and fondle them with their dirty parts. Be careful! It's difficult to tell at first sight, because they often look like respectable gentlemen!"

My parents had never talked to me about love, let alone about sex. Once or twice, Aunt Markella had let slip veiled references to what grown-ups did in bed. At school in Pangrati and also at the White Tower, the boys would blurt swear words and innuendos and were constantly making a strange gesture whose meaning I did not understand: hand loosely closed, they shook it rapidly up and down. At ten years old, I was entirely ignorant, even though at night I would unconsciously squeeze my only doll, Dadouna, between my legs. What my mother had said about monsters had its intended effect: I was thoroughly horrified. For a long time afterward, I avoided all contact with unknown men, and if someone, even a neighbor, were to greet me on the street, I would conspicuously turn away.

ON THE LAST day of each month, at two o'clock sharp, come rain or shine, I had to be standing on the sidewalk of Syngrou Avenue, near the Church of Saint Sostis, on the side with the traffic heading toward Faliron. I would walk slowly, pretending to be lost in thought. After ten to fifteen minutes at most, I would hear behind my back the agreed-upon blast of the horn. The car would brake beside me, and I would open the door and sit myself down next to Aunt Markella.

Aunt Markella had begun driving. A little coral-colored car made in Italy that resembled a windup toy.

"So where shall we go today?" she'd ask, before stepping on the gas. As for me, at the first scent of her perfume, I would immediately let my guard down.

Before going somewhere to eat, I always looked forward to taking a spin in the city center between Syntagma and Omonia Squares. I loved watching the people sitting in patisseries, the chic misses walking out of boutiques loaded with packages, the traffic officers on their raised stands. The civil war raged ever more fiercely in the mountains, but the capital seemed to be flourishing and fancy-free. *London, Paris, New York, Budapest, Vienna, you can't hold a candle to Athens*, were the words of a song of the period. As we passed by theaters and cinemas, Markella would tell me about the new plays, the new films on the bill, and a whole heap of gossip about various personalities in the world of entertainment, excluding any "spicy" details not suited to my young ears. It was as if I were skimming through a news magazine full of color photographs and satirical cartoons like *Romanzo* or *Bouquet,* which my mother considered utter rubbish and never allowed me to bring into the house.

Finally, we would end up at one of those out-of-the-way restaurants far from the city center, which were frequented by clandestine couples. Markella wanted, at all costs, to avoid running into any acquaintances. How would she introduce me? Everyone believed that her brother, Antonis, had fled the country with his family. We would order the very best dishes on the menu and chatter away like two bosom buddies, but as the hands on the clock turned, my good cheer would surrender to melancholy. Generally, Markella pretended not to notice. One day, however, she decided it was time to have a frank conversation.

"Why so gloomy, young lady?" she asked.

"Because soon, I'll be back in my prison." I sniffled.

"And may I ask why it is a prison?"

"You know very well."

"Yes, I grant you, it's not all fun and games. You're not going to school, you can't see your grandmother and Aunt Fani, and you have to use a fake name. But things could be a lot worse. Ask yourself, what does a regular student in elementary school do that is all that different from your life? Do you imagine that she goes to the cinema every day or spends the entire day gadding about having fun? No, she's at home doing her homework and helping her mother with the house chores!"

She didn't understand! Not even Markella understood what it meant to live with the constant, implacable dread that the police might at any moment barge in, grab my parents, and execute them! She had no clue what it was like to be bursting with life, with sociability, and yet be forced to tame your every impulse, watch your every move, monitor your every word; to be constantly looking back as you walk the streets to check if you are being followed by a snitch. (That abrupt turn of the head very quickly became a tic that I carried with me to the end of my life.) And since she didn't understand, what was the point in trying to explain?

"You're right, Auntie," I conceded, as I cut into the last piece of my pork chop.

Needless to say, my amusement was not the sole purpose of my meetings with Markella. I served, first and foremost, as a "mule," to use a term that was coined later. I transported news, letters, and small items back and forth. Most important, I picked up and delivered to my father the money for our rent and all other expenses. The Maestro was having us fork over five gold sovereigns a month in rent for that hovel. His protection cost as much as a luxurious mansion in Kolonaki. Needless to say, after us, he was the person most invested in preventing our arrest.

IV

IN SEPTEMBER 1948, two big boxes arrived at the White Tower addressed to the "honorable Mr. Panteleimon Dimitriades." As a result, most of our neighbors' suspicions about us disappeared. Deceived by the postal stamp, they read it as proof that my father not only was not hiding anything but that he also had nothing to hide. Especially since the sender, whose name was writ large all over the boxes, was a certain Mr. Walter Johnson—clearly an American.

In actuality, Aunt Fani had mailed the boxes at my father's request. What they contained would, from that time on, fill our days and render our hiding a little less intolerable.

The first contained a Philips radio set, the last word in technology, despite vacuum tubes that required three minutes to warm up. A fairly large piece of furniture in polished wood, its speakers were covered in high-quality wickerwork. We rearranged the furniture in the living room to give it pride of place, and then sat in front of it enthralled, as we had in the past before the fireplace and would in the future before the television. In preparation, my father read and translated word for word the instruction manual, which was in French. In his opinion, the operation of such a piece of equipment was not child's play; it demanded delicate handling. When he finally pressed the On button, the dials lit up and the names of cities—"London," "Paris," "Rome," "Budapest," "Moscow"—twinkled on the high-frequency receiver like stars in a magical galaxy.

During the day, we listened to the National Radio Foundation on the medium frequencies. As soon as night fell, however, and we could barricade ourselves in without arousing our neighbors' suspicions, we turned down the volume, switched to the high frequencies, and eagerly pricked our ears: "London calling," "Moscow speaking," "*Govorit Moskva.*" Mostly, though, we listened to Radio Free Greece, which was broadcast from Bucharest[69] and informed us that the Democratic Army was going from victory to victory and before long would crush the monarcho-fascists once and for all, leading to the establishment of the people's rule in our country.

THE SECOND AND heavier box contained some fifty or so books, of which more than half were destined for me.

"Which elementary school will Koula attend, Mrs. Meropi? The 3rd or the 11th?" the neighborhood women would ask my mother in our early days at the White Tower.

"We're going to wait until she settles in," she would reply. "In any case, she has lost this school year. We'll see come September."

September came and went, but there was of course no question of enrolling me in school, seeing that neither I, Koula Dimitriades, nor my parents existed for the Greek state.

"Our daughter will be homeschooled," my mother announced to the White Tower community. "It's common

---

[69] Given that they were outlawed in Greece, the KKE established its head-quarters in Bucharest.

practice in the United States and has been scientifically proven to lead to better educational outcomes."

"Who will be her teacher?"

"What a question! Her father! Telis is a graduate of Constantinople's Robert College. If you'd like, he can tutor your children, too."

WHEN A MAN raises a daughter, he more or less consciously chooses a role to play. In my day, most fathers acted as masters; others, the more sophisticated ones, acted as mentors. The most popular role was, and still is, that of father heartthrob, whose confidence and virility depend on his daughter's unconditional adoration. My father drew the role of teacher, and he assumed it with impressive avidity.

"Next Monday, you begin sixth grade!" he announced enthusiastically. "Even if the monarcho-fascists cut off our food and water, they will not deprive you of your education! The two of us will build an exemplary school that will leave nothing to be desired when compared to other establishments out there. When we come out of hiding, you will be better educated than all your peers!"

"When will that be?" I asked for the umpteenth time, even though my parents had stopped answering that question long ago.

That same evening, Antonis began feverishly poring over the manuals of the Textbook Publishing Organization, with their characteristic owl logo. Their humanities

curriculum struck him as quite limited and, most important, ideologically unacceptable. He decided to revise it
completely. Between 1948 and 1955, the most radical educational reform in Greece took place in our little shack on
the White Tower's premises.

Religious education and home economics textbooks
went straight to the garbage—"We don't mean to make a
sanctimonious housewife out of you!" They were replaced
by classes in political economy—"to introduce Niki to
socioeconomic structures and thereby gradually acquaint
her with the basics of Marxist theory."

For history, my father of course complied with the
distinctions among the ancient, Byzantine, and contemporary periods. But he taught almost everything through
the lens of the relentless struggle between exploiter and
exploited. What was the uprising of 1821? "A failed social
revolution." The Nika riots? "A revolt of the Byzantine
people against the palace." Even the Trojan War had not
been waged for the sake of the beautiful Helen but was,
in fact, "an imperialist war for control of the Straits." As
for Prometheus's theft of fire, for which he suffered untold
torments on the Caucasus mountains, it was the first act of
revolt by the human race.

"When socialism comes to our country, we'll erect a
statue to Prometheus across from parliament!" he would
promise, expecting to see my eyes light up, as if he had just
announced the launch of a giant ice-cream machine in Syntagma Square serving free scoops of vanilla and chocolate.

Literature classes saw the most beneficial improvements. While children at my grade level were bored to tears by antiquated verses of doggerel (like: *Oh, land of genius! From your bosom springs, of yore and evermore, oh, beloved homeland! The greatest of ideas!*), I was reading Solomos, Palamas, and Ritsos. A devotee of memorization, my father had me learn long poems off by heart: *Step aside, rock, that I may pass! The wave made so bold as to ask, Turning turbulent and thick with sand, As she struck the rocks along the strand,*[70] or *Child, this, my garden, shall be yours one day; Leave it as you have found it, as easy on the eye as of yore,*[71] or even "Ithaca" by Cavafy, whom he had heard about in Egypt. (He made sure, of course, to keep the Alexandrian's erotic poems carefully under wraps.)

He had also added two foreign languages to the curriculum: French and Russian. I would need Russian because it had been decreed that I would pursue advanced studies in Moscow. Even though the Party had turned its back on us, Moscow's Lomonosov University was impatient to welcome me when the time came. My parents lost no opportunity to encourage this absurd belief in me.

Proceedings at the White Tower schoolhouse were modeled, as much as possible, on the regular school day. We hung a curtain in the middle of the living room by way of a screen to provide privacy, at least visually, from my mother, who would wander around doing her chores. Every morning, at

---

[70] "The Rock and the Wave," Aristotelis Valaoritis (1824–1879).

[71] "The Fathers," Kostis Palamas (1889–1943).

seven thirty sharp, I would appear dressed in my blue uniform, notebooks tucked under my arm, and sit at one side of the dining table. At twenty-five to eight, my father made his entrance. I would stand as a sign of respect, like students at school when their teacher enters the classroom. During class time, I would address him formally with the prefix Mr. He had designed a carefully scheduled program, which we followed faithfully. Monday: modern Greek, arithmetic, geography, fundamentals of political economy. Tuesday: Russian, history, composition, arithmetic. Six days a week, morning and afternoon, with a three-hour recess so that I could do the shopping. Absences due to illness where not permitted if the mercury did not rise above a hundred degrees on the thermometer. Vacation days were markedly fewer than in regular schools. Ours celebrated only New Year's, March 25,[72] September 27 (the anniversary of the founding of the EAM), October 28,[73] and November 7 (the anniversary of the October Revolution). Starting in the second year, at my mother's insistence we added Christmas and Easter, not as religious holidays but rather as a way to honor the rituals and customs of our people.

WHEN YOU ARE the only student of a teacher devoted to and passionate about the task of transmitting knowledge, who

---

[72] Beginning of the War of Independence from the Ottoman Empire (1821).

[73] Date of commemoration of the beginning of the Greco-Italian War (1940).

makes you get up and come to the board every day—we actually had a blackboard!—and quizzes you mercilessly, you cannot help but improve. Every three months, my father had me take exams. On the following day, he would convene my mother and me and provide a detailed report of my improvements and weaknesses. At its conclusion, he would hand my mother a self-designed "performance report," on which she had to append the note "read and approved," before signing and returning it to him. On June 15 each year, I received my "diploma": My parents would congratulate me and then we'd share a celebratory meal of moussaka and semolina walnut cake.

After overcoming his initial anxiety, my father became increasingly proud of his homeschooling. Often, when I was chatting with the other children at the White Tower, he would eavesdrop and delight in the fact that my vocabulary was richer and my knowledge deeper than theirs.

"You see, life underground isn't all disadvantages," he said to me one day. "You would not be getting an education like this at a regular school!"

He probably had no clue how much I missed having classmates, teachers that one could both respect and tease, not to mention recess in a playground, passing notes in class, horsing around, playing hooky. It probably never even occurred to him that the only thing I truly longed for was not to become a paragon of socialism's New Man (confined, to cap it all off, to two and a half rooms) but to be a normal little girl.

V

I BEGAN KEEPING a diary when I was ten. It was my father who had suggested it, not only as a way to practice my writing but also to serve me as a type of confidante to whom I could divulge everything I held deep in my heart.

"Write in it whatever you feel, whatever you want. Your mother and I will never even touch it," he assured me.

I believed him. Even so, reading my entries one cannot escape the impression that I am writing under the pitiless surveillance of an imaginary eye right next to my elbow, judging my every word, my every comma.

January 2, 1949. This evening, after dinner, something terrible happened. I don't know what got into me, but suddenly I started screaming at my parents. I told them that I couldn't bear it any longer, that they had to do something to get us out of here! That all the better if we get caught because it will bring an end to this thing sooner! And so many other crazy things! I surprised even myself. Had I gone mad? I was screaming—in a whisper, of course, as we always do at night when we talk among ourselves—and even saying bad words that I had never said before in front of my parents. I felt like my face was burning and my hair was standing on end. At one point, I thought I had peed my pants. I went and took a quick peek inside and all I saw was bright red. I really lost it then! Thank goodness that my mother was there. She took me to my room, sat beside me on the bed, and explained that my period had arrived. A period is what all women get once a month. It lasts three to four days, and we must use a special napkin to absorb the blood. Mama also told me that a period is very useful: It helps the body cleanse itself.

"You're all grown up, Niki!" she said, and kissed me. Later, when we returned to the living room, Papa was not angry. He smiled a kind smile and told me that tomorrow will be a school vacation.

"Don't expect a day off every time you get your period! You're in luck because it's the first time," he said. Now I'm all mixed up. On the one hand, I'm ashamed I spoke to my parents like that. On the other, I'm glad to have grown up.

"Becoming a woman is a beautiful thing," my mother said. Also, my belly hurts. But Mama says that's normal.

April 12, 1949. Today, early in the afternoon, Mr. Karassoulas's howls got everyone at the White Tower up on their feet! Even Argyroula, eyes swollen from sleep, rushed to the back balcony to ask what was going on. No one really knew, and then we saw Aristomenis dragging his sister, Miss Mary, who was only in her slip, out of the house and into the yard. He was calling her very obscene names, as Papa said ("obscene": a new word that I wrote down in the glossary I'm creating). He had grabbed her by the hair and was hitting her every which way. Mr. Psaltis and Mr. Attonis had to step in the middle to pull them apart.

"There's no reason to commit murder!" they said to Aristomenis. And while Miss Mary, who had collapsed into Mrs. Psaltis's arms, sobbed and wailed, he went back into the house, emptied all his sister's clothes onto a sheet, tied it up into a bundle, and carried it out to the yard.

"Take your things and go! Hit the road, slut!"

That's what he called her: "slut." Then he marched over to the bachelors' house and started banging on the door, calling for Mr. Neris to come out and settle their score like men. Mr. Neris is a law student from Tyrnavos. He wears little round glasses and a brown suit, and works the cash register at a movie theater to pay for his studies. All the grown-ups at the White Tower like him—they call him "a good boy." In fact, Mrs. Attonis, if I heard correctly, would really like him to marry her eldest daughter, Thaleia. Even my father, who doesn't have much to do with the neighbors, has had coffee with him a couple of times in the yard. What I mean to say, dear diary, is that everyone is openmouthed with shock at Mr. Karassoulas's sudden madness. In the end, Mr. Neris was not there, so for the moment we were spared an even worse drama. Mr. Karassoulas tossed the bundle of clothes out onto the street, and sent Miss Mary along with it.

"Don't you dare step foot here again. Go on now, shoo!"

Miss Mary hesitated for a moment, but then she undid the bundle, pulled out a dress and shoes, put them on, tied the bundle up again, threw it over her shoulder, and started down Imvrou Street, head bowed. We were all watching, but no one went to help her.

"The show is over. Go back inside!" Mr. Karassoulas barked, his face still completely red. After advising us to warn Mr. Neris to make tracks and fast, because if he happened upon him, he'd "smash his ugly face in," he went home and closed his door. Until nightfall, it was all everyone could talk about. What I gathered from listening to the grown-ups was that Mr. Neris had secretly seduced Miss Karassoulas, and Mr. Karassoulas was avenging "his sister's honor."

"And there you have a woman's role under capitalism: the private property of her father or her brother," my father remarked to me. "Then she gets turned over to a husband like a piece of livestock or a wheel of cheese."

But the children were whispering a different story. They said that Mr. Karassoulas was secretly married to his sister! Not a real marriage in a church—that isn't allowed—but because at night they slept in the same bed and he climbed on top of her! And when she put the horns on him and went with Mr. Neris, Mr. Karassoulas had found out and almost slaughtered her in a fit of jealousy. The children at the White Tower tell a whole lot of lies, but perhaps this one is not one of them. I remember Mrs. Chaïtides and Mrs. Psaltis exchanging whispered asides and sneering every time Mr. Karassoulas and Miss Mary crossed the yard arm in arm on their way to church.

"Ah, there they are! The little lovebirds of Saint Paraskevi," they'd say, among other such gibes. Go figure! I, in any case, feel sad for Miss Mary. God knows where she is right now, and whether she will even find a bench somewhere to spend the night...

IN FACT, IT was my own fate that was making me sad. I was certain that Mary Karassoulas would manage just fine. But I, when would I finally find my way out from the murky bottom of this pit that we euphemistically called the White Tower? When would I no longer have to live among creatures who spent all day and all night stewing in their own rancid juices? Complete brutes who had not offered any help—the idea had not even occurred to them—to a woman (their friend, their neighbor) kicked out on the street like a piece of garbage? (It would be the same with us, if not worse; they would neither protest nor lift a finger, I thought, if the police showed up at the White Tower to arrest my parents.) True oafs, that's what they were, incapable of seeing anything beyond their own noses or any further than their stomachs, their base interests, and their tedious tittle-tattle.

Precipitated into a precocious adolescence, I had become a misanthrope.

Even though I didn't show it, they all sickened me, no matter what their age: old, young, or innocent. Even tender or charming scenes made my stomach turn. I would see, for example, Sitsa Attonis nursing her newest babe, the sixth in succession, and I would have to grit my teeth so as not hurl myself at her and spit in her face: "Where did you get the idea, you moron, that it's your duty to fill the planet with your beautiful but feebleminded babies?" I would watch Mr. Psaltis help his daughters up onto a low wall to have them sing Schubert's "The Linden Tree" as he directed them with his pudgy sausage hands and the puffed-up airs of the conductor of a symphony orchestra, and instead of being touched by this artistic effort, or at least finding some amusement in the comical picture presented by the two little roly-poly songbirds, all I wanted to do was throw a bucket of shit right in their kissers. I had cut off all relations with children my age. Whenever I went out to the yard, I held a book in front of my face and rarely looked up from it. This was not because of a passion for reading but rather from a refusal to take part in their conversations and games. They were, naturally, irritated by my behavior, and lobbed all manner of spiteful comments at me behind my back, "show-off" and "ass-kisser" being among the most benign. This did not stop them from staring in fascination at my chest, which seemed to be growing before my eyes. I began hunching in order to hide it.

Even my parents, whom I had always considered heroic figures free of any fault for as long as I can remember, had started to get on my nerves.

With my mother it was simple, we clashed on an almost daily basis and usually over trifles: "Why is the towel hanging all crooked like that?" "I asked you, didn't I, to wash the pan?" But these reproaches surged into quarrels that necessitated my father's intervention, fruit of the hormonal tempest raging inside me, as well as my mother's obsession with cleanliness—a symptom of our life underground. Up and about at the crack of dawn, all she did all day was housework, relentlessly hunting the very last particle of dust, furiously scrubbing laundry on the washboard to banish even the faintest stain. She was like a lioness relentlessly cleaning and recleaning her cage.

My relations with my father were of a different order entirely, and much more congenial. Despite our close quarters and lack of privacy, he had not lost any of his sheen in my eyes. The stories he told me—about Mudanya, about the heroic early days of the Party, about Egypt—I always found captivating no matter how many times he repeated them. I also continued to find him handsome, despite the almost fifty pounds he had gained and his graying mustache. The only thing that irritated me was his hopeless optimism, his conviction that sooner or later History would vindicate us and that together we would build the new socialist state. "With whom are you going to build your new socialist state?" I wanted to shout and shake him. "With incest-is-best Karassoulas? With Attonis the half-wit? Or with that bastard of a Maestro?" Unless finer people were to be found in other houses, other neighborhoods, he didn't have a hope. But at times, I would begin to believe in what he had to say. Especially when he talked to me about his time in the Soviet Union—its parks, schools, the Moscow metro, all of which he described in vivid Technicolor. *High in Soviet Russia's snow, where the north winds always blow, the immortal clouds they scatter, the chains of slavery they shatter…*[74] He would sing this to me, and I would imagine myself as one of the Soviet Pioneers, the children with the red scarves

---

[74] A song by Mikis Theodorakis.

around their necks, and then, when I got older, joining the Komsomol, the Leninist youth union.

AUGUST 29, 1949: The National Army crushed the Democratic Army on the Grammos mountain range.[75] The survivors were forced to flee to Albania, and from there were found passage to other Soviet countries.

The National Radio Foundation triumphantly trumpeted the end of the Civil War by proceeding to play military marches and folk songs for an entire day without interruption. The KKE, for its part, was in no hurry to publicly announce its position. Six weeks had elapsed before Radio Free Greece proclaimed from Bucharest: "The Democratic Army has not surrendered; it has merely put down its arms close at hand. It did not bend at the knee; it was not crushed. All its powers remain intact. The Democratic Army did not capitulate..."

While listening to this declaration, my father was hard-pressed not to pull out his mustache.

"Why won't they admit it? The war is over!" he marveled. "What in the blazes are they thinking? Don't they understand that all this bluster about 'arms close at hand' is giving the monarcho-fascists the perfect pretext to settle their differences with all the leftist militants or, for that

---

[75] The National Army was the official government army; the Democratic Army was founded by the Communist Party. The final battles of the Civil War took place on the mountains of Grammos and Vitsi, near the Albanian border.

matter, anyone on Greek soil with leftist leanings? What exactly are they after? To keep Makronissos in business until time immemorial? To keep that living hell churning out martyrs and heroes without end?"

Apprehended at the end of 1948 in a cleanup operation after the battle of Karditsa, Uncle Petros was currently on Makronissos. Despite Markella's insistence, Lyssandros Mavrides had not succeeded in reducing his sentence nor in improving the conditions of his detention. The fact that he was a cripple did not soften the prison guards.

"Wasn't he wounded in the December insurgency, Mr. Delegate, sir?" the camp commander had asked Lyssandros. "God only knows how many of ours he butchered..."

Uncle Petros was suffering the torments of hell. In absentia, the Party awarded him a medal for the Order of Glory. As for Radio Free Greece, they paid him tribute in their program *The Faces of Our Warriors*, which aired every evening. Except that this time, the program was titled *Two Brothers*. After singing praises to the bravery, fortitude, and, most of all, the dedication of Petros Armaos, he was pitted against Antonis.

"One of the brothers, faithful to the cause of the people, is drinking vinegar and gall on Makronissos. The other brother, whom we once had the naïveté to entrust with the leadership of our Party, is, as we speak, to be found in the United States—smuggled out by his new patrons—and is living large on the fruits of his thirty pieces of silver. One braved the enemy in the trenches with exemplary valor. The other ran for cover like a mole rat diving into its hole."

The actress—or was it the hostess?—continued in this vein for a full ten minutes. Meanwhile, the veins on my father's temples were pulsating at full gallop; his bottom lip trembled. Yet when my mother got up to turn off the radio, he nudged her hand away. Almost masochistically, he wanted to make sure not to lose a word.

Then he lit a cigarette, smoked it down to the butt, and forced a bitter smile.

"Every cloud has a silver lining... The Bureau for the Repression of Communism follows all the broadcasts coming out of Bucharest. After tonight they'll no longer have any doubts: We're abroad." He made no further comment. Nor did he move the dial from the Radio Free Greece frequency.

This took place in early 1950. Two years later, Beloyannis[76] was executed as a hero, crowned in glory. Four years later, Ploumbides[77] was shot, accused of treason, and covered in opprobrium.

VI

ON FEBRUARY 3, 1952, I turned fourteen. At my full five feet seven inches (I wasn't going to get any taller), I towered over

---

[76] Nikos Beloyannis was a leader of the Resistance and the leading cadre of the Greek Communist Party whose execution led to worldwide outcry against the authoritarian postwar establishment.

[77] Nikos Ploumbides, a leading figure in the KKE, was accused of being a double agent by the Party. He was arrested by the police, tried, and executed.

my mother, my aunt Markella, and most of the women I knew. I had a rather developed chest, a rather small waist, and a rather perky bottom. At fourteen, I could easily be mistaken for a twenty-year-old, especially if one overlooked my face bare of makeup, my badly tweezed brows, the pimples on my cheeks, and my airs of a child. On the street, men would whistle at me. "Hey there, dollface!" they would cry, when they were not shouting racier or, depending on your preference, more florid comments. I would bow my head and pick up my pace—my shoes, flat, without the least bit of heel, nervously tapping the ground. I did not feel at ease in my new skin—no, not at all.

Aunt Markella, who was supervising my wardrobe (she was the one who would buy me my brassieres, slips, and panties—the most virginal she could find so as not to scandalize my mother, I reckon), was also charged with my sexual education. During one of our monthly meetings at the deserted café in Kavouri, she plucked a leather-bound volume on human sexuality out of her bag, flipped to the pages she had dog-eared in preparation, took a sip of her lemonade, coughed, and began to read in a monotone voice a screed on the reproductive instinct, the virginal hymen, the labia minora and majora, the vagina, the penis, the testicles, pregnancy, and childbirth.

The dated, highfalutin language used by the doctor who was the author of the book struck me as absurd, and I found the pictures, scientifically accurate but wanting any aesthetic sensibility, utterly repellant. Essentially, sex was presented as a cross between a medical intervention and a crime, an unpleasant but unavoidable human act, which one would do well to exercise in a sterile environment to guard against venereal disease and unwanted pregnancy. I knew—and I had absolutely no doubt about it—that sex was not like that! Why was it, then, that my aunt, a woman of the world, a bohemian, was choosing to vilify it with these airs of a catechism teacher?

When she finished reading the chapter "Anatomy and the Physiology of Wedlock," and before moving on to the next one, "Sexual Perversion," she took a break to light a cigarette.

"Do you have any questions, Niki? Is there anything that's unclear?"

"Auntie, why are you bothering me with all this!" I burst out. "I couldn't care less! I'm a child."

"Come now, you're hardly a child, you're a woman grown. These are things you ought to know about."

"I'll have plenty of time to learn when I get married," I retorted, hiding behind an even more retrograde attitude.

Markella's face clouded for a moment; she was obviously thinking. "You know, Niki, why you find all this frightening and disturbing? Because the book makes no mention of love. Without love, sexual relations, for the woman at least, are pure misery."

"And what is love?" I asked in the hope that she would repeat the magic sentence she had told me when I was very little: "Love is what happens when devotion catches fire."

Instead, Markella began reeling off mawkish platitudes and poetic nonsense: Love is how angels embrace the stars; love is blind; we each have a missing half and it's only when we find it that we know the true meaning of happiness. Then, she became more personal. "One day, you will meet the man who is your intended partner," she promised me. "You will both know it, from the moment you set eyes on each other. No matter the obstacles that rise in your path or the storms that threaten you, nothing will pry you apart. Because you will have become one and the same being, one soul in two bodies."

I stared at her, more dismayed and distrustful than ever. How could she rehash—to me, a "woman grown"!—more or less the same fairy tales full of Cinderellas and Snow Whites that she used to read to me not that long ago when she put me to sleep? Out of all the adults in my life, who had found their "missing half" and true and lasting happiness after marriage? Had she, perhaps, with Stratos Vranas or Lyssandros Mavrides? Her relationship with the latter, she had confided, was hanging by a thread and was as likely to end in marriage as a pig was to fly. What about Aunt Fani and Savvas Bogdanos? I remembered their relationship as a tender, affectionate, and strong one, but not once had I detected the least hint of erotic passion—it was more like a relationship between a father and a daughter. My parents? They were above all comrades in arms. They themselves made no bones about repeating it at every available opportunity, and I had never seen them kiss, not once—if indeed they desired each other, how could they always exercise such restraint? Out of our neighbors at the White Tower, the only ones who were convincing as one soul in two bodies, the only ones who bloomed (and were fruitful and multiplied) together, were the Attonises. But who would ever dream of pointing to the Attonises—those dim-witted clods!—as a paragon of marriage?

"Love does not exist," I concluded. "And if it does, it lasts next to nothing. It's a complete waste of time."

Three weeks later, I fell in love.

I cannot describe his face in any great detail. I never took the time to observe it closely. What I remember are two coal-black eyes and very thick hair, cut short in a brush cut, or an American, as it was called back then. "Give me an American!" is what the boys would ask of the barber. He must have been five years older than me, or perhaps as much as ten and just looked younger. The one thing I'm certain about is that he was tall and lanky, you could tell from the shadow that he cast on the ground next to me. Artakis was still a dirt road back then, awash in dust and potholes, with very few passing cars. I was walking up it, my father's trousers under my arm, on my way to the seamstress for an alteration: Antonis was getting fatter by the day and no longer fit in them. The boy's lanky shadow surfaced at my side, and then, mere seconds later, I heard him whistle.

At the time, men whistled at any halfway decent-looking woman who happened to be passing by. They'd stick their fingers between their lips, like shepherds marshaling their flock, and I wondered whether there was a woman born who would respond favorably to such an overture. But the lanky shadow's approach was completely different: He struck up a foxtrot that was in vogue, and whistled the whole thing with great fervor and bravura—as if he had a microscopic orchestra in his mouth. He was following right behind me, and instead of crossing to the other side of the street or slipping into a shop to escape him, I unconsciously attuned my footsteps to his. Before exchanging a word, before even looking at each other, we danced in the middle of Artakis Street, enveloped in the scent of spring, he behind and I in front. "What are you doing, Niki? Have you lost your head?" I pulled myself together, and darted into the seamstress's semibasement shop.

When I stepped back out, the boy was still there. I spied him out of the corner of my eye, leaning against a tree trunk, smiling impishly. He began shadowing my footsteps again. Now he was not whistling but was singing in a deep, slightly brash voice: "*Coachman, let loose the reins! Storm or deluge can't detain, at such a drunken time as this, heart and soul madly thirsting for your kiss.*"

We must have traveled half a mile like this, perhaps more, when I realized that I was leading him straight to my house. Then and there, all the fears instilled in me over the years stirred and grabbed me by the throat. "He must be a snitch," I said to myself and shuddered. "He'll lead the police to us and have us arrested! Or he's one of those monsters who is trying to entrap and abuse me!" Panic-stricken,

I stopped a passing taxi and gave the driver all my remaining change to take me the five blocks to my house.

Three days later, when I went to retrieve my father's trousers, the boy was in the same spot where he had first set eyes on me. I imagined that he must have lain in wait on the preceding two afternoons, perhaps even until nightfall, before resigning himself to the fact that I wasn't coming. We acted out a replica of the previous time. The "coachman" whistled all the way as he escorted me to the seamstress's, then launched into song on the way back to the corner of Artakis and Kasamba Streets, where we had parted the first time. Not a taxi in sight this time around, I simply made an irritable gesture with my hand at the boy, as if shooing away a cat: "Time to move on!" He understood, and turned on his heel.

The following day, I had no excuse to return to his stomping grounds. But the thought of him gnawed at me, and I kept losing my concentration in class.

"Is Pericles's funeral oration not interesting enough for our young lady? Or is Thucydides in general not to your liking?" quipped my father in frustration. Two days later, I came up with a pretext and was there at five o'clock sharp. As I was every afternoon after that for the following two and a half weeks.

Wouldn't any man, upon realizing that a woman is responding to his advances, or at least that she is always constant to their rendezvous, raise the stakes on his bid? Wouldn't he try to get her to give him a little something more each time? Yes, any man, except for the lanky shadow. Not only did the boy never attempt to lay a finger on me, he didn't even address a word in my direction, not even to ask my name. (This question did not cease to torment me. If I said "Niki," I'd be breaking the cardinal rule of our lives underground. If I said "Koula," it would be as if I were introducing myself wearing a mask—the dreadful mask I had been forced to wear since I was ten years old— as if I were acquiescing to my miserable fate.) But he didn't ask me anything. He just kept whistling a new song every afternoon, all the big hits of the time. "Come, if Only for One Night" or "Marina's Song": *everything is blue, the waves so blue, the seagulls, white.* All the top songs on the radio, but interpreted in his own particular manner, both more playful and more serious at the same time. As for me, I would give myself over to their rhythms.

Was he a professional musician? Did he spend his nights performing in a popular tavern or at one of those cabarets frequented by Aunt Markella? Or was he simply one of the neighborhood youths, who lacking the courage to speak, preferred to whistle and sing? And, if he'd spoken to me, what would he have said? How would I have replied? Tossing and turning in my bed, I would concoct a heap of scenarios of greatly varying likelihood and rehearse imaginary dialogues, all the while pondering the best way to react should he either invite me to a patisserie or get down on his knee to ask for my hand in marriage. Naturally, I had not confided to anyone what it was that had me on pins and needles in my heart, but at the same time, no one had noticed anything. I was surrounded by perfect indifference.

On the twentieth afternoon (I tallied our meetings in code, by drawing a line in my diary), as I walked up Artakis Street, I saw him waiting for me, standing next to a bicycle. A tall "professional" bicycle as we called them at the time, because the grocery and butcher boys used them to deliver shopping. He gave me a wide smile, let me get ahead of him by five steps or so, and then he straddled the bike and approached slowly with short pumps on the pedals. My heart was beating fit to burst; I sensed that something was about to happen. Not to mention that he was whistling "The Coachman" again, like when we had first met—it could not be a coincidence.

Usually, we walked together to Skatzouraki Square. Once there, we turned back to walk down Artakis Street and part ways at the intersection with Kasamba. But this time, the boy turned everything upside down. With one big stroke of the pedals, he overtook me, twisted the handlebars to one side, and barred my way.

"Jump on!" he said, his voice hoarse—throat tight with nerves, no doubt. He couldn't even look me in the eyes, his face lowered as if the sun was blinding him, even though it was turning to dusk.

"Jump on and I'll take you for a ride!" he said pointing to the bicycle's horizontal crossbar, which could easily hold a passenger and even accommodate a girl riding sidesaddle.

"Jump on!" he repeated, and in his nervousness managed to ring the bell. That's when I noticed his hands, his long fingers and square nails with what appeared to be traces of paint embedded in the cuticles.

I was trembling like a leaf. I knew—I was sure, and no argument could have convinced me otherwise—that if I got on that bike, I would never be able to return to the world that until that moment had been mine. It would mean leaving the White Tower forever; it would mean kissing my parents goodbye and abandoning them to their fates, to their battles and their worries; and if one fine morning I happened to hear that they had been caught and executed, I would shake my head with something akin to indifference, as if to say, "You made the bed, now lie in it." All I had to do was lift my leg and sit on that horizontal crossbar for my guilty conscience and my doubts to disappear once and for all. It wasn't that the boy represented a fairy-tale prince to me but rather more of a Hermes, a conductor of souls, whose role was the exact inverse: He would tear Niki away from the land of the dead to return her to the world of the living. I was yearning, I was burning to put my arms around him, to hold him tight, to do nothing but become one with him.

And then the boy made the wrong move. "Jump on, will you?" he repeated impatiently, and grasped my shoulders as if to pull me on. In a flash, the spell was broken, without my really understanding why. His touch might well have been what I needed to banish my final doubts and make me go with him. Yet it had the exact opposite effect. Startled, I shoved him back with all my strength and took to my heels. Dashing through the back streets of Nea Smyrni, I arrived home panting, my heart in my throat.

I was in a state of unspeakable agitation. My parents, thankfully, didn't notice anything: My mother, as usual, was absorbed in her chores, and my father was bowed over an algebra textbook preparing his lesson for the next day. I grabbed a poetry anthology and ran to cloister myself in the White Tower latrines. I searched for the Cavafy poem about the "great Yes or the great No."[78] Sobbing, I read it over and over again. Then I tore out the page, ripped it up into tiny pieces, threw it in the hole, and pissed on it.

VII

MARCH 5, 1953: Iosif Vissarionovich Dzhugashvili, also known as Stalin, died in his country house on the outskirts of Moscow. For hundreds of millions of people around the world, it was as if the sun had suddenly gone out. First, throughout the rest of the world, and then, after a big delay, in the Soviet Union.

TASS probably leaked the news, which was then disseminated in all the Western capitals. We first heard it on the BBC on the evening of March 5. Immediately, my father

---

[78] C. P. Cavafy, "Che Fece...Il Gran Rifiuto."

turned the dial to Radio Moscow. They were broadcasting sports bulletins and music. We didn't know what to say.

"It must be a lie!" my mother concluded. "It reeks of dirty capitalist propaganda!"

Her supposition did not strike me as irrational. How else might one explain that the entire world was in the know except for Stalin's own people? Hour by hour, Radio Moscow's programming was becoming more somber. Oratorios gave way to requiems, priming their audience the way one primes a child. After barricading ourselves in our house, like we did every night, we positioned ourselves around the radio set. Sleep was out of the question.

At two in the morning, the national anthem resounded: *Soyuz nerushimy respublik svobodnykh*: "United forever in friendship and labor, our mighty republics will ever endure." Instinctively, the three of us rose and stood to attention—I no longer remember whether we turned to face the northeast like Muslims looking toward Mecca during prayer. The hymn lasted six minutes. The lyrics referring to Stalin were reprised four times. An agonizing silence of two minutes followed. Then the voice of Yuri Levitan, the legendary broadcaster who announced all the Soviet victories, never the losses, during the Second World War, rang out: "The Central Committee of the Communist Party, the Council of Ministers, and the Presidium of the Supreme Soviet of the USSR announce with profound sorrow to the Party and all working people of the Soviet Union that on March 5, at 9:50 p.m., Stalin died. The heart of Lenin's comrade in arms and the inspired continuer of his great cause has stopped beating. Our enlightened leader, the global proletariat's guiding torch, is, from this moment on, a part of eternity."

Papa was translating for Mama word by word. I, however, was delighted by the fact that I could understand everything—my Russian-language classes had paid off. As soon as the announcement concluded in affirming that the Party, more united than ever, was "as strong as steel and mobilizing all its forces in the great cause of building communism," the Armaos family became lost in their own thoughts.

"It had to happen one day," Antonis said, breaking the silence.

"Why could he not have lived at least until we won in Korea?" Anna said and moaned.

"What matters is that we have the atomic bomb!" Antonis observed. "The imperialists will not dare to yank our chain!"

"What now?" I asked in alarm.

"Now, it's bedtime," my father replied. "Tomorrow, there will be new battles to fight."

Tomorrow, there will be new battles to fight! If there was a sentence that truly rose to the pinnacle of absurdity in that house, it surely was that one. What battles? What tomorrow?

MY PARENTS, ALMOST immured as they were in the White Tower, deprived of even the most minimal change of scenery—the shopping trips and meetings with Aunt

Markella that allowed me to fill my lungs with fresh air—had to make do with watching the days pass by, or rather trample right over them. I don't mean to minimize the sufferings of those who were tortured on Makronissos, the struggles of those trying to put down roots in Tashkent[79] and the other socialist countries they had adopted as homelands, or those who lay down each night in their cells in the Averoff and Syngrou Prisons, not knowing if they would be woken by the sun or the voice of the warden crying, "Get ready. It's time for some fresh air!"—in other words, for their execution. I'm not claiming that my parents' lot was worse than theirs, but I am saying that theirs was the most absurd.

Convicts facing ironclad death sentences, the most hardened of criminals, even they can wrest a sense of purpose from the passing moments of their lives. They can demand a retrial, apply for a pardon, battle their remorse and their demons, hatch plans for a jailbreak, or spit blood to survive and prevail over their prison mates. If not criminals but political prisoners, enemies of the regime, revolutionaries, then we are dealing with people who endure the worst by keeping a fast hold of their ideals; who see themselves on the vanguard of the struggle, as catalysts, as symbols; who stride toward the place of martyrdom with head held high; who smile into the barrel of a gun as if at a camera, the camera

---

[79] Twelve thousand combatants of the Democratic Army were relocated to Tashkent in Uzbekistan in 1949, at the end of the Civil War. This was the largest community of Greek political exiles stationed in various Soviet-bloc countries.

of eternity. They wink their eye at future generations. They know that a comrade-poet will dip a pen in their freshly spilled blood to compose a heroic elegy in their honor that one day will be taught at school.

My parents, too, of course, were counting on the future. "History will vindicate us," my father continued to declare, but my mother, without disputing the fact, now added "some day": "History will vindicate us." "Some day." For the time being, History and the world at large could not have cared less about us. The name Antonis Armaos seemed to have been wiped clean from the memories as much of his former comrades as of his former persecutors. Not one newspaper, not one radio program made any reference to the man who during the 1930s had been the parliamentary delegate and second-in-command of the Party. And why would they? These were cobwebby stories of the past. My father maintained that if he were arrested, before his execution, he would first be defamed and Ilias Balassis's depravities pinned on him. I had no reason to doubt him. But no one seemed to be especially bothered by the fact that he had evaded capture for so long. In any case, his persecutors had an abundance of men at their disposal of whom to make either martyrs, like Beloyannis, or scapegoats, like Ploumbides.

How much longer could we hold on at the White Tower? My father had it all figured out. "If we manage everything prudently, the gold sovereigns will see us through August 1966, and if we tighten our belts a tad more, until 1970. Of course, this all depends on the rate of inflation, too…" In 1970, he would be almost sixty-five; my mother, sixty; and I, thirty-two. We would have spent a total of twenty consecutive years underground. How many had Jonah spent in the belly of the whale?

"We can't wait until the cows come home to live our lives and be happy. We've got to try, here and now!" my father would exhort, digging with forced enthusiasm the little vegetable patch the Maestro had allowed him to grow behind our house. One end contained our coop, the two hens and a rooster that kept us supplied with fresh eggs. As I did my homework, I would hear my mother mollycoddling them with a tenderness that she had never shown to me. "Come, my lovely! Come, my lady! And you too, my big pasha!" she would say to the rooster. "Come and grow big and strong! I've got some top-quality corn for you!" And when one day Yolanda laid a double-yolked egg, my mother, beside herself with joy, paraded the cracked the egg in a bowl around the White Tower so that the neighbors might admire it.

No, my parents had not lost their marbles. They knew that they were floundering at the bottom of a muddy well and were deliberately grasping at the slenderest branch growing along its walls so as not to go under. The fact that my father had spent eighteen months in translating Victor Hugo's *Les Misérables*, and that my mother had dedicated an equal amount of time to copying it out calligraphically, using a fountain pen and violet ink, into seven hardbound notebooks—her premature cataracts had worsened, and she needed the light of three lamps at her side to see anything—was not to assuage unfulfilled ambitions, literary for one and artistic for the other. The fact that they made love almost every night, even though physical desire had never been the foundation of their relationship, was because it served to remind them that they were still alive, still full of fight.

I never heard them, not even once. As a couple, they lived and breathed the puritanism of the communist ethos. First, they would make sure that I was asleep, then they would turn the key to their bedroom door, douse the lights, and turn and clasp each other silently, without haste, without passion, and almost without any variation. Anna would squeeze Antonis tight inside her, while he kissed her neck, her nipples, his hand descending the length of her spine, vertebra by vertebra, to her thighs. Her orgasm was a mute spasm. She would then climb off him and take him in her mouth, knowing exactly how to use her tongue to make him come. Finally, she would curl up in his arms. His breath now turning into a snore, far from irritating her, would soothe her to sleep. Stroking the graying hairs on his chest, she slipped softly into sleep. My parents' lovemaking was not that of a married couple, it was that of castaways, clinging to each other for dear life, the way a drowning man clings to a lifeline.

THERE WERE ONLY two things they truly dreaded: accidental pregnancy and an illness that called for professional medical care.

On New Year's Day 1953, my father, knife in hand, was preparing to cut into the vasilopita.[80] One piece for the people's struggle and another for the Soviet Union; then one piece each for the three of us, Aunt Markella, and the rest of the family whom we hadn't seen in years: Grandmother Sevasti; Uncle Petros; Aunt Fani and Uncle Savvas Bogdanos and their progeny, my cousin Toula, a round, red-haired little girl based on the photograph Markella had given me; and, bringing up the rear, my mother's relatives, whom I barely knew: Grandmother Elpida, Aunt Theone, Aunt Alcmene and her husband the lawyer in Kalamata and their sons. ("Why do they all get a piece?" I'd wonder. "If they get the coin, are we going to mail it to them?") At that moment, as my father prepared to slice into the cake, he felt an invisible blade slice into his entrails, plunging deep and searing right through him. Turning livid, cold sweat springing to his temples, he crumpled onto the table. We grabbed him under the armpits and dragged him to bed.

"It's a colic. It's a renal colic!" he moaned, issuing the correct diagnosis.

"Run to the pharmacy!" my mother ordered as she made him some compresses.

The pharmacist, who had been ogling me for quite some time for my beautiful eyes (although more likely for

---

[80] A sweet, challah-like cake with a coin baked in it used to celebrate the beginning of the new year. It is customary to cut the cake and dedicate the first few pieces to the Greek Orthodox God and saints, and then each subsequent piece to family members. Whoever gets the piece with the coin is said to have a blessed year.

my beautiful cleavage) agreed to give me an opiate pain-killer—morphine?—in injectable form.

"I would come with you, but I can't leave the shop," he said to excuse himself, and under the pretense of showing me how to inject the needle, he made me take off my jacket and pull up my shirt.

"Soak the cotton in alcohol to disinfect the skin...like this..." he explained, his mouth watering as his hand stroked my stomach.

I gritted my teeth so as not to bite him. A few years later, our paths would cross by chance on Akadimias Street; he claimed then that he had worked out who my father was and actually had the gall to say that he had "risked all for our sake out of a sense of democratic duty."

When I returned home, I found my father burning up with fever, a handkerchief clenched between his teeth to stifle his screams.

"When I can't take it any longer, Niki must go find a taxi. Throw me in there by myself and tell him to go straight to Evangelismos Hospital," he urged us. "Ask Markella to get Mavrides to find you a new hiding place. Don't even think of setting foot either in the hospital or the courthouse!"

The injections only brought him temporary relief. During the forty-eight hours that followed, my father moaned and raved. The fever gave him hallucinations, especially at night when I kept watch by his side. This is how one time I heard him rail against his accusers at a court-martial: "Go ahead, kill me, honorable collaborators and good sirs of the Security Battalions! My ideals, however, are immortal!"

Another time, I heard him delivering an important speech at a KKE congress on "conditions necessary for the passage to socialism." The imaginary audience must have given him a standing ovation, for obviously flattered, he kept saying at every opportunity "Thank you, comrades!" while calling for silence with flourishes of his hands. Finally, I heard him conversing behind closed doors with Stalin, trying to convince him that Nikos had betrayed the people's movement. "And who will replace him?" in obvious perplexity, my father kept repeating Dzhugashvili's question. Before daring to point to the fact that he was the right person for the job, he sank back into a stupor. When he woke up the following day at around noon, he found a stone as big as a dogtooth in between the damp bedclothes.

"If Papa had turned himself in, I would immediately have turned myself in, too!" I decreed after the fact. "And too bad if they send me to an orphanage, a juvenile detention center, Makronissos, or who knows where." I held back from sharing with my parents this inconsequential resolution. Why spoil their joy at the fact that the stone had been expelled in my father's urine and that our confinement at the White Tower could now continue uninterrupted.

I RETURN TO the 5th, or probably the 6th of March 1953. March 6 in the evening, as Stalin's corpse is being transferred to the House of the Unions to lie in state and hundreds of Muscovites are trampling each other in the attempt to get nearer, the Armaos family is attending to their regular domestic activities: My mother is darning socks; my father is doing the crossword in the newspaper while slowly sipping his well-sweetened coffee (he uses a very sharp pencil to make it easier to erase before he passes it to my mother for her turn); and as for me, I am reviewing for the next day's lessons. We hear a timid knock on the half-open door and looking up we see Mr. Chaïtides on the doorstep, the waiter who lives in the neighboring house with his wife and their two sons. A full five years at the White Tower and all we've ever shared with the Chaïtideses are the customary salutations: "Good morning" and "Good night."

"Good evening…may I come in?" he says timidly.

"Why are you asking?" My father smiles warmly. "Anna make a coffee for Vlassis. How do you take it, neighbor?"

"Don't bother! A glass of water will do. May I have a private word with you, just the two of us?"

These words seem to put a bug in my father's ear, because he responds: "I have nothing to hide from my family, so let's just stay here!"

Chaïtides appears to hesitate for a moment, but finally perches on the very edge of a chair, brings the glass of water to his lips, stares at the walls and the furniture while avoiding our eyes, and swallows dryly. He's trying to buy time and muster some courage before jumping into the fray.

"What's new, Vlassis?" my mother asks.

With that, his forehead furrows, his eyebrows knit, and he finally comes out with the words that must have been rehearsed over and over again: "I know who you are. Your name is not Telis Dimitriades. You are Antonis Armaos, a communist commander. And those two are your wife and daughter!"

My father smiles as if he doesn't have a worry in the world, almost with sweetness.

"Where did all this come from, Vlassis?" he asks, as if addressing a child.

"One of my relatives who was visiting. He saw you and recognized you!"

"And he's a hundred percent sure, this relative of yours? Bet his boots on it, would he? We live in troubled times, Vlassis. Even those closest to us—sometimes our very own brothers—might be taking us for a ride, and instead of going for gold, we end up in a whole heap of trouble. You are aware that defamation is a most serious crime, aren't you?"

Antonis's composure is staggering, and it partly soothes my distress. He suddenly shoots up in my estimation. That's my father, my hero!

"Cut the crap!" Chaïtides exclaims angrily. "I may not know much about politics—I have always kept my nose out of other people's business because I have work to do and mouths to feed—but this relative is a former police officer. Under Metaxas, he was the one who personally carted you off to the clink! As well as that little lady over there," he adds, pointing to my mother.

"So why didn't he make straight to the first police station?"

"I stopped him!"

"You? That was a mistake, a big mistake, dear Vlassis! The invasive weed of communism ought to be extirpated wherever it crops up!"

"Are you having me on?"

"Call them and have them arrest me then. Go on!" my father says, changing his tone.

"I'm no fink!" Vlassis parries. "And if you really want to know, I haven't even told my wife. I respect you, as the holy Virgin is my witness, I think you're all right. Even though you never get off your high horse here at the White Tower. Whenever I hear gossip running wild behind your back—your neighbors weren't born yesterday, you know, they know there's something fishy going on, but hey, the Maestro's got your back, right?—whenever I hear them peg you as either a smuggler or fugitive, I speak up. 'Shut up! Mr. Pantelis is a true gentleman,' I say."

"I owe you a debt of gratitude," my father says with a sneer.

"Debts are meant to be paid off," Vlassis replies in all seriousness.

"Spit it out, what do you want?"

Chaïtides finally sits back in his chair, sensing that things are falling into place and the hard part is over.

"You know, Mr. Antonis—" he says, assuming his usual unctuous airs.

"Don't ever call me Antonis again! Pantelis is my name!" my father cuts him off.

"You know, Mr. Pantelis, we too are poor, simple working stiffs. After the Turks sent us packing from Samsun in 1922, that was it for us. We've been living from hand to mouth. Have you seen my wife's hands, what all the years of dishwashing have done to them? Or her legs covered in varicose veins? Not that mine are any better. As for my boys, what have I been able to offer them besides a plate of food? They are strong lads, you'll say, they'll find their way. But easier said than done, no? The poor never get their day in the sun!"

I get the sense that he is capable of whining on like this until nightfall.

"Come on, out with it! What is it you want?" my father asks.

Vlassis heaves a deep sigh. "I sweat blood to send my eldest to Sivitanidios[81] after he left the army. He always liked tinkering with things. Anything handy—an alarm clock, a moped, he'll take it apart and put it back together again, bing, bang, boom. He's finishing his training as a car mechanic this year."

"Well done! And he can hold his own?"

"He's the best of the best, and that's not saying anything. But what's the point? What is his future? Working his fingers to the bone for some big shot? Getting his hands dirty only to end up with lungs rotten and body broken at the age of forty? And all for chicken feed? Unless he leaves for abroad, of course."

---

[81] The public arts and crafts school in Athens.

"You're the nationalist, Vlassis. Run to your delegate and ask him to find him a position somewhere." My father smiles ironically.

"We all know how these delegates work. If you don't come with a dozen votes in tow, you'll have your work cut out to get even a hospital bed. But you, Mr. Antonis . . . Sorry! Mr. Pantelis, you are a superior person, with ideals and means."

"Means? What are you talking about?"

"Good wine needs no bush!"

"In a nutshell, then, you're asking me set up your sonnyboy in his own garage?"

"How did you know?"

"Yes, I'll set him up and then off you go straight to the police to turn me in and you end up sitting pretty with the entire business. How much of a fool do you take me for?"

"I don't mean for you to lend us the entire sum all at once." Chaïtides changes tack. "There's a body shop for rent nearby, on Amfitheas Avenue. It's a great little business; it's doing well, and the owner is retiring."

"How much is the rent?"

"From what I know, he's asking for ten sovereigns a month. I can get him down to six."

"I see you came to me with *i*'s dotted and *t*'s crossed on your plan, Vlassis."

"We would share the profit, it goes without saying—"

"Oh, yes, share the profit, my foot! Three sovereigns— you'll get him down to three. You won't get another cent out of me. Three sovereigns, not for the rent but for your silence."

"Silence about what? I have already forgotten!" Chaïtides replies, in an attempt at levity that falls completely flat.

"And I warn you, Vlassis, if anything happens to me or my family, if so much as a hair on our heads is harmed, I will hold you personally responsible. Remember that we communists—'Bulgarians' and 'throat-cutters' as they like to call us—don't mess around when it comes to settling scores. We'll set fire to the garage with your precious son inside, and you'll be hard-pressed to find anything standing."

And so it came to pass that instead of sending a garland in Stalin's memory, and in addition to our contributions to the glitter and gold of Argyroula's lifestyle, we ended up forking out for Sakis Chaïtides's grease and motor oil. Thinking about it from this vantage point, it strikes me as truly absurd: Deep in hiding, my father was playing the role of the rich "American uncle." Those who did not believe his stories—who either were aware of the truth or had good reason to suspect it—were the ones to either extort him or bleed him white as if he truly were an American uncle.

VIII

THE TWO YEARS that followed were the grayest of my life. As bubbly and vivacious as I had been at the beginning of my adolescence, so I became apathetic toward its end. Perhaps a specialist would have diagnosed depression. I certainly exhibited many of its symptoms. I usually spent my spare time flat on my back with a book in hand, which would take me months to get through. I had cut off all relations with children my age at the White Tower. I no longer took any joy in my shopping trips, not even as a change of scene. They had become yet another tedious chore.

To all appearances, however, I was fine. Fine, in terms of the way my parents understood the word: I continued to study my lessons with unflagging zeal, got top marks in all my subjects, and pretended to believe that one day I would study at the university in Moscow. I took equally good care of my physical health and hygiene (a cold shower three times a week; exercises every morning and evening: stretching, extensions, deep inhalations and exhalations under my father's supervision). But I had stopped plucking my brows and no longer had any desire to varnish my nails (I had done so once at the age of fourteen, and my mother had almost bitten my head off). Beauty and the ability to please were the least of my worries.

IN THAT ENTIRE period of time, I recall only one moment of joy. A moment of joy that was followed by the deepest sorrow.

In early February 1954, Aunt Markella picked me up at our usual meeting place on Syngrou Avenue. As soon as I stepped into the car, I knew that something truly marvelous had happened: She was beaming from ear to ear. We ended up, as always, at the little café in Kavouri. First, she gave me my birthday gift, a mohair pullover ("You'll be all the rage in that!" "Where? At the White Tower?" I wanted to say, but bit my tongue, as usual). Then, she beat about the bush a little before announcing the great tidings: "I'm going to have a baby!" Overjoyed, we fell into each other's arms. At that moment, a song from the radio rang out through the café: *Let your hair down, loose and wild.*[82]

"I no longer thought I had a hope of getting pregnant. Despite what I say to everyone, I was not born in 1921—it's actually 1916. In December I'll be thirty-eight. With Lyssandros things have been going downhill and fast. But now our love has caught a second wind. At the beginning of March, his divorce will be finalized, and on the very next day, he's taking me straight to church."

I didn't even know that Lyssandros Mavrides was married. Suddenly I had to reckon with the image of my aunt as an adulteress like Zola's Nana, both a sinner and a romantic at the same time.

"I'm going to have to leave the theater, of course. But in any case, I was growing tired of it."

"May I tell my parents?"

"Do as you think best."

---

[82] "Let Your Hair Down" is a song by Fotis Polymeris released in 1950. Polymeris was considered one of the most successful singers and composers of early Greek popular music.

I could not hold my tongue. Contrary to my expectations, they betrayed only a tepid enthusiasm, which angered me. Later in my life, I realized that their years in hiding had deprived them of the capacity to truly feel. Is the fish confined to the aquarium capable of rejoicing in the delights of the sea?

The next time we met, Markella was wearing black. "I lost the baby," she said bluntly. We drove twice around the block. I didn't know what to say to console her, and she too didn't say another word but kept driving, lost in her thoughts. She handed me the envelope with the cash for the month and dropped me off on the sidewalk.

On my way home, I sobbed inconsolably. "Nothing good ever happens to us," I was thinking. "There is no hope. Whenever it looks like life might be smiling at us, it is only because it is getting ready to jeer as it slaps us in the face." I felt such bitterness, such defeat that I contemplated suicide. I thought of throwing myself under the tram, like a lovelorn little maidservant had done two weeks earlier. The story had shaken all of Greece: Her enlarged photograph had appeared in all the newspapers, and the writer Spyros Melas had declared the tragedy the inspiration for one of his plays. Only the thought of my grandmother (or at least that's what I made myself think) kept me from carrying it out. How could I do that to her? How could I deal her such a bitter blow? My grandmother, my beloved grandmother! The only time I had ever felt truly free of fear and trouble was at her side, nowhere else. I had not seen her since 1948.

I resolved to thumb my nose at the demonic forces conspiring to keep us apart. Abruptly, I turned back onto Syngrou Avenue, hailed a taxi, and asked the driver to take me straight to our old building in Pangrati, where she still lived with Aunt Markella.

Everything was exactly as I remembered it, even the mortar hole in the wall next to the glass of the front door—a memento from the Dekemvriana. I dashed past the doorman as if possessed, and heart thrumming in my ears, I took the elevator—second floor, third floor... I rang the bell. Someone turned down the volume on the radio, and then I heard the distinctive flap-flap of her shuffling slippers approaching.

"Who is it?" she asked. At my "It's Niki!" there was a frantic scramble of movement—the safety chain was almost torn out of its settings. I practically jumped when I saw her before me: It was as if she was a compressed, miniature version of the Grandmother Sevasti I used to know. Had I gained three feet in height? Or had she shrunk one, while I gained two? In any case, instead of huddling in her arms, I was the one who ended up wrapping her in mine. Her hair had gone completely white and her face was covered in wrinkles, but her smell, that smell of my early childhood, was exactly the same and it soothed me, softened my pain.

Eyes streaming with tears, she clasped me tight, both hands patting my back, but she suddenly drew back in alarm.

"What happened? Have they been arrested?"

"No, Granny. I just ran off to come and find you."

She made the sign of the cross over both of us and led me to the kitchen—she spent most of her time there, having relinquished the parlor to her daughter and her daughter's friends—where she scrambled some eggs with pastourma for me. Then she got up and retrieved from her bedroom all the linens that over the years she had embroidered for my dowry: multitudes of birds and flowers on pillowcases, hand towels, slips.

"Look at you, my love, grown so tall, a veritable Amazon! I'm going to have to take all these out and lengthen them some, too. Boy, oh, boy, you've got your granny up to her ears!" She was beaming.

"May I stay here tonight, Granny?" I asked timidly. She swallowed the "yes" that had sprung to her lips, seized by misgivings: "What about your parents? They'll go crazy with worry! God forbid!"

"We could ask Aunt Markella to let them know—"

"Markella won't be back until late. She's still wasting her time with that good-for-nothing."

"I can't bear it anymore at the White Tower, Grandma."

"Be strong, my dear. Time brings all things to pass."

"But I can't bear it."

"It will come to an end one day. You'll see, mark my words!"

She knew she would give in if I continued to pester her, so she hastened to send me on my way, arms filled with three bags of treats.

"My parents will hit the ceiling when they find out that I came to see you!"

"Oh, they'll get over it!" Making the sign of the cross over me one more time, she practically pushed me to the door.

This is the way of devotion: It loosens the knot around your neck, just enough so that it doesn't hurt; occasionally, with time, it may even completely undo it. But only love can cut through it in one blow.

IX

ALMOST A YEAR later, in early 1955, Lyssandros Mavrides appeared out of the blue at the White Tower. He did not venture as far as the mud-brick houses. It was not a preelection period, so he was not out fishing for votes. He installed himself comfortably in the Maestro's parlor, and the latter sent Argyroula to call my father.

"What a pleasure to see you, Mr. Delegate, sir!" Mavrides declared, as he stood to welcome Armaos. The Maestro turned every color of the rainbow. He knew that he had been bleeding a person of influence all these years, but a parliamentary delegate? It hadn't even occurred to him. Moreover, there was Mavrides, a delegate himself, former undersecretary of transportation, a centrist, admittedly, but one who was a regular guest of Queen Frederica's, addressing him with such deference!

"May I offer you a cognac? A vermouth? My ward could pop into the patisserie or the chophouse for a little something…"

"It's eleven o'clock in the morning. A couple of coffees will do. Then, make yourself scarce." Lyssandros sent him packing.

"We have a lot to talk about," he began, turning to Antonis, who thought that an apology was forthcoming for the churlish treatment of Markella, left high and dry by Lyssandros after the miscarriage. But Mavrides didn't even utter her name.

"I'm the bearer of good news!" he announced, as he pulled a typewritten paper from his briefcase and held it out to Antonis. My father donned his glasses and read out loud: *All persons guilty of acts of subversion or of a criminal nature, conducted individually, as a group, or in any manner whatsoever, who shall appear of their own accord and surrender unarmed to the authorities, shall benefit from the advantages enumerated in article such and such, paragraph such and such and such and such pertaining to the adjudication of aforementioned offenses.*

"What does this mean?" he asked suspiciously.

"It's a bill for a new law. A clemency program!" Lyssandros exclaimed triumphantly. "It means that as soon as parliament votes to ratify it, you may, as of the following day, leave this absurd quasi-captivity that has strangely and unjustifiably lasted so long—no thanks to the guerrilla war,[83] of course! You must voluntarily report to a police

---

[83] This term was used by the government and political conservatives to delegitimize the partisans and portray them as the opposite of an organized army. The term "civil war" was not used until later.

station and after some brief, pro forma administrative nuisance, you will finally be free! Without a trial or other proceedings. The past is forgotten, and you get a new start!"

"As long as I renounce communism, of course—"

"You're not going to be asked to renounce anything, absolutely anything! Do you truly take us for such petty idiots as to hope that a man of your caliber will bow his head and renounce his convictions? We know very well that you won't flinch."

"And what happened? You all suddenly decided to play nice?"

Lyssandros Mavrides, more so than my father, was experiencing their meeting as a historic moment. He was delighted to be representing, in the Maestro's parlor, an enlightened bourgeois politics.

"Listen, Mr. Armaos. The fact that we crushed the rebels in Grammos and Vitsi and kept Greece in the free world does not mean that we do not acknowledge the presence and accomplishments of the left. What do you think? That we aim to wipe you all out and leave no one standing? We see, all too clearly, that to continue your persecution would only make a hero of you! Let me speak frankly, Mr. Armaos: I prefer a thousand times over to share the parliamentary backbenches with someone like you, than with former collaborators and Metaxas's lackeys, utter crooks who have tried to rehabilitate their image by joining the war against the rebels."

"You nationalists are the ones who covered for them," my father said.

"Fanaticism is nonpartisan. There's no shortage of idiots, in my camp as much as in yours."

"So why the need for 'certificates of social conscience'[84]? And what about exile, why not abolish it?"

"I just answered that."

"There's also the EDA[85] party. Despite all the hurdles you've thrown their way, they haven't given up the fight."

"Unfortunately, the EDA is, on the whole, an instrument of the KKE, a mouthpiece for Moscow. Our country is crying out for people like Armaos! We urgently need you back on the front lines!"

"Either my near brother-in-law is putting me on, or he is trying to entrap me," Antonis thought. "What's so special about Armaos?" he asked. "He's a working man, a communist militant, a devotee of Marxism-Leninism."

"In a Western democracy, one should not be hounded for one's ideas. In Greece we must make progress in this direction." Mavrides then added, becoming even more complimentary, "And Antonis Armaos rose to the leadership of the labor movement on his own sweat and merit. He was not delivered ready-made from the workshops of

---

[84] These certificates attested to the fact that the signatory was neither a communist nor a communist sympathizer and therefore upheld the values of patriotism. Possession of such a certificate was necessary for access to a number of important social benefits, including employment in the public sector, enrollment in a university, and conferral of a driver's license. Along with the declaration of repentance, the certificate was one of anti-communism's ideological weapons.

[85] United Democratic Left founded in 1951 by center-left and leftist politicians.

the Third International. Most important, he played no part in the fratricide of the Civil War. By expelling him, by leaving him on the sidelines, his party ended up protecting him."

"I participated in the Middle East uprising."

"And that, too, was rejected by the KKE. Whether you like it or not, from this point on, you are an independent political figure of the left. You are beholden to no one. Above all not to the Party leader, who, despite his criminal history, continues to call the shots from the Soviet Union and decimate lives. But don't worry, the star of the infamous Nikos is on the wane!"

This prediction of Nikos's fall, as far-fetched as it may have sounded barely a year before it was realized, made my father smile. The ice began to crack.

"I trust the clemency measures will apply to all?"

"It goes without saying! We want all the partisans who were indicted and are at large to come down from the mountains and tend to their lands! We have faith in the concept of national reconciliation!"

"You speak as if you are in power, Mr. Mavrides. But from what I know, you are a member of the centrist opposition party."

"You're splitting hairs, Mr. Armaos. The necessity for clemency measures has mobilized delegates of all factions."

"Personally, I very much doubt that I will return to politics. Certainly not before my party reinstates me."

"Personally, you may do as you like."

"What will happen with the Ilias Balassis file? Will the crimes he committed under the Occupation come to haunt me?"

"Leave that to me. I swear to you on the memory of my unborn child" (and this was the only indirect reference to Markella) "I swear to you that you will not be held responsible for someone else's actions."

"If Lyssandros can now clear me of this little 'gift' of Balassis's, why couldn't he do it seven years ago?" my father wondered, suddenly beset with suspicion. But there was no need to lose any sleep over the issue, it was blatantly obvious. In 1948, Armaos was not indispensable to the regime, there was nothing to be gained from him, not even from his trial and execution. He had therefore been wrapped in mothballs and put on the shelf in the White Tower. In 1955, however, Armaos had become a valuable ace in the hole. He represented a moderate, pacifist left that any nationalist with an ounce of common sense wished to see entering the political arena, even if only in a tightly circumscribed corner, to vouch for the system. "That's it! That's why they need me. To vouch for the system!" Antonis mused, his revolutionary fervor fully aroused. "Very well, and so now what? Dig my heels in and stay underground until I'm a doddering old man, or get out of here and foil their plans?"

How exactly he would foil their plans, he would see to later. The prospect of freedom was so exhilarating that he could barely refrain from bursting into laughter, into tears, into song. There was a skip to his step as he made his way back to the house from the Maestro's. When he caught a glimpse of his double chin in the latrine mirror, he was, for the first time, distressed by his corpulence. "I'm going to have to lose all this excess baggage before going back out into the world!" he told himself.

X

HE WAS IN no hurry to break the news to us, my mother and me, and was even contemplating keeping it under wraps until the very end so as not to raise our hopes needlessly in case the clemency measures were withdrawn. But we would have caught wind because of our neighbors' change in behavior.

The Maestro kept nothing from Argyroula, and she, in turn, was someone who could not hold her tongue when it came to other people's business. (When it came to her own personal matters, on the other hand, she was as silent as the grave.) In the span of a few days, the news had spread like wildfire through the White Tower, and with all manner of embellishment, each one more fanciful than the next, fanned by the grapevine. Suddenly everyone knew that my father was an important figure who had been holed up among them all these years, most likely with the blessing of the authorities. How else could the tête-à-tête with a dignitary like Lyssandros Mavrides be explained? It was therefore impossible that he was a leftist, at least this is how the simple folk there reckoned it. So what was he? A Cypriot who was soon to throw himself into the struggle for independence? A northern Epirote, awaiting the signal to invade Albania and liberate the Greek villages from the yoke of Enver Hoxha?[86] Yet he did not at all have the look of a commando leader. Perhaps he had been a minister under the Occupation? An American spy? A philosopher or astrologer, secret adviser to the palace? Flights of fancy were running rampant. The funny thing is that Chaïtides, the only one who knew the truth, did not say a word.

No matter who this Pantelis Dimitriades character really was, he and his family, from one day to the next, suddenly acquired an unexpected prestige in their eyes. They began to address us all, even me, much more formally, and to offer us their gifts and services, to show themselves in their best light so that we would remember them when we came into our kingdom.[87] Unlike my parents, who were irritated by all this (as they were every time their fellow men revealed their pettiness and inadequacy to socialist ideals), I was delighted. To suddenly be admired as a princess, the princess Koula, was, if nothing else, truly funny.

Our kingdom was slow in coming. Spring passed, then summer, and the clemency measures had not yet been ratified. There were occasional references in the newspapers, but

---

[86] Northern Epirus, a region populated by an important Greek minority, was annexed by Albania after the fall of the Ottoman Empire.

[87] A reference to Luke's account of the crucifixion, where the penitent thief says: "Jesus, remember me, when you come into your kingdom."

they were vague and inconsistent. The issue of such critical importance to us kept getting eclipsed by other events: the Cypriot problem, the pogroms in Constantinople against the Greek minority, Prime Minister Papagos's rapidly deteriorating health. The wait had worn our nerves raw.

"Perhaps you ought to contact Mavrides and find out what is happening?" my mother would suggest every so often.

"Have you gone mad, Anna!" my father would burst out, almost angrily.

Even within the White Tower itself, we had gradually taken the backseat. An infinitely more thrilling event, a true scandal, had left everyone dumbfounded: the impending nuptials of Argyro Mazza—Argyroula, the Maestro's lover!

ONE SWELTERING AFTERNOON—IT must have been during one of those mid-August heat waves—the Maestro, freshly shaven and in a suit, came down all the way to our mud-brick houses and called us to an urgent assembly. We all poured out into the yard and lined up in front of him, every single one of us almost standing to attention. Aristomenis Karassoulas was the last to appear at the door to the latrine, his pajama pants crookedly buttoned and lightly stained with urine.

"I'll go throw on something more suitable," the tsarouchi-maker mumbled. After banishing his sister, and especially after taking his retirement, he had aged dramatically and was a ruin of his former self, perhaps even bordering on senility.

"Stay right there!" the Maestro said and stopped him. "We are all family here. There is nothing to be ashamed of." He then pointed to Mr. and Mrs. Attonis among the group and beckoned them to his side. They must have been in on it because Theodoros was wearing a starched white shirt and Sitsa was in her newest calico dress.

"We are all family here!" repeated the Maestro, without, of course, abandoning his airs of a great lord addressing his peons. "You should therefore be the first to hear the happy news: I am marrying my ward, Argyroula, to Dimitris, the eldest and most accomplished son of these good, honest people. Come here, Mitsos, so that I may kiss you!"

Mitsos, a great handsome hulk of a lad who in another time and another place could have easily had a career as a top model, emerged from his house in a visible state of shock, approached the Maestro, stooped, and kissed his hand. The latter smiled paternally and gave him his blessing. Then, he turned toward us once again.

"The ceremony will take place on September 18th, at the Church of Saint Fotini. I count on you all being there. Afterward, we'll have the party here, in the yard!"

At that very moment, only after the Maestro had already announced the engagement in her absence, Argyroula emerged from the back door of the big house. She was almost unrecognizable, prim and proper, eyes down, hair pulled back in a bun, and dressed in a simple little frock.

(How had she agreed to take part in this farce, she who did not deign to go to the grocer's without getting dolled up and decorated like a barrel organ?) She took her place to the right of her future husband. They did not kiss; they barely even glanced at each other. The Maestro had to take her hand and place it in Mitsos's.

We were all speechless. Argyroula—and there was absolutely no doubt about this—was not the Maestro's ward but his lover. Even the deafest among us had heard (or, more precisely, kept hearing almost every evening that summer) the moans and even occasional shrieks of pleasure emanating from their bedroom. And if they more or less kept up appearances at the White Tower during the day, at night when they were headed to a tavern or a bouzouki club, they seemed to want to flaunt it, radiant as they clung close to each other. They were not a couple bound by expediency, corroded by boredom, longing for the flame of passion. Despite their difference in age, they were well matched— I've said this before. For all that the Maestro was a great bastard, he was no less of a fully virile man with his large hands, square shoulders, and indomitable mustache. He filled both a room and his trousers.

The first version of the story that made the rounds of the White Tower was that Argyroula had fallen in love with Mitsos Attonis, and the Maestro, instead of ending up a cuckold or having the girl abandon him completely, had made a virtue of necessity and decided to accept his lot with gallantry and gala, to give her away in proper form, with a

priest and a best man. It made sense, as long as you didn't
know any of the three characters involved, especially Mitsos. Besides his parents' good looks, he had also inherited
their temperament in spades. Slow and somnolent of voice
and gesture, he was listless, with big bovine eyes. It was
completely outside the bounds of possibility that Mitsos had
even raised them to look at Argyroula, let alone gone on to
seduce her and claim her as his wife.

"Still waters run deep," some of our neighbors kept
repeating, unconvinced by their own words.

No one really knew what to believe. With the passing
of each day, it was becoming clearer and clearer that the
entire situation was pure smoke and mirrors. Argyroula
performed the responsibilities of a bride-to-be by spending
the afternoons with her betrothed's family, drinking coffee
or sipping on a taffy submarine[88] while seated on a chair at
the entrance to the mud-brick house. (The new couple was
going to move to the Maestro's house after the wedding.)
This spectacle broke my heart. Nothing could be more
tedious than keeping company with the Attonises. Theodoros smoked and gawped, head in the clouds. When not
wiping the noses of her younger brood, Sitsa was invariably
bowed over some handiwork. Mitsos would sit staring at his
wife-to-be in a besotted trance and, every once in a while,
would stroke her arm, as timidly and awkwardly as if it was

---

[88] A traditional Greek dessert consisting of a spoonful of usually mastic-
flavored taffy dunked in a glass of cold water.

his first time touching a woman. Argyroula looked like she was caught and suffocating in a painting (an allegory titled something like *Pulchritude and Purity*), a living, breathing being held captive among magnificent but one-dimensional and soulless figures.

Exactly two weeks before the wedding, the mystery deepened, or depending on one's point of view was finally cleared up. Overcome by sudden bouts of nausea, Argyroula revealed to her mother-in-law that she was pregnant. Mrs. Chaïtides overheard and wasted no time in singing it from the rooftops. In any case, the Attonises were not going to keep it a secret. With a smile of triumph, Mitsos accepted his neighbors' congratulations and good wishes: "To an easy delivery for your little one!" and all the rest.

The neighborhood gossips had a field day.

"There's no way that moron got her pregnant!"

"He's such an idiot, it wouldn't surprise me to learn that he believes you can make a baby with only a kiss on the cheek!"

"And his parents, they swallowed that story, too?"

"You must be joking! They're in on it! It suits them just fine to see their pride and joy married off so well! At least they won't have to worry about him. In case it hasn't occurred to you yet, our rents are going to be keeping Mitsos Attonis in food and drink from now on. And when, sooner or later, the Maestro kicks the bucket, he will inherit the White Tower!"

"He or Argyroula?"

"Same difference."

The heart of the matter, the critical question, was to what end the Maestro had hatched the entire preposterous scheme. The only convincing interpretation came out of the mouth of Mr. Psaltis, the fishmonger and opera aficionado, who until that point had always had the appearance of a rather naïve and romantic sort, the last person in the world one would have thought capable of plumbing the darkest recesses of the human soul. Appearances can be deceptive.

"The Maestro has an incredibly high opinion of himself," he explained. "He considers himself so powerful, peerless, and unique that he would never stoop to the common lot of family life, to the worries and responsibilities of a child to call him 'father' and monopolize his attention and love. The Maestro sees his life not among people but above them."

"Even kings have heirs!" his wife observed.

"Look at the tales of the ancient Greeks, which said everything there is to say and more on any given topic," Mr. Psaltis retorted sharply. "Kings either devour their children or are devoured by them. Kronos gobbled up all the offspring borne by Rhea. Oedipus, for his part, killed his father."

Believing my father to have the monopoly on education at the White Tower, I had no idea that Mr. Psaltis was so well-read.

"You're saying that the Maestro is a Kronos?"

"For all intents and purposes, yes. Think about it: This farce serves him well. In Mitsos Attonis he gains a stalwart errand boy in the guise of an adopted son. In the mean-time, Argyroula is there to take to bed whenever he fancies, and, mark my words, he will end up baptizing their baby while playing the part of the proud godfather. All things being equal, he may even reveal the truth to the child someday. The Maestro has it all planned out like clockwork!"

Mr. Psaltis's words literally made my stomach turn. I was thoroughly disgusted not only with the Maestro but with everyone else as well. Even with Argyroula, despite the compassion I felt for her.

"A case study in what bourgeois decadence does to people," my father declared in the dogmatic tone of the political instructor. Did the story not remind him of Adam Kremos's five thousand sovereigns?

"When are we finally getting out of here?" I rejoined, all aggression. "All I truly want is to get out of this place!"

"We'll be out before winter," he replied, more to appease me than from true conviction.

XI

THE CLEMENCY MEASURES were ratified and implemented on September 9. Lyssandros Mavrides triumphantly announced the news to my father by sending a telegram addressed for the last time to Mr. Pantelis Dimitriades, c/o the White Tower.

The time has come to reclaim your true name. Stop. Tomorrow report to 22nd Precinct Station in Nea Smyrni. Stop. The commissioner has been informed.

Holding the telegram in my hands, I read and reread it, hard-pressed not to cover it in kisses.

"So we'll be going together?" I exclaimed.

"No one is going!" my father said, leaving me dumbfounded.

He then explained to me the final directive of life underground: While still in hiding, one had to remain invisible and protect information of one's whereabouts at all costs; but once apprehended, and even more so if one were to turn oneself in, it was best to do so with as much pomp and circumstance, as much splash and dash as possible.

"Why?"

"Think about it, Niki. Do we trust the state, or the police for that matter? Who says that these famous clemency measures aren't a mousetrap, a way of luring indicted partisans out of hiding? Can anyone guarantee that if I 'appear of my own accord' at the station, I won't suddenly disappear into the night? What's to stop them from throwing me into a dungeon for as long as they like, without even submitting an official arrest record? Or to throw me out of a window and then claim that I committed suicide, riddled by the guilt of my treasonous actions?"

"What do we do, then?" I asked, horrified at the thought that we were going to ignore Mavrides's telegram and stay at the White Tower forever.

"Oh, we are going to turn ourselves in all right, but in front of as many people as possible! All of Nea Smyrna, indeed all of Athens, must know that Antonis Armaos has delivered himself of his own free will into the hands of the authorities. And all the better if the newspapers write about it. Publicity is our only shield."

With the telegram in hand, he headed to the Maestro's house. Twenty minutes later, he returned, a big smile on his face.

PREPARATIONS FOR ARGYROULA'S wedding lasted five days and five nights. Not only did we whitewash the entire yard and the mud-brick houses, not only did a tanker truck arrive to empty the cesspool (a truly unprecedented event), but a seamstress and her dedicated assistant were installed in our midst to dress all the women, old and young, or at least alter and update what they had on offer. She applied herself to the task with breathtaking zeal. The sewing machine had been placed outdoors, in front of the latrines and the shower, and was surrounded by a dozen or so rolls of fabric of every color and quality under the sun. She was truly a sight to behold, taking measurements, pinning fabric, sewing, chatting away, smoking, complimenting her customers, even predicting their fortunes from the grounds in their coffee cups—and all this at the same time!

For the first time in all our years at the White Tower, my father let loose the purse strings. He had two dresses made for us: for my mother, a loose-fitting, navy blue one (which, truth be told, looked more like a robe, if not a priest's cassock, but my mother refused anything fancier), and for me, a shorter, slinkier, cream-colored number with pink polka dots and a wide red belt nipping my waist. He even sent me off to buy pumps. But as soon as he saw me all decked out with my hair styled (it was the first time I put my hair up in a ponytail), his face puckered with displeasure.

"You look like one of those girls in the ads!" he said. "Throw something around your shoulders, please, a shawl or something. And could you manage not to have your brassiere jut out like that?"

He was going to wear the linen suit that he had brought back with him from Egypt in 1944. After following a strict diet for the last few months, he was back in fighting form.

The seamstress left us the night before the wedding. In the space occupied by the sewing machine, three spits were installed cheek by jowl to an improvised stage for the musicians. This wasn't going to be any old party—we were going to raise Cain! The Maestro was orchestrating it all and footing the bill besides. The Attonises simply watched on the sidelines, onlookers and strangers even to their own joy.

On September 18, everyone was up and ready before dawn. The men accompanied the groom to the barber, while the young women dressed the bride and decorated the wedding bed. The older women were busy making salads, peeling potatoes, boiling the sugar syrup for the baklava and kataïfi. A fleet of roasting pans traveled back and forth between the White Tower and the two neighborhood bakeries, leaving only to return piping hot and cooked to perfection.[89] A truck arrived from Spata and disgorged four big barrels of wine. "Goodness! How many people has he invited?" "Who hasn't he invited is the question!" The Maestro wandered among us, thumping backs and pinching cheeks, issuing directives, paying the suppliers. The day seemed to belong to him exclusively.

"Perhaps he'll change his mind and end up marrying Argyroula himself," Mrs. Psaltis kept saying to herself, in the hope that things would return to their proper order, even if only at the eleventh hour.

But it wasn't to be. The Maestro, with us in joyous procession trailing behind, led the bride to church and handed her over to Mitsos Attonis. All the way from the White Tower to Saint Fotini, my parents stared hungrily around, completely stupefied. It was the first time in seven and a half years that they were out in broad daylight, walking with their heads held high. They were impressed by the cars, whose numbers had grown appreciably, and the apartment blocks that had bloomed sporadically among the refugee shacks. A new world beckoned—was there a place for them?

Argyroula was more beautiful than ever, resplendent in her wedding dress, which incidentally had not come from

---

[89] Traditionally, large roasting trays were taken for cooking to local bakeries whose wood-burning ovens could more easily accommodate them.

the hands of a neighborhood seamstress but was instead
the pièce de résistance of a fashion house in Kolonaki and
had cost the Maestro a king's ransom. Nevertheless, more
than her beauty and her wedding dress, what I remember
most are her eyes: eyes that shone with a carnivorous glint,
the eyes of a wild cat raring to eviscerate her prey. Her eyes
shook me; they terrified me.

Now, when I look at her through the preternaturally
lucid eyes of the dead and I see her there, posing for photographs on the landing of the Church of Saint Fotini, bouquet
in hand, I know exactly what she feels. Since she had been
betrayed by the love of her life, since he had disposed of her
by marrying her off to that half-wit ("Either you marry an
Attonis or off you go to the gynecologist for an abortion!"
he had declared cynically, and she had chosen to keep the
child, hoping that the Maestro might come to his senses,
even if only at the eleventh hour), since she no longer had
any choice but to bow her head—suicide and melodrama
in general were not at all her style—she would wreak her
revenge in a traditionally feminine way: She would have
them both, the Maestro just as much as Mitsos, eating out
of her hand. With all the subterfuge and sweet nothings at
her disposal, she would gradually gain the upper hand in
the house. Without their realizing it, they would find themselves at her beck and call. She would lead them by the nose,
at times playing the role of the hypersensitive mother, at
others the temperamental lover. When the Maestro, horny
and hard up, would throw himself at her, she would turn on

her heel and leave him, pecker in hand, nine times out of ten, and before letting him take her on the tenth, she would really make him sweat for it. Nor would she, naturally, settle for just Mitsos and the Maestro: She would have her way with any man she took a fancy to, without scruple, without shame, and let people call her a whore to their hearts' content. What mattered to her was that everyone know that these two fools were cuckolds. She'd make them a laughingstock, the pair of them!

Strong in her resolve, Argyroula flounced proudly down the red carpet as if there was not a priest waiting for her in the church to officiate the marriage but a panel for the beauty pageant at which she would be crowned Miss Nea Smyrni, Miss Greece, Miss World.

THE SPECTACLE POOR Mitsos presented was worthy of tears. He was smothered by his suit, strangled by his tie, and, to crown it all, he was painfully embarrassed by the Band-Aid that the barber had stuck on his cheek after almost butchering him with the razor.

"It's not my fault! He was the one who suddenly turned his head—you saw him, didn't you?" the shaken man had cried in his defense to the future groom's companions. "Are you trying to die, my man, on the day of your wedding?"

In fact, that is exactly what Mitsos Attonis longed for: death. Or at least for the earth to open up and swallow him. That very same morning, he had as if by a miracle seen the light. Accidentally overhearing a conversation between Mr.

and Mrs. Chaïtides, he finally understood the predicament in which his own parents had landed him. Weak-willed and slow-witted as he was, he still had his limits. It was as if the sky had fallen on his head and crushed him, shattered him. Not having found the courage to turn tail and run, he had surrendered himself like a sacrificial lamb to his best men who had dressed and groomed him, and now, here he was, next to Argyroula, climbing the stairs to the church the way one might climb Calvary.

In short, it was a complete calamity of a wedding. But the rest of us were oblivious of the fact. Blithely, we showered them with rice, handed out tulle sachets of sugared almonds, and, on our return to the White Tower, threw ourselves on the wine and grilled meats. The musicians, two guitars and an accordion, got onstage and began with a waltz, *In the morning, you wake me with a kiss*. The Maestro took hold of Argyroula's waist and spun her all around the yard, before almost forcing Mitsos to get up. The guests, more than two hundred of them, were sitting every which way, wherever they could find, and the children had climbed up onto the roofs of the mud-brick houses.

My father, a rose in his buttonhole, was standing on our doorstep. I had rarely seen him look so handsome. His dolphin smile had returned, and it lit up his face, as well as everything around him. What was he waiting for, I wonder, to steal the limelight from the reigning protagonists?

"Would you allow me the next dance?" asked Sakis Chaï-tides with the airs of a dandy as (I kid you not!) he bowed and kissed my hand. At that precise moment, my father saved me from the awkward predicament. He approached the stage and begged the musicians to pause their playing. Then he made his way through the crowd and came to a stop in front of the newlyweds' table, across from a burly man in a uniform who was gnawing on a crispy piece of grilled skin.

"Are you Adamantios Kiosses, the commissioner of the 22nd Precinct Station in Nea Smyrni?" he asked in a loud voice.

"The very same!" The man hastily wiped his greasy hands.

"I am Antonis Armaos, a member of the Political Bureau of the Communist Party of Greece, Athens delegate, director of the central office of the National Liberation Front!" (He recited all his titles in the present tense—they were not medals that could be removed, they were his body, his flesh.) "In light of the clemency measures ratified by the Greek parliament, I willingly surrender myself to your custody Mr. Kiosses. As does my wife, Anna."

My mother grabbed my arm and we hastened to take our places on either side of my father. The man had probably been instructed by Lyssandros Mavrides to follow Armaos's lead. He rose and put on his cap. It wouldn't have surprised me had he actually stood to attention.

"You are under arrest, Mr. Armaos! You are under arrest, Mrs. Armaos!" he declared in a solemn tone.

As we turned toward the entrance to the White Tower, I felt dozens of eyes trained on us, eyes brimming with admiration if not reverence. But in crossing from one moment to the next that line between deep hiding and freedom, I too, in one fell swoop, came to see my former neighbors in a completely different light: I no longer despised them, no longer disdained them. Deep down, they were good, honest souls who might have flown high had they had the opportunity to break their chains.

Three weeks later, a news item brutally severed any lingering pangs of nostalgia I harbored for the White Tower: *Yesterday, at approximately three o'clock in the morning, Attonis, Dimitrios, twenty-five years of age, manual laborer by profession, resident of Nea Smyrni, 46 Imvrou Street, did slaughter in their sleep by means of a military bayonet, his wife, Argyro, née Mazza, as well as the woman's adoptive father, Ligouras, Charilaos. The horror of this heinous crime is only exacerbated by the fact that the hapless woman was pregnant. Immediately following the double homicide, the perpetrator fled to the communal latrines, where he hung himself without leaving a note or any other explanation of his actions. Interrogated about a possible motive for the crime, Attonis's neighbors claimed complete ignorance. "Everything was going so well for him. He was the toast of the neighborhood and well liked. It must be that he lost his mind," was a characteristic declaration by Mr. Aristomenis Karassoulas, a retiree from the Evzone Palace Guard, to our criminal justice reporter.*

THE STORY OF the White Tower concluded in a bloodbath. A cousin of the Maestro's from Thessaloniki inherited the big house and the surrounding shacks. He gave all the occupants six months to clear out. Then bulldozers arrived and left nothing standing. Two years later, the lot was sold to the Israeli community in Athens, who turned it into a small cemetery for the Jews of the southern suburbs.

In 1975—perhaps even as late as 1980?—as I was driving down Imvrou Street one afternoon, I'm not sure what came over me: I parked and walked into the cemetery that had once been our yard. I wandered around for quite some time, scanning all the headstones, in search of something, although I didn't know what exactly, until I found it: an unassuming little grave, glued to the northern wall of the lot. A marble slab covered in mold on which were engraved the Star of David and a weathered inscription: "Argyro—Sylvia—Mazza. Thessaloniki 1931–Athens 1955."

I don't know if anyone had truly mourned Argyroula, had shed heartfelt tears for her. But someone in any case, a charitable soul perhaps, had taken it upon themselves to return to her her true name and hidden faith so that she might finally fly free to the New Jerusalem. *And the soul longs to rush into Abraham's warm embrace, to kiss his beard of straw.*[90]

---

[90] From a poem by Kostas Varnalis (1888–1974), "The Ballad of Kyr Mentios."

ON THE OUTSIDE

I

MY FATHER'S FEARS that the clemency measures were a ruse designed to entrap hunted leftists proved to be exaggerated. But Lyssandros Mavrides was also exaggerating when he promised that once they had turned themselves in, my parents' exoneration was a pure formality that would take only a few hours to process. Their arrests were conducted punctiliously, by the book, and until they were fully cleared, and the sentences with which they had been charged before the war declared null and void, four months had passed for one and almost six for the other. Anna spent Christmas in the Averoff Prison; and Antonis, Ash Monday in the Alikarnassos Prison on Crete. For me, that was a time entirely free of care; indeed, they were the most carefree days of my life.

Needless to say, after September 18 I didn't set foot at the White Tower again except to collect our clothes and the radio. The furniture and kitchenware we left for our former neighbors to share among themselves. I moved to Pangrati, where Grandmother Sevasti, Aunt Markella, and the other members of the family welcomed me with open arms. You'd think that I had truly risen from six feet under, or at least that I had recovered from a life-threatening illness. In no time at all, Grandmother Sevasti had prepared for me a sun-drenched bedroom all to myself that even boasted a full-length mirror hanging from the door to the wardrobe. You cannot imagine what a gift, what an endless source of pleasure that mirror was for me. Up to that point, I had never seen my new woman's body in its entirety! While I had not overcome the habit of abruptly turning my head to look behind me, it now had a new purpose: I was no longer checking if a snitch was following me but rather to see if my ass looked good in the skirt I was wearing.

For the first time in my life, I was on vacation. The adults did not deny me anything, and plied me with generous amounts of pocket money every time I ran into them.

"She needs to recover and learn how to smile again! What would you like me to cook for you, Niki? What do you have a hankering for? Shall we go to the cinema or the theater this evening? There's a truly fantastic variety show on at the Acropol. We could get some granita during intermission! And how about a drive to Kifissia this Sunday?"

They found my experience at the White Tower unsettling, confusing. At times, they treated me as if all the trials I had endured had matured me beyond my years; at others, as if I were still a child. I will never forget the look of bewilderment on my grandmother's face when she found a sanitary napkin among my dirty laundry.

"We must keep an eye on you. Someone might steal you away!" she murmured, but she never did anything, or even said anything, to rein me in. On the whole, I was at complete liberty to wander around as I pleased, at least until nightfall. I went out when I liked, returned when I liked, and—oh, pinnacle of emancipation!—did so with my own bunch of keys in hand.

More than going to the theater and the movies, or eating the meals served in my honor, what I enjoyed the most was simply walking around. Going out by myself come rain or shine, roaming the streets without a particular goal or destination for hours and hours on end; gawking at shop-windows; buying magazines and leafing through them perched on a bench in Zappeion or Klafthmonos Square, my legs smartly crossed; trying to learn to smoke, until, after the five-hundredth coughing fit, I had to relinquish this noble ambition. All the dejection, timidity, and inhibition of the years in hiding had momentarily taken wing. Once again, I was the girl with the devil-may-care attitude, who looked people in the eye and skipped in the rain just like Gene Kelly (I had already seen *Singing in the Rain* twice at the Pallas theater in Pangrati). Once again, I was Niki Armaos. Proudly, I clutched the identity card I had hastened to have made. I had it always at the ready to pull out and show to whomever might be interested, so that they could bear witness to the fact that I was no longer hiding from anyone, that I was walking around freely and could go wherever struck my fancy!

The truth is that I was not as spontaneous with my family and their friends. And they, for their part, with the exception of my grandmother and Markella, did not feel completely at ease with me. They wondered whether the seven-year sentence I had served without being guilty of any crime had poisoned my heart, had filled it with bitterness, had perhaps transformed me into a communist fanatic who looked on them, without openly saying so, as her class enemies.

I can't shake the feeling that there was a measure of guilt in Bogdanos's warmth and generosity. Indeed, Uncle Savvas had gotten off exceedingly lightly. Even with the best intentions in the world, it was undeniable that he had been a high-profile collaborationist through and through. The fact that, a mere ten years after the Occupation, he had regained his status as a distinguished member of polite society and had a foot in every powerful door—while others who had resisted the invaders were still rotting in exile—was a scandal of untold magnitude. Not that his fellow collaborationists had received harsher punishment, the very opposite, in fact. Some even had the gall to boast about their participation in the Security Battalions. Uncle Savvas, however, had a sense of honor. Even though he firmly believed that he had done the right thing, even though he was an anti-communist to the bone, his conscience still gnawed at him every now and then. This is why (as I found out a lot later) he provided financial support, under cover of strict anonymity, to a number of families of imprisoned leftists.

After the death of Uncle Savvas's heirless brother in 1951, the Bogdanoses had inherited the vast and sumptuous apartment on Stisichorou Street, which they had moved into from Kypseli. They were now living the life of the haute bourgeoisie, or the haute bourgeoisie à la grecque, in a country where the ruling classes, in their great majority, had neither roots nor particular aspirations, other than to ape the West and ensure that they played their cards right and got off scot-free no matter the circumstances. They had two aproned and bonneted maidservants in their employ, as well as a cook and a Swiss governess for their daughter, Toula.

For Aunt Fani, her forties were her golden age. Shedding all traces of youth, she could finally shine in the role of a grande dame. She organized dinners, where the cherry-picked guests were methodically arranged around the table so as to foster both interesting conversation and the occasional romance. She put on card-playing soirees, during which she discreetly surveyed each player to ensure that no one came to ruin. She participated in philanthropic galas, never missed a classical music recital at Parnassos or a National Theater premiere, and would badger Savvas to travel to Europe once a year to "keep abreast of the latest trends." The only thing she didn't devote herself to was her daughter. To be precise, she dedicated two afternoons a week to her, during which she reviewed the girl's progress at school, obliged her to play the piano, and bored her stiff with advice, primarily sanctimonious in nature.

My cousin was truly pitiful in every way. She was a listless little girl who addressed her parents as if they were strangers, was ashamed of her red hair and freckles, and collected every award for academic excellence at Arsakeio.[91] Whenever I set eyes on her, I was almost consoled for the years I had spent at the White Tower. "Things could have been worse!" I would say to myself. I wouldn't be surprised, of course, if she was thinking the same about me.

Uncle Savvas was completely emotionally disengaged from his family, and had probably been so for quite some time. Even though he fulfilled all the responsibilities of a father and a husband, in letter at least if not in spirit, I don't believe that he cared much any longer for Fani and Toula. Perhaps I'm mistaken, but he seemed more affectionate to my grandmother, Aunt Markella, and me than to his wife and child. At almost seventy years of age, Savvas looked fifteen years younger. Sturdy and strong, with raven hair and boundless reserves of energy, he always had things to do and people to see. He would leave Stisichorou before dawn and return only when it was time for the evening meal. He had his own bedroom, his own bathroom, his own telephone line. I remember him always closely shaven and impeccably dressed, when not in a suit, in a violet robe with a velvet border under which

---

[91] Originally founded in 1836 by the Society of Friends of Education as a girls-only boarding school, Arsakeio quickly established campuses throughout Greece and acquired a reputation for excellence and prestige. The school started enrolling boys in the 1980s.

he wore a white shirt and tie. He smoked strong English cigarettes—John Player Special—and whenever he saw me, he would insist on treating me to at least one Leonidas chocolate bonbon.

What did he do for work? "Consultant" is what he would say—a business and investment consultant. But he avoided talking about his business concerns at home. I am not implying that he was lying. In any case, it was obvious that anyone who wanted to participate in the country's economic recovery through entrepreneurship or simply by playing the stock market would be well advised to seek the counsel of Savvas Bogdanos, who had served as the governor of a bank, a minister (even if under the Occupation), and (this was truly the most remarkable achievement of all) had resettled half a million Asia Minor refugees in the villages of Macedonia. Uncle Savvas knew Greece and the Greeks inside and out.

WHEN I RETURNED to the world, Uncle Savvas's most recent success, the masterstroke that, in contrast to his habitual reticence, he talked about with great pride, was called Afroessa. It had formerly been known as Buenos Aires, and before that, Bosporus.

The place had a checkered past. It first opened its doors in 1908, at the intersection of 3rd September Street and Omonia Square. At the time, it was a high-society café, founded by a Constantinopolitan—hence its original name—frequented on a daily basis by hundreds of devotees who flocked there for the freshly ground fragrant coffee, the raki that never caused a headache no matter the quantities consumed, the syrup cakes, and the superior quality of its hookahs. In 1935, his son took over and turned it into a brewery-restaurant. He hired an orchestra to play tangos and foxtrots and hung from the facade what was probably the first neon sign in all of Greece, bearing the words "Buenos Aires" accompanied by the silhouette of a raging bull. The owner's Nazi sympathies, but chiefly his inspired idea to print the menus in Italian and German, transformed Buenos Aires under the Occupation into the beloved haunt of the invaders. All day and all night, men in uniform came and went, hell-bent on revelry so provocative that short of being a collaborator or a whore most people wouldn't be caught dead passing outside but would cross over to the other side of the street. Inevitably, then, after liberation, Buenos Aires suffered the consequences and was plundered by the ELAS during the Dekemvriana. It was later reopened by the proprietor, but instead of its former brilliant clientele, it was now favored only by the working men of the neighborhood and rustic types from the provinces, seeking a simple plate of bean soup, and in a pinch, a serving of smoked herring for starters. A handwritten sign spoke volumes about how far the place had fallen: "Customers are kindly requested to leave all toolboxes by the entrance." In other words, the place was essentially catering to shoeshines. Gradually fading away behind the register, the proprietor finally gave up the ghost on an icy evening in 1952.

About a year later, a certain Terpsichore Papadodimas secured an interview with Uncle Savvas after pulling a few strings through mutual acquaintances. She was a big bag of a woman in her forties who had been twice divorced and sported dye-fried hair and a gold incisor: in short, a complete wreck.

"Save me, Mr. Bogdanos," she began whimpering immediately. "You are my last resort before suicide! I entrust to your hands the inheritance left to me by my poor late father!" Without batting an eye, Uncle Savvas let her speak, and when he realized who the father in question was, his first impulse was to unceremoniously show her the door—he wanted nothing to do with Germanophiles and their offspring. But as Terpsichore Papadodimas recounted her misfortunes and pressed her suit, he began having second thoughts. "What a crying shame—nay, a sin!—to let an establishment like that, and in the heart of Athens to boot, go to the dogs! If I can't restore it to its prewar glory, then no one can!" Before half an hour had elapsed, the deal was sealed: Terpsichore had given him carte blanche, and he had promised to underwrite the costs of renovation and had secured thirty percent of the business's future profits.

He then immersed himself in the dictionary in search of a new name. Afroessa[92] was poetic and struck him as

---

[92] The *Afroessa* was one of the Greek navy's first steamer ships, commissioned and built in England in 1857. It was the ship used in the scientific expedition that discovered a new volcanic island near Santorini later named Afroessa. The term *afroessa* also evokes the word foam or seafoam in Greek, *afros*.

quintessentially Greek in its seafaring resonances. A name as far removed from the shameful past as possible. "I'll get Giannis Tsarouhis to paint the sign. I want a work of art that will stop passersby in their tracks and have them clamoring for a photograph under it!" Then he turned to more critical issues: What kind of restaurant did he want it to be? Carefully, he pondered the nuances of its ambiance, cuisine, and clientele.

At that time, the center of Athens boasted a handful of upscale restaurants and another dozen or so in the second tier: vast, high-ceilinged rooms done up in Viennese furniture, chandeliers, and frescoes, and waiters in bow ties and waistcoats serving a large selection of dishes, from fried calf liver in Madeira sauce to boiled grouper in mayonnaise. Also on offer year-round for lunch and dinner was tripe soup to settle the stomach.[93] There were Ideal and Pantheon on either end of Panepistimiou Street, Kostis on Korai Street, Kentrikon on Kolokotronis, as well as a profusion of wine taverns, hole-in-the-wall groceries-cum-eateries, and souvlaki joints, where the smell of seared fat clung to the clients' clothes. Inside the arcade on Voukourestiou Street, two competing ouzeris located across from each other, Apotsos and Orfanides, were doing booming business. At the foot of Omonia Square, on Ionos Street, Marios's bar was the haunt

---

[93] Traditionally eaten to break the fast on Easter Sunday, tripe soup is also served at many late-night eateries in Greece as it is believed to be a good antidote to a hangover.

of bouzouki players, among them the two leading names in rembetiko, Tsitsanis and Mitsakis. A few backstreets farther along was a dive frequented exclusively by homosexuals, where sailors billeted near the Botanical Gardens and soldiers barracked at Rouf sold themselves for some extra cash.

For two months, Savvas Bogdanos made the rounds of all the restaurants on a quest to pinpoint what was missing and identify how Afroessa might entice the Athenian audience. He knew that the competition would be won not on quality alone (they all were serving choice dishes of quality ingredients) but also depended on a certain novelty, as was the case at the Belarussian Niki Iakovlev's Petrograd on Stadiou Street, which had introduced piroshkis and vodka with caviar to Athens.

In the end, Uncle Savvas came up with not one but two inspired ideas. The first was to offer Coca-Cola, the American drink that Greeks at the time had seen only at the movies. Even if they found its brown color off-putting in the beginning, it would be no time at all before they were queuing up to try it. Like it or not, it would become part of their lives, as was the case with everything that came from their superpower protector.

Uncle Savvas's second idea was even more daring: He was going to hire young women as waitresses. This was something unheard-of for any self-respecting restaurant aspiring to a serious clientele.

"Girls? What are you doing? Turning this place into a cabaret?" a shocked Terpsichore Papadodimas exclaimed.

"Even under the Occupation, we had no business with the women of the Italians and the Germans! Tolerate them is all we did."

"I'm not talking about loose women!" Bogdanos explained. "They won't be there as escorts or to bait the clients in any way. They will be irreproachable, as beautiful as the caryatids, but as modest as young girls just out of Arsakeio."

"Why the need for them, then?"

"Beauty, Terpsichore, is always a draw. And the more inaccessible it is, the more it enchants."

Afroessa opened its doors on New Year's Day 1955. From its very first week, it was evident that Uncle Savvas had struck gold. Two months later, daily overcrowding had obliged him to rent the neighboring pharmacy and tear down the separating partition to accommodate another twenty tables. (The pharmacist had been paid a king's ransom to vacate the premises.) The scandal caused by the female staff resulted in extensive press coverage. The most prominent cartoonist of the time, Fokion Dimitriades, no doubt in cahoots with Bogdanos, drew a sketch of Afroessa as the Erechtheion, with aproned caryatids carrying serving trays amid pillars in the shape of Coca-Cola bottles. Savvas had this page from *Athinaika Nea* enlarged and hung in a conspicuous spot over the register.

Whenever he talked about Afroessa, Bogdanos never failed to point to Markella's contributions: After abandoning the theater once and for all, she had taken charge of the selection, training, and management of the girls.

"Without you, we would be nothing! You are the one who brings measure and harmony to the place!" He would shower her with praise, and she would happily accept his compliments.

Even though she never commented on it, Aunt Fani was not at all pleased. Indeed, she was far from thrilled to see her husband, who had gone from an established banker to a fledgling restauranteur (a glorified tavern keeper in other words!), and her sister, who had been flighty from the cradle, playing the role of brothel madams. No, she was certainly not buying that cock-and-bull story about Afroessa's waitresses being as modest as girls in a prep school. Even if one had to keep up appearances, Foteini Bogdanos, née Armaos, wasn't born yesterday! Thankfully, she was not aware of the dream that had shaken Grandmother Sevasti right out of her sleep: She dreamt that Savvas had married not Fani but Markella and that I was their daughter.

ON JANUARY 3, 1956, my mother was released from prison. We met her at the entrance to the Averoff Prison in Bogdanos's car and drove her straight to Afroessa. In my sublime innocence, I had thought it a good idea to celebrate her freedom with a sumptuous meal. From the moment we were seated around one of the most prominent tables, next to the piano and the Christmas tree, and the waiters began their to-ing and fro-ing bearing trays with the best the restaurant had to offer, Anna would not stop casting murderous glances all around. She did not touch the food. "I'm not used to this type of food, it will upset my stomach!" she said in a tone heavy with reproach to Bogdanos, who was trying to calm her down. She wouldn't even deign to smell the wine and Coca-Cola. All she had was a glass of water and a Turkish coffee at the end.

As soon as the two of us were alone, she exploded. "Is this what we fought for? To end up drinking and toasting in the company of black marketeers? To have working men" (she meant the waiters) "pass around their caps for tips? To have to witness our own men salivating for whores in front of our very eyes? Why did you take me to that place? My executed comrades will be spinning in their graves."

I could not find the words to calm her down.

"And don't even dream that we're going to stay in Pangrati, with my mother-in-law under my feet and your aunts breathing down my neck! We're renting our own place as soon as possible, a hovel if need be. And you, young lady, seem to be taking it too damn easy. This is what happens when you are spoiled and allowed to run loose as you wish! It's time to turn a new leaf, and don't you forget it! Or else when your father sees you again, he won't recognize you!"

Poor mother! Little did she know what lay in store.

II

AUGUST 1956: THE Armaos family, reunited and free for the first time in eight years, is living in a most respectable single-family house in Koukaki. We have a yard out back with a well and a pergola, a gas stove in the kitchen, and an oil heater. Our rent is a quarter of what it used to be at the White Tower.

Only a few days after his release, my father tasted the choicest of dishes served cold: revenge. The sixth plenary session, convened in Romania, removed Nikos from leadership and expelled him from the KKE. The charge of "sectarianism" leveled against him was so specious as to be practically laughable. Nikos had not accepted the sentence. "Who's making the decisions here?" he had asked scornfully. "It was the Soviet Union that placed me at the head of the Greek movement in 1934, and only the Soviet Union can send me to hell…" He pretended to be unaware of the fact that it was the Soviets who were pulling the strings in this instance, too, as they had before.

These events were a triumphant vindication of Lyssandros Mavrides who, at a time when it was still unthinkable, had predicted the wave of de-Stalinization that in very short order ousted all of Dzhugashvili's clones. Men like my father, who had survived without being brought to heel, were primed to take lead roles in the imminent new order.

"Petition for an annulment of your expulsion, and at the next meeting of the Central Committee you will be reinstated with all pomp and ceremony," they let him know.

"I'm not petitioning for anything!" Armaos replied, imperiously. "My Party expelled me in 1945 without deigning to hear my side. It's now up to the Party to acknowledge its mistake and exonerate me. It also owes a humble apology to all the comrades who were defamed and eliminated by Nikos and his lackeys."

"The Party does not apologize."

"Then I'll wait until it learns how to," Armaos replied. "In the meantime, I'll work for the EDA."

THE EDA SERVED, on the one hand, as the legally recognized arm of the still-outlawed KKE. On the other, it was casting, or attempting to at least, a much broader net. In its midst could be found not only communists but also democratic leftists from both the EAM and even the prewar Liberal Party. The latter, by advocating for national reconciliation and social democratization, often tempered the KKE's hard-line ideology. While the exiled Party leadership was still deluding itself with dreams of a "third round"[94] and the seizure of power in Greece through revolution (the catastrophe of the Civil War had not taught them anything), the motto of the EDA militants was "de-escalation, peace, and demilitarization." There was constant bad blood between communists on the "outside" and those who remained on the "inside" in Greece. At times the viewpoint of one side prevailed; at others, the other. My father had, by force of circumstance, chosen his camp.

---

[94] After the first uprising of partisans against the German occupiers (the Resistance), and the second against the Greek government (the Civil War).

He reported to the EDA central offices, where its leadership welcomed him with open arms. "You know who that is?" one of their parliamentary representatives asked his younger assistant. "Antonis Armaos! While we were just getting started, he was finishing the race. He's leaps and bounds ahead of us! Every time you see him, make sure to stand to attention!"

He was assigned a dual role: management of the trade unions and the education of younger members. For all that, they did not grant him the status of professional cadre or allot him a salary. Clearly, the KKE had vetoed such a move.

My father had to find paying work. We still had approximately half of the gold sovereigns that had supported us during our time at the White Tower, but Antonis refused to keep eating away at our nest egg. "God only knows what tomorrow will bring. We might have to go into hiding again..." But fundamentally it was a question of principle to him: He who does not work, neither shall he eat. This was the mantra that had shaped his formative years.

Of the few opportunities for employment that came his way, he chose the most uncertain: He was hired as a representative—a salesman, in other words—for a business importing farming machinery. Half the month he spent wandering the countryside selling tractors to farmers. He knew nothing about tractors and even less about farmers.

"A chance to learn!" he said as he excitedly showed off the suitcase he had just bought. "I also informed the EDA.

In the evenings, I will visit the Party cells in the provinces and provide guidance to our comrades!"

"And what about your salary?" my mother asked.

"The salary is nothing special" (in reality, it was a pittance) "but I'll be getting a percentage on each contract!"

There was no doubt in my father's mind that his knack for commerce would once again save the day, as it had when he was twenty and he had sold Emilio Lichnarakis's carpets like hotcakes.

It did not take long for him to be disabused of his optimism. At the end of three months, after spending forty-five days and as many nights on the bumpy back roads of Thessaly and the Peloponnese, he had sold only two tractors and had earned enough to cover only the costs of the rent to our new home and his cigarettes. Admittedly, his experience of the rural countryside—"tending its war wounds and rediscovering its dreams"—was valuable. "The stories I could tell! They'd take hours..." Unfortunately, our grocer did not accept stories in exchange for soap and cheese. And the stamp on our most recent bill from the gas company read "Notice of termination of services."

"Niki, we must find you some work," my father declared, his voice serious.

WHAT ABOUT THE university in Moscow that was allegedly awaiting my arrival with open arms? Had that gone flying out the window? And what about sitting for the qualifying exams for my high-school diploma, which by all accounts I ought to pass with my eyes shut and an arm tied behind my back seeing that each year I excelled at our model school at the White Tower?

I accompanied my father to the Ministry of Education and Religious Affairs.

"You were homeschooled?" the presiding official said and grimaced as he stared at me incredulously. "Why? Are you handicapped, Miss Armaos? Or are you afflicted with an infectious disease?"

My father was obliged to explain our situation, and the bureaucrat, his suspicions about our identity confirmed, resolved to do everything in his power to make the life of the communist leader's daughter a living nightmare.

"Convening a special examining committee for you alone is completely out of the question, of course. You will have to sit for the exams for each class separately, one by one, beginning with fifth grade of elementary school, which you quit, from what I see here, in 1948. At the end of each academic year, in June that is, you will take the end-of-year exams with the rest of the students in your neighborhood school. If you pass and are admitted to the higher grade, you will sit for the next grade's exams the following June."

"But at that rate, it will take me seven years to graduate! I'll be done in 1964!" I exclaimed, seething with fury.

"Those are the rules," he said, shrugging his shoulders.

"If Niki passes the high-school qualifying exams, does it not go without saying that she has mastered the curriculum of all the preceding grades?" My father tried to intervene.

"Listen, Mr. Armaos, the Old Testament, for example, is taught in the second year of high school; inorganic chemistry in the fourth. For students to climb the ladder of their studies, they must prove their knowledge at each step. Nowhere in the world, not even in the Soviet Union, can someone just catapult to the very top," he said with a sadistic smile.

"We'll get the courts to intervene!" my father threatened.

The bureaucrat looked at us almost with pity. "It will take at least five years to have this reviewed by the State Council, which has jurisdiction over such matters. In all respects, it is to Miss Armaos's advantage to follow the route that I have pointed to."

Bingo! I would not be getting my high-school diploma until I turned twenty-five. As for the university, there was no point in even thinking about it: To sit for the entry exams, one had to have a certificate of social conscience, and it's not as if anybody had a spare one lying around to give me.

"We will consult a lawyer to see what can be done!" my father promised. "We'll ask for a summary procedure!"

I had no idea what he meant by "summary procedure" nor did I care. All I knew was that History would vindicate me—if indeed it ever vindicated me—a lot later than my parents. Of course, they were not to blame. Perhaps no one was to blame. In the meantime, I had to find work and make a living.

This prospect was not at all disagreeable to me. I was already working anyway, had been for a number of months, and what's more without pay. As soon as my mother had me under her tutelage again, in addition to putting a stop to my outings and forbidding me from accepting all pocket money even from Grandmother Sevasti, she anointed me as her assistant in Solidarity Action.

Solidarity Action, a women's initiative under the aegis of the EDA, aimed to provide aid to political prisoners. They were in a constant flurry of activity, organizing informal fundraising drives and in-kind donations; dispatching packages with sheets, medicine, and books to the detainees on the islands and in prisons; collecting the signatures of prominent foreigners on petitions demanding general amnesty (as if the Greek government would soften its stance because Picasso and other personalities of his stature—bohemian artists of an avant-garde that was incomprehensible to the Helleno-Christian ethos—had a soft spot for local leftists). They actively supported the families of those who were "on vacation." Almost every day, at the end of the day, arms laden with gifts, we would visit a home where the father and often the mother were absent, and the children were either being raised under the good care of wrinkled and embittered grandparents or were dependent on the generosity of the neighborhood.

My mother was in her element in Solidarity Action. Long gone were the days at the White Tower, where the only thing that seemed to excite her was housework. She was an entirely different person now, full of energy and ideas to spare, and displaying impressive organizational skills. Without a doubt, under different circumstances she could easily have been the one wearing the pants, relegating my father to the role of proud but invisible husband.

I, on the other hand, had had it up to my ears. I could not endure one more tragic story of families decimated by the wars: "One of our brothers was killed in Albania, the second slaughtered by Sourlas's men[95] to stop him from joining the partisans, the third executed by court-martial." Or one more story of heroic resistance in Makronissos, where despite all the broken bones in his body, the beleaguered partisan still refuses to sign the declaration of repentance. I'd had enough of playing the clown to children who would never laugh truly, with all their hearts, unless their parents were freed. The pain and dismay of defeat steeped everything, and conversations returned again and again to the same burning question: "Since the people were on our side, why did we lose?" No matter what my father said, it seemed to me that everyone on the left was taking masochistic pleasure in reopening the wound. I preferred a thousand times over to work for my living than to have to bear witness, each and every day, to that same old lamentation.

"SINCE YOU DON'T trust me, why don't you fit her with a chastity belt!" Aunt Markella said, almost beside herself.

---

[95]   The captain of an anti-communist militia, Sourlas was armed by the Germans, and he and his men sowed terror among communists in Thessaly.

"Or take her to the gynecologist every month to vouch for her virginity!"

"Why won't you let this go, sister?"

"Because Niki won't find a better job! It's a most civilized environment, where she'll meet many new people, and I will be keeping an eye on her—"

"We approve of neither the restaurant's environment nor its patrons!" my mother interrupted.

"Do me a favor, Antonis, and come to Afroessa just one time," Aunt Markella said, turning to her brother. "If you don't find it respectable or, for that matter, anything else isn't to your liking, I will resign instantly."

After much effort, she persuaded him. One Sunday, Antonis took us each by the arm—I beaming beside him, my mother dragging her heels and only after making a lot of fuss and bother about having a headache and not finding anything to wear—and off we went to Afroessa. It turns out that not only did he not disapprove but he had a wonderful time, even though he would not admit it. He delightedly devoured the escargots and cut the schnitzel into tiny little pieces so as to prolong the pleasure. It was only the Coca-Cola that he refused for ideological reasons.

"What are your impressions?" Savvas Bogdanos asked, as he personally uncorked a bottle of burgundy for us.

"It reminds me very vividly of the Tsentralny in Moscow," my father observed.

"True, Afroessa is inspired by that particular air of Central European restaurants, Antonis. But we also want to give it a distinctively Greek identity. We are considering adding gardoumbakia[96] and Epirote pies to the menu. And perhaps certain dishes from Asia Minor may prove a draw. What do you think?"

It was as plain as day that Bogdanos was using flattery to win Armaos over. Even more so, after the chef was summoned from the kitchen and the three started to talk about how to augment the menu.

"I remember that kebab was a staple at even the best restaurants in Constantinople—our late father took us a couple of times at the beginning of the '20s. Why don't you try something similar?"

Bogdanos's face lit up. "Excellent idea!"

"But we'll need someone good to man the grill," the chef observed.

"I know someone, and there's no one better!" my father exclaimed. "But he is one of us, a Party member from the cradle practically! He was released from the Alikarnassos Prison shortly after I was and has been looking for work ever since."

"No problem!" Uncle Savvas announced. "Tell him to stop by tomorrow morning. I will owe you one."

During the entire meal, no one referred to me even once. But as we left the restaurant, there was no doubt in my mind: Along with the water poured for the basil (the griller), the pot (Niki) would also be getting something to drink.

---

[96] A grilled dish made out of lamb or goat organ meats wrapped in intestines.

It took two weeks for Antonis to finally overcome Anna's objections.

"It was a waiter at Ideal, Vrassidas, aka Carob, who initiated me into communism," he reminded her.

My mother finally beat a strategic retreat. In other words, she countered with strict, nonnegotiable conditions: I would work the lunch shift only, and I would be home before sunset; my skirt was to go below my knee; I was not to pluck my eyebrows, varnish my nails, or paint my face like a clown.

"You're a waitress, not a trollop!"

My contract at Afroessa was signed on August 31, 1956, by Savvas Bogdanos as the establishment's legal representative and by Antonis Armaos as my guardian. I was a minor. Until I turned twenty-one, I did not have the right to decide my own fate.

III

A SKIRT OR loose pants in gray; a white silk shirt, a forest green vest; a black tie or bow tie: This was the uniform specially created by Tsouchlo House for the Afroessa girls, who were permitted three changes of uniform, as well as two pairs of low-heeled, comfortable shoes from Lemisios shoemakers. Markella put the finishing touches on our appearance with a rigor that almost matched my mother's. Our hair had to be either cropped close or gathered back in a bun or, in a pinch, in a ponytail; our nails, short and neat, coated in clear varnish; and only an imperceptible trace of makeup was allowed to cover any imperfections of the skin.

When it came to physical hygiene, Markella was a veritable Cerberus: Before the beginning of each shift, she would have us line up and succumb to a meticulous inspection of her discerning eye and sensitive nose. Whoever was not fragrant with soap—strong perfumes were strictly forbidden—would be sent straight to the bath and would lose that day's wages. Whoever was afflicted with facial hair (bushy brows were allowed as a special exception, since the rising star Irene Pappas had legitimized them as a particularity of Greek charm), whoever had the slightest trace of a mustache or sideburns was, from the moment of hire, obliged to make regular visits to the beauty parlor under contract with Afroessa. At that time in Athens, most women had a bit of a mustache—it was not something that bothered men, who, on the contrary, considered it a sign of a warm temperament. Nevertheless, Afroessa girls had to look like porcelain dolls.

Afroessa was run like a factory with two parallel lines of production. One concerned cuisine; the other, service. One was headquartered in the kitchen; the other in the restaurant's main dining hall, which was abutted by the annexes, namely the former pharmacy and the two sidewalks where we put out tables from April through October. The head chef reigned over one, while the maître d' over the other. There was also, of course, the accounting office, located in the attic, with its four employees. Savvas Bogdanos, as general manager, was everywhere with a finger in every pie. Terpsichore Papadodimas, even though the majority owner of the business, would make an appearance only twice a week, during which she would imperiously deliver a handful of ridiculous comments and hasten to cash in on the profits, only to—according to malicious tongues—lose it all on the gambling table.

When I worked at Afroessa, the dining hall employed almost eighty people (including the cleaning staff) and the kitchen, another thirty. The maître d', Mr. Tolis Bouas, a former head waiter on an ocean liner, managed his men with military discipline. There were two floor managers, five chief waiters, thirty waiters, and another thirty busboys. The female staff were an independent squad under the iron fist of Markella Armaos. Even though there was no love lost between Markella and Tolis, they tried not to step on each other's toes.

As soon as a group of people crossed Afroessa's threshold, four employees rushed to their service. If they happened to be people of importance, the maître d' himself, all bows and scrapes, would welcome them. Otherwise, they were led to their table by one of the chief waiters. Their order would then be taken by a waiter, and the busboy would bring the plates—that is, unless they had chosen a truly special dish, in which case they were due the full pageant: the ceremonial lifting of the silver domed cover to reveal a lobster or a venison steak. We girls were responsible for water and drinks. We carried pitchers, uncorked bottles of wine, served liqueurs and cognac, and inducted neophytes into the delights of Coca-Cola. For the duration of the entire meal, one of us would stand two feet from the table, diagonally across from the waiter's assistant, ready to respond to the smallest signal from the diners.

Of my early days at Afroessa all I retain is a memory of unimaginable exhaustion. I literally could barely stand on my feet, either because I was not accustomed to working like that or perhaps because Markella, in trying to whip me into shape, was pushing me too hard. The lunch shift began at eleven in the morning and ended at six in the evening. I, however, had to be there at nine thirty for training. She taught me everything, even the most basic things, from scratch: how to walk, how to smile, how to address the customers. She even tried, in vain, to teach me how to roll my *r*'s properly. "Doesn't matter, it has a certain charm," she said, giving up. She made me try all the dishes, all the wines, all the alcoholic drinks. Needless to say, I ended up getting drunk, but instead of sending me home and exposing us both to my mother's ire, she made me lie down on the divan in her office. There were also theoretical lessons to be learned from *A Guide to Good Waitering*, a manual translated from the French, that addressed all of Afroessa's needs. There I learned, among other things, the correct way to open a bottle of champagne (you don't let the cork shoot out but gently pull it out by hand), as well as the hierarchy of royal titles: baronet, baron, count, marquis, duke, prince, archduke, king, emperor.

"Do we have baronets and marquises in Greece?" I asked, stunned.

"Nothing but goatherds," replied Markella. "But you never know."

Until November, I was entrusted with purely secondary tasks. I emptied ashtrays, carried ice, held on to clients' coats. In early December, I was formally anointed as a waitress and placed in the second dining room, which we still called the pharmacy among ourselves. Aunt Markella's squad consisted of twenty-five girls. The pharmacy, distinctly less popular than the main dining room and the sidewalks, required the presence of only six of us. When the room was empty of customers, we would congregate in groups of twos or threes by the windows and prattle away, our voices low. The male waiters made their own clusters on the other side. We did not have much to do with them: My squad mates looked down their noses at them, and they, for their part, scorned us as useless window dressing if not bona fide whores. (During my time at Afroessa not a single waitress dated a male colleague, with one notable exception...)

The other girls gave me the cold shoulder too at the beginning. Taking me as an example of nepotism, they distrusted me as my aunt's snitch.

"Oh, come on, you really think Niki will rat on us? Can't you see she's a little puppy! She doesn't know her ass from her elbow!" Niove reprimanded them one day, after deciding to break the ice.

"My name is Niove. Want to be friends?" she asked, with the candor of a schoolgirl. She had a gap between her two front teeth. Ever since the day Niove gave me that big, broad smile, I have immediately been drawn to anyone with the same characteristic.

IV

FOR TWENTY-ONE YEARS, Niove Papadaki had enjoyed what I had been most deprived of: a normal life. Born in the neighborhood of Patissia, she had never left, and almost all the comings and goings in her life revolved around Agamon Square, later to be renamed Amerikis. Her parents owned a grocery store there, as well as the three-room apartment above it. It's there, in the square, where she had gamboled in the sandpit as a toddler, where later she had learned to skip rope and play Chinese jump rope, where she had spent her free time hanging out on its benches with her eighth-grade friends from the local girl's school, and where she had first kissed a boy behind one of the trees. All of Niove's stories were rosy. She never referred to the Occupation and the Dekemvriana, the hunger and the killing. Nor did she ever show any interest in hearing about how that time had been for me. She did not want to remember that period, let alone talk about it.

"HAVE YOU EVER kissed a boy?" she asked one day, point-blank.

"No," I confessed awkwardly. "What about you, Niove? Have you kissed lots of boys?"

"When I like a boy, I will often do more. But I protect my virginity with my life. I'm saving it for my husband."

Since the age of fourteen, Niove had her wedding dress hanging in her wardrobe. Twice a year, her mother would take it up to their roof deck to air it out. Then she would make the sign of the cross over it and put it back inside its cover.

This family custom of theirs made a huge impression on me. I imagined thousands of white veils billowing over the roofs of Athens, like windblown streamers or specters.

Thanks to Niove, I became one of the girls, timidly at first of course, barely opening my mouth. In any case, what could I possibly have contributed? Their conversation, their gossip, their jokes all revolved around the same subject: men. From customers and waiters (even though they looked down on them, they still scrutinized their every move, so much so that they could identify whose member hung to the right or the left of his pants) to any and every kind of man. Men with whom they had only exchanged a few charged looks. Men with whom they had trysted in the most improbable places: parks, construction sites, and the rare love den.

The eldest of my colleagues was twenty-seven—by the standards of the day, an old maid—and the youngest was one year my elder. None were married. Four were engaged, two with sailors who docked in Piraeus only once in a blue moon, but who sent them packages with American hosiery and French lipstick. Most of them were on par with Niove: technically virgins yet exceptionally experienced, experts in the art of pleasing boys—perhaps even of pleasing themselves—while at the same time protecting their chastity. They all had some dowry—a small house or a plot of land—which they took care to publicize so that every possible prospective groom would be fully apprised.

Yet for an Afroessa girl there was no dowry as valuable as her own person. Aunt Markella had handpicked each one according to stringent criteria based not only on their physical beauty but also on their capacity to truly shine as young ladies of high society, after the requisite training, of course. Even the ones plucked from the lowest echelons of society were convincing in the role of daintily raised Siamese cats. Little would anyone dream of the vulgarity with which they talked about men among themselves, of how they assessed, in one swift look, the thickness of one's wallet or another's anatomical endowments.

"You're not going to be waitresses all your lives. I'm preparing you for your role as brides!" Markella would often repeat with a meaningful look toward the tables reserved for the distinguished clientele. She would also remind us that six months before I had started working, one of the waitresses had married a regular client, a successful business man, while another, shortly before that, had become pregnant by the pampered son of the mayor of Ioannina, a fact that had obliged the old Epirote family to welcome her into their fold.

"This here," Markella said, placing a hand on Tetas's lower abdomen (I found the audacity of the gesture almost

shocking), "this here is our atomic bomb. It destroys homes,
sets hearts on fire... But you must aim very carefully, at
exactly the right time. Be on your guard, you poor fools:
You don't have a second bomb!"

As much as my aunt's analogy dismayed me, it seemed
to impress the others, no doubt flattered by the thought of
themselves as little airplanes flying over male Hiroshimas.

V

FLIRTING WITH THE customers was officially prohibited on
pain of dismissal. Savvas Bogdanos was not joking around
about it—he even explained that he could read lips from a
distance of twenty-two yards, and if he happened to catch us
saying anything remotely suggestive, we'd be sent packing
without so much as a goodbye. Markella, on the other hand,
demanded only that we keep her informed about which client was making eyes at which waitress, and that we share
every detail of every budding idyll so that she might steer
it—"God willing!"—toward a felicitous conclusion. In any
case, the customers devised various stratagems to divulge
their feelings and desires. The most common was the table
napkin.

They were aware that after their departure from
Afroessa, the linen napkins would be collected by the waitress charged with their table. If they had taken a shine to
her, they would take out a fountain pen and scrawl sweet

nothings on the fabric. When their intentions were purely sexual in nature, they had no compunction about pinning a banknote or two on the inside, above and beyond, of course, the sum left for the tip, something which, according to Markella, was a terrible insult, as much to the girl as to Afroessa.

"Anyone who leaves money for you like that will not be darkening our door again! As for you, my dolls, if you dare pocket it instead of handing it over for me to donate to the orphanage, I'm sending you straight to the vice squad!"

At the end of each shift, we harvested a crop of at least a dozen napkin notes. For the most part, we would read them together, relishing the opportunity to have yet another good laugh at the bottomless stupidity of the male species. There was poetry, of course, either filched from various authors—Palamas, Mavilis—or extemporaneous; confessions of every kind, sometimes lyrical, sometimes explicit and peremptory, *Tomorrow, six sharp, meet me at the Nikoloudis Arcade* ("Too big for your britches, aren't you, my bald friend!" Kiki would jeer); there were even promises of marriage and drawings of hearts and flowers ("Now what on earth is that? A gardenia or a thistle?" Elissavet would ask, unleashing gales of laughter). To ridicule men, to witness them ridicule themselves and fall off their pedestals, was an immense source of pleasure for all the girls.

Naturally, not all billets-doux were surrendered to our mockery. When an admirer was deemed of consequence by a waitress, she would slip the napkin into the pocket of her vest on the sly: the first step in a game for two that in the best-case scenario led to the altar, and in the worst, to the hymen-repair surgeon.

Innocent that I was, it took me a long time to realize that, joking aside, the napkin notes represented true trophies to my colleagues. That deep down there was fierce competition, an undeclared war, each one of us pitted against the other for who would get the most. And that my numbers happened to be intolerably, indecently high.

One day, when I was in the bathroom peeing, I happened to overhear from behind the closed door Elissavet and Nionia gossiping about me.

"The little one, she plays it as if butter wouldn't melt in her mouth, doesn't she?" one was saying. "But you see how she swings her ass around, don't you? Or how she bends over the tables to tease the customers? The other day she wasn't even wearing a bra! You could get an eyeful of her boobs! Not that it takes much, given their size, the cow! And Markella, of course, just looked the other way!"

Lies! Lies, through and through, from beginning to end! Even now in recounting it, my blood boils. I would never, ever have gone without a bra. As for the way I walked, I looked like a windup toy soldier more than anything else.

"You realize Markella won't say a word, don't you? Why on earth do you think she brought her here in the first place? To palm her off on some moneybags for heaven's sake! Or you think that Bogdanos was born yesterday? He's in on it, too, of course! All they are after is to get the niece married off and settled. And the cherry on top? Word is that our little Niki is a communist! I spit on such communists!"

I was holding my breath so as not to give myself away. Immediately afterward, I ran to find Niove, and fell trembling into her arms. She could not stop laughing.

"What did you expect? That they wouldn't be jealous of us? That they wouldn't talk behind our backs? We're the youngest and the most beautiful! Look, look here!" Triumphantly, she unfolded a napkin and pointed to an illegible scrawl.

"What does it say? I can't make out a thing," I admitted.

"How could you? Don't you know that doctors have the worst handwriting, and the better the doctor, the worse the writing? Do you know who this is? Papastylos! Why are you staring like an idiot? Papastylos, you know, the son of the director of the clinic on Acharnon Street! His father sent him to Paris to study. He was there for ten years and only just got back this summer. Don't go thinking he's an old man. He's in his thirties, thirty-two at most. And handsome, too, a fine figure of a man. He was here with his parents for the Christmas Eve party and has been courting me ever since. He was waiting for me one day after work, holding a red, red rose. He didn't say a word. He just handed me the rose, turned on his heel, and left. Have you heard of anything more romantic? No, go on, tell me? And now, he's asking me to go out. The four of us! You, a friend of his, he, and I—"

"I don't go out with strangers," I interrupted abruptly.

"Why? It's not as if you go out with people you know! Come on, Niki, come out of your shell! Do it for me, your friend, if nothing else!"

SHE PULLED OUT all the stops to persuade me. Not that I didn't want to, if only for curiosity's sake, but on the one hand, I had no evening dress, and on the other, what could I possibly say to my parents? That I was going out with an admirer? In desperation, Niove called my aunt to the rescue and found in her an enthusiastic ally.

"Is she truly trying to fob me off on some tycoon?" I wondered, almost horrified at the thought. The plan was that I would be staying overnight in Pangrati (I don't know if Grandmother Sevasti was in on it as she didn't betray the least hint) and that Markella would lend me one of her strapless crinoline dresses in a beautiful burgundy velvet. Together, we took it to the seamstress to let down the hem.

"I think I know who Papastylos's friend is. It must be Zarifis, the criminal attorney. He comes from a big and eminent family, with roots in Asia Minor, just like us. He's brilliant! Even though still very young, he's already the star of the courts. Of course, his surname must have helped: Zarifis, 'the refined!' You're going to have a wonderful time! But make sure, young lady, to keep your head! Watch that atomic bomb of yours and all will be well! No smooching on the first date, mind you. If you really have to, a quick one on the cheek will do!" Aunt Markella was so excited and talking a mile a minute, it was as if she were the one making her social debut.

Zarifis was indeed the one. Epaminondas Zarifis, who in a few decades was to become a leading name in the administrative courts. In 1957, Eddy—as he introduced himself—still had a respectable amount of hair, which he slicked back against his skull with very liberal applications of brilliantine. One could almost see one's reflection on the mirrored surface. The same applied to his stylish oxfords and his car, which was waiting for us, headlights doused for discretion, in Amerikis Square, before driving us the five blocks to Fokionos Negri Street. The men sat in front and the girls in the back.

Premier dance hall! Eleven-member orchestra! Musical stars of international renown! I read all this on a poster at the entrance while our companions waited for the maître d' and Niove handed her mother's fur to the coat girl. (I only had a shawl with me and was chilled to the bone.) Our table, especially reserved for Eddy, was right next to the dance floor. A huge bottle of vermouth sat in the center, surrounded by ice cubes, cold drinks, pistachios, and an enormous tray of sliced apples and pears sprinkled with cinnamon, all arranged in concentric circles. Eddy took a seat next to Papastylos. They were rather similar in general appearance, although the latter was softer and red-cheeked, one of those boys who pass for good-looking at school but turn to fat as they age. Nonetheless, Niove, despite her efforts at discretion, was gawking at him moon-eyed, as if he were the cat's whiskers.

When we arrived, the club was already abuzz and hopping. Latin rhythms, maracas, steel guitars. Onstage, a modish singer in a silvery tux was crooning in a fake foreign accent while three young women, one of whom was Black, did the backup vocals behind him. Eddy pulled me onto the dance floor. I didn't know how to dance the samba, but in letting the music take control, I managed to hold my own. He was a great dancer—I'll give him that.

"A round of applause for Mr. Zarifis and his lovely lady!" the singer announced through the microphone. "Lovely? My foot! When in the company of the great Eddy, one's loveliness is par for the course," I thought to myself and smiled half in earnest, half in jest. During the slow dance that followed—*An old friend is returned tonight*[97]—Niove clung to Papastylos, arms wrapped around his neck, while I kept at a safe distance from Zarifis. On our return to the table, we paired off and sat as couples. The doctor's hand was already stroking Niove's bare arm.

Eddy was a rather skillful flirt. He kept his deep voice quite low—to follow what he was saying, you had to keep your ear almost glued to his mouth—as he rattled on about one criminal case after the other. Secrets and scandals, passions and hatreds in spades, eliciting at once goose bumps and little shivers of pleasure. Within an hour, I had heard, in all their prurient detail, the stories of Spyridoula, the servant girl who had been tortured with a hot flatiron by her

---

[97] A slow foxtrot from 1950, sung by Sotos Panagopoulos, and with music by the prominent Greek composer Giorgos Mouzakis.

employers (the Zarifis practice had taken the case), as well as of the depravity of a famous pastry chef, who was allegedly at the head of a prostitution ring. Clearly aiming to impress his interlocutor, Eddy would pepper the description of his handling of the cases with frequent questions: "What do you think about this?" "What would you have done in my position?" Even without being a complete chump, it was difficult not to feel valued. And even in the full awareness that he most likely said the same thing to all women, it would not have taken much to succumb to his charm and persuade yourself that you were the special one to steal his heart, the only one equal to the delicate diplomacy—"your ring for my virginity"—at the heart of a lover's game full of blind turns and pitfalls.

"How about a drive to Vouliagmeni this Sunday?" he asked, as he refilled my glass.

"Why are you asking?" I suddenly found the nerve to reply, shooting straight from the hip. He lowered his lashes with the earnest air of a movie heartthrob and sucked in his belly—without being fat, he already had the paunch of a drinker.

"Because I like you, Niki, and not only because of the way you look. I know what you've been through; I know your story." Straightaway he started singing my father's praises. "It's men like Antonis Armaos who ought to be taking the lead in the political life of the country!" he declared, voice solemn, supercilious. "It's true that I am on the other side of the political spectrum, but you cannot imagine the depths of my respect and appreciation for his intelligence and patriotism. The guerrilla war could have and should have been avoided—I am sure that we agree on this. Personally, I did not shed my brothers' blood. I did not fight at either Grammos or Vitsi. As soon as I heard that I was among those called to the draft, I left to begin my studies in France."

This great genius of the courtroom had no suspicion how laughable he became to me with this last sentence. What exactly was he trying to say? That he was a deserter, a draft dodger? That while young working men butchered each other out in the rocky backwaters of the country to defend his regime, his privileges, he had been sitting pretty, living the good life in Paris? That once a measure of peace prevailed again and he had his distinguished degree in hand, he had returned to Greece and continued living la dolce vita while donning the mantle of a pacifist into the bargain? I preferred a thousand times over to be with someone drenched with communist blood on the battlefield, than with that whey-faced fop! But those who had saved "Helleno-Christianity" from the "Red plague" very rarely possessed the qualities that made for a renowned lawyer. They became waiters, in the best-case scenario public servants at some ministry, or else they returned to their villages.

"Are you tired, Niki?"

"No, I feel like vomiting!" I started to say, but bit my tongue. I should have spat in his face, got up, and left him there, but I had been brought up to be polite, and I didn't want to do anything to prejudice my friend's romance with the doctor. When Eddy repeated his proposal about the drive to Vouliagmeni, I hemmed and hawed: "We'll see…I'll let you know through Niove…if possible." On our way back to Pangrati, I stared out the window. At least he was smart enough not to try to kiss me when he said good night.

SLEEP EVADING ME, I twisted and turned in my bed. I was in pain—truly, without exaggeration. "I will never find a man!" I was thinking. "No one will ever be right!" The tragedy was that I did like men; I liked them a lot. When a good-looking boy passed me on the street, or even just a boy who had a special something about him, I would furtively peer at him and flare my nostrils wide to breathe in his smell. When one of the customers at Afroessa flirted with me, not via napkin or other such nonsense, but by looking me straight in the eyes or by glancing mischievously at my breasts, and he happened to be manly and sure of himself, I'd turn bright red and be in an agony of turmoil. And then there were my dreams, a constant Sodom and Gomorrah that would leave me aghast when I woke up: I dreamt of them, long, thick, pulsating, more menacing and magnificent than anything described by the waitresses in their ribald repartee. Had my father known, his reprimand would have been blistering: "You have a sick imagination, Niki!"

Every Saturday afternoon, my father gathered all the EDA youth in our parlor to teach them the history of the workers' movement. Through all the years of my "schooling" at the White Tower, he had acquired a knack for teaching, and in trying his hand on me, he had perfected the art of explaining clearly in plain language and conveying information. His students hung on his every word—his revolutionary credentials endowed him with a surfeit of prestige—and kept asking that he recount, again and again, the story of the heroic strikes of the '30s, his conversations in Moscow with Dimitrov and la Pasionaria (Tito, now considered a traitor, had been expunged from the picture),[98] and the Middle East uprising. As soon as dusk fell, we'd put out some ouzo and meze—cheese and salami, usually brought by the young people themselves.

"Why don't you join us," they'd say to my mother and me. "Sit with us, sister comrades."

I'm convinced that these Saturday meetings were conducted at our house and not in the Party offices for my benefit, to coax me into joining the EDA Youth. My parents were crestfallen that all I read of the *Avgi* newspaper[99] was its arts and entertainment pages. And each time they tried to encourage me to take part in a demonstration, I would say that I was too tired from work. I don't think they expected me to devote myself body and soul to the communist cause, as they had done, but there was no denying that I was getting older and

---

[98] Tito (1892–1980) was a communist revolutionary, military figure, and politician who is recognized as the chief architect of the Socialist Federal Republic of Yugoslavia, which he led as president from 1953 until his death. He fell out with Stalin in the late 1940s by defying Soviet hegemony and supporting independent roads to socialism.

[99] The EDA newspaper. In Greek the word means "dawn."

would begin going out, making friends, flirting—and with whom would that be? With the other waitresses at Afroessa, or with these young people, who slaved away all day to make a living and studied with undiminished zeal as they worked to build a better tomorrow for everyone?

These concerns were legitimate, I have never claimed the contrary. But the fact of the matter was I didn't know how to tell them that nothing about the young people who flocked around my father appealed to me. Sensible and serious, all knitted brows and irreproachable conduct, they reminded me of Sunday school scholars or, to be a bit more magnanimous, of Byzantine saints. And how was a saint to seduce me? By regaling me with tales of the socialist resurrection? By persuading me that I ought to lay my life on the altar of that cause? Having already sacrificed to it more than most young people my age—my entire adolescence, in fact—I could no longer tolerate more talk of sacrifice. I had been given one egg in this life, and I was raring to crack it and eat it. Not for love or money was I going to just sit there stoically waiting for the chick to hatch.

Clearly, then, it didn't look like I was going to find a man. A man to truly fall in love with that is, like in books and films. Not a nice little cookie-cutter, groom-material mélange of good intentions and serious goals. I meant a man with whom I could not help but become one, not some partner to set up house and raise our two and a half rug rats.

Well, what about the other girls, one might ask, were they going to find a man like that? Perhaps they weren't even looking. Perhaps they had their feet firmly planted on the ground. Perhaps, from a young age, they had accepted that this was the way of life, all limitation, while I, locked away in my White Tower, had idealized the outside world. As I tossed and turned in my bed in Pangrati, Niove, in Amerikis Square, was as happy as a clam dreaming of her doctor. The wedding gown rustled in her wardrobe. Even if I wanted to, I could never be anything like her.

In that case, I might as well come to terms with the fact as soon as possible: My path in life was to be a solitary one. I was and would always be Niki the puppy, Niki the wild child, Niki never at home no matter where she is, neither at her parents' nor at Afroessa. I might as well come clean with Markella and tell her to stop fantasizing about me in a wedding dress on the arm of one of the restaurant's distinguished customers. I might as well gird my loins and dare one day to know true love. Not by bargaining for a ring with my virginity but by taking that breathtaking dive with a beautiful boy I chanced upon in the street, or with a customer of Afroessa who would crook his finger at me and I could not help but follow.

VI

"YOU SPEAK RUSSIAN, don't you? Come with me now!"

I was at my post in the small dining room, the pharmacy, my teeth chattering because, even though it was almost March, it was a bitterly cold day and the heat was never turned on only for us, the staff; there had to be at least a few customers at one of the tables. Uncle Savvas could be unreasonably miserly like that. Even though he had brought us all French perfume from his last trip to Paris, he did not give a damn if we got frostbite.

Alexandros Strofalis had rushed into the pharmacy, taken me by the arm, and practically dragged me into the big dining hall to act as interpreter for a group of Soviets from the embassy, all intent on wining and dining even though it was barely past noon. To cap it off, he would not let me take their order as I normally would but kept interrupting me nonstop and obliging me to translate every little flash of wit that popped into his head, even launching into a debate with the cultural attaché about the affinities between *Anna Karenina* and *Madame Bovary*, which I had to translate.

"The books are poles apart!" I finally whispered, thoroughly irritated.

"Oh, really? And how do you know that?"

"I've read them both."

"Careful now...I'll test you and see how you do!" he retorted, mischievously.

The Russians rewarded us handsomely for our zeal, leaving a third of their considerable bill as a tip.

"It's yours!" Alexandros said.

"Fifty-fifty!"

"You're the one who translated."

"And you're the one who kept them entertained!"

He pushed the money toward me. I pushed it back at him. At this point, he snatched it up, folded it in two, and stuffed it in the pocket of my vest.

"Back to your post!" he commanded.

"WHAT DID THAT weirdo want with you?" the girls asked. "Weirdo" was not meant with any affection. They all thought there was something strange, unsettling, pretentious about Alexandros. Almost everything about him rubbed them the wrong way, but most of all the fact that during breaks, instead of horsing around with his colleagues, he preferred to sit alone in a corner of the restaurant, either smoking with a faraway look in his eyes or engrossed in one of those pocket books he always carried in his trench coat.

"He finished university, didn't he? What's he doing with his head in a book all day?" Teta asked one day, full of suspicion.

"Where did we unearth such a fine specimen of a waiter?" the maître d' muttered on another occasion, thoroughly exasperated because Alexandros, for the second time running, had confused table 6 with table 9, and had their orders sent to the wrong tables. But it was Bogdanos himself who had hired him, and there was no other option but to turn a blind eye.

Truth be told, Alexandros had neither the manner nor the appearance of a waiter. A garçon ought to be discreet and unobtrusive, like a house servant (which is why they're

called that, irrespective of age). Even when physically striking, their beauty must not be of a type to distract the customer, much less eclipse him. It was unheard-of, then, for
a waiter to be almost six feet tall, two hundred and thirty
pounds, and sport a big thatch of unruly hair—the more
he tried to tame his curls, the more they seemed to rebel—
along with a gold watch!

"I recommend that you take that off," Uncle Savvas had
said to him on his first day.

"It's the only thing I have of my father's," Alexandros
had replied.

"Well then never take it off, son!"

Truth be told, Alexandros was not even really doing
the job of a waiter. He was not assigned to certain tables.
He leapt into the breach only when foreigners crossed
Afroessa's threshold. Even though tourism in Greece was
still in its infancy, it was growing rapidly. A fine fellow like
Alexandros, with his perfect command of French and English, his serviceable Italian and smattering of German, was
completely indispensable to a chic restaurant. Especially as
his exchanges with these foreigners was not limited to discussions of the menu. He talked to them about Athens, its
landmark sights and attractions as well as its hidden corners
and gems; he knew a thing or two about history, geography,
music, and cinema. Our guests, impressed by his knowledge
and eloquence, would often ask him to give them a tour of
the city, and even to accompany them on their excursions
to Delphi or Epidaurus. As a general rule, he would refuse.

"What I make at the restaurant is enough for me," he later explained to me. "There's no reason to waste more time."

WHEN I FIRST started working at Afroessa, I used to walk back and forth from Koukaki. But after an eight-hour shift spent on one's feet, even a nineteen-year-old is ready to drop. Indeed, once back at home, an immediate footbath in warm water and Epsom salts is generally advisable. As a result, I started taking the bus that ran on the Akadimias to Neo Faliro line, which would let me off at the Syngrou stop, five blocks from my house. I would board at the terminus, and therefore usually found a seat. If that wasn't the case, I waited patiently for the next bus. As a young woman using public transportation, it was critical to keep one's backside covered at all times. Otherwise, some handsy pervert was sure to brazenly cop a feel. There were legions of them, and they were not at all easy to spot.

Three days after the episode with the Soviets, I had curled up on the very last seat next to the window and was just beginning to doze off behind my dark glasses, when I heard a familiar voice.

"Perhaps you are right, Niki Armaos."

I turned my head and saw him. When had he boarded the bus? When had he sat down beside me?

"After all, female infidelity is a theme throughout world literature. Before Bovary and Karenina, the petite bourgeoise and the aristocrat, there was the beautiful Helen. In fact, perhaps it all began with Eve, when she was led astray by the snake!"

I gawked at him, dumbstruck, probably exactly as he had intended.

"But there's an adulterous woman of the nineteenth century who is much more interesting than the French and Russian examples," he continued at full tilt. "The German, Effi Briest. Have you heard of her?"

"No," I admitted, wanting to add something, but not knowing what exactly.

"It's a great novel by Theodor Fontane, but it has never been published in Greece. I translated the first chapters from the English edition, because my German, unfortunately, is not up to the task. If you like it, I will translate the rest for you."

He pulled a blue notebook out of the pocket of his trench coat and held it out to me. "I want to hear what you think!" he said and got up.

The bus opened its doors with an explosive belch and Alexandros leapt onto the sidewalk. The sun blushed red behind the pillars of the Temple of Olympian Zeus.

Every time I tried—both then and in the years that followed—to read the opening of *Effi Briest*, I failed. I could not bring myself to concentrate on the text. Alexandros's handwriting kept me from it: the swooping *v*'s like seagulls hovering over the blue lines, the lavish *l*'s full of feminine flirtation, the vibrant vulgarity of his *w*'s and *o*'s. I was also riveted by the two coffee stains on pages 18 and 43, the cigarette burn on the back cover, and the obviously rubbed-out words under the title. Had he written his name before taking an eraser to it? Or had he written a dedication to me? I never found out.

When I first cracked the notebook open, I was lying in bed in Koukaki, and I imagined him sitting at his desk—an oil lamp, a steaming pot of coffee, and an ashtray stuffed with cigarette butts at his side—preparing to translate until dawn, eyes feverish, lips pursed in a charming, somewhat childish pout.

What more could Alexandros Strofalis have expected from this intrusion into my life?

VII

ALMOST TWO WEEKS later, he starred in an event unprecedented in the restaurant's annals.

Spring was arriving in all its splendor. Even the center of Athens was fragrant with it. At the time, Omonia Square was abloom with lilacs and bitter orange trees. During a break, Alexandros lit a cigarette and sat down to enjoy it at one of the tables on the sidewalk by the restaurant. Outraged, the head waiter hastened to inform the maître d'.

"What do you think you're doing there?" Tolis Bouas demanded, his dyed hair already standing on end.

"What am I doing?" Alexandros replied, as innocently as a newborn babe. "I'm taking a little rest to gather my strength before returning to work!"

"Get up immediately! The tables are not for the staff!"

Alexandros complied, but vowed to get his revenge. At the end of his shift, after taking off his waiter's uniform and donning a khaki overshirt—the kind covered in pockets that the British used to wear in the colonies—he parked himself at one of the most prominent tables, stretched out his long legs, and made a show of poring over the menu. In short order, Mr. Tolis appeared, more daunting than ever.

"Ah, your timing is impeccable! An ouzo, please, and the special assorted platter of meze!" Alexandros threw down the gauntlet.

"Shove off, you little shit! You're fired! Away with you!" the maître d' bellowed, shaking with fury.

"Mr. Savvas Bogdanos hired me, and only he can fire me," Alexandros replied, without raising his voice.

"If he doesn't clear out, then I quit!" Tolis Bouas cried in a threatening tone to my uncle.

"The role of employee and all responsibilities pertaining thereto cease to exist at the end of one's working hours. My shift completed, I enjoy all the rights and privileges of any other client. *N'est-ce pas?*" Alexandros explained with a crooked grin.

Half the staff was glued to the window, the better to enjoy the spectacle of Bogdanos booting out Strofalis with a good kick in the pants. Against all odds, however, Uncle Savvas donned the mantle not of martinet but of peacemaker. He beseeched Tolis Bouas to return to the floor. "We'll talk shortly," he said reassuringly. Then he linked his arm through Alexandros's and they walked out of our sight, talking in low voices.

The next day, it was as if nothing had happened, no harm, no foul. Mr. Tolis, of course, kept well away from Alexandros, and if their paths happened to cross, he would conspicuously turn his back on him. Strofalis, for his part, was on his best behavior and did not strut his victory—gloating was beneath him. In any case, the Afroessa staff was far from appreciating his exploit. They called him a show-off, accused him of being a know-it-all. I was the only one, I suppose, who had admired his conduct, which struck me as almost revolutionary. It confirmed my conviction that this strange young man, at only twenty-five years old, had moxie. He was neither a yes-man nor a bookworm buried in his books. But I did not dare congratulate him.

I did not even dare offer my opinion, not that I had been able to form one, of his translation of *Effi Briest*. I could not even thank him. And he, too, seemed unable to decide how to make another overture, feeling in any case that I was too beautiful for him and, most important, too inexperienced. For the following month and a half, we only exchanged furtive smiles at Afroessa.

To cap it all off, I made the mistake of telling Niove about what had happened on the bus. She had burst out laughing as soon as she heard the story.

"What an idiot!"

"Why?"

"Who thinks of translating an entire book? What's wrong with writing a poem on a napkin?"

"Perhaps he doesn't write poetry."

"Oh, come on, Niki, he's just so full of himself! Looking down his nose at us like he's little Lord Fauntleroy! I just don't understand why your uncle likes him so much."

I did not know what to say or do to defend Alexandros. What's more, Niove was annoyed with me for not accepting Eddy Zarifis's advances. She was now going out regularly with the doctor and was in the midst of deploying a detailed, step-by-step plan designed to ensnare him once and for all.

"If all goes as planned, by Christmas, he'll have popped the question!" she bragged.

Things with Alexandros could very well have ended there, his fledgling advances relegated to a charming memory of youth, one of those sweet regrets, an "imagine what might have happened if" moment that one chews over in one's dotage. Life would have widened the distance between us before we had a chance to truly get a hold on each other. Don't misunderstand me, I am not underestimating the power of love. But I believe (and the fact that I am speaking beyond the grave adds great clout to this conviction), I believe with all my being, that destiny is a web woven by the thread of coincidence.

IN OUR CASE, it was an entire chain of coincidences: First, the shipping magnate Joachim Bavelas finally agreed to his sister's marriage; second, he decided to celebrate the

wedding on Spetses, where they had a distant family connection; third, that summer of 1957, the kitchen in the hotel
Poseidon was closed for renovations; and fourth, Joachim
Bavelas insisted—at all costs, and even ended up paying a
king's ransom for it—that Afroessa take charge of the wedding dinner.

A sizable ship was chartered to convey the guests, along
with Afroessa's entire staff, to Spetses. The restaurant closed
its doors for the weekend: Waiters, cooks, even dishwashers
were included in the expedition. For days, the restaurant
was abuzz with joyful anticipation, less because of the fact
that Uncle Savvas had promised all his employees, no matter their station, an exceptionally generous travel bonus,
than because most of them—children of the war and the
Occupation, and for the more advanced in age, the indelible traumas of the Asia Minor Catastrophe—had never
had the chance to take an excursion. Forced expulsions,
massacres, terror, and a life led day to day under the constant fear of what tomorrow might bring: This had been
their lot, if not worse.

At first, my parents got on their high horses: It was out
of the question that I spend the night outside my own home,
and in Spetses to boot, a notorious bastion of the right and
favorite summer resort of the royals, as my father lost no
time in pointing out. As always it was Markella who talked
them out of it. She swore up and down that she wouldn't
let me out of her sight, even though she knew full well that
as the deputy director of personnel she would be lodged at
the Poseidon, while we, the waitstaff, would be scattered

throughout various rooming houses rented for the occasion. She argued that I'd be getting half a month's wages for one day's work, and even went so far as to suggest that my presence was absolutely indispensable.

"You mean, our daughter has truly distinguished herself as a waitress?" Anna quipped in a sneering tone. She could no longer tolerate my working at Afroessa and kept badgering my father day in and day out to have me begin my studies, if not in Moscow, "at least in Uzbekistan, or another popular democracy," or that I be hired at one of the EDA offices.

"Niki is our little mascot, our good luck charm! Without Niki the egg-and-lemon soup curdles and the wines turn to vinegar!" Markella replied with the utmost seriousness.

Had she suspected what would transpire in Spetses, she would have been of an entirely different mind.

I COULD HAVE written an entire novella about that parody of a wedding, where the bride, on the wrong side of fifty and afflicted with a corpulence that added considerably to her age, had at least a decade on the groom. I could mock their saccharine behavior, their longing looks, their comical misalignment of appearance: Luigi, as lean and lanky as a telegraph pole, and Melpo, small and roly-poly, folds of flesh bulging from her dress, face on fire and streaming with sweat as she danced. Or, conversely, I could laud the power of their love, which had withstood the ire of Joachim Bavelas, the distinguished captain, who for years had refused to give his sister to an Italian carpenter, a prisoner of war whom Melpo, as a volunteer nurse, had met in Athens in 1941, and had loved and stoically waited for, rejecting all suitors that her brother foisted on her until she had succeeded in finally forcing him to bend. And in so doing, she had brought together the crème de la crème of Piraeus and the Greek ship-owning classes of London with Naples's hoi polloi, all of whom together were making the parquet floors of the imposing Poseidon hotel shake under their tarantellas.

I could have written an entire novella about it, if I had paid any attention to what was going on around me. But I had eyes only for Alexandros. During the crossing to Spetses, while the other waitresses were singing their hearts out, I was nervously pacing the decks looking for him. When I finally spotted him on the foredeck, having a laugh with a group of Italian girls, I was in turmoil. I bit my lip and ducked behind a pillar so that he wouldn't see me (but he must have seen me, and it probably sparked the courage he had lacked up to that point).

"You're jealous, Niki? Have you lost your mind? Don't tell me that you have fallen for that big bear?" I reprimanded myself. No, I was not in love with him, I swear. I didn't even find Alexandros Strofalis particularly good-looking—by the day's standards, to be considered good-looking one had to resemble, even if only faintly, a movie star. Nor did I find him particularly charming. Yet he intrigued me more than any man ever had. I wanted to—no, I absolutely had to—get to know him.

As soon as we arrived on the island, we were up to our ears in work. The wedding was going to take place at the cathedral at seven in the evening. The guests would begin arriving at the hotel shortly after the conclusion of the ceremony. We had a mere six hours to get everything ready. And to cap it all off, the hotel's permanent staff seemed to have no intention of pitching in. They barely deigned to unlock the storerooms for us so that we might retrieve the hundreds of linen tablecloths that needed ironing before we could set the tables, as well as the innumerable pieces of silverware and crystal glasses all in need of washing and shining. It was the first time that I ever saw Uncle Savvas fly off the handle.

"You dirty bastard! Didn't you promise to have everything ready and waiting for our arrival!" he roared as he laid into the Poseidon's manager, but instantly realized that even if he were to beat the living daylights out of the man, it wouldn't do any good. At around six, a rumor made the rounds that the prime minister of Greece, Konstantinos Karamanlis, had arrived incognito on the island and would be attending the reception, and the tension mounted to a fever pitch. All ajitter, Aunt Markella dropped a soup tureen, which shattered and left a shard lodged in her calf, and Teta and I had to rush her to the doctor. At some point, in the general hurry-scurry, Alexandros intercepted me on the way from the kitchens to the dining room.

"Two, two thirty at the latest, the reception will be done," he said. "Don't stay to clear the tables. Find a way to get out of there without the others seeing you, and come meet me under the statue of Bouboulina."[100]

"Where is it?"

"Ask and find out!" he replied in a tone that brooked no objections. Brushing the feathers off his uniform—the waiters had been charged with plucking the poultry—he disappeared.

It didn't even occur to me to stand him up. At midnight I was already staring angrily at the guests, who were showing no signs of tiring of the revelry. "When will they finally decide to clear out?" I thought, champing at the bit. When the dining-room clock rang two in the morning and the party was still in full swing, I decided to take things into my own hands. I drew Markella aside and whispered that I had just got my period and could barely stand up straight.

"Do you want one of the girls to walk you to your room?" My aunt swallowed the lie hook, line, and sinker.

"No, I think you have enough on your plate with me leaving. I won't deprive you of another waitress!"

She was impressed by my conscientiousness. "Before I got married, I too would be flat on my back every time I got my period," she commiserated.

I dashed to the changing rooms, threw on a frock, and took one of the back doors out into the moon-bathed night.

---

[100] Laskarina Bouboulina was a naval commander and heroine of the Greek War of Independence in 1821.

"SHALL I COME down, or do you want to come up?"

I raised my head, and all the breath went out of me. The reckless rascal had climbed up onto the gigantic bust of Bouboulina, which at the time presided over the Spetses harbor (it was taken down some years later). He was leaning against her marble chest, his curls tickling her chin. He had removed his tuxedo jacket but was still wearing the ruffled shirt and bow tie. A bottle of wine and two glasses stood beside him. If the island folk had woken up and seen him, they would have either stoned him or taken him for a madman.

"All right, all right, I'm coming," he said and leapt down with an agility astonishing for someone his size. He landed between a wilting laurel wreath—"A nation eternally grateful" read the ribbon—and a bag that looked like Santa's sack. He threw the sack over his shoulder and entrusted me with the wine and glasses.

"Let's go!" he said.

"What's in there?"

"Ah! All sorts of goodies! Sausages, for one, and even some French cheeses!"

"And where are we taking it?"

"You'll see!"

We followed the coastal road out of town. A little over a half mile out, we spied some huts to our right.

"That's where the oars live," he told me. "In other words, the boatmen who row out to passenger ships and bring people to shore. They don't own the boats, so they cannot use them to fish. They live in penury..."

"You've been to Spetses before?"

"Never! I met them this afternoon." Then, he called out: "It's Alex! From the Poseidon!"

An old man in a woolen undershirt and long underwear, accompanied by two children with shaved heads, appeared out of the darkness.

"Here you go, as promised," Alexandros declared. "I swiped everything that was left."

The children undid the sack and pounced on the vittles.

"Blessings to you, lad! May you live long and prosper!" the old man replied. "And the young woman? Your wife?"

"Niki is her name," Alexandros said elusively.

I was staring at him in admiration that was not unalloyed with a small dose of suspicion. Was he truly such a philanthropist, or was he simply trying to impress me by any means? Even if the latter, I have to say he had succeeded marvelously.

We walked on and on, the twinkling lights of Spetses now faint in the distance. I would have asked about our destination had I not realized that he too had no idea where we were going. When our feet began sinking in sand, he said, as if he were the master of the house, "Let's take our shoes off. It's time to enjoy the wine!" Half an hour later, I was nestled in his arms. He was drinking from the bottle, and I from his lips.

What was it that drew me so strongly to Alexandros Strofalis? What was it about him that conquered my every resistance, my every hesitation? How many times did those close and less close to me ask the question, "What do you see in him?" at times under the pretense of kindness—"We're just trying to understand, because we care"—and at others in a manner deeply hurtful and offensive? I, of course, never bothered to explain to anyone. Not even to Niove, who would not have understood if I had told her that Eddy Zarifis and all the well-heeled Lotharios of his ilk could not hold a candle to Strofalis, because he had not tried to win me with smoke and mirrors, by playing the famous lawyer or showing off his car and the empty celebrity he enjoyed in the haunts of the era's golden youth. How could I have explained to my father that Alexandros offered me the pure love for life that I had so sorely missed as a child? That his every word, his every kiss made me see the world in a new light: It was neither a battleground nor an altar on which to sacrifice oneself in the name of grand ideals. That the world was, above all, a garden of flowers in full bloom.

That June night, on the narrow stretch of beach facing the Anargyreos and Korgialeneios School,[101] was the night of my rebirth. The Niki that the sun caressed with its soft light at six in the morning in the crumpled dress and with the tousled hair full of sand, the Niki who found a crab clinging with its claws to her brassiere, was not a daughter, a granddaughter, a niece, a colleague, a puppy, or a wild child. That Niki was a woman.

---

[101] A prestigious school for the children of affluent families.

WOMAN

I

WOMAN! WHAT A triumph it was to feel like a woman! How proud I was of the fact that I had not auctioned off my "purity" and "honor"; that I had not used them as leverage to secure a wedding crown[102] but had offered them spontaneously to a boy! The fact that Alexandros had not told any tall tales, had not tried to sway me with promises; the fact that he conveyed his love in caresses and not grand declarations endeared him to me even more. Naked, we dove into the morning sea, and then he dried me in his arms and together we walked back toward town. On the way, we stopped at a greengrocer and he bought me cherries. I hung a couple from my ears, like I used to do when I was little. He stooped, kissed me, and bit into one of my earrings, and in that moment, I wished he were still inside me. I knew that it would hurt less than the first time, that

---

[102] *Stefana*, in Greek, wedding crowns are an integral part of the Greek Orthodox marriage ceremony that symbolize matrimonial union in the eyes of God.

I would quickly become intimate with that insolent little creature maddened by even the most fleeting caress (and how difficult to appease it once aroused)! I would learn to straddle it, ride it to its rhythms, gallop away with it, as if it were my horse. Or rather my magic broom, my flying broomstick!

I tiptoed into the room I shared with Niove. She was not asleep; she had been up waiting for me, worried sick.

"Another ten minutes and I would have called your aunt. Where were you all night?"

My wicked smile betrayed me.

"You're no longer a virgin, Niki?" she howled as if someone had died. "Where? When? With whom? With him?" She didn't even dare utter his name. "Don't tell me! Actually, yes, tell me! No, no, drop it. I don't want to know! And you better forget it, too. When the time comes, we'll think of a way to sort things out."

When two days later I asked her to cover for me (I had already told my parents that I was going to her house after work under the pretext that it was her birthday), Niove balked.

"You're going out with him again?"

"He's taking me out to dinner."

"Seriously? Here at Afroessa perhaps in order to create some more drama? Come to your senses, Niki! I wouldn't trust Strofalis with my coat!"

"But why?" I asked naïvely.

"Oh, my!" Niove heaved a deep harrowing sigh that suddenly reminded me of the White Tower's sanctimonious matrons. "If he was a decent sort, he would have respected you in Spetses!"

"What do you mean 'respected me'?"

"You really don't learn unless it's the hard way, eh? What a little simpleton!" She looked as if she was about to beat her head against the wall. Yet she still covered for me.

"WOULD YOU LIKE to see where I live, and I'll make spaghetti with a sauce I invented?" Alexandros suggested, and even though we were already on the threshold of Petrograd and the smell of piroshkis was tickling my nostrils, we turned on our heels and hailed a taxi.

"Take us to Kypseli!"

"Has the young lady finished high school?" the taxi driver muttered as he stared at me pointedly in the rear-view mirror.

"What about you? Have you finished school?" Alexandros shot right back. I loved how he never let anyone have the last word.

On Agias Zonis Street, across from the psychiatric hospital, stood a single-family house, one of those houses that in a few years would be razed to the ground by the explosion of urban development,[103] and that even later, Athenians, now

---

[103] In the Greek, a reference to the land-for-apartment exchange program, which ceded lots with individual family homes to developers for the building of the high-rises now typical of the Athenian urban landscape in exchange for a specified number of apartments in the building.

snug in the comforts of apartment living with their radiators and watertight window frames, would lament and christen "neoclassical," thus anointing them as symbols of a lost city, once human in dimension and now buried under layers of cement. It was, to be precise, 48 Agias Zonis Street.

"Villa Violetta" announced the marble plaque by the front door. The term "villa" was, by all indications, an exaggeration, but Alexandros's mother had had every reason to take pride in the house: She had not come into its possession through either dowry or wedding gift. She had it built after purchasing the land by the fruit of her labor—that is to say, with the money she had received for the sale of her business before getting remarried in 1935.

"My stepfather made it a condition of their marriage that she stop working," Alexandros explained. "The income from his notary office was more than enough."

"What was your mother's line of work?"

"She ran a fashion house. She and her sister, Aunt Ioulia, created it from nothing when they arrived in Athens after fleeing Smyrna during the Catastrophe. As my mother liked to say, it was not at the bottom of the top-tier fashion houses but at the top of the second tier. In other words, she was not dressing the ladies of the court but the wives of high-ranking public officials."

He unlocked the front door and, as we stepped over the threshold, the bright afternoon sun abruptly gave way to a gloomy penumbra. All the shutters in the house were closed. A subtle smell of mustiness filled the air. Alexandros showed me around the three large bedrooms, the bathroom—where the tub rested its cast-iron paws on a black-and-white tile floor—and even went so far as to open the kitchen cabinets so that I might admire his mother's porcelain. He found the role of estate agent amusing.

"Here we have some choice bottles of prewar cognac. Will you take them along with the house?"

"Where is your family?" I asked.

"They're waiting for you in the parlor."

I found myself in front of a wall covered from floor to ceiling in photographs: all four of his parents—father, mother, stepfather, and stepmother—flanked by grandfathers and grandmothers, uncles and aunts, an interesting and motley crew, judging by their clothing and primarily by the look in their eyes. There was an old star of the National Theater next to a doorman; a military type sporting a crested helmet and a sword at his belt—"my great-grandfather"—and one of the belles of yesteryear, immortalized at Faliro's *bains mixtes*, in a bathing suit down to her knees. Their only common trait: They were all dead. Almost all of Alexandros's family had perished during the 1940s.

"The scourge began in 1939 with Aunt Ioulia, who was taken by cancer, but at least not before she had secured the family vault at the First Cemetery. Her parents followed a year later. At the Albanian front two of my first cousins remained under the snow. In the winter of 1941, Uncle Loukas had gallbladder surgery. They did not have medicines back then. He got sepsis and *Arrivederci, Roma*! His son,

Lelos, whom we all thought a daddy's boy, a little limp-wristed if not an outright queer, astounded us by deciding to go fight in the Middle East. The ship on which he was traveling was torpedoed. But it was my cousin Roula who had the most absurd death of all: She was slaughtered by a Chite, not because of ideological differences but in a fit of jealous rage. He was her fiancé and caught her making eyes at an ELAS lad. *Rizospastis*, which was banned at the time, depicted her as a heroine of the Resistance. Poor Roula! She knew as much about politics as I know about entomology! But look at the cleavage on her, Niki! When we were kids, she would let me cop a feel now and then..."

This roll call of the dead was conducted almost cheerily, in a tone that verged on the blasphemous. Only when we got to his parents did Alexandros change his tune.

"In May 1944, my father was executed. Myrto went to visit him at the Patras Prison, where he was being held. They told her, 'Your husband is waiting for you in the square,' so she made her way up there, to Psilalonia, only to see her husband hanging from a plane tree. They let the executed hang there for two days as a cautionary tale to everyone else. Then she had to fork over a small fortune to have the gravedigger put him in his own plot and not toss him into a mass grave. After the ninth-day memorial, Myrto returned to Athens in a state of near collapse. She begged me to go live with her: 'Alexandros, please, I don't have anyone left in the world.' But I had my mother. I was only thirteen years old and could not bear to leave her. I thought it over and over again—it was my decision to make, no one else's—but I just couldn't do it. Two weeks later, Myrto killed herself."

I kept glancing from Myrto—a coquettish brunette in her midthirties posing in a garden with a cat perched on her knees—to Alexandros. He looked like a little boy fighting to hold back tears.

"And it's not like my mother had that much time left. On May 1, 1946, she and my stepfather were killed at Cape Sounion. They had just bought a car and had gone to pick flowers.[104] They drove off a cliff."

"And you've been by yourself ever since?"

"No, with Smaragda!"

A small side table on the other side of the parlor was also covered with photographs, happier in nature: Alexandros and Smaragda as infants and then a little older, as children, both of them blond and curly-haired, either mounted on little bicycles or seated in small boats.

"Here I am rowing on Lake Geneva. Where were you, Niki, in the summer of '38?"

"In exile on Sifnos, with my mother."

"I was in exile on Tzia in '39, with my father. I've never tasted better fish!"

"Where is Smaragda?" I asked him, trembling at the thought that she too had died.

"My little Smaragda?" he said, his face lighting up. "My princess?" He pointed to an adolescent with a cascade of hair, huge eyes, and the allure of a Hollywood diva.

---

[104] It is traditional to pick flowers on May 1st to make May garlands.

"She was barely fourteen and the cobblestones simmered under her feet when she walked along the street! All the boys in Kypseli were in love with her. Oikonomides, the radio host, even wrote a song for her, *In the castle of my childhood nights, you always reign as my Snow White*. In the end, she dashed all their hopes. She married an American and moved with him to San Francisco!"

"You raised her?"

"I had no choice! When our mother and her father were killed, Smaragda was ten years old and I was fifteen. Technically, since we were without a guardian, we ought to have been remanded to an orphanage. Fortunately, my mother's youngest brother, out of the goodness of his heart, assumed the responsibility of our care. For a price...Once a month, our dear uncle would turn up and make off with half of my stepfather's pension. In exchange he would lecture us: 'Keep your eye on the little one! God forbid she be led astray! Spare the rod and spoil the child!' He was full of such pearls of sanctimonious advice, each more disgusting than the last. He claimed he was investing the money in the stock market to add to Smaragda's dowry. He was a grocer, what did he know of stock markets? The night before her wedding, he announced, all crocodile tears, that the money had vanished into thin air 'because of the international crisis.' As if we gave two hoots! As if Smaragda had need of a dowry! All right then, Niki? You've met the relatives? Shall we go up to my quarters?"

The Villa Violetta's roof terrace was the epicenter of Alexandros's world, his flourishing kingdom, his own personal universe. By connecting the laundry room with the servants' quarters, he had constructed what he described as his "alchemist's lair": a large, sun-bathed studio with a view of the Acropolis and climbing plants posing as curtains. A huge iron bed presided over the center of the room. Alexandros did almost everything on that bed: reading, eating, daydreaming. It was the only piece of furniture in the room. A radio set and a turntable rested on the floor. There were towers of books, a colorful carpet of magazines, and plates tottering in high piles until he remembered to take them down to the kitchen or at least out onto the terrace. There weren't even any wardrobes. His underwear was folded into two crates that he pushed under the bed. His ties—he had inherited an entire collection from his elegant stepfather— were tied like silk ribbons around the bedposts. His shirts and jackets hung from nails in the wall.

On the opposite wall, there was an enormous world map. Alexandros spent as much time devouring foreign newspapers and magazines (he bought them secondhand from a newspaper vendor in Monastiraki) as he did dreaming about the continents and oceans he contemplated on that map. Since his adolescence, he had been a passionate reader of travel literature and had seen so many films that he could talk endlessly about the lost civilizations of the Inca and the Maya, the Scandinavian sagas and the Norse epics, as well as the bars of New York and the opium dens of Hong Kong.

The longing to travel both exhilarated and plagued him. At eighteen, shortly after his acceptance into the literature department of the School of Humanities, he had applied for and been issued a seaman's permit. His sister's care had provided him with the perfect alibi not to set sail. The fellow whom Smaragda had married at the age of nineteen, a mechanic stationed at JUSMAG, the American Military Mission, had repeatedly suggested that he follow them to California. "It would be a shame to quit the university without my diploma after five years of studies," Alexandros had said to account for his resistance.

To me, however, it was crystal clear that he was hostage to his dead. Despite his having them under lock and key in the parlor, despite making light of them at every opportunity, they held him fast in their clutches, had him trapped in their invisible web, sucking on his marrow so that they, in turn, might escape the swallow of oblivion.

"Why don't you sell the house, Alexandros? Why don't you at least rent it out?"

"What would I do with the furniture? And the four thousand volumes in the library?"

"Give them away! 'A gift from Alexandros Strofalis in memory of his parents...'"

He stared at me for a moment, stunned, as if I had asked him to cast pearls before swine, as if I had committed the ultimate blasphemy. Then immediately, his face lit up, his eyes sparkled triumphantly, the sorrow that appeared to dim even his brightest moments seemed to dissipate.

"Now that I've found you, everything will begin again from the start! You will be my Niki, my victory!"

He kissed me and threw me on the mattress.

How many times did we make love? Four? Or was it five? His desire fueled mine. My body was coming undone, blooming, alive under his eyes and his touch. The more I had him, the more I wanted him.

At one point, I collapsed on top of him, exhausted, and my bleary eyes fell on a record jutting out from under the bed. On the sleeve, there was a smiling young man who could easily have been taken for Alexandros's younger brother—true, he was a lot smaller and wore the thick glasses of myopia, but he had the same curly hair, the same smile.

"Who's that?" I asked.

"Buddy Holly. A kid from Texas with an incredible talent! He plays rock and roll, a new kind of music. Do you know it?"

"No."

"Of course, how would you? Last year, *Blackboard Jungle* was screened in Greece, a film with dancing scenes set to rock and roll. But I suppose few people saw it, and it came and went. The American Library on Stadiou Street gets all the new records. Katy, a friend who works there, lends them to me for a couple of days. Do you want to hear some Buddy Holly?"

He put "That'll Be the Day" on the turntable, a song that had come out barely a month earlier. I didn't speak a word of English so the lyrics meant nothing to me, but the music thrilled me, the rhythm gripped me from the very first note. Naked, lying belly-down in Alexandros's arms, I swung my ass, rolled my hips. He held me hard and still for a moment, lifted me gently, and slipped inside me again.

"Now, keep going!" he said.

The spaghetti dish he had talked about making turned out to be wishful thinking, of course. We fell asleep on empty stomachs. When I woke up, it was pitch-dark. I glanced at Alexandros—it was the first time I had seen someone sleep with his legs crossed—and then at the clock. It was a quarter to two! I had promised my parents that I would be home by midnight. I threw my clothes on, gave him a quick kiss, and ran out into the street. Fortunately, there was a taxi stand on the corner of Agias Zonis and Kallifrona Streets. I paid the night tariff, my entire day's earnings, for the ride.

The front door opened before I had the chance to take the key out of my bag. My father was standing at the doorstep, grimmer than Charon.

"Where were you, Niki?"

"At Niove's..."

That's when he slapped me. A hard, heavy slap, its force and trajectory carefully considered and calibrated. A slap dealt by someone who had been dealt many in his life. A slap of the kind that sets fire to the cheek and numbs the jaw.

"Who were you with?"

Suddenly, it seemed absurd to lie. I had no reason to be ashamed of my joy. "With Alexandros Strofalis," I said simply, not at all expecting that his name meant anything to my father.

"Takis Strofalis's son?" my father asked, his expression suddenly transformed.

"Yes."

"Tell him to come see me and ask for your hand."

II

WHILE TAKIS STROFALIS was neither folk nor national hero—no song had been written about him, no statue erected in his memory—he had, nonetheless, left an indelible impression on those in the inner circles, the elite of both the left and the right.

Uncle Savvas was categorical: "If Takis Strofalis were alive today, he would be playing a leading role in public life. He had such charm, such erudition. Yes, many others also studied in Europe, but only Takis had the stuff of a European intellectual. I met him at the beginning of the '30s, both of us still died-in-the-wool Venizelists. I was part of the right wing of the Liberals, and he, on the left. Afterward, he turned even further left and tried to establish a socialist party, unfortunately with little success. In Greece, if you challenged the regime, you were labeled a communist, true or not. Under the Occupation, he made the mistake of enlisting in the EAM, like many other progressive citizens. It was at that time that I sent him a message: 'Do as you like in Athens, where you have a network to protect you, but do not go to the mountains, because that will be the end of you.' He didn't listen. Out there in the backwoods, the partisans rolled out the red carpet for him. They needed social democrats to water down the bite of the Stalinist brew. But instead of sending him to the Middle East with the delegation charged with negotiating the Lebanon Agreement—no one else had his chops for something like that—they said, 'Go to Morea[105] and organize the illegal elections.' They threw him to the wolves."

"Are you saying they set a trap for him?" I asked.

"I'm convinced of it, but I cannot prove it. Someone must have denounced him. After all, he was intercepted by a German patrol while crossing from the mainland to the Peloponnese on a boat in the middle of the night! If I had known that he was being held in the Patras Prison, I would have moved heaven and earth to get him out. And then they executed that gem of a man as retaliation on a trumped-up pretext, because some drunken ELAS louts killed a German soldier in a brothel! Out of hundreds of prisoners, they chose to hang ten, Strofalis among them. Oh, I know that it wasn't by chance, but I cannot prove it. That's why I have never discussed it with Alexandros. What would be the point in upsetting the boy?"

I, however, did not have my uncle's scruples. I could not bear the thought that things of such immediate concern to him were being discussed behind Alexandros's back.

"I've heard the story before," he told me. "I can neither confirm nor deny it. I have no proof either way and I don't

---

[105] An ancient, popularly used name for the Peloponnese.

know if I have full confidence in Bogdanos. While my father and yours were fighting in the Resistance, he was a minister under the Germans. Yes, he's a great fellow, but one shouldn't lose sight of this fact. In any case, I am not really all that interested in determining if my father was a hero or a victim, if he was truly charismatic or if he has been lionized after his death. To me, the main issue is that he was taken away from me when I needed him the most."

Antonis Armaos's version of the Takis Strofalis story was a lot more measured than Savvas Bogdanos's. "I never met him in person. I have been told that he was a truly exceptional character: dynamic, educated, selfless. His death was a great blow, as were the deaths of so many others, but also an example of self-sacrifice to you, the younger generation. Oh, Niki, what's the point? The Resistance and then the Civil War decimated the flower of our people."

In other words, my father had not been dazzled by Alexandros's pedigree. He was simply relieved that the young man to whom I had given my heart came from good stock, that he was "one of us" and not one of those dandified daddy's boys who frequented Afroessa. He had invited him to the house, then, so that they might get to know each other. (Not for Alexandros to ask for my hand—fortunately, my father had almost immediately recognized and corrected the absurdity of that formulation; he also rued the slap, and had hastened to explain that I had earned it not because I had a boyfriend but because I had lied.) Indeed, he had invited him to the house in full expectation of encountering a young man who embodied all the virtues of the left—simplicity, integrity, an exemplary work ethic—a young man who would conduct himself less as a prospective groom and more as a disciple yearning to learn from his wisdom, like the young people from the EDA who came to our house every Saturday.

My mother's attitude before meeting him was at once kinder and more feminine. She was truly moved to hear that he had been orphaned and had raised his sister by himself.

"Is he tall?" she then asked. Height was to her an indispensable characteristic of male beauty, not at all surprising given that her father and brothers were well over six feet tall.

"Very tall!"

"Of course! I knew you wouldn't choose a midget!" she said with a big smile.

OFFICIALLY, THERE WAS another motive for the family dinner at Koukaki scheduled on the first Sunday of July 1957: The KKE had finally reinstated my father with great pomp and circumstance. Immediately after the annulment of his expulsion, the EDA hired him with full membership rights and promised to submit his candidacy at the next elections. Even if he was not reelected as the delegate to Attica, as he had been in 1932—after all, he was no longer the young and fiery revolutionary of yore—the anticipated proportion of Party votes would assure him a seat in parliament. The political career so unjustly interrupted in 1945 now looked to be back on course, and with a fair wind blowing in its sails. Even though my father, a partisan of the left, did not place rank and recognition high on his list of priorities, to see himself vindicated like this could not fail to warm the cockles of his heart.

Flattered by the invitation, Alexandros went to great lengths to create the best possible first impression as soon as he set foot in my family home. In preparation, he asked me to tell him in detail about each one of my relatives.

"I want to know how to break the ice," he explained.

"Would you also like a dress rehearsal?" I asked, almost doubling over with laughter.

That Sunday, our doorbell rang at one o'clock sharp. I opened the door and found myself face-to-face with an unrecognizable Alexandros looking as if he had stepped right out of the pages of a men's fashion magazine: linen suit, silk tie, gold cuff links. He couldn't have looked more overdressed. All the men, even Uncle Savvas, were in shirt-sleeves because of the heat wave. He held a huge bouquet in his left hand and a leather-bound book in his right. He offered the flowers to my mother and then bowed to kiss her hand, as he did with all the other women, including Grandmother Sevasti. He then extended what he called his "gift of introduction" toward my father: the *Manifesto of the Communist Party* in a sumptuous French edition from 1905. Antonis kept glancing up and down, from Alexandros to the book.

"Where did you dig this up?" he asked.

"In our library."

"This must have cost a fortune," my father muttered, leafing through it. "Certainly, no working man could afford something like this…"

The venom of this remark left me aghast. I had not expected such boorish behavior from my father. But he too had not expected to be welcoming his daughter's lover— a moment come so soon and out of the blue! Beneath his veneer of civility, he was in the clutches of an almost primal panic.

"Let's go eat. The meze will get cold!" he said, putting his arm around Alexandros's shoulders with a heartiness that was as clumsy as his earlier blunder.

We were not seated next to each other. Alexandros was placed between Grandmother Sevasti and Uncle Petros, and I was at the other end of the table to help mother serve the meal. To disguise the prevailing awkwardness, we chitchatted about food: how camel made for the tastiest pastourma; how one always ought to stuff the vine leaves for dolmadakia the night before serving them. Trying to loosen the mood, Markella attempted an amusing anecdote from Afroessa, but ran aground on the icy look from mother, who balked at any mention of that "restaurant for the wealthy." Finally, clutching at straws, they all turned to my little cousin, Toula, and began interrogating her in unison: What was her favorite subject in school? What did she want to be when she grew up? Poor Toula, accustomed to going unnoticed, stumbled over the simplest questions.

Alexandros had barely uttered a word. No one spoke to him, and he was probably coming to terms with the fact that they all had to get used to his presence first before relations warmed on both sides. Accordingly, he was sitting there quietly, sipping his wine, nibbling on a chicken wing, and throwing me the occasional tender glance. Everything seemed to be portending a conclusion to that first family meeting as colorless and commonplace as its beginning. (Alexandros would have found my family cold and they would have pronounced him exceptionally reserved.) But then, Uncle Petros suddenly turned toward him and asked, as if about to bite his head off, "Who in the blazes are you and what in God's name are you doing here?"

I had, of course, warned Alexandros. I had explained that Uncle Petros's mind had come unglued after the terrible tortures he had bravely endured at Makronissos. Not that he was what we call fit for a straitjacket. But he would often go off the rails, cursing under his breath and picking fights for no apparent reason with the first person to cross his path, be it at the café or on the bus. Stalin's denunciation was the straw that broke the camel's back. He simply could not swallow the fact that "Uncle Joe," for whom he had literally shed blood, sweat, and tears, was now being labeled a criminal by his very own heirs, so-called enlightened communists. On his return from Makronissos, he had cut ties with the KKE and renounced his medal of the Order of Glory. He had been living as a pariah ever since, aimlessly wandering around all day, dragging his crippled leg behind him, and whenever he felt that someone was looking at him oddly, he would pull up the cuff of his pants to bare the leg and recite, word for word, the story of his wounding during the Dekemvriana. Uncle Petros was the third cross my grandmother had to bear after Giannos and Iordanis, who had shown no signs of life in the past twenty years, and had been lost without a trace in the maws of South America. Naturally, the family had not abandoned Petros to his fate: Fani had rented a studio for him in the same building in Pangrati where Sevasti and Markella lived; my grandmother cooked for him, washed and ironed his clothes, and generally made sure that he was presentable; and Antonis also regularly put his hand in his pocket. The Armaos family was knit together by a love without bounds. Even though Petros occasionally vilified one sister as a collaborator, the other as a whore, my father as a revisionist and a sellout, and my mother as a Pisspotaria—a play on Pasionaria—to our eyes he was not only blameless but also crowned with the halo of a martyr.

"Who are you, you shit?" he demanded again.

"Alexandros Strofalis. Graduate of the School of Humanities. I am here with Niki," Alexandros replied with remarkable aplomb.

"With Niki? What does 'with' mean? Are you fucking her? Is the fine gent here fucking your turtledove?" Petros turned to my parents and burst into demented laughter.

"Stop it!" snapped Antonis, the only one able to occasionally prevail on Petros, but the latter turned a deaf ear.

"Did you say a graduate from the Humanities? Ah, there's a scholar among us! Which means that when young men your age were fighting in the Democratic Army or rotting on Makronissos or elsewhere, you had your head buried in books without a care in the world. And now you just show up here and take up with Antonis Armaos's daughter. You have some balls on you!"

"To be honest, I ought, by rights, to have been 'taking classes' at Makronissos," Alexandros said, without betraying the least offense or anger. "I also ought to have been barred from the university for political reasons. They already had quite a file on me because of both my father's activities and that whole racket with the photograph…

"In the final days of the Dekemvriana, the ELAS had begun recruiting even the children in their districts, at first only to help with backup tasks, although if you happened to have a few hairs on your upper lip, you were sent to fight the British and the monarcho-fascists. My friends and I in Kypseli, we were raring to go. They called us the EPON's '20th Platoon' and charged us with keeping the local EAM branch supplied with provisions. The ELAS lads had commandeered and then holed up in the home of a high-school principal on the corner of Lesvou and Megistis Streets. Our job was to deliver water and anything edible we managed to scrounge. Needless to say, we looked on our elders, the ones who were armed, as if they were gods. One day, I approached one of the men who was standing guard and begged him to let me hold his rifle. He liked me, so he swung it off his shoulder and passed the belt over my head. As my evil luck would have it, that morning a French war correspondent was reporting in the area. 'May I take your picture?' he asked, and thrilled by the request, I struck a fierce pose. Two weeks later, my big mug was on the front page of *L'Humanité*. 'Greek Youth Up in Arms' read the caption. I doubt that the newspaper gave a thought to the repercussions the publication might have on me.

"Not that I was suddenly a household name, but when I turned sixteen and had to go to the police station to have my identity card issued, the commander thrust the newspaper in my face.

"'That was a long time ago. My views have changed,' I told him.

"'It's always the same song and dance with you lot!' he retorted, landing a fist on the desk. I realized my troubles were only beginning, so I proclaimed, my voice blaring, 'I have no relationship whatsoever with communism and its offshoots!'[106]

"'I prefer concrete proof of your commitment to the nation,' he said, winking at me. You understand what I'm trying to say, don't you? He was looking for a snitch."

The more Alexandros made headway with his story, the more my family's eyes popped out of their heads.

"Don't worry. I didn't become a snitch. I came up with a better solution," he reassured them. "My late stepfather was a famous cardplayer, renowned in all the best clubs."

"Cardplayer or cardsharp?" my father asked.

---

[106] A stock formulation in the declarations of repentance required of communist political prisoners by the regime.

"You're a cardsharp if you get caught," Alexandros replied mischievously. "Before he died, he managed to teach me some tricks, which I then perfected. From the age of seventeen to twenty-two, I made out like a bandit every Sunday in the cafés lining Fokionos Negri Street. One afternoon, the precinct commander showed his face.

"'On your guard, Alex, my lad!' he bragged. 'When I have a deck of cards in my hand, I mean business!'

"'You do me an honor, then, Commander, sir!'

"We played until sunrise. I stripped, tarred, feathered him, and left him for dead.

"'What do I owe you?' he asked at the end.

"'I don't want any money. I want you to burn my file and place me, as pure as the driven snow, back among the ranks of our stalwart nationalist citizenry.' He did what I asked. Deep down, he was a decent sort. I have not encountered another obstacle, either in the army, at the university, or anywhere else, ever since."

"Certificates of social conscience are kept at the central offices of the Security Forces," Antonis observed, with a tone of suspicion.

"What can I say?" Alexandros replied. "Perhaps my case was of interest only to the local authorities."

"You're telling us that you gambled your past away, that you cold-bloodedly sold off your father's memory in a game of cards! And you dare boast about it to boot!" Uncle Petros lambasted him.

"And you're telling me that my father would have preferred me to sacrifice my university studies to his memory?

I doubt it. Yes, our past belongs to us, but we don't need to be held captive by it."

"Do you still play cards, Alexandros?" my mother asked.

"No. One morning, I woke up and knew that I was done with them. I've taken up billiards instead."

Watching my parents, there was no doubt in my mind that Alexandros had been a terrible disappointment. They didn't even understand what he was. A traitor? An opportunist? Or simply a smart aleck trying to scandalize them with stories whose veracity my father deemed highly dubious? Most of all, they could not understand how someone like that had ensnared their daughter, their Niki, who not only had never betrayed her parents but, at barely ten years of age, had left school in order to stand bravely by their side.

III

MY FATHER WAS in no hurry to talk about Strofalis. His silence a slow-burning torment, he let me stew for three days before taking me aside and letting me have his opinion in the same imperious and absolute tone with which he announced, all the time and at any opportunity, that History would one day vindicate him.

"That boy is not right for you, Niki. I don't know how he took advantage of your innocence and got you eating out of his hand, and I don't want to know. I could insist that

you not see him again. You are a minor and it is my right
under the law. But it would be against my principles. What's
important is that you realize, of your own accord, what a
corner you have painted yourself into."

He was speaking to me not as a father but as a priest.
I bristled. "I love Alexandros. I want to live with him!"

"You think you love him, but you don't. You're just confused. If I asked you to tell me what you love about him you
wouldn't be able to get a word out."

"That's not true!"

"Well, I have no interest in putting you in a difficult
position. The only thing we care about, your mother and
I, is that you not make an irreparable mistake. Very soon,
within a matter of weeks, or at worst months, this boy will
no longer mean anything to you. And then you will come
to me and ask—not in tears, I hope- -how you could have
been so completely misled. And then I will take you in my
arms and console you. I will say that you have your entire
life ahead of you and that it is through errors like these that
we learn and grow and continue moving forward. For the
moment, I want you to promise me one thing: that you will
be careful, Niki. Promise?"

"I'm always careful."

"Well, now be even more so. You don't want to end up
paying for the Strofalis episode for the rest of your life, do
you?"

It wasn't clear to me if my father feared a pregnancy or
simply the loss of my virginity, and I had no desire to seek

clarification. Besides, his position did not surprise me at all.
My father was the kind of man who aspired not to impose
his opinion on those around him but to instruct and guide
them to it; he was the kind of man certain, almost intrin-
sically so, in his possession of the truth, a certainty that
never failed him, even in the most tumultuous moments of
his life; the kind of man who had the intelligence not to
strong-arm without reason but to apply diplomatic means
whenever possible. He was constitutionally incapable of
reacting differently. Besides, it was evident to my father that
if he openly clashed with Alexandros, I would dig my heels
in and defend my choice come hell or high water. Not to
mention that he would be giving me the biggest gift of all
by endowing Alexandros with the allure of forbidden fruit.
The best *line* to follow (this is the word he used in conversation with my mother, as if he were addressing a political problem) was to give him enough rope to hang himself,
undermining him as discreetly as possible and keeping him
close to hand so as to trip him up all the more easily.

Politics, in other respects, was the last thing—or at least
the next to last thing—that stood between them. Armaos
felt for Strofalis a deep, visceral dislike, which gradually
turned into loathing.

This was not the proverbial hostility of a father toward
the younger man who appears, out of the blue, to carry off
his only daughter. It was the fury of the man who aspires
to convince everyone of everything when confronted with
someone who lacks all desire to prove anything to anyone.

It was the scorn of the man for whom "we" encompasses not only the Party, not only the working classes, but also humanity in its entirely; the scorn directed at the younger man who in using "we" points only to himself and his girl. Even more than the enemy, the soldier detests the traveler who wanders blithely through the battlefield, observing all parties from the same distance, with the same understanding and the same sense of inanity at their death. The fact that Antonis Armaos harbored such a traveler in the innermost recesses of his being—although buried alive, he would occasionally feel him stir—only added fuel to the fire. I am sure that my father would have preferred a thousand times over to see me with the worst of right-wing scum, an Eddy Zarifis for example, than with Alexandros.

From a practical point of view, my father's stance was convenient. While his opinion of Alexandros certainly did not thrill me (I had hoped, naïvely, that he would take a liking to him), it was not the cause of contention. In fact, it actually made my daily life easier. My parents, needless to say, had not given me free rein because of the mere fact that I now had a boyfriend. I still had to hurry home and barricade myself in as soon as it got dark, even in the summer, even when the night air was heavy with the scent of evening primrose. At the time, the Ilisos River still flowed next to the stadium, song and laughter poured from the outdoor taverns and movie theaters, and Athens was an open invitation to roaming and romance. I, however, was allowed out only on the balcony or in the backyard. And only until midnight, at which point the Armaos household was doused in silence.

Fortunately, there were three full hours from the end of my shift at Afroessa until my obligatory return to Koukaki, and I had devised the perfect excuse to spend those three hours in Alexandros's "lair": I told my parents that I had enrolled in a private language school, where I was allegedly taking intensive English lessons.

But "allegedly" isn't quite right. I was, in fact, learning English, except instead of taking place in a schoolroom, the classes were taking place in bed. Alexandros was as passionate about Shakespeare—whom he had learned to read by himself, poring through lines and passages with the dictionary in hand—as he was about American gangster films. And because Shakespeare's plays were not staged in Greece in the original language and he had not had the opportunity to familiarize himself with the British accent, he would reproduce Romeo and Juliet's pleas, Othello's fury, and King Lear's despair in Humphrey Bogart's raffish American. As it happens, I was not in a position to see the humor in the situation, and even if I had been, it would have done nothing to change my feelings for Alexandros.

MY ADMIRATION FOR him grew day by day. I did not know if I preferred his lips kissing me or talking to me. No matter what he did, no matter what he said, I found it madly thrilling, charming, exciting. And yet, with the exception of the successive deaths that had afflicted his family, Alexandros's life had not been very different from that of any other boy his age in Kypseli. He would tell me about silly adolescent pranks, stories of playing hooky from school or taking a spin with his friends, and they captivated me a lot more than any of my father's heroic adventures. Was it because he didn't pair each one with a neat little lesson at the end, as my father had a habit of doing? Because he refused to amputate life of its nuances and contradictions in order to make it fit the mold of a particular moral or worldview? Because he'd had to develop, from a very young age, an inimitable sense of irony and humor in order to endure misfortune? Or was I simply a girl besotted?

And what about him? Had he ever fallen in love before meeting me?

"Who were you in love with before me?" I summoned all my courage to ask one day, my voice almost trembling.

He hesitated for a moment.

"With Pari Kordova," he replied with a smile. "At the time, her name was Paraskevoula Pantazopoulos. She lived with her mother and her idiot brother three streets down that way. I pursued her relentlessly from the age of eighteen until I turned twenty-one. I serenaded her—I, who can't carry a tune in a bucket!—I wrote her poems; I even went so far as to go out with one of her cousins to make her jealous. In the end, I succeeded. I slept with her twice all in all, and, as was to be expected, the whole thing fell far short of what I had imagined. To put it bluntly, Niki, I had a much better time when I masturbated at the thought of her, than when I had her in my bed."

"Here? In this bed?" I said, shocked.

"You asked! Then she entered a beauty pageant, without letting me or anyone else know, and that's where she met the fellow who got her into the movies. Her first husband was a gaffer. Now, if I am not mistaken, she's about to marry her third, someone to provide ample financial security."

I was relieved by the fact that even though I could discern condescension in these remarks, there was no bitterness.

The following day, I spied Pari Kordova on the cover of *Romanzo* hanging on the rack outside the corner kiosk. I bought it and proceeded to scour the "exclusive details of the green-eyed star's new romance" and scrutinize the photographs of the filming of her new movie.

"What an idiot to let Alexandros slip through her fingers like that!" I thought to myself.

Clearly, I was a girl head over heels in love.

SATURDAYS AND SUNDAYS were my only official, parentally approved, meeting days with Alexandros. Saturday nights, usually spent at the movies followed by a patisserie, I was allowed out until midnight. On Sunday mornings, he would pick me up and we would go to the beach, usually Faliro, and very occasionally farther afield to Glyfada. We had to be back at two in the afternoon at the latest, or else lunch would get cold on the table. Strofalis's incursion into my life had rallied the Armaos clan. During those meals at

Koukaki, the entire family was invariably in attendance, and if occasionally Uncle Savvas was absent due to "urgent matters at Afroessa," Aunt Fani was more than capable of filling his shoes. Those family meals were my father and Alexandros's favored battleground.

We were never able to get to the fruit and coffee without their being at loggerheads over one pretext or another, either serious or completely meaningless.

"A literature teacher, is it? And when do you expect an appointment?" my father said during their second encounter, already planning ahead for Alexandros's future.

"Me, teach? Never!" the latter protested. "Why would I want to bore those poor children to tears with Helleno-Christian preachifying of the genre *I have a sister, dear; a true doll, far and near; her name is Northern Epirus*, or by having them parrot things like *Of Darius and Parysatis were born two children*.[107] God forbid!"

"What do you plan to do, then? Be a waiter all your life?"

"In the near future, I'd like to travel. I've been saving money for some time to go to America. California doesn't excite me all that much, even though both my sister and Hollywood are there. I'd love to spend some time living in New York. But since I don't want to end up washing dishes, I need to take a good cache with me."

"New York. What do you intend to do there exactly?" Antonis spat the words out one by one.

---

[107] The first line in Xenophon's *Anabasis*.

"I have no idea. I'll know once I get there."

They all sat there openmouthed, Uncle Savvas included.

"Since you're dreaming about adventure and la dolce vita, my friend, what are you doing with Niki?"

"She'll come with me, of course! Or did you really think that I would leave her behind with you? *Our country is closed in*," he said, throwing in a line by Seferis for good measure.

"What if, as her father, I don't allow you to take her abroad?"

"I'll wait until she comes of age on February 3, 1959. Or we could always elope and get married," Alexandros announced with disarming aplomb.

My father blanched, then immediately blushed as the blood rose to his head. No one, absolutely no one, neither friend nor foe, had ever addressed him with such bald-faced cynicism. No one had ever attacked the very core of his being with such equally bald-faced impudence.

"How dare he, the little bastard!" he said under his breath. "I'm going to crush him! I'm going to tear him into little pieces! No, no, I must not stray from my line." He immediately pulled himself together. "I must not give him the pleasure. I will be the one to decide if and when we take the gloves off for the final showdown." So Armaos gritted his teeth. "Keep on dreaming, my friend," he muttered and moved on to something else.

Even Grandmother Sevasti, who until that point had had a real liking for Alexandros, was horrified at the thought of seeing me leave for America.

"America, my child, is a cancer! It will chew you up and swallow you whole!" she kept saying, traumatized by her eldest son's fate.

"Uncle Iordanis disappeared in South America, Grandmother. We'll be traveling to North America," I explained.

"North or South, it's the same thing: Scylla and Charybdis!" she replied, and begged me not to leave before I closed her eyes for the final time.

MY FATHER KEPT needling Alexandros, and he, for his part, always had to have the last word.

"Why do you smoke like that?" my father asked him one day out of the blue.

"Why? Smoke how?"

"A cigarette ought to be held between the fingers, not by the fingertips. Are you aping gangsters in the movies?"

"How did you know?"

"It looks so fake...so mannered."

"Fortunately, in the Soviet Union, American films are banned and there's no risk that young people will go to the dogs like me."

"Smoke however you like. Why should I care?"

"That's exactly what I was asking myself."

Their jousts would come to an end along with the Sunday dinner. Neither one ever spoke to me of them afterward, nor did they demand that I take a side. I tended to view these exchanges as all bark and no bite, a bizarre but fundamentally amicable form of communication between two competing males, both of whom refused to back down. "They will keep quibbling like this all their lives, but in the end, they'll learn to appreciate each other. Although they will probably never admit to it," I would think, basking in the newly acquired feeling of female superiority.

THIS CONCLUSION WAS reinforced by Alexandros's reaction when he discovered my father's most closely kept secret.

"Look here!" he said to me during one of our afternoons in the "lair" as he pointed to an article in the arts section of the *New York Times*. I saw a picture of a handsome young man posing in front of a strange labyrinth of fluorescent tubes. He was wearing a form-fitting velvet jacket, a huge polka-dot bow tie, and a blasé expression: Oscar Wilde was clearly an influence.

"Who is that?"

"He doesn't remind you of anyone?"

"No."

"His name is Chrys Kremos. He created a new style: neon sculpture. Apparently, it's all the rage. To be on the front pages of the *Times* there must be a lot riding on him."

"You think that we too will have such opportunities open up for us when we go to New York?" I asked in banter and completely unsuspectingly.

"For you, Niki, no doubt. It may be in your blood."

I stared at him, surprised. That's when Alexandros translated Chrys Kremos's interview for me.

You're a Greek from Egypt? the reporter asked. *Not exactly,* Chrys replied. *My biological father was a Greek from Greece—a communist leader, believe it or not, by the name of Antonio Armaos. Please don't tell my mother that I've let the cat out of the bag, because she will have a fit! An illegitimate child, and by a communist! Oh, my! What a stain on her aristocratic pedigree!*

IN THIS INSTANCE, I was the one almost having a fit. I asked Alexandros to read the critical sentence three times over and then I reached for the dictionary to check it myself, word by word.

"So that means that he is my father's son?"

"That's what it looks like," Strofalis replied with an impish grin. "Or do you know of another Antonis Armaos in the communist leadership?"

I looked at the picture again. "They don't look alike!"

"That doesn't mean anything! And, moreover, it's wrong. They do. It's their difference in expression that's confusing. If you look at their features, they're two peas in a pod."

"But how? When?"

"How would I know!"

"The truth is that in '43 my father was in the Middle East."

"In '43? That doesn't work. Chrys Kremos is in his thirties."

"My parents got married in 1933."

"A youthful indiscretion of your father's, then."

"Why did he never say anything?"

"You, too, Niki, must not say a word. Not even a hint. Promise?"

"…"

"No one should have to lay bare their entire lives, Niki. Much less to their children."

"In other words, just like that, I have a brother?"

"And a famous one into the bargain! Doesn't that make you happy?"

"I don't know…"

"As soon as we get to New York, you can ask the newspaper for his address and write to him. He seems like the type who would be happy to meet you. You see? I am not asking you to follow me into entirely unfamiliar waters."

The episode left me in a state of confusion that lasted for days. But when it began to clear, I was flooded with a strange sense of joy. First, I was grateful to Alexandros for the supremely decent and honorable way in which he had handled it. Second and most important, I fully agreed with what he had said: I felt—no, I knew—that there was another world out there somewhere for me, a world as much mine as the one I had known until then, but incomparably brighter, a world as resplendent as my brother's (my brother?) sculptures that was waiting to welcome me with open arms.

"How much money do we need to get us there?" I asked, almost giddy with excitement.

IV

ON SEPTEMBER 10, 1957, my mother's mother, Grandmother Elpida, died.

I had met her all of three times in my life: The first was before we went underground in 1948, and the other two recently, when they had brought her to Athens for medical tests. She was an old woman ravaged by bereavement, hair smothered under a kerchief, face lacerated with wrinkles. She had never recovered from the loss of Kyriakos at the Albanian front, and even the birth of her grandsons, Alcmene's twins, had not brought a light to her eye or persuaded her to shed her mourning weeds. After the death of Grandfather Giorgos in 1942, Alcmene had taken her to Kalamata, along with her youngest sister, Theone.

Alcmene's husband, Uncle Vangelis, was a well-to-do lawyer of undisclosed political affiliations. They all lived together in a beautiful house, a veritable palace, on the coast of Kalamata. Aunt Theone, unlucky in love, had devoted herself to the care of her mother and her nephews. After our liberation in 1955 and our move to Koukaki, they began sending us a Christmas card each year, a family photograph taken in front of the decorated tree. They were figures from another world, whose lives were utterly foreign to me: Uncle Vangelis, so exceedingly comme il faut, with his gleaming bald pate and double chin; Alcmene, tall, dark, and ample, beaming like a goddess of fertility with a son on each side;

in one corner, Aunt Theone, with her beautiful but prematurely fading face, blond like my mother and looking like a pale copy of her; and in the middle, my grandmother, just like an ancient figurine tarnished by the centuries, a creased and skeletal doll whose grim eyes were the only things to betray that she was alive. When, years later, I read about the Mayan—or was it Aztec?—custom of mummifying the dead and keeping them at home, I thought of Grandmother Elpida.

Her death, as may be clear, barely affected me. My mother, on the other hand, was devastated. After Kyriakos was killed, she was tormented by guilt about her parents. As if her own flight to Athens, more than ten years earlier, had opened the floodgates to their woes. "I wasn't there to support them," she kept repeating, even though in 1941 she had escaped exile in Sifnos with me, a tot, in her arms and headed straight to her village. Even though she had joined the partisans on the mountains only after Grandfather Giorgos's death. Not surprisingly, then, her misgivings led her to lash out at Alcmene.

"Why didn't you tell me that mother was on her deathbed?" she screamed into the grocer's telephone—we did not yet have a line in the house.

"Because she wasn't on her deathbed. It was very sudden. She went in her sleep, like a little bird."

"Who closed her eyes?"

"She died with her eyes closed—I just told you. Should we perhaps reopen them so that you can come and close them yourself?"

In addition to being in the right, Alcmene was gifted with a strong streak of black humor. But if Anna had had the slightest inkling of the Kalamata clan's original intentions, she would have been justified in lunging at her throat.

"**WE WILL BURY** her in the village, next to father." Alcmene had decided.

"In that case, do not notify your sister, Anna, until after the funeral," Uncle Vangelis had replied.

"Why?"

"Don't you see why, Mene? Especially at this particular time, the beginning of September? Do you want to get us stoned?"

Uncle Vangelis was not exaggerating. My mother's village was forbidden territory, strictly off-limits to her and to anyone who had allied themselves with the left in those critical years.

Meligalas in Messenia. Meligalas and its well, a site of holy pilgrimage to nationalists throughout the country.

On their departure from Kalamata on September 5, 1944, the Germans had left behind squads of officers to maintain the peace. These officers had refused to surrender to the ELAS and had retreated, three days later, to Meligalas, where some thousand Security Battalionists were already in hiding. After besieging them for two days and nights, the ELAS prevailed. At the end of the battle, the situation quickly deteriorated: More than seven hundred Security Battalionists, as well as collaborators and their families—perhaps even

just plain civilians whose only fault was a personal difference with a member of the ELAS—were lynched, hanged,
or in the best-case scenario shot after an expedited trial. The
scenes of horror—floggings, rape, and dismemberments with
an ax—were no doubt exaggerated by the apologists for collaboration, who had now found the perfect counter to their
own crimes. In any case, only one thing is certain: All the
elementary rules governing the treatment of prisoners of war
were trampled underfoot at Meligalas. After all the dead
were thrown into the well, the ELAS celebrated their temporary triumph in the southern Peloponnese.

When the tide turned, the left made haste to abandon
the region. They were safer as street vendors of sesame
bagels in Athens or factory workers in Germany—even
as prisoners on Makronissos—than staying in their home-
towns and crossing paths on a daily basis with the siblings
and children of those lost in the Meligalas well.

"I cannot keep this from Anna!" said Alcmene.

"Well, then, Mother will be buried in Kalamata," Uncle
Vangelis concluded in a definitive tone.

This was all presented to us as a fait accompli when, after
a fifteen-hour train ride, we finally arrived at their house. I
accompanied my mother, and Alexandros accompanied us
both. When he had offered to travel with us, my father, needless to say, had frowned with displeasure. But he had thought
it over and changed his mind. He, of course, could not even
dream of setting foot in Meligalas, and it was far from desir-
able, perhaps even dangerous, to have the women in the

family travel unaccompanied. Since Strofalis was doing as he wished with his daughter, he might as well be of some use. "Go on, then," he had said curtly, as if doing him a favor.

Before our departure, my mother sprang the most absurd of surprises on us: Taking us aside, she slipped wedding rings on our fingers.

"People in the village are sticklers for convention," she explained. "Let's at least keep up appearances."

"In other words, we're engaged?" Alexandros asked.

"In a manner of speaking…" Anna replied, without a trace of enthusiasm.

"I could take exception to your tone, but never mind!" he said with a big smile, and bowed to kiss her hand.

"ARE YOU CRAZY?" my mother screamed. "You're going to bury Elpida far from Giorgos? She's going to claw her way out of that grave and hound you!"

"Well, how about we bring father's remains to Kalamata?" Alcmene suggested as a compromise.

"No!" Anna cried even louder than before. "Meligalas is where our parents lived, and Meligalas is where they shall rest!"

This conversation, which was showing signs of turning into a full-blown altercation, was taking place after midnight in the parlor, around my grandmother's open casket, in the presence of the silent and grieving Theone and my adolescent cousins, who were picking at their pimples.

"Do you realize, Anna, that in Meligalas almost every second family has lost someone to the well?" Uncle Vangelis intervened.

"I had no part in that! It all happened when I was crossing mountains on foot to get to Athens!"

"You think anyone gives a damn? Are you forgetting that Achilleas and Kyriakos were the first communists in the village? Are you forgetting that you are Antonis Armaos's wife? Or you think that the people of Meligalas have forgotten?"

"What can they do to us?" Anna asked.

"Heckle us, make sure that there's no priest willing to officiate the funeral, or, as soon as we have our backs turned, they might very well decide to dig up your mother and toss her into a ravine, like the ELAS did with their relatives in the well. Your village is seething with hate, Anna. Please be reasonable. And on a final note, I will not allow my family to travel with you to Meligalas," Uncle Vangelis added, in a sterner tone. "If you refuse to compromise and can convince Mene to skip her own mother's funeral, then be my guest and go with Niki and her fiancé. I wash my hands of the whole thing. You're sisters, settle the issue between yourselves!"

Anna and Alcmene exchanged fraught looks, like two wildcats smelling blood.

That's when Alexandros opened his mouth for the first time. "May I have a word in private?" he said to Uncle Vangelis.

Twenty minutes later, they returned from the kitchen, relief written on their faces as if everything had been resolved.

"What did you say?"

"I asked him if he has a gun."

"Why do you need a gun?"

"Wait and see," Alexandros whispered enigmatically.

"Mr. Strofalis and I are departing at dawn for Meligalas to lay the groundwork," Uncle Vangelis declared. "At ten, eleven at the latest, we'll call you to tell you to get started."

And that's exactly what happened. The hearse arrived to take grandmother. My mother and Alcmene squeezed in next to the driver while Theone, my cousins, and I followed them in a taxi.

When we entered Meligalas, I broke into a cold sweat—it felt like we were entering the lion's den. The commemoration of the battle was in a couple of days, and the main street was covered in flags. On the walls, laurel-wreathed portraits of King Pavlos and Queen Frederica peered at us, and banners hung from the electric pilons: "Honor and Glory to the Dead at the Well" read one; "Meligalas = Thermopylae," the second; "Communism Stops Here," the third.

All my life until that day, I had believed that my parents' enemies, our persecutors, were rich people defending their privileges, foreign imperialists striving to keep Greece under their thumb and the Greeks at their beck and call; that the Civil War had been a popular uprising of a people drowning in the bloodshed wrought by English tanks and

American fighter planes. The fact that simple country folk, plain working people were calling us "Bulgarians" and "cutthroats," and were prepared to die for a free Greece— a Greece free from us!—I could understand it rationally, in my head, but not in my heart. Had I been a little younger and a touch bolder, I would have stood myself in the village square and explained to all passersby that it was all a grotesque misunderstanding.

"Meet us at the café across from the monument to the dead," Uncle Vangelis had instructed on the phone.

"It's probably better that I not get out," my mother announced as she rolled up the hearse window, her bluster having suddenly evaporated.

As I entered the café, I saw that my uncle was standing and talking to a fellow from the ESA,[108] whose back was turned to me. The mere sight of the golden lanyard on his shoulder made me quake. Perhaps the ESA was not yet the gang of torturers it became under the junta, but its men were already sowing terror throughout the country. Big hulking men in white gaiters and belts, with royal blue caps pulled all the way down to their eyebrows, they were out every day, patrolling Omonia on foot or in their jeeps. Officially, they were part of the military police—charged with monitoring soldiers both on and off duty—but they were steadily expanding their jurisdiction to include the citizenry. They were regular visitors to Afroessa. Fondling their wooden

---

[108] The Greek military police.

batons or the guns hanging from their waist with vaguely vulgar gestures, they would order chocolate cakes to appease their sweet tooth. Savvas Bogdanos had given us strict orders: "Do not accept payment from the military police. No female waitresses anywhere in their vicinity. Serve them first and keep your fingers crossed that they leave as soon as possible."

I therefore immediately came to the conclusion that the ESA had prohibited the funeral and was forcing us to take grandmother back to Kalamata. You can imagine my surprise, then, when the uniform turned toward me and I came face-to-face with Alexandros!

"What do you think? Does it suit me?" He winked at me. He wasn't holding a baton, but the gun bulged in its holster and the stripes glittered on his shoulders.

"Start heading to the church." He turned to Uncle Vangelis. "I'll go bring the priest, the cantors, and the gravediggers. Don't get out of the car before I return!"

The ESA's protective presence poured oil on the troubled waters of the village. Only our small family circle attended the funeral ceremony, but as our procession crossed the village to make its way from the Church of Saint Giannis to the cemetery, passersby took off their hats and crossed themselves.

"I want her name on the headstone," Alexandros instructed the stone carver. "As well as her son's, Kyriakos, who gave his life for his country, and instead of erecting a statue for him in the square, you all behave as if he didn't exist. You hear me?"

"At your service, Sergeant, sir!"

"When we return for the nine-day memorial, I want this grave to be gleaming!"

Now on a roll, Alexandros led us, almost forcibly, to the café. "Drinks all around on me. I want everyone to drink to the memory of the deceased and in forgiveness of her sins!" he ordered the café owner and paid for two bottles of brandy.[109]

One by one, the customers filed by our table to give us their condolences—or, more accurately, to pay their respects to Alexandros's uniform. My mother and her sisters, eyes cast down like frightened virgins, barely raised their heads from their coffee cups. Alexandros, on the other hand, gawked at everyone with the hard eyes of power.

"You're all in their crosshairs," he murmured in my ear. "In particular, that group over there, sitting by the door, must have had some fatal differences of opinion with your family. They must be with the Security Battalions. Not to worry though! The crown on my cap and the rings on our fingers will keep them to heel. They're probably thinking: 'The girl's engagement is a sign that the Milonas clan have embraced our nationalist ideals.' The people of your village, Niki, are model citizens! Truly spineless bottom-feeders!"

"But you...are you really in the ESA?" I asked.

"Only in case of an emergency," he replied with a mischievous smile.

---

[109] After a funeral it is traditional to treat guests to a coffee and a brandy.

V

UNLIKE ME, MY father would not accept ambiguous responses. "What did you do?" He hauled Alexandros over the coals as soon as we returned to Koukaki and my mother had described the goings-on related to the funeral.

"What did I do? I succeeded in getting your mother-in-law buried in the village of her birth, and I protected your family from the people of Meligalas."

"Did you serve with the ESA?"

"Why is that so important to you? Perhaps the uniform was mine—you keep it, you know, once you return to civilian life—and in foreseeing what was to come, I put it in my suitcase in Athens. The most likely scenario, however, is that I borrowed it from a friend in Kalamata, or that I bought it at a military surplus store. In any case, the important point is that for Grandmother Elpida's sake, I risked being charged with impersonating an officer and getting thrown in jail!"

"In Nazi Germany, would you have dressed up as the SS?"

"If I thought there was no other choice. But don't compare Greece in 1957 with Hitler's Germany. You are doing an injustice to both everything you fought for and your intelligence. Deep down, you know this very well: We are living in a country that is still barely picking itself up from a civil war, and no matter which side had come out victorious, the defeated would be suffering. If the Democratic Army had prevailed, do you think that there would be no concentration camps and certificates of social conscience for the monarcho-fascists? And not only for them. You, especially, would not have gotten away with only seven years underground in a socialist Greece. They would have ferreted you out from wherever you were hiding and hung you from a meat hook. Your very own like-minded comrades—"

"How dare you talk about my struggles!" Antonis exclaimed, landing his fist on the table. "Why won't you admit to being in the ESA? Are you ashamed?"

That's when I noticed the flash of fury in Alexandros's eyes.

"Me? Ashamed?" he roared, hair standing on end as if he had been electrocuted. "Me ashamed? You are the one who ought to be ashamed! For months now, instead of rejoicing in the fact that your daughter is happy, you've put me under the microscope in the hope of finding some fault! You've skulked in the shadows, itching for an opportunity to declare me a good-for-nothing! Not surprising! After all, have you ever really cared for her? The only thing that seems to matter to you is to serve your grand ideals, and too bad if Niki has to pay the price, as long as she stands by you!"

My father had regained his composure and returned to his line. He could smell victory in the air. "Please continue," he said to Alexandros.

"Continue? Continue what? And why? You think I give a damn about your opinion of me? That I need your approval? That I place any importance on these rings that you half-heartedly forced on our fingers only in order to keep the village tongues from wagging? Frankly, I did not expect it of you, died-in-the-wool communists, to care so much about what people say! Our marriage already took place months ago, on a beautiful beach in Spetses, worlds away from you, fortunately. I wipe my ass on your rings!"

Looking almost triumphant, he whipped the ring off his finger and threw it in Antonis Armaos's face. The silver ring bounced off my father's right brow and fell onto the tile floor. It spun around itself like a top, before gradually flagging and falling flat on the doorstep.

"We're done!" Alexandros declared, glaring at my parents. "Come on, Niki, let's go!" He turned toward me.

Even though I had taken everything in with bated breath, I refused to acknowledge, I refused to understand, what had just happened. My only desire was to bend over, pick up the ring, and put it back on Alexandros's finger in the irrational hope that this gesture would return everything to what it had been; that the two men's fury (these two overgrown boys fighting over me like rabid dogs even though they already had me, even though they were both my heroes) would vanish, that my life would resume its sweet rhythms—afternoons of love at the "lair" in Kypseli, Sunday dinners at my house—and time would soften their differences and teach them how to coexist.

"Let's go, Niki, we're out of here!" Alexandros repeated, looking me straight in the eyes.

My mother was also looking me in the eyes, but—oh, miracle of miracles!—not to beseech me to stay true to my parents. Instead, she was exhorting me to make up my mind, to cut the umbilical cord, if that was my true heart's desire; to heed the call of my passion and shoulder its risks. As she too had done, when at only eighteen years old, she had left her village for Athens and enlisted in the Communist Youth, turning her back definitively on the gold-coin-festooned wedding dress that her father was preparing. Like Grandmother Elpida, who without a backward glance had followed the man who had laid waste to nearly half her family, before giving herself to him in a cave.

But I was like a bird blinded and paralyzed by the light.

After the fact, I readily invented every possible excuse, claiming that I did not appreciate being the apple of discord, the trophy at the heart of a confrontation for which I served perhaps only as a pretext; that Alexandros was not the one speaking but all the glasses of ouzo he had downed at the Isthmus of Corinth, when the train had stopped to let us out for souvlaki; that I was worried about my father's health, fearing that he might have a heart attack if I up and left him out of the blue like that.

Poppycock! The simple fact was that I froze. If things had happened the other way around and it was Armaos who had said, "Come on, Niki, let's go!" I would have reacted in exactly the same way: rooted to the spot, unable to breathe a word. Even though I had spent my entire childhood in the shadow of tales of heroism, or perhaps precisely for that reason, because they had exacted their pound of flesh from me, I could not endure any more conflict and heartbreak.

"You're not coming, Niki? All right then," Alexandros said. He got up, patted his hair with a slightly tremulous hand, picked up his suitcase, and left.

"*Alea jacta est*," said my father, locking the front door.

VI

THE MOST TERRIBLE thing of all was that everyone believed I had made a life decision that night.

Not only my parents, who didn't deign to mention the name Strofalis again; not only Aunt Markella, Grandmother Sevasti, and the Bogdanoses, who embraced me with the exaggerated tenderness of that first period after my release from the White Tower; not only the girls at Afroessa, who found their suspicions corroborated in my misfortune ("What a silly puppy, falling blindly head over heels like that! What did she expect?"); but Alexandros himself.

On the very next day, he resigned from the restaurant. He surrendered his waiter uniform to Tolis Bouas instead of Savvas Bogdanos, preferring to stomach the maître d's derisive sneer rather than have to explain himself to my uncle. He left through the back door without a goodbye to anyone. Usually, when someone quit Afroessa, they would leave a home address just in case. Not Alexandros.

"What's the point? I'll be leaving Greece soon." This, at least, is what my friend Niove Papadakis reported he said.

"To be frank, he didn't look at all sad, but more as if a burden had been lifted," she added sadistically.

I, however, could not resign. Resign and go where? And do what? So instead, I threw myself headlong into the work. I polished my fake professional smile and became the best waitress around. I coaxed customers into ordering the most expensive bottles of wine, and with alcohol flowing like water and the bills' totals climbing higher and higher, napkins were swamped with sweet nothings written for my beautiful eyes. I didn't even glance at them. At the end of my shift at Afroessa, I would return to Koukaki, cloister myself in my room, and stare at the ceiling for hours. One night, I peered up at the bare bulb hanging over my bed for so long that it fizzled out. At least that's what it felt like to me: that I had caused its demise. This small miracle, performed despite myself, left me almost completely cold. Even if I had raised someone from the dead, I doubt that it would have done anything to ease my sorrow.

One afternoon, after leaving Afroessa, I made my way like a sleepwalker to Syngrou, but instead of turning left toward my house, I continued straight down the entire length of the avenue past the Hippodrome until I reached the shore. There, I sat on a rock and finally cried my eyes out. I cried with remorse for my cowardice, for not having seized the hand offered by my love, for having treated it as if it were a dead branch. Most of all, I cried for Alexandros and how easily—how easily?—he had renounced our love.

Night was falling, and the sea breeze turned cold and piercing. It was already October. I got up from the rock, mainly because I had to pee and was not used to doing it outdoors. I dashed into a little café, a shack smothered in smoke and teeming with cursing old men pounding pawns on their backgammon boards. As I walked out of the bathroom, the jukebox was playing the big hit of the day, *You're so beautiful when you cry*.[110] I had always found it corny, and hearing it there, with all the patrons' eyes riveted on me, I imagined that it had been written with the sole purpose of mocking me.

"May I treat you to something, miss?" the café owner said with the sleaziest of smiles as by force of habit he licked his mousy mustache. I turned tail and ran.

What could I do, I wondered, to get away, even if only temporarily, from the sorrow that was stifling me? What could I do to stop the echo on automatic loop in my head of my father's words and then Alexandros's, and then the ping of the ring hitting the floor, and finally my own idiotic, catastrophic, shameful silence? What could I do to forget everything, even if only for one night, and be free of the unbearable weight of my being?

What if I stepped into the bouzouki club I had just passed, Triana Wine Bar and Brasserie, in Tzitzifies, with its long lines of people at the entrance, its multicolored lights blinking on the marquee, its lottery and balloon vendors and the banner announcing, "Today: The

---

[110] A very popular rembetiko song from 1954 by composer Stelios Chrysinis.

Papaioannou—Chiotes Band!"? What if I went in and drank until the world started spinning around me and then followed the first random stranger, the first man who just happened to be near?

These were laughable thoughts, befitting the protagonist of a silly romance novel. In any case, I had no real desire to either flee or forget.

Where was Alexandros?

ON ONE OF the following nights, as I strolled along Patision gaping at the shopwindows, my feet took me, of their own accord it seemed, to Kypseli. I found myself "by accident" in front of his door. The lights were out and the shutters closed and padlocked. "He's gone!" I thought, panic-stricken, "He's already in America!" But at that moment, I heard his voice. He was on the roof terrace, outside his "alchemist's lair," explaining something to someone in English. I caught only a few scattered words, and then waited apprehensively for his interlocutor to respond, trembling in case it was a woman. It was a man—what a relief!—and it was clearly a serious conversation. I had my back up against the wall and was holding my breath. I wanted to avoid being seen at all costs, to avoid having him call in my direction with ironic good cheer: "Hello there, Niki! What brings you to these parts?" A cigarette butt landed at my feet. What I had failed to do with the ring, I did now: I stooped and picked it up. On the still smoldering paper, I read Santé—it was his brand; he had smoked it! I regretted the fact that I hadn't thought to make a wish as it swooped down, as if it were a shooting star. Was I losing my mind?

MY PARENTS' BEHAVIOR toward me was unrecognizable, abounding with unprecedented and predominantly clumsy expressions of affection. One day I caught my mother ironing my waitress uniform.

"What are you doing?" I asked.

"Your clothes got mixed up with mine..." she stammered, blushing a deep red.

They had even tacitly relieved me of the responsibility of washing the dishes after each meal and didn't ask why I was so often late in returning from work. My brokenhearted expression was all they needed to know that I had not patched things up with Alexandros.

It was a Sunday when my father, practically jumping for joy, rushed into my room and announced that the People's Friendship University would be opening its doors in Moscow any day now.

"It's an institution of higher learning that will be accepting progressive students from all over the world, based on their true inclinations and learning, and without requiring a highschool diploma if the circumstances in their country made it impossible for them to obtain it! It's designed for young people like you, Niki! You must apply as soon as possible."

"Wonderful," I replied, barely getting the word out.

He ignored my complete lack of enthusiasm; perhaps it didn't even register. "What would you like to study?" he asked. "Architecture? Archaeology? Nuclear physics? They say it is the science of the future."

"You choose what you think will suit me best," I replied, yawning.

And that's exactly what he did! He decided—in my place and in my name—that I would study medicine with a specialization in the suitably feminine field of pediatrics. He even drafted in Russian a three-page letter of application addressed to the People's Friendship University, to which he attached a CV (more his than mine, truth be told) that he then had me copy and sign. And that's exactly what I did, without so much as a raised eyebrow. I believe that I would have boarded the airplane for "our great Soviet homeland" with equal docility. How much worse could my life get there?

The only person who went out of her way to have a forthright conversation with me was Aunt Markella.

"I can see how much pain you are in, my sweet Niki, and it breaks my heart," she said. "But that's how love is. That's how life is: a long, hard, topsy-turvy fight. There's only one person we can ever count on in the end, ourself."

"I don't want anything to do with myself. I can't stand myself!" I burst into tears.

"Don't ever say that again! The wheel turns, pain ends. Do you know that you're a shadow of yourself? You're not eating; you're not sleeping. When is the last time you weighed yourself? You're swimming in your clothes."

"I'll have them taken in."

"Take care of your health!"

"I don't care about my health!"

"If you get sick—God forbid!—you'll remember this conversation!"

"If only I got sick!"

And that's exactly what I did: I got sick.

IT BEGAN WITH a stabbing pain in my lower abdomen that I tried to ignore. It was during a packed Saturday shift at Afroessa, and we were up to our ears. We, the waitresses, were coming and going like robots, opening wine bottles and Coca-Cola as if on an assembly line. I was taking orders at the table of a minister lunching with his friends, when I felt a sudden tidal wave of nausea. I don't know how I managed not to throw up all over them. I dashed toward the toilets, but halfway there I couldn't hold it in any longer and barely managed to dart into the checkroom, where I emptied my guts on the customers' coats. By the time the ambulance got there, my shirt was soaked through with cold sweat.

"Appendicitis. Presenting very typically. Absolutely nothing to worry about," decreed the doctor at the Aretaeio emergency room. "As long as it comes out as soon as possible."

As they wheeled me down freezing corridors, I could hear the surgeon reassuring my parents.

"She'll be right as rain in a week!"

Two overweight nurses undressed me, cut through my underwear—I was so ashamed that on top of everything else, I was also having my period—and lifted me off the stretcher and onto the surgical table.

"You are a very beautiful young woman!" the anesthetist complimented me with the sardonic smile of a butcher salivating before the kid goat he is about to eviscerate. "Can you count backward from ten?"

A voice somewhere in the back of the room said something about the Olympiakos soccer team.

"Nine, eight, seven..." At "six," I was lost to the world.

I came to in a huge ward, containing some thirty beds. Screens shielded me from the sight of the other patients, but I could still hear their moans, their paroxysms of coughing. I could still smell the hospital miasma: antiseptic, urine, bargain-basement detergents, and chicken soup.

"All went really well!" my mother informed me. "Tomorrow you can get up, and on Wednesday you'll be released!"

The next morning, I had a fever of 103. By the afternoon, it had climbed to 106.

VII

WHEN I FINALLY awoke without a fever, I had no idea if hours or days had gone by. All I retained were a few scattered images: white uniforms bowed over me, needles prodding me, anguished whispers: "107 and climbing," "108," "white blood cell count skyrocketing," "administering supplementary dose of antibiotics."

Now I found myself in a small private room, flooded with sunlight, and my parents staring at me as if I had risen from the dead.

"You made it, Niki! You gave us the scare of our lives, but you made it!" said my father. He truly must have stared death in the face, because he looked like he had aged ten years. As for my mother, she was squeezing my poor tormented arm as if she could barely believe that my pulse was still beating.

"You're hurting me, Mama!"

"Forgive me, my child, forgive me! Would you like some orange juice?"

She held the glass so that I could drink from it and then patted my lips almost devoutly.

Ten minutes later, there was a knock at the door.

"Come in, come in, she just woke up!" my father exclaimed, eagerly opening the door. "Niki, let me introduce you to your savior!"

I watched him walk into the room: a tall man in his mid-thirties, dark and athletic of build, with the head of a roman statue; a doctor plucked straight out of a Hollywood film.

"I'll introduce myself!" he said, all smiles, as he approached my bed. "Gerassimos Liakos, general surgeon."

"And a swimming champion at the Balkan Games!" my father added. "And a former member of the EPON!

And, despite his democratic leanings, a professor at the Aristotle University in Thessaloniki! The world of higher learning couldn't afford to freeze out such a scientific luminary! Dr. Liakos traveled all night from Thessaloniki to come to your bedside, Niki! Our doctors here had thrown in the towel."

"To speak plainly, the doctors here almost killed you, Miss Armaos!" said Liakos. "They kept talking about a mysterious infection, kept ordering test upon test, kept losing their way in erroneous diagnoses, if not outright conjectures, each more implausible than the last! When I arrived, I found them wagering on your chances of survival based on the death rate. Can you imagine that? They were essentially ushering you into the next world and using statistical probability to account for it!"

"Public health care, what do you expect?" my father quipped.

"I immediately read them the riot act: 'Why the deluge of antibiotics? We must operate again, immediately!' 'We risk losing her on the operating table! She is presenting arrhythmia, fevers,' the cowards retorted. 'We're scrubbing in now for emergency surgery and I take responsibility!' I put my foot down. Of course, I had your parents' trust."

"So Gerassimos opens you up and what does he see?" my father asked, as if posing a riddle.

"What?"

"A piece of gauze! They left a piece of gauze inside you!"

"And your body, naturally, was reacting to this foreign matter with all its might! Your central alarm bells were ringing a code red! As soon as I took out the gauze, all your values returned to normal."

"Colombus's egg!" My father smiled.

"Criminal negligence!" Liakos corrected him.

"What do you say, Gerassimos, should we press charges?"

"It would be a first in the annals of Greek history. A doctor has never been charged and convicted of murder, let alone endangerment of a patient's life. They have each other's backs, and the system itself covers for all of them."

"Well, everything has to start somewhere," said my father.

"We'll see. The important thing is that Niki has been saved. May I call you Niki?"

What could I say to that? That we barely knew each other? On the pretext that he was checking my temperature, he stroked my brow and then my cheek. His hand was big and smelled of cologne.

"You'll remain in the hospital for a week or so to regain your strength. And I too will stay in Athens to oversee your convalescence."

"But we'll keep in touch after that, Doctor!" said my mother.

"Naturally, dear Anna!"

I COULD SEE it in their eyes: They had found the perfect son-in-law. And I could see in his that he was prepared to turn a blind eye to all my shortcomings: the fact that I had no dowry; that, on paper, I hadn't even finished elementary school; that I worked as a waitress (he had, of course, made inquiries and had learned that Afroessa was as upscale as you could get); that I had barely surfaced from an unfortunate relationship—to avoid him hearing about it from a third party, my father had hastened to let him know about my "silly passing fancy."

Over the next few days, Gerassimos Liakos seldom left my bedside. He played the role of doctor, nurse, butler, and entertainer, all with the same zeal and success. He was in that category of men who, in setting a goal for themselves, will use any and every means at their disposal to realize it; who give chase to it without respite and with unflagging tenacity. And immediately after their victory—for it is inherent to their nature—they move on to a new goal. In his heart of hearts, Gerassimos Liakos had made it his goal to win over Niki Armaos.

Had he fallen in love with me, or was it simply a question of conceit, a sense that my love was his due? After all, every girl adores her savior, doesn't she?

At night in my solitary room—he would tuck me in and switch off the lights at eight thirty, but I couldn't fall asleep before midnight—I had plenty of time to ruminate over what had passed between us and ponder his intentions. And I'd come to the conclusion, because everything led me to it, that they were serious. Otherwise, why would he have invited the entire family to Thessaloniki as soon as I recuperated? Why would he have told my father, when the subject turned to the People's Friendship University, that he too was thinking of postgraduate work in Moscow and that "we could kill two birds with one stone"? Could one kill two birds with one stone without marriage, or an engagement at least?

What was it about me that charmed him so? Gerassimos Liakos, a man who must have had countless women at his feet given his looks, social status, and charm—he had no shortage of charm, indeed the very opposite; he was what we call "the complete package," a real catch, a man of class both in appearance and manner. (I had observed all too clearly how not only the nurses but also my friends from Afroessa fairly drooled whenever they saw him.) I certainly must have attracted him physically. The ordeal with my health had caused me to lose even more weight, and I looked fragile and virginal. Even my breasts were smaller. And frail women always appeal to strong men. But in my opinion the biggest point in my favor was something else. Having heard my history, he knew the depths of my devotion to those I loved. If I had sacrificed my adolescence to my parents, the mind boggled at what I might be capable of for him and our children! I would burn like a candle at the altar, an exemplar in every way in my role as spouse, mother, mistress of the house, professor's or even parliamentary delegate's wife, should he decide to accept the EDA's insistent invitations and adorn their ballot with his name. I would be exactly like his mother, Mrs. Symela, who had raised three sons by working her fingers to the bone as a washerwoman. The same, if not better!

I didn't even ask myself if I actually liked Gerassimos Liakos, because the crux of the matter lay elsewhere: I could easily imagine my life with him. We would live in a brand-new penthouse apartment overlooking the sea. He had shown me the pictures.

"I bought it last year and have not yet had the time to furnish it," he had said with a meaningful look, as if entrusting me with my first assignment.

We would hobnob with the city's who's who. On Sundays, we'd go on outings to the nearby countryside, and our summers would be spent on Thassos, where he had grown up. He would make love to me in that vigorous, athletic way of his: his endurance inexhaustible, his sperm prodigiously fertile. For our anniversaries he would present me with a piece of jewelry, either in gold or studded with diamonds. And even if he cheated on me occasionally, he would do it in a way calculated to spare me the least suspicion.

Life with Gerassimos would not leave much to be desired. No, not at all. And if sometimes—very rarely— all that normalcy and salubrity began to bore me, I would pull myself together. Sternly, I would remind myself of all I had endured during my childhood, and of all the comforts—most important, all the security—offered to me by this man, who had, after all, saved my life!

Where was Alexandros?

VIII

"ALEXANDROS IS RIGHT here!" Niove Papadaki announced. "In the café across from the hospital. He has been camping out there for the past three days, standing watch from dawn till dusk, waiting for me to let him know when to come up and see you. I, in turn, was waiting until you were alone, so I kept an eye on when your family left. But whenever your parents and aunts and uncles decamped, Dr. Liakos took over, and I didn't think that you'd want them to cross paths."

"How did he know I was in the hospital?"

"I went to his house and told him. We thought we were going to lose you, Niki, and I thought he had a right to know."

I was speechless.

"He even canceled his ticket to New York on the *Olympia*. When I confirmed that you were no longer in danger and were on your way to a full recovery, he bought a new one on the *Queen Frederica*."

"When does it sail?"

"Tomorrow. He sent you this," Niove said, handing me a large envelope.

When I tore it open, a vinyl record fell out. Buddy Holly, the one we had listened and "danced" to in bed that first afternoon in the "lair." "That'll Be the Day," which he had translated for me, chuckling as he did so, as if trying to banish what the lyrics portended: *That'll be the day when you say goodbye, that'll be the day when you make me cry, that'll be the day when I die...*

There was also a note in the envelope, scrawled hurriedly on a piece of writing paper, the kind with the faint blue lines that they used to sell at the corner kiosks.

It's lucky that I did not see you again before leaving, because if I had, I would most likely not be leaving. I will always be grateful to you: You pulled me out of the shadows cast by my dead. You freed me of their burden. You proved to me that the world can be a garden full of flowers, that we can laugh without care—truly without care—and not just to banish the disaster that is inevitably lurking around the corner. I wanted so much to offer you the same happiness. But perhaps it was not possible. You, Niki, are bound by strong ties: to your family, to your principles, to the path you have mapped out since your infancy. It was very egotistical and very stupid of me to ask you to give it all up to follow me. Like demanding that a tree grow some feet or a pair of wings. Flight is only possible once all the roots have been cut. Even if you had joined me that night when I fell out with your father, you would have been racked by guilt sooner rather than later, and your regrets would have ended up suffocating us both. Here is the Buddy Holly album. I leave it to you. As soon as I arrive in New York, I'll buy another one and keep it with me always. Every time you put yours on the turntable, I will know and will listen to mine, too. While an ocean, and many—so many!—things may lie between us, we are tied by a thread both invisible and unbreakable.

Outraged, I crumpled the note in my hand. Not only had Strofalis not had the guts to climb the stairs to my room and take me away from my family—to come to blows with my father and Liakos if need be!—but he was inventing excuses after the fact! He was washing his hands of me by saying I was like a tree. And then he was trying to gild the pill for us both with this ridiculous talk of listening to the same record at the same time. What a histrionic joke! He did not deserve me—I was now completely sure of it.

"Here, take this record, it's yours. Take it, because if not I'm going to shatter it!" I said to Niove.

"You don't want to keep it as a memento?"

"I hate mementos. They're just dead weight. I am going to marry Gerassimos."

"Are the girls chatting? Am I interrupting?" said Liakos, as he walked into the room, after knocking first, of course.

"I was just getting ready to leave," said Niove and discreetly slipped the record and Alexandros's letter into her bag.

"I heard that you are very close to my colleague Giorgos Papastylos. An excellent doctor and a very good sort, from what I hear. We should go out one night, as soon as Niki is feeling stronger."

"With great pleasure!" Niove exclaimed, her face beaming.

"No hello for me, Doctor?" I complained, all sighs and simpers. He went to kiss me on the cheek, but I gave him my lips. He hesitated a second before giving free rein to his ardor.

IX

I AWOKE AT dawn. A strange light was shimmering through the window. Even stranger was the fact that my right arm was once again hooked to the IV and two tubes hung from my nostrils.

"There must have been another unexpected complication," I thought.

In trying to prop myself up, I realized that I could no longer move at all. Only my left hand seemed to work, with great difficulty, as if it weighed a ton. What's more, my head was horribly itchy. "No wonder, it's been days and days in the hospital, and I haven't washed my hair." I touched my scalp. It was completely bare. All my hair had fallen out. Where had it all gone? Panic-stricken, I started shrieking.

"It's the death rattle . . . it's beginning," I heard an unfamiliar voice say. "I'll leave you alone with her. My presence is no longer needed."

"How long will it take?" asked another voice.

"Difficult to say. By morning it will all be over, I reckon."

I opened my eyes wide and tried to ask for an explanation, but only an inchoate whine came from my stiff, parched lips.

"What is it, Mommy?" the second voice asked.

That's when I finally saw him. A man—or, more accurately, a big boy—in his early forties. At first, I took him for Alexandros. He had the same look, the same hands, the same hair, but there was also something different about him, something that rendered him even more familiar to me.

The big boy—that's what I decided to call him since I had little interest in a name—soaked a white towel in a metal bowl, wrung it, and placed it on my cheek. The coolness soothed my skin. And as he bent over me, caressing me and looking at me with more tenderness than sorrow, I suddenly recognized my father's smile. That lovely dolphin smile that lit up his face and everything around him. And I felt like I had long ago, when they had taken me, little girl that I was, to the Corfu Prison, and my father had wrapped me in his arms and made me forget his rags and the sinister surroundings, delighting me with his whistling and the shadows he had summoned on the wall with his hands: a rabbit, a cat, a rooster.

"He's Alexandros and my father all in one. My father and Alexandros at the same time. How is that possible?" Even though I couldn't, in my condition, comprehend the obvious, I was overwhelmed by an unimaginable feeling of triumph and serenity. "The two men of my life, my two heroes, not only reconciled but now united in one body!" I rejoiced.

"Come on, Mommy, dear…hang in there just a little longer," the big boy said, and this sentence took me even further back, to February 3, 1938, in Kifissia, snow falling fast and thick, and I, battling to be born, fighting my way toward the light. For the first time, I remembered how hard it had been, how painful, and with what terror I had abandoned my mother's belly to come into the world. This is what I had to do all over again.

Fate was kind to me: The deep breath I took to gather my courage was my last. I died on June 8, 2008, at 6:02 a.m., according to the almanac, the exact moment when the sun was rising.

Then, the big boy closed my eyes. Hovering now somewhere at the height of the ceiling, I could look down at him. The big boy made as if to ring the bell next to my bed to call the doctors, but thought better of it. He bent over my body one last time and covered me, as if trying to protect me from the cold.

"Not that the dead feel cold..." he chuckled with Alexandros's sense of humor, and then, without taking his eyes off me, took two steps back, opened the window, and lit a cigarette.

"You did well, Niki! You lived a good life!" he said.

That must have been exactly what I was waiting to hear. Mingling with the cigarette smoke, I drifted away into the sky.

X

NOW THAT I am dead, laid out in my coffin, I know that my dream on November 5, 1957, at the Aretaeio Hospital, was a scene from my future that traveled full and intact into the past to visit the sleep of the nineteen-year-old girl I used to be. At the time, though, owing to my age and my upbringing, I scornfully rejected any form of metaphysical belief. There was no doubt in my mind that what I had dreamt had been entirely forged by my unconscious mind: that the big boy who resembled both Strofalis and Armaos was just a symbol, an expression of my deepest longing. In other words, that I had confused my destiny and my desire. One can reject one's destiny, rail against it, strive to escape its pull. One's desire—especially when it surfaces pure, palpable in a dream so vibrant—one cannot but jump on it and ride off at full gallop!

It was far stronger than me. I leapt from the bed and hurriedly threw on the waitress uniform I had been wearing when I was admitted to the hospital. At the very last moment, I had the presence of mind to reach for my wallet. With my heart in my mouth, trembling lest I be seen, I took the service staircase and left out of one of the side doors. When I hailed a taxi, it was seven a.m. sharp.

"To Piraeus!" I said. "To the pier for the *Queen Frederica*."

The liner looked like a gigantic apartment building. It was weighing anchor at half past ten, but none of the gangways had been lowered yet. There was already a crowd on the pier: emigrating farmers, their entire lives packed in baskets; young women on their way to an arranged marriage. I sat on a mooring post and waited for him. Three hours passed as if they were minutes.

I knew he had arrived before I saw him by the salvo of effusive blasts of the car horn. Who else would have asked the taxi driver to make such a racket "to confer the requisite pomp to the moment," as he would have said? He got out of the car, stretched, plucked a wad of bills from his pocket, and pressed it into the taxi driver's hand.

"These are the last of my drachmas," he said. "Take them, and you and your friends go drink to my health!"

I REALIZED THEN why I had fallen so desperately in love with Alexandros: In everything he did, in everything he said, there was always an inner music—at times, somber; at times, joyful; at times, triumphant—a music that usually only he could hear. And all I longed for was to take him in my arms, squeeze him tight, and get into the groove of that inner music.

"Niki!"

"Alexandros!"

"You came!"

"I came…"

The music stopped for a moment. He caught hold of my waist and lifted me up high.

"You'll come with me to America?"

"I'll go with you to the ends of the world."

Music filled the air again, louder than ever.